Tall, dark
Dest

L

OF THE
DESERT

CHOSEN BY THE SHEIKH

Three fabulous, exotic novels by
three beloved writers:
The Sunday Times bestselling author
Penny Jordan,
Laura Wright & Alexandra Sellers

LORDS
OF THE
DESERT

CHOSEN BY THE SHEIKH

PENNY JORDAN
LAURA WRIGHT
ALEXANDRA SELLERS

M&B™ and M&B™ with the Rose Device
are trademarks of the publisher.
Harlequin Mills & Boon Limited, Eton House,
18-24 Paradise Road, Richmond, Surrey TW9 1SR

CHOSEN BY THE SHEIKH
© Harlequin Enterprises II B.V./S.à.r.l. 2010

Taken by the Sheikh © Penny Jordan 2006
The Sultan's Bed © Laura Wright 2005
Sheikh's Castaway © Alexandra Sellers 2004

ISBN: 978 0 263 87703 8

10-0210

Harlequin Mills & Boon policy is to use papers that are natural, renewable and recyclable products and made from wood grown in sustainable forests. The logging and manufacturing processes conform to the legal environmental regulations of the country of origin.

Printed and bound in Spain
by Litografia Rosés S.A., Barcelona

TAKEN BY
THE SHEIKH

PENNY JORDAN

Penny Jordan has been writing for more than twenty years and has an outstanding record: over one hundred and sixty-five novels published, including the phenomenally successful *A Perfect Family, To Love, Honour & Betray, The Perfect Sinner* and *Power Play,* which hit *The Sunday Times* and *New York Times* bestseller lists. Penny Jordan was born in Preston, Lancashire, and now lives in rural Cheshire.

Look out for Penny Jordan's latest exciting novel, *The Wealthy Greek's Contract Wife,* available in February 2010 from Mills & Boon® Modern™.

PROLOGUE

'So THE negotiations went well, then?'

Drax frowned, his dark, arrogantly slanted eyebrows snapping together over an equally arrogant aquiline nose. Although his brother had welcomed him back to the small Arab emirate they ruled together with his usual warmth, Drax sensed that there was something on his elder twin's mind that Vere had not yet revealed to him.

'The talks in London went very well,' he confirmed. He and Vere had ruled Dhurahn together now for almost a full decade, having come to power just after their twenty-fifth birthday, following the death of their parents in a car accident during a state visit.

Despite their closeness, they had never talked about the horror of that time—or the loss of their strong, energetic and forward-thinking father and their beautiful Irish mother. There had been no need. As twins they instinctively understood each other's feelings. Physically they were identical, but when it came to their personalities sometimes it seemed to Drax that they were two halves of one whole—sharing the same basic mind-set and understanding, and yet manifesting a desire to follow their shared life path in different ways.

Drax had come straight to his brother's private audience room from the airport without bothering to go to his own quarters first to change. So, while Vere was dressed traditionally in a robe of dark blue embroidered with gold, worn over his white dishdasha, his head covered, Drax was wearing a formal dark blue business suit, the jacket open over a crisp white shirt worn with a discreetly striped dark red silk tie.

However, although their mode of dress could not have been more different, that faded into insignificance against the impact of their identical and magnificent physical appearance.

They were both tall and broad-shouldered, with the same slightly hooded ice-green eyes which could glitter with fierce heat, and the same distinctive predatory profiles. Their Berber blood, mixed with French and then Irish, had ensured they possessed an aura of power and sexuality that went beyond easy good looks to something that would have been dark and dangerous enough in one man, but when doubled possessed a force that was unnerving and compelling.

'We both know that we aren't the only Middle Eastern country wanting to establish ourselves as not just the Arab world's recognised premier financial centre but the one with the strongest links to the recognised financial centres throughout the world. However, from the talks I had in London I gained the impression that we are the favoured choice. As we agreed, I made it clear that Dhurahn is prepared to put aside an enclave of one hundred acres of land to house the buildings needed to develop and grow a "knowledge economy", and that we favour the use of English mercantile law because of its principles of equity and fairness. I also told them we envisage developing a financial exchange that will equal anything that New York, Hong Kong or London has to offer, with a regulatory system that investors and the business community can rely on and trust. But that's enough about what I've been doing in London, Vere. Something's on your mind.'

Vere raised one eyebrow in silent recognition of his twin's astuteness.

'Yes,' he admitted. 'We have a problem.'

Drax looked searchingly at his twin. 'And that problem is?'

'While you were in London we were contacted by both the Ruler of Zuran and the Emir of Khulua.'

Drax waited. There was nothing particularly unusual in them being contacted by their closest neighbours; they were on good terms. Dhurahn did not have the large oil reserves and revenues enjoyed by its neighbours, but its long river made the land rich and fertile, and Dhurahn had become the 'greenhouse' that supplied Zuran, in particular, with fresh produce for its expanding tourist industry. The days when the fiercely warring tribes had fought bitterly over the hot desert sands were long gone, and the people of Dhurahn lived in peace with their neighbours, enjoying a mutual and shared prosperity.

But certain tribal methods of ensuring peace still endured.

'Both the Ruler and the Emir have, in the mysterious ways of such things—the desert wind is, as ever, capricious in where it blows—heard rumours of our plans,' Vere told his brother dryly. 'Not that they said as much, but of course it is obvious why they are both now so eager to cement the existing good relationship we share with them.'

'You are telling me this—but what is it that you are *not* telling me?' Drax demanded, easily recognising that his brother was withholding something. 'To keep on good terms with our neighbours makes sound business sense…'

'What the Ruler and the Emir are so keen to discuss with us is the matter of our marriages.'

'*Our* marriages?' Drax frowned again. They were thirty-four. One day, of course, they would both marry, choosing their wives carefully and with due consideration for the future of their country, but that time was not here yet. Right now they had far more important things to do—like establishing Dhurahn as the strongest financial powerhouse in the region.

'Our marriages,' Vere repeated grimly. 'Yours to the Emir's eldest daughter and mine to the Ruler's youngest sister.'

The two brothers looked at one another.

'Such marriages would strengthen our ties with both countries, but it would also strengthen *their* potential involvement with Dhurahn,' Drax pointed out. 'While we stand between them, and get on well with both the Ruler and the Emir, there are issues on which they do not agree. The Emir has never approved of the Ruler's decision to expand Zuran's involvement with the tourist industry. Currently we hold the balance of power between them, and ours is in many ways the stronger position.'

'And, while he is loath to admit it, the Emir is jealous of the growing financial status and success of Zuran, and eager to match it. If we agree to their suggestion and take as wives members of their families both of them will try to use the link marriage creates to demand greater allegiance and support from us: in effect to control the power we hold. We can't let that happen. Apart from anything else it could, theoretically, mean that there might come a time when our loyalty to one another and Dhurahn could be in conflict with the loyalty demanded of us by our wives and their families.'

'And if we don't agree we'll risk offending both the Ruler and the Emir, causing them to lose face, and we can't afford to be on bad terms. It could harm our plans to establish Dhurahn as the financial and business capital of the region.'

'Yes.'

Angrily Drax paced the floor. 'We cannot allow ourselves to be manipulated like this.'

'Neither of us wants to be tied via marriage to either of our neighbours,' Vere agreed grimly. 'Dhurahn must always govern its own future, and it is our duty to ensure that it does.'

'But, as you said, if we refuse then we risk offending two very powerful men.' Drax thought quickly. 'Unless, of course, we tell them that we are refusing because we are committed to marriage elsewhere. That way they'd stop pressuring us and they wouldn't lose face.'

'And when they discover that we are *not* getting married?'

'Do they need to discover that?' Drax asked. Vere was frowning but Drax persevered coolly. 'Both the Ruler and the Emir know that it is the tradition for our family and our people to take only one wife. It is not, surely, an insurmountable task to find women—the right kind of women—we could marry, and then—'

'The right kind?'

'You know what I mean.' Drax shrugged dismissively. 'The dispensable, disposable type—morally decent enough to be acceptable and naïve enough to agree to be divorced with the minimum of fuss and pay-off.'

'Oh, that kind,' Vere said cynically. 'A naïve virgin ready to fall in love with a sheikh and be so grateful to him for marrying her that she willingly accepts being divorced and put aside without wanting a penny. Do they still exist? Somehow I don't think so,' he told Drax dryly. 'Certainly if you could find us such a bride apiece then I would gladly marry mine. But we both know that the kind of woman who would agree to the sort temporary marriage we would want is hardly likely to be the sweet virgin our people would expect. The reality is that she is more likely to be an adventuress, who would demand an extortionate amount of money to go through with a temporary marriage in the first place and who would then probably attempt to sell her story to the press. That kind of media attention would be bound to have a damaging effect on how we are perceived by the rest of the world as men of integrity.' Vere shook his head. 'No, Drax. It sounds like the perfect way out of our current dilemma, but my view is that it would be impossible to find even one woman let alone two of the right type—and fast enough to bring an end to the Ruler's and the Emir's determination to have us marry into their families.'

Drax's eyes gleamed like those of a predatory black panther. 'Is that a challenge, brother?'

Vere laughed. 'I know better than to issue you with any challenges, Drax. But if you can find a woman—'

'*Two* women,' Drax corrected him. 'I promise you I shall find them, Vere. And you shall have the first of them.'

'Mmm…' Vere looked unconvinced. 'Very well. But in the meantime the only way to keep our neighbours at bay is to continue negotiations with the Ruler and the Emir while avoiding making any kind of commitment. The Ruler has invited us to make an unofficial visit to Zuran,' Vere continued. 'And I rather thought you ought to be the one to go, Drax.'

'You mean that the Ruler wants *you* for his sister, since you are the elder,' Drax guessed shrewdly, 'and you want me to put up some delaying tactics. Why not? They want to talk to you in London, by the way,' he told Vere. 'I said that you would be free to fly there for more negotiations once I was back in Dhurahn.'

'One of the benefits of dual rulership—one pair of hands always available to hold onto the helm of leadership here in Dhurahn, no matter what matters of state require our presence elsewhere.'

'But you are the one who prefers to remain here in

the desert,' Drax pointed out. 'I am the one who welcomes the cut and thrust of pursuing our business activities elsewhere.'

'A perfect partnership—built on a trust nothing can destroy and absolute loyalty.'

Silently they clasped hands, and then, in the manner of their Arabic ancestors, they exchanged a fierce, brotherly embrace.

CHAPTER ONE

'YOU are useless—totally and completely useless. I cannot imagine why I ever thought you were up to the demands of this job. You claim to have a degree, and an MBA, and yet you cannot do the simplest thing you are told.'

On and on went the harsh, critical voice of her Lebanese employer, while Sadie dutifully bowed her head beneath the weight of the venom being directed towards her, all too aware that if she looked directly at Madame al Sawar now the other woman would see all too clearly the angry hostility in her own eyes. And Sadie could not afford to give *madame* the opportunity to threaten, as she had done many times already in the two months that Sadie had worked there, to withhold the wages still owing to her.

To be accused so unfairly and so vindictively was bad enough, but to have to stand here and be berated in a voice loud enough to carry to the rest of the al Sawar household—a traditional Arab household, where loss of face was something to be dreaded and avoided at all costs—made it even worse. It was typical of her employer, Sadie recognised, that she should choose to accost and accuse her while she was enjoying her legitimate lunch-break in the peace of the pretty courtyard garden of the al Sawars' traditional Moorish-style Zuran home. Sadie knew perfectly well that, although she could not see them, most of household staff would be lingering in the shadows of the building, listening to their employer hectoring her assistant.

Not that they could *avoid* hearing what was going on, with *madame* screaming and shouting so loudly. The whole street could probably hear, Sadie reflected miserably. She wasn't the only recipient of her employer's vile temper. Scarcely a day went by without *madame* losing her temper with someone.

Sadie could have defended herself against her employer's unfair accusations, of course, and told her that she did indeed possess both a First Class Honours degree and an MBA. And she could have told her, too, that as much as Madame al Sawar regretted employing her it couldn't come close to her own regret at having taken the job. But the truth was that she simply couldn't afford to lose this job—not with *madame* having consistently refused to pay her since she came here.

'I have no use for such a deadweight as you in my business. You are dismissed.'

'You can't do that!' Sadie burst out, panicked out of her determination not to be forced into a verbal battle.

'You think not? I assure you that I can. And don't think that you can walk out of here and get another job,' *madame* screeched. 'Because you can't. The Zurani authorities impose very harsh measures on illegals who try to take work from the locals.'

Illegals! Now Sadie *had* to stand up for herself. 'I am not an illegal,' she protested. 'You know that. You assured me yourself when I took this job that all the necessary formalities would be completed on my behalf. I remember signing the necessary forms...' Sadie was beginning to feel slightly sick with panic now, as well as from the heat burning down on her exposed head. She was being made to wait and listen to *madame* ranting in the full burn of the sunlight, whereas *madame* herself remained in the shade.

Sadie could see a smug look of satisfaction in the older woman's eyes as she affected nonchalance with a dismissive shrug.

'I do not remember saying any such thing. And if you try to claim as much now, it will be the worse for you.'

Sadie could hardly believe what she was hearing. She had thought her situation bad enough, but that was nothing to what she was facing now.

With no job, no money, and no legal status here in Zuran her situation was dire indeed. And it had all seemed so promising at the time...

Six months into her first job as an MBA graduate with one of London's premier hedge funds, she had been made redundant to make way for the son of a very senior member of the bank's latest lover. Or that was what she had been told via the office grapevine. It had certainly been easier to swallow that explanation than it had been to accept the jeering comment from one particularly unpleasant male colleague that she was being dumped because she couldn't hack the testosterone-loaded male environment in which she worked.

A top-flight, good, money-earning job in the financial sector—one which would make her completely financially independent—had been her goal all the way through university, and she had initially been devastated by this unwelcome setback to her career plans.

Her parents had divorced when she was in her early teens. Her mother had then married again—a very wealthy man, with children of his own from his first marriage, and with whom she now had a second and younger family. When her mother had first become involved with the man who would become Sadie's stepfather he had lavished time and attention on Sadie, forever telling her now much he wanted her as a daughter. But as soon as her mother had married him he had changed completely towards Sadie, instilling in her the belief that male love, both sexual and paternal, was something that some men could assume to suit themselves.

After her mother's marriage to him Sadie had grown up enduring her stepfather's unkind comments about her father's inability to provide for her as well as he provided for his new children. She had been torn between anger against her parents for divorcing and a protective love for her father, who had remarried as well, and had a young wife and a very young family, and had looked far older and more careworn than his age the last time she had seen him. Unlike her stepfather, her father was not a wealthy man.

It had been pride that had made her refuse to ask for financial help from her stepfather to get through university, and that pride had left her weighed down with a very large student loan. The loss of her first job had meant that she would have to crawl back to her stepfather and ask for his help—help which he had given willingly to his own sons, both of whom had been given a car and an apartment apiece when they had started work—and that was the last thing she had wanted to do.

She could still remember how he had sneered at her when she had announced that she was going to study for her MBA, suggesting that she'd be better off looking for a rich husband to support her instead.

'After all,' had been his comment, 'it isn't as though you haven't got the looks—and the body.'

Yes, she had those. But Sadie had sworn when she had seen the way her obviously highly-sexed stepfather behaved towards her mother, making it plain that he expected her to repay his financial support in bed, that she would never, *ever* let any man think he had the power to demand her sexual compliance just because he paid the bills. Either inside marriage or outside it. And she had stuck to that vow—even though its by-product had been an unexpected and unlooked-for celibacy that had left her partnerless. For Sadie, her financial and sexual independence were strongly interlinked. Thirteen was a very vulnerable age for a girl to witness the kind of relationship Sadie had witnessed between her mother and her stepfather.

When she had seen her current job advertised, in the columns of a national broadsheet newspaper, she had been so excited that she had had to warn herself that there would be hundreds of applicants and that she probably wouldn't stand a chance.

But then, when Monika al Sawar had interviewed her and told her that she specifically wanted to employ a female MBA—'Because my husband is very much the Arab male, and will not tolerate me working one to one with another man'—her hopes had started to rise.

The job Monika had described to her had sounded perfect—challenging and exciting, with plenty of room to grow. Monika's business, she had told Sadie, involved advising new residents to Zuran in the wake of the tourist boom on investment, the buying of Zurani property, and arranging finances for property purchases. Monika had further told Sadie that she wanted a keen young assistant she could train up to work as a financial adviser in her own right.

Sadie had been in seventh heaven when she had got the job—even when the promised business-class flight to Zuran had somehow turned out to be an economy-class flight, and the promised advance of funds to pay a lump sum off her student loan had not materialised.

But then had come the discovery that the accommodation she had been promised was the not the apartment in a modern executive block she had somehow imagined, but instead a very small and basic room in the al Sawar house—and, more disturbingly, that Monika was deducting what seemed to be an overly large sum of money from Sadie's wages to cover her 'bed and board'. Sadie's awkward attempt to discuss her dissatisfaction with this situation had led to the first of the now regular and familiar outbursts of Monika's temper, and with it the withholding of Sadie's wages.

Now, with only a very small sum of money left from the funds she had brought with her, Sadie was getting desperate. Very desperate. But she was not going to let Monika see that.

'Very well, then. I'll go,' Sadie said quietly. 'But not until you have paid me the wages owing to me.'

The scream of fury that erupted from the other woman made Sadie wince, and it could be heard all over the house.

And also outside in the street, where Drax, having parked the hire car he preferred to the Ruler's offer of a chauffeur-driven limousine—mainly because of the privacy it afforded him—was walking towards the house. He slowed his pace to match that of Amar al Sawar. The kindly older man had been a close friend of the twins' father, and neither of them ever visited Zuran without calling to see him. Drax had found him on this occasion at the Royal Palace, and had reluctantly accepted his invitation to return to his home with him. Neither Drax nor Vere liked their father's elderly friend's younger second wife.

'Oh, dear me. I'm afraid it sounds as though Monika is a little upset,' Amar apologised. 'And I had so hoped that this time she would take to the new assistant she hired. Such a delightful young woman. English, and well-educated—a good, kind girl too, modest and sweet-natured.'

If she *was* all of those things then she was certainly no match for Monika, Drax reflected.

'I cannot understand why it is that such an attractive young woman should choose to work instead of marry.

If I had a son she is just exactly the kind of girl I would want for him as a wife.'

Now Amar had surprised Drax. The older man was very much of the generation and outlook that followed the old ways and looked for the kind of virtues in a young woman that very few now possessed. Drax suspected that the older man, who was no match for his aggressive wife, deeply regretted having allowed Monika to bully him into marrying her.

From inside the courtyard, the piercing sound of her wrath could still be heard quite plainly by the two men as she berated her young assistant.

'Wages? You expect me to *pay* you for practically ruining my business? Hah!' Monika screeched at Sadie. '*You* are the one who should be paying me. Be glad that I am letting you go without demanding any recompense from you. If you are wise you will leave now, this minute, before I change my mind and set my lawyers to work on you.'

Before Sadie could object Monika had turned round and begun walking away from her, leaving her standing in the courtyard.

'My clothes...' she began, too stunned and battered by Monika's loud ranting and merciless tactics for logic or argument. 'My passport...'

'Zuwaina has packed them for you. Take them and go,' Monika said triumphantly, as a young maid appeared in the courtyard, pulling Sadie's case on wheels with one hand and holding her handbag and passport in the other.

It gave Sadie a sharp sense of revulsion to know that

Monika had been through her personal belongings, but the real cause of the sickness making her feel so clammy and light-headed was the reality of what she was now facing. No job, no money, no plane ticket home. All she could think of to do was throw herself on the mercy of the British Consulate—although it would mean a long walk in to town to get there.

The courtyard gates were being opened and two men were walking through, both of them wearing traditional Arab dress. One of them was the elderly husband of her employer—a charming, educated man who made Sadie think yearningly of the grandfather she could just about remember—while the man with him... Sadie made an involuntary sound deep in her throat, her eyes widening and her heart thudding heavily into her chest wall. The other man was quite simply so compellingly male, and so arrogantly alive with raw sexuality and power, that he was mesmerizing. All Sadie could do was stand there gazing—no, not gazing at him so much as gaping in awe, Sadie mentally derided herself. She who had not only never gaped at a man before, but who had never imagined she would want to do so.

She could feel her face turning pink as he turned his head, so that instead of just seeing his profile she met a full-on swift, hawkish assessment from a pair of narrowed, shockingly unexpected ice-green eyes. Ice-green? Her hands were trembling so much she almost dropped her handbag, grabbing hold of it as it threatened to slip sideways from her grasp.

What was happening to her? Her instinctive and immediate response to her physical reaction was to take

refuge in the safety of denial and tell herself that what
was happening was caused by her defences having been
undermined by Monika's attack on her, not by anything—or anyone—else. But she couldn't escape from
the knowledge that with just one glance from those far
too knowing green eyes a total stranger had stripped
from her the protection with which she had previously
kept his sex at bay.

Without saying or doing anything he had broken
through her barriers and made her so intensely aware
of his male sexual driving force that her whole body was
now a mass of chaotic, over-sensitised and far too re-
ceptive sexually attuned nerve-endings.

So *this* was physical desire, then! This white-hot unstoppable flood of bitingly intense, dangerously seductive longing mixed with promise, possessing her and
dominating everything she was feeling and thinking—
changing her from what she had been into something
else as surely as though she had been given into the
hands of a sorcerer.

CHAPTER TWO

'ARE you all right, child?'

Sadie could hear the gentle voice of her employer's husband, but somehow it was impossible to drag her imprisoned gaze away from the dangerous, almost cruelly handsome perfection of the man standing beside him. She felt as though she was having to bring herself back up to the clear light of day from the darkest depths of some secret hidden place.

'Yes. Yes, I'm fine,' she managed to gulp—even though she knew that both men must be perfectly aware that she was not.

She risked another look at Professor al Sawar's much younger companion. To her relief, he wasn't searching her soul with that too-intense glittering look any more, and some of the turbulence inside her subsided, allowing her to tell herself that she had over-emphasised his earlier effect on her—no doubt because of the trauma she had just experienced. Relief poured through her like cool, soothing water on over-heated skin.

She could see in the Professor's face that both men had overheard Monika's angry tirade. Her now ex-

employer's husband reached into his robe and withdraw
a wallet. Normally such an incongruity as the sight of
a modern wallet concealed within the folds of such a
traditional garment would have made her smile, but
now she was struggling too hard to rationalise the rush
of unfamiliar sensations seizing her to do anything other
than note vaguely that the older man was opening his
wallet and withdrawing some money.

'Please—take this…' he was urging her.

Now she *had* to force herself to focus on him.

'I don't know how much my wife owes you, but…'

There was a look in the ice-green eyes that burned
her pride. Her reaction was instinctive and immediate.
Shaking her head, she stepped back mutely.

'Please…' the Professor was insisting.

'No,' Sadie refused fiercely. Whether his act was a
kindness to protect her or a bribe designed to protect his
wife, she didn't know; all she did know was that she
would not and could not take his money, his charity. She
had *earned* her wages, and it was her wages she
wanted—not the professor's generosity.

'No,' she repeated in a calmer, more rational tone,
even if her voice was shaking slightly. She grabbed
hold of her suitcase and hurried towards the still open
courtyard gates.

Drax watched her go, protectively shielding the intensity of his desire by lowering his eyelids to hood his
focused concentration on her. The familiar, dry, sand-
blown scent of the desert in the air he was breathing into
his body was sharpened and flooded by the heat of his
own arousal. Dismissively he mentally shrugged off the

warning his body was activating. He was man, wasn't he? And a man who had perhaps been voluntarily celibate longer than was wise. Drax didn't take women to his bed on sexual impulse. His sense of his position was too strongly developed for that. Actions that potentially shamed him did not just shame him, they shamed Vere—and they shamed the reputation that had been handed down to them. Nevertheless, while it was not his habit to go in for casual serial partner sex, it was perhaps time that he found himself a discreet mistress.

The gates had been closed behind the young woman for several seconds when, as though she had been surreptitiously watching from inside the house, Drax recognised, Monika came into the courtyard, beckoning them both inside. Reluctantly following the Professor, Drax almost missed seeing the small maroon oblong lying on the ground. Bending to pick it up, he frowned when he realised that it was a passport. He opened it, flicking through. Sadie Murray, twenty-five years old, single, light brown eyes, dark blonde almost brown hair, her only distinguishing mark a small mole on the inside of her left thigh…

'Vere—it is always such a pleasure to see you,' Monika was gushing, causing Drax's eyes to narrow as she hurried forward to envelop him in the overpowering strength of her scent. Tucking the passport away, he stepped back from her.

'Sadly for both of us, I'm not Vere,' he told Monika coolly. Over a decade ago, in the early days of her marriage to the Professor, when Drax himself had been a young man in his early twenties, Monika had offered

herself to him. She would never forgive him for rejecting her, Drax recognised, and he would never forget that
she had so easily planned to betray her husband.

'I appreciate that you have your reasons for doing so,
my dear, but, really—that poor child…to dismiss her like
that…' the Professor was saying with a worried frown.

'She deserved it,' Monika returned sharply. 'She
refused to carry out my instructions with regard to one of
my clients, and in doing so cost me a great deal of money.'

'But, my dear, she's so young, and all alone in a
foreign country,' the Professor wavered unhappily.
'And morally—'

'Morally? Hah! It is her *morals* that have caused me
so much of a problem. Why should I have to suffer the
disadvantages of employing a young western woman
who has chosen to behave like a traditional virgin?'

'My dear…'

Drax could hear the distress in the older man's voice,
but Monika chose to ignore her husband's shock.

Tossing her head, she continued sharply, 'I need a
female employee who knows how to *persuade* men to
become my clients, not one who freezes them away.'

'Sadie should surely be praised for her virtue,
Monika?' the Professor protested.

'I did not employ her for her virtue. She is pretty
enough, but plainly she doesn't know how to use that
prettiness to her own advantage.' Monika gave a dismissive shrug. 'Now she has to learn the hard way that that
does not make good business sense.'

'You have ensured that she has sufficient money to
pay for her air ticket home?'

Drax watched as Monika's mouth hardened. 'That is not my concern. If she hasn't, then it will teach her much needed lesson. Let me summon the maid and get her to bring you both some coffee,' she told her husband, determinedly changing the subject.

As a Lebanese woman, Monika lived a far more independent life than that of a traditional Zurani wife, who would never have dreamed of even appearing in front of a male guest of her husband, never mind addressing him directly. She was certainly far too strident for his taste, Drax acknowledged, and he shook his head and refused. 'Not for me, Monika. I'm afraid I can't stay. I have an appointment.'

It might only be March, but Zuran did not have a spring. Its climate went straight from a welcome 'cool' winter temperature of around twenty-five degrees in February to a swiftly climbing forty-five-degrees-plus in the middle of summer.

For Sadie, having to walk all the way into town with her case, and without the hat she normally wore for protection, the rising temperature felt distinctly too hot. Her hair might be thick and long, its burnished light brunette warmed with natural gold highlights, but it was no protection against the sun. At least she had her sunglasses to shield her eyes from the harshness of the sunlight as it bounced off the white-painted walls of the houses lining the roadside.

No one walked in Zuran—which was no doubt why so many male drivers slowed down as they drove past her. At least, that was what she was going to tell herself,

Sadie decided, gritting her teeth as she ignored yet another car driver crawling along beside the kerb, murmuring to her words she was relieved she could not understand before thankfully he drove off when he realised that she had no intention of acknowledging him.

Her dismissal was so unfair. She had been good at her job, she knew that, but no way had she intended to coax and tease men into signing up with Monika by hinting at providing them with a sexual reward that she was not going to deliver. Sadie loathed that kind of female behaviour, and she loathed even more the kind of men who expected it.

Perhaps she was naïve, but it had shocked her to discover that a female employer should expect it of her—especially out here in this predominantly morally conservative part of the world. About her reaction to the man who had been accompanying Monika's elderly husband she did not want to think at all.

Drax was just about to put his foot down to join the fast lane of traffic when the car phone rang. He knew it would be Vere calling him. It was typical of Drax that he never questioned why or how he should know that without looking at his phone. It was just an accepted part of their twinship.

'How did the meeting go with the Ruler?' Vere asked.

'Well enough—although I don't think he was too pleased that I turned up in your place. And, speaking of people who weren't as pleased to see me as they would have been to see you, I've just seen the Professor. Monika asked to be remembered to you.'

'So you've been too busy to find me a wife, I take it?' Vere responded, ignoring Drax's dig about Monika.

Up ahead of him, in the dust of the roadside, Drax could see the lone figure of a young woman walking and dragging her suitcase behind her. She looked weary—forlorn, almost.

What was it Amar has said about her? That she was modest, the kind of young woman he would be happy to see his son marry. Drax remembered the passport he had picked up. By rights he should have handed it over to the al Sawars, because the girl would surely return there to look for it once she realised she had lost it.

She certainly wasn't greedy, he acknowledged. He had seen that with his own eyes. And she *had* to be naïve if she'd let herself be persuaded into working for Monika.

'Drax? Are you still there?'

'Yes, I'm still here, Vere. As to your bride—well, that's where you are wrong, my brother. It just so happens that I may have found you the perfect temporary wife.'

Drax switched off his phone before Vere could say anything, and then started to cut the speed of his car.

Sadie could hear the now familiar tell-tale sound of a car braking to a crawl just behind her, but she refused to look round. However, this car didn't pull away as quickly as the others had when she did not respond. Instead it continued to keep pace with her, casting a long shadow in front of her. She tried to walk a little bit faster, wishing she could move away from the side of the road, but the land beyond was too rough for her to wheel her case over it.

There was no need for her to panic, she assured herself. It was broad daylight and, even if he was being more persistent than the others, surely whoever it was would soon get bored when she didn't respond, soon put his foot down to race past her in a cloud of sandy dust.

Only he didn't. And out of the corner of her eye she could see a long black bonnet edging just ahead of her, then keeping pace with her.

She couldn't walk any faster; she was panting slightly already, her skin soaked with perspiration caused not just by the heat now but by her anxiety as well.

'Ms Murray?'

Hearing her name spoken in crisp accent-free English gave her such a shock that she froze. Just as he had estimated she would, she reflected bitterly several seconds later, when the car stopped, the driver's door opened and the driver himself stepped out in front of her, trapping her between his body and his car.

'You!'

Why had she said that? It had sounded so personal and so betraying somehow—as though she were deliberately creating an intimacy between them. And that hadn't been her intention. She was just so shocked to see the man she had last seen standing in the Al Sawars' courtyard with her employer's husband standing in front of her.

Unlike her, he wasn't wearing sunglasses, and something about the look she could see in his eyes made her feel like some poor creature of the desert caught in the predatory searching stare of a falcon.

'If Madame Al Sawar asked you to come after me...' she began uncertainly.

Before she could finish what she was saying Drax silenced her with a swift frown.

'I can acquit you because you do not know me well enough to know that I do not act as an errand boy for others,' he told her arrogantly. 'But do you really know Monika so little that you think she'd show that kind of remorse?'

Sadie looked away from him. He was right, of course. Monika was not the type to suffer from second thoughts, much less guilt over what she had done.

'I came after you because there is something I want to discuss with you. The Professor speaks very highly of you. He considers you to be a young woman of good morals and intelligence.' Drax was not going to tell her that the Professor had also confirmed his own assessment that she was more inclined to think the best of others than the worst, and that this made her vulnerable to the selfish machinations of the unscrupulous.

Sadie could feel a pink flush heating her face as she listened to this praise.

'You are fully qualified to work in the financial services industry, so I understand?'

His question startled Sadie. 'I have a degree and an MBA,' she acknowledged. She could see Drax nodding his head, as though her words had confirmed what he already knew.

'It could be that I can offer you a job to replace the one you have just lost.'

Now he could see uncertainty and suspicion in her eyes, along with the kind of female wariness that made Drax congratulate himself again on his own intuition. She would be perfect for the plan he had outlined to his twin.

Sadie looked at him with a challenging expression. She wasn't so naïve that she wasn't aware that there was a certain type of Arab male who looked to western women to satisfy his sexual needs via a series of brief sex-only liaisons.

'Thank you, but my plan has always been to return to the UK to work.'

'But not without the money to pay your fare or your passport?' Drax suggested.

Her passport? Sadie looked at him, and then looked down at her bag. But there was no need for her to look inside it, because Drax was already holding her passport in his hand.

'What…?'

'Why don't you get in the car?' Drax looked at his watch. 'I can tell you about the job that's on offer over a late lunch in the city.'

Did he really expect her to fall for that kind of line? She wasn't that naïve. 'I'm sorry, but I'm not interested—in anything,' she emphasised firmly, reaching for her passport.

Drax stepped back from her, sliding her passport out of sight somewhere within the folds of his dishdasha.

'Very well,' he said calmly, and turned back to his car.

'My passport…' Sadie protested frantically.

'What passport? If, when I reach the airport for my return flight to Dhurahn, I find that I still have the passport I found lying on the ground in Zuran City, then I shall naturally see that it reaches the nearest British Embassy.'

'What?' This was getting worse by the minute. Not only had he got her passport, he was also planning to leave the country. 'No, you can't do that!' Sadie told him wildly.

'No?' The ice-green eyes had hardened.

Ignoring the warning in them, Sadie tried to grab her passport back from him, crying out as she stumbled over a sharp piece of rock jutting out of the earth and then fell heavily against Drax.

Drax's reactions were quicker than Sadie's. He caught her easily, and could have held her away from him so their bodies didn't come into contact, but for some reason he wasn't prepared to explain to himself he didn't. Instead, he wrapped his hands around her upper arms to steady her, and let her body rest against his own. He could feel the soft rounded swell of her breasts, and the temptation to slide his hands from her arms to her hips, to pull her more intimately against him, was so strong and instinctive that it startled him. She smelled hot and sweet, and her scent caused an unexpected surge of sexual awareness to grip him. It took him off guard.

What the hell *was* this? He didn't normally react with this kind of easy arousal. A man in his position had to be careful about his sexual liaisons. Drax had learned that long ago. He had a responsibility towards the position he held. He and Vere had a shared duty to give their subjects a good example and to set high moral standards. Casual sex wasn't something he indulged in, and yet here he was so stiffly erect that he felt down-right uncomfortable—and all on account of this dusty young woman with her topaz eyes and her pale skin. A woman he had already decided to offer to his brother.

Which was, of course, why he was testing her moral standards. If she took advantage of their shared intimacy now to come on to him he would know there was no point in pursuing his plan. Neither could he afford to become sexually involved with her—it wasn't for sex that he wanted her. She must be proved to be the kind of woman the Professor believed her to be. The kind of woman who was the opposite of women like Monika al Sawar and who would not try to institute sex with a man without being invited to do so.

After Sadie's shock at being so unexpectedly close to Drax, with all its drugging excitement, came recognition of her vulnerability—and with it panic.

'Let go of me!' She sounded more pleading than assertive, Sadie recognised weakly, as she heard the emotion in her own voice. Being this close to this man wasn't good for her, she admitted. It reactivated everything she had felt in the courtyard, and underlined her inability to override her physical response to him.

So why wasn't she doing more to make him release her? Why, in fact, was she leaning into him as though she couldn't stand without the support of his body? Did she really not care about the danger of her own actions? Not just via the casual sex with a stranger he might think she was inviting but, just as dangerously, via the effect her proximity to him was having on what she had always believed to be givens about herself. Givens like the fact that she wasn't a woman who had strong sexual urges; like the fact that she wasn't a woman who could ever be overwhelmed by desire for a man just by looking at him; like the fact that she was far too sensible to take risks with her sexual and emotional health.

It was the heat of the sun that was making her feel weak, she hurried to reassure herself. Nothing else. She certainly wasn't entertaining the kind of fantasies she had heard some western women had about sexy Arab sheikhs—even if this man was everything that such a man should be, right down to the aura of danger surrounding him.

'This is Zuran,' she heard him telling her coldly as he thrust her away. 'Here it is not acceptable for a man and a woman to embrace in public, no matter what you may be used to doing elsewhere!'

What *she* might be used to doing elsewhere? He was making it sound as though he thought she was coming on to him. Mortified, Sadie pulled away from him and stepped back. She was right about one thing. She *had* been out in the hot sun for longer than was wise, and her own sudden movement had caused a wave of faintly nauseating dizziness to swamp her.

The sight of Sadie's suddenly too pale face accompanied by her soft gasp of shock had Drax reacting with instinctive speed as he recognised the onset of heat sickness. He bundled her into the car so quickly that Sadie didn't have time to do anything more than make an incoherent protest. She could feel the car depressing as he slid into the driver's seat and switched on the engine. She could hear too the sound of the doors locking as he set the car in motion and pulled away from the kerb.

'Stop,' she said frantically. 'You can't do this!'

'What would you have preferred me to do—leave you where you were to suffer sunstroke?'

'There's plenty of shade in the city.'

'You would never have made it that far,' Drax told her bluntly, before adding, 'And you needn't look at me like that. You have nothing to fear from me.'

'That's easy for you to say,' Sadie retorted shakily. 'You've practically kidnapped me, and—'

'And now you're worried that I might be carrying you off to my harem to have my wicked way with you?' Drax mocked her, raising one dark eyebrow. 'Do you really think that's likely? Let's be honest with one another—in today's world, if I wanted to indulge myself sexually with a disposable partner I would hardly need to kidnap one, would I?'

Her eyes were the colour of clear warm honey, Drax noticed, her tawny hair as polished and silken as the coat of one of his cherished pure-bred Arab mares. He sensed within her the same pride that possessed his falcons—a pride he had the power and the skill to tame, so that they came to his hand as softly, as though they were doves.

Her skin was too pale, though, for the harshness of the desert's midday sun, and she was paying for her folly in ignoring that fact now. Perspiration beaded her forehead and her head drooped on the slender stem of her neck. Drax guessed that in addition to her obvious apprehension at being bundled into his car she was probably also feeling slightly nauseous. She was certainly likely to be dehydrated.

He reached out and tapped open the centre console

that separated their seats. 'You will find a bottle of water in here. Take it and drink some,' he advised her sternly.

Water! Until he had spoken she hadn't realised how thirsty she was. Sadie's tongue-tip flicked against the dry saltiness of her lips as she reached eagerly for the unopened bottle.

Removing the top, she lifted the bottle towards her mouth.

The traffic was heavy enough for Drax to slow down and watch her. Her lips were soft and full, and as she closed them around the head of the bottle she also closed her eyes, as though she was giving herself over to a much longed-for sensory pleasure. She drank quickly, the muscles of her throat contracting and expanding as she swallowed and then drank more deeply.

The arousal Drax had felt earlier returned, thrusting past the barriers of civility and necessity. Was she aware of just how intensely erotic her actions were? Drax wondered, as between one breath and the next he became trapped within the sexual urgency and immediacy of the images his own brain was creating from her actions. Inside his head the soft fullness of her lips clung eagerly not to the water bottle but to his flesh, greedily absorbing its texture and taste. A pothole in the road caused water from the bottle to trickle from her lips down her throat and beyond, filling the hollow at its base and then spilling from it. If he were to lap its wetness from her skin now it would taste of her flesh and her heat, and the taste would feed his tongue to taste her more intimate wetness, to...

The sudden sharp blare of a car horn somewhere up

ahead of them wrenched Drax out of his fantasy and back to reality. His heart was the thudding in slow, heavy erotic beats as it urged his body to greater arousal. He reached for his own bottle of water, and drank fiercely from it, as though to quench the heat of what he was experiencing.

The air-conditioning was on, so why was she suddenly feeling aware of a heat so physical that it not only seemed to be filling the interior of the car, it also felt as if it was actually touching her, pressing against her skin as though in a caress? Because she wanted to be caressed? By him? What kind of craziness had possessed her? Was this some kind of heat-induced lust that was a by-product of too much exposure to the sun? Sadie's thoughts spilled dizzily on top of one another, blocking her rational exit from them. She fought valiantly against them, making herself focus on the scenery outside the car.

'We're almost in the city,' she told Drax. 'It's kind of you to think about offering me a job, but really there's no need. If you give me my passport and drop me off—'

'You're rejecting the job without knowing what it is?'

Sadie's words had aroused two very different and competing instant reactions inside Drax—one, that he should stop the car, give her the passport and forget that he had ever seen her; the other that there was no way he was going to let her go.

He pressed harder on the accelerator, swinging the car into the outer lane that led away from the city.

CHAPTER THREE

'As JOINT rulers of Dhurahn, my brother and I have for some considerable time been looking into ways to provide our country and our people with a prosperous future once our oil runs out.'

Did he really expect her to believe that *he* was a ruler of Dhurahn? She had heard of Zuran's neighbouring state, but she had also seen the protocol and the hierarchy of personnel that attended Zuran's Ruler whenever he left the palace.

'To this end, as you may know, we have developed an agricultural policy that has led to us provide other Gulf States with fresh produce. That is all well enough in its own way, but my brother and I both believe that we need something more. To effect this we have been in negotiation for some time now with various organisations in the City of London, with a view to establishing a business and financial centre of excellence within Dhurahn.'

Sadie started to frown. She *had* heard vague rumours of something like this, she acknowledged. In the way of such things word had got out of this ambitious plan by an unnamed gulf state, and she had also heard the

young male MBAs with whom she'd worked stating
that if the plan went ahead it would be a golden opportunity for the ambitious.

'My brother and I are now at a stage in our negotiations where we are looking to put together a team
of young MBAs to work with the experts we'll be
bringing in to implement our plans. Professor al
Sawar, who was a long-standing friend of our late
father, speaks very highly of you, and naturally it
occurred to me that you would be an ideal candidate
for our team.'

Drax gave a small shrug. 'Of course I appreciate that
offering you a job in this manner is not exactly orthodox
business procedure, but events have moved ahead with
more speed than we had anticipated. Interviewing and
selecting a large number of the right young graduates and
MBAs is going to take time. We have therefore decided
to set up a small, specially selected team with all speed.
The fact that you are here in Zuran and in need of a job
makes you an ideal candidate for a place on that team.

'Time is very much of the essence here. My brother
has to leave for London for further negotiations, and I
need to return to our country to allow him to do so, since
one of us must always be resident in Dhurahn. If I can
take you back with me and set you to work, initially as
my PA with regard to the preliminary paperwork and
the setting up of procedures and negotiations, that will
allow me to have more time to work on other aspects
of this ground breaking project.

'You will be well paid. My brother and I have already
agreed upon a salary scale for our young graduates—it

is almost double the best rate paid in London, and I assure you that you *will* be paid. As rulers of Dhurahn our word is our bond, and we do not operate the same kind of business ethics as Monika al Sawar.'

'You don't really expect me to believe that you're a ruler of Dhurahn, do you?' Sadie challenged him. Just what kind of idiot did he take her for?

'You're accusing me of lying to you? Why should I bother to do that?'

'Rulers of Arab states don't drive themselves around without escorts, or—'

'You know this for a fact, do you? So, how many rulers of Arab States exactly are you familiar with? Have you any idea just how insulting you are being?' he asked Sadie softly. 'Under traditional Dhurahni law people can be locked away for the rest of their life for such an insult to a member of its Ruling Family. In ancient times they would have had their tongue cut out so that they could never speak another lie. That was if they were allowed to live.'

Sadie shuddered, sickened by the graphic image he was forcing on her. He was certainly every inch the haughty all-powerful potentate whose word was absolute law, she admitted, wishing now that she had not spoken out so rashly.

'I do not lie, Ms Murray. I do not need to. I could drive back to Zuran City and take you to the Ruler to verify my identity for you. Indeed, I could ask the same of your own Embassy. But I don't have time. I need to return to Dhurahn before my brother leaves.'

Sadie saw the look in his eyes as his mouth curled

downwards in hard dismissal, and knew that he meant what he said.

It was still hard for to take what he was saying at face value—especially after she had been so naïvely taken in by Monika.

'I find it hard to accept that you're willing to offer me a job without knowing anything about me, or—'

'Here in the Gulf we believe very strongly in fate. It is true that when I left the Royal Palace earlier today with Professor al Sawar the thought of employing you or anyone else was not something I had planned. However, a clever man does not ignore the opportunities that fate offers to him.' Drax gave another shrug. That was certainly what he believed, even if the opportunity he believed 'fate' had given him on this particular occasion was not the one he was now promoting to Sadie Murray.

'A contract will be drawn up that allows us both a probationary period in which to assess the consequences of what might seem to be a too-hasty decision. I have no desire to keep you in my country against your will. An unwilling worker is of no benefit to Dhurahn. As co-rulers of Dhurahn, both my brother and I are well aware of that. Neither of us would ever tolerate anything that prejudices the progress or the reputation of our country. And, just for the record, I have no desire to keep you in my bed unwillingly, where the same principle applies. I see no pleasure to be gained in a woman who is not there of her own free will and her own desire.'

Sadie was struggling to get her head around not just

what Drax was saying but also the whole *Arabian Nights* fantasy of being told by the ruler of a Gulf State that he wanted to whisk her off to his kingdom.

However, his purpose in taking her there was not because he wanted her to give him one thousand and one nights of pleasure, as Scheherazade had given her Caliph master with her fabulous stories, but—far more mundanely—so that he could use her expertise to help build a world-class knowledge economy with a world-class financial exchange to rival those of London, New York and Hong Kong. If what she was being told was the truth…

Surely rulers travelled in cavalcades of cars, surrounded by courtiers and security men? They did not drive themselves around in ordinary, if up-market, saloon cars. The ease with which Monika had deceived her still stung. This man—Drax, as she recalled hearing the Professor call him—might physically possess the kind of arrogance that went with high estate, but that did not mean he actually was what he claimed to be.

'I…it all sounds so far-fetched,' she told him doubtfully.

The green eyes glittered a look over her that was a combustible mixture of savage fury and arrogant disbelief.

'You *dare* to persist in trying to accuse me of being a liar?'

'I have a right to protect myself from being tricked into another situation in which I end up being out of pocket,' Sadie defended herself. 'There is a saying—"If a man makes a fool of me once, shame on him. If twice, shame on me." You *say* you are a co-ruler of Dhurahn.'

'I say it because that is what I am,' he retorted. 'I am not Monika al Sawar. I *am* co-Ruler of Dhurahn, with a moral responsibility towards my brother to act in a way that cannot possibly leave any stain on his honour, just as he has that responsibility to me.'

So much had happened in such a short space of time, the changes in her circumstances had been so seismic, that Sadie suspected she wasn't in any fit state to make any kind of decision—never mind one as potentially reckless as agreeing to accept the job she was being offered.

And yet what alternative did she really have? She had no money, no family in the true sense to love and support her in England, should she choose to return, no job to return to there, and no passport to return there with, thanks to the man seated next to her, she reminded herself grimly. And what kind of message did that give her—the fact that he was prepared to use such an under-hand method to force her to do as he wished?

'What if I choose not to accept your offer?' she demanded.

Drax could hear the uncertainty in her voice. As though he could see into her head, he could imagine her thoughts. She had come to the Gulf in order to change her life in some way; that desire would still exist, despite Monika al Sawar's behaviour towards her.

'Why would you do that?' he asked her coolly. 'Dhurahn can match everything that Zuran can offer you and exceed it. You would be a fool not to accept.

And since I have offered you a job, and I do not offer jobs to fools, you cannot be one.'

Such arrogance. It was breathtaking. And exciting? Was she excited by it? By him? Thoughts she had never imagined were whirling through her head like grains of sand being whipped up by the desert wind, to create a mesmerizing, whirling force that changed the known to the unknown.

This man—powerful sheikh or lying braggart—possessed that same power as the dessert wind, and for better or for worse she was being swept into the maelstrom of excitement and uncertainty he was creating within her.

If he was speaking the truth then surely she would be a fool to turn down this kind of opportunity? Especially now, with no earnings to show for her time in Monika's employ and the burden of her student loan still hanging over her.

'If I take this job you are offering me, there will be two conditions,' she told him firmly.

She was attempting to *bargain* with him? A woman? Powerless, jobless, trapped in his car, and wholly at his mercy? She was either very foolish or very brave. Vere would appreciate neither of those qualities. He was a fair man, but very autocratic. Whereas he…

He, Drax admitted to himself, was not always fair and autocratic—only when it suited him. Vere often teased him that he was Machiavellian. Drax preferred to think that he understood people and their weaknesses.

'And those conditions are?'

Sadie took a deep breath.

'That you return my passport to me and that you pay

me—*before* we leave for Dhurahn—an advance on my salary sufficient to pay for a return ticket to the UK.'

So she had learned something from working for Monika after all.

'Certainly.'

Sadie looked at him uncertainly, wondering if she had misheard his prompt and affirmative response.

'You agree?' she questioned him.

'I'm beginning to see why Monika found it so easy to manipulate you,' Drax told her. 'A good negotiator behaves as though he or she believes themselves to be in an unassailably strong position even if they know that they are not.'

His instincts about her had been right. There was a softness, a vulnerability about her, that would make her perfect for his plans. The fact that in asking for an advance of her salary all she had asked for was the price of her air ticket home added to his confidence in his own intuition.

'Yes, I agree—but with a condition of my own. And that is that while I am prepared to advance you the money you require before we leave Zuran, I am not prepared to return your passport to you until we reach Dhurahn. Still, you have at least shown some initiative—and I must say that I am impressed that you believe you are in a position to make conditions,' Drax told Sadie smoothly.

'And I am amazed that you would want someone working for you who was not aware of their value,' Sadie countered. When his eyebrows lifted and she saw the cynicism in his eyes, she added swiftly, 'The fact that Monika cheated me out of my wages does not lessen the value of my qualifications.'

'I agree. But it does raise questions about your judgement. Academic qualifications on their own are all very well, but the shrewdest and most successful entrepreneurs will admit that it is the instincts they have honed and come to rely on that create the alchemic effect to turn the base metal of mere scholarship into the pure gold of financial genius. And that, surely, is true of every sphere of achievement?'

'You are the one who offered me a job, not the other way around,' Sadie felt bound to remind him.

But instead of responding to the anger in her voice Drax changed the subject, demanding coolly, 'Monika's accusations against you interest me. What exactly did she mean?'

His question had caught her off guard. Sadie looked away from him, not wanting him to see her naked expression and read in it what she would prefer to keep hidden.

'She wanted me to…to persuade her clients that certain investments were of better value and more promising than she knew them to be.'

A tactful and evasive answer, Drax acknowledged. But, knowing Monika as he did, it wasn't one he had any difficulty in interpreting.

'She wanted you to use your sexual allure to sell unsafe investments, you mean?' he suggested. It was no less than he had worked out for himself, but it interested him to witness her obvious discomfort in talking about it. Because she had felt obliged to give in to Monika's bullying?

Drax's good humour evaporated. A woman who had sold herself sexually, even if she had been forced to do so by someone else, was not the kind of woman who could become the wife of a ruler of Dhurahn— even in a marriage that was to be both temporary and unconsummated.

When Sadie didn't say anything his mouth compressed. The light mockery disappeared from his voice as he demanded, far more sharply, 'It was only sexual allure she expected you to use, I trust? And not something more intimate…?'

'There was a suggestion from her that I might flatter some of the clients a little more than I felt was morally acceptable,' Sadie told him reluctantly. He was, after all, a friend of Monika's husband, even if he had made it plain that he did not like Monika herself.

'She wanted you to have sex with her clients in return for them giving her their business? Is that what you mean?'

'She never said that in as many words, but it was plain enough what she expected me to do.'

'And did you?'

Sadie was too outraged to think of being tactful.

'*No*. I did not. That is *not* the way I live my life,' she told him furiously. 'And it never will be. So if you are thinking of suggesting that I—'

He stopped the car with such force that she was thrown against her seatbelt.

'*What?* You would dare to suggest that I, a ruler of Dhurahn, would sink to such depths?'

Sadie could see how much she had offended him. Where before she had seen arrogance, now she could see a fierce, steely pride.

'I wasn't making any accusations. I was simply stating what I am not prepared to do,' Sadie defended herself.

She was speaking the truth. Drax could see that. Everything was as he had hoped—and expected. She was perfect for Vere, and he was a genius for having found her—and for having seized the opportunity she afforded so swiftly and effectively, he congratulated himself.

He turned his attention back to the road, setting the car in motion again.

'So it is agreed that you will accept the job I have offered you and will return with me to Dhurahn?'

Was it? Sadie hadn't given any verbal agreement to do anything, but somehow she wasn't able to say as much to him. And she couldn't really blame him for taking her silence as a sign that she had accepted what he had said, she acknowledged, when several minutes later he told her, 'We should be at the airport in less than half an hour.'

'I'll need my passport,' Sadie felt bound to point out.

The look he gave her reduced her to immediate silence.

'We will be returning to Dhurahn in my own private jet. Naturally, as an employee I have personally appointed, there will be no need for you to go through passport control either in Zuran or Dhurahn.'

However, he would have to telephone the palace and make his excuses to Zwar's Ruler for returning to Dhurahn at such short notice, Drax acknowledged.

His own private jet. Sadie struggled not to look too overwhelmed.

'I am not sure…er… That is… I'm afraid I don't know your correct title or how I should address you,' she managed to say uncertainly.

He gave a small shrug of the powerful shoulders she had already noticed.

'My brother and I both had a very liberal upbringing. Our mother was Irish and our father wanted us to follow in his footsteps and be educated in England and Paris. While the traditionalists in our country still use our titles, since we are modelling our new venture on modern lines everyone will be on first-name terms with one another. Therefore you will address me as Drax.

'Drax…'

She made his name sound as though she was tasting it—a soft whisper of sound as her lips parted round the 'D' and then closed softly on the 'x'.

'It is a family name,' he told her dismissively, irritated with himself for the images that were forming inside his head. He had seen far more beautiful women and had known far more sensually explicit and carnal women—so what was it about this woman that uniquely invested so much of what she said with such an intense sensuality that just being with her had his body in an almost constant state of arousal? It was a reaction to her he would have to destroy, since it was Vere who would have the right to claim her sexually—if he chose to do so.

The sudden savage surge of male possessiveness that gripped him made him frown. He was engaged in a matter of great diplomatic importance—one that must not be prejudiced by some ill-considered sexual lust. He had been too long without a woman. That was all that was causing him to feel desire for her, Drax reassured himself. It was over a year since he had ended his last relationship, and it was no wonder that his body was reminding him of its needs.

There was a very discreet and elegant retired belly dancer who had returned to Dhurahn after the death of her elderly husband and would be more than glad to welcome him into her bed, and she understood the rules that would govern their relationship without him having to spell them out to her. She was only just thirty, and stunningly beautiful.

They were at the airport. Sadie felt her stomach muscles start to clench. Was she doing the right thing? Was it too late for her to change her mind?

Change *her* mind? So far all the decisions had been made for her, not by her, Sadie forced herself to admit. And yet, if she was honest with herself, there was something exciting and energising about the thought of the career challenge that now lay ahead of her. If he—*Drax*—this Arabian sheikh who had swept into her life like the hot desert wind and taken her over, was telling her the truth.

CHAPTER FOUR

ZURAN airport was world-famous for its elegance and the number of shops in its duty-free shopping mall.

A snap of his fingers and a few quiet words from Drax had ensured that they were ushered through the airport's security system by Zurani officials, and her case had been politely but firmly taken from her.

Without knowing quite how it had happened, Sadie discovered that she was obliged to walk behind her new employer, following in his wake as he strode arrogantly through the brightly lit mall with its designer label shops. He spoke into his mobile phone in Arabic, holding a conversation with someone who made him laugh several times. A woman? Sadie wondered. *His* woman?

The ferocity of the sensation that spiked through her shocked her into stopping abruptly, and it took the hasty apology of someone bumping into her to break her out of the paralysis that had seized her. It wasn't quite so easy to move her thoughts on. Why on earth had the thought of a man she hardly knew having a sexual relationship with another woman stopped her in her tracks and filled her with such a fierce surge of envy? *Envy?*

That wasn't what she had felt at all, she hastily denied to herself.

She needed to find something else to focus her thoughts on. Determinedly, she looked around the impressive terminal hallway.

Huge gold palm trees reached up the full three floors of what was claimed to be the world's biggest and most exclusive duty-free airport shopping mall. Tiny sparkling lights illuminated the trunks and the leaves, and beneath her feet the marble floor was immaculately clean. Everywhere she looked she could see evidence of Zuran's wealth and status—and that of the travellers filling the mall. Being here reminded Sadie of how she had planned to treat herself to a few new things before returning home, thinking that the salary Monika had agreed to pay her would allow her some small indulgences.

Her wardrobe badly needed revamping; that was for sure. The cheap business clothes she had bought for her first job were now worn and shabby, and not really suited to the Gulf's hot climate. Monika had promised her that she would provide her with a working wardrobe of clothes on her arrival in Zwar, but as with everything else the promised new clothes had never materialised. Now, looking at the displays in the windows of the shops lining the mall bearing the exclusive logos of well-known high-profile designers, and being surrounded by elegantly dressed women, Sadie couldn't help giving a small sigh. She was not a materialistic person, but she still paused wistfully to look towards the windows, all too aware of how unfavourably she compared to both the mannequins in the shops and the women around her.

Yes, it would have been fun to treat herself to some new clothes. Fun, but now, thanks to Monika, impossible, she told herself sturdily. She quickened her pace to catch up with her new employer, the co-Ruler of Dhurahn—she still wasn't sure she would be able to get used to addressing him informally as Drax. She just hoped that she was doing the right thing, that she wasn't jumping out of one bad situation into another that was potentially even worse—because it was obvious to her that she couldn't change her mind now. Drax had her passport and she had no money.

Up ahead of them several small electric buggies were waiting.

'These will take us to the Royal runway,' Drax informed her matter-of-factly as he was ushered into the first buggy. Accompanied by the same officials who had escorted them through the airport, Sadie had to travel behind him.

A group of uniformed and robed officials were waiting to receive them when the buggies came to a halt, and Sadie watched as the waiting men salaamed respectfully to Drax, who in turn merely inclined his head, indicating that there was no question of who was the highest ranking person there.

An immaculate strip of beautiful carpet ran from the exit to the foot of the steps leading up to a gleaming jet waiting on the tarmac, and overhead a canopy had been erected to protect them from the sun. This was travelling as Sadie had never experienced it before.

The robed officials surrounded Drax, their dark silk cloaks billowing in the wind as they escorted him to the plane. Sadie's escort consisted of a small group of men dressed in white tunics, traditional baggy trousers and richly embroidered waistcoats bearing the device of the Royal Ruling Family of Zuran. One of them was carrying her shabby case. She felt as though she had stepped into some kind of parallel but very unfamiliar world, and if she was honest she was beginning to feel completely overwhelmed by it.

Several smartly uniformed men, who looked as though they must be the pilots and crew, were waiting at the bottom of the steps to the aircraft. Like the officials, they too bowed respectfully to Drax, and Sadie caught an unmistakably Australian twang in the voice of one of them as he murmured respectfully, 'Highness.'

As Drax started to mount the steps, Sadie hung back. It was almost as though she didn't exist, as though he had forgotten all about her. Her throat had gone tight, and suddenly she felt very alone and forlorn.

As though somehow he had sensed what she was feeling, Drax turned round to look at her. Although he didn't say a word, somehow Sadie found that she was climbing the steps towards him, as though compelled to do so by some power that was emanating from him. There was something in the commanding intensity of those green eyes that exerted as much of a pull on her senses as any magician from an Arabian fairytale might have done. A man like this could be dangerous to know for a woman like her, an inner voice warned her, but Sadie refused to listen to it. This was the twenty-first century, and she was far too much of a modern woman to let herself drift off into some foolish fantasy about powerful, sensual desert men and their effect on her sex.

Assuming a businesslike expression, she followed Drax into the plane. Inside, the jet was nothing like any aircraft she had ever flown in before. There were no rows of seats. Instead there was a large open space, its walls painted a subtle shade of blue-grey and its floor covered in off-white carpet. Several very modern-looking leather chairs were artfully placed around the space, which also held a large black desk with a computer, on which Drax was already working.

A uniformed steward came towards her, guiding her to a chair. 'There is a TV screen concealed in the wall opposite you,' he told her, offering her a handset and earphones. 'And on the opposite side of the dividing screen you will find a guest bedroom and bathroom, should you wish to rest in private. However, the flight time to Dhurahn is only one hour, and I shall be serving champagne and canapés before we take off, followed by a meal. If you have any dietary preferences…?'

'No, none,' Sadie answered, trying to perch upright on the edge of the leather chair in a businesslike manner, resisting the temptation to subside into its luxurious comfort. There was something about its shaping that invited the human body to abandon itself into a languorously sensual pose that she didn't feel was appropriate for an employee on probation.

Putting an automatically dialled call through to his brother, Drax swung round to look at her while he waited for Vere to answer. She looked uncertain and slightly overwhelmed. That was good. He wanted to ensure that he kept the upper hand, and the slight apprehension she was betraying reinforced his confidence in what he was doing. He was pretty sure she didn't speak Arabic, but just in case he swung back to face his desk, away from her, keeping his voice low as he answered Vere's, 'Yes, Drax?'

'I am just about to leave Zuran, Vere, and I am returning with a very special gift for you. Perhaps it will give you a hint as to what it is when I tell you that its price is above rubies.' When his brother made no response Drax added softly, 'I have found you the perfect temporary wife, and I am bringing her back to Dhurahn with me.'

'*What?*'

Drax laughed. 'It is true. I have found you a wife, Vere, and she is perfect for our purpose. Wait until you see her.'

'Seeing her is all I shall have time for, Drax. I am leaving for London as soon as you are back.'

Vere had sounded more incredulous than pleased by his news, Drax admitted when the call ended. He frowned as he looked across at Sadie, who was still struggling to sit upright in a chair that was designed for reclining. She looked unsure of herself, and slightly stressed. His brother was a man who liked elegant, immaculate women—and, no matter how perfect she might be in other ways, as far as her personal appearance went she was not dressed or groomed in a way that would appeal to Vere.

Sensing that she was being watched, Sadie looked toward Drax, colouring up when she saw the way he was scrutinising her. It was not a flattering look she was being given—quite the opposite—and her face started to burn.

'I have some business to attend to before we take off,' Drax told her. 'But it won't take more than half an hour. Beyond this office there is a private suite, which includes a bedroom and a bathroom.'

'Yes, I know. The steward has already told me that,' Sadie interrupted him hurriedly, wondering if she looked as flustered and uncomfortable as she felt. The truth was that she simply wasn't used to sexy, powerful men telling her in drawling, wickedly sensual voices about bedrooms and bathrooms being on hand, should she require them.

The now familiar lift of one dark eyebrow signalled its owner's disdainful reaction to her interruption.

'Excellent. I appreciate that you left the al Sawars' in some haste, and that you may wish to refresh yourself and change your clothes prior to our arrival in Dhurahn, when I hope to be able to introduce you to my brother before he leaves for London. Ali will show you where everything is, and bring your bag to you, should you need it. And now, if you will excuse me, I must attend to a small matter of business I have overlooked.'

He was leaving her here alone on the plane? She had to fight not to spring up and cling to him, begging not to be abandoned. Abandoned? By a man she barely knew? She was being totally ridiculous.

But he had taken control of her life, Sadie recognised as Ali salaamed him out of the doorway, and received another of those regal inclinations of Drax's dark head in response. And in doing so he had thrust her into a kind of lifestyle in which she felt totally alien and insecure.

And was she being over-sensitive, or had he been

hinting that she looked as though she was in need of a change of clothes? He had mentioned that she would meet his brother. Meet him, or be inspected and then potentially rejected by him because of her appearance? Did it matter if she was? The extent to which she felt mortified by the thought of being considered not smart enough to work for the Rulers of Dhurahn told her that it did. And yet hadn't she always despised the attitude of men like her stepfather, who judged others on their outer appearance and their material possessions?

There was a big difference between being judged for one's physical beauty or lack of it and being considered unkempt and slightly scruffy, Sadie told herself. To be fair, she knew that the majority of employers in the financial sector preferred their employees to look smart and businesslike.

She reached down for her handbag, intending to open it and find a mirror to check to see if she looked as bad as she was beginning to feel, but before her fingers had curled round its handle Ali had materialised at her side, holding a tray on which she could see a full glass of pale, bubbling champagne and a plate of deliciously mouth-watering canapés. At the sight of her food her stomach gave a betraying rumble, which Ali effected not to notice.

'His Highness informed me that you may wish to use the guest suite. Please allow me to show you.' He had bent down and picked up her handbag before Sadie could stop him, leaving her with no real option other than to trot obediently alongside him as he guided her through the office-cum-lounge area into a narrow corridor that led to a pair of closed doors.

'This is the guest suite,' Ali told her, somehow managing to open the door while still carrying the tray and her handbag. 'The door next to it leads to the private suite of Their Highnesses. It is kept locked at all times, unless Their Highnesses specify otherwise.'

A subtle warning to her not to think of going snooping around to see what the Royal suite looked like? Sadie wondered as Ali held open the door for her to precede him into the guest suite.

To her amazement, it contained not only a large double bed but a wall of fitted cupboards and a built-in dressing table, plus two chairs and a small table. In the adjoining bathroom there was full-size shower and a basin.

Sadie looked at the shower. The thought of standing under it and washing the dust of Zuran off her hair and body was tempting—and not just because her skin felt so grubby and gritty from her hot walk. There would be something metaphorically beneficial about having a clean, fresh start to her life and her new job.

She would need a change of clothes, though. She had no idea where her case was, but as though he had read her mind Ali put the tray down on the table, placing her handbag beneath it, and then went to open the cupboard doors. Inside were her clothes, neatly hung up and looking undeniably tired and out of place in their luxurious new setting. A bit like her?

'Thank you, Ali,' she said to the hovering steward.

'You wish me perhaps to prepare the shower for you?' he asked politely.

'What? Oh, no…no. I can manage, thank you,' Sadie assured him swiftly.

It was silly of her to feel so overwhelmed. The Al Sawars had employed a large staff, and Monika's personal maid had done everything for her including running her bath. Sadie knew that.

Was it safe to have a shower now, while they were on the ground? she wondered. What would happen if they took off while she was in it? She had visions of water sloshing everywhere, ruining the carpets and perhaps even flooding into the forbidden Royal suite. She looked uncertainly at Ali.

'Is it all right to use the shower now?' she asked him self-consciously. 'I mean, before we take off?'

'It is very good,' he assured her solemnly. 'The airplane, he does not go until His Highness is back on board. I will tell him that you use the shower and he will tell the Captain.'

If she was quick she might have time to be in and out of the shower and dressed before Drax returned. It would certainly give her pride a much-needed boost if she could present herself to him looking freshly groomed.

'Thank you, Ali,' she said to the steward again. 'I shall shower and change now, then, if that's all right?'

'It is very good,' Ali repeated. 'You will call me, please, if you wish anything? Perhaps more champagne?'

There was no lock on the bedroom door—but then there was no need for her to lock it, Sadie assured herself. She had never found the al Sawars' staff to be anything other than respectful and polite, and Ali certainly hadn't struck her as being anything other than trustworthy.

Five minutes later she stepped beneath the shower

and felt the bliss of its warm water on her skin, even better than she had anticipated. To see the fine grains of sand sluicing down with the water into the shower tray made her change her mind about not bothering to wash her hair. If she couldn't dry it then she would plait it, and at least it would be clean—even if it meant taking a longer shower than she had planned.

Drax frowned as he watched the line of immaculately dressed young women handing over the glossy designer logo carrier bags to his waiting staff. He had bought what he had thought most suitable—not just for a young woman about to enter the employ of the ruling house of Dhurahn, but also for the prospective bride of one of them. Guessing Sadie's size for the clothes hadn't been too much of a problem. He had enough experience to make a pretty shrewd estimate of her measurements. But to be on the safe side he had instructed the boutiques to supply the shoes they had suggested went best with the outfits in two sizes. Now she would have a wardrobe fit for a young woman well-groomed enough to catch the eye of his fastidious brother, complete with some discreet pieces of costume jewellery and a Cartier watch.

Drax stepped into the interior of the jet and the waiting stewards closed the doors.

'Where is Ms Murray?' he asked Ali as the steward offered him a glass of champagne, which he waved away.

'She asked me if there was sufficient time for her to take a shower before takeoff.'

Drax glanced at his watch.

She should be out of the shower by now. He got up

and headed for the guest bedroom. He had no intention of warning Sadie of his plans for her, but he would have to give her some acceptable explanation for the new clothes he had bought her and make sure she wore them from now on.

Sadie was crouched on the floor, wrapped in a large bath towel, going through her almost empty suitcase with increasing disbelief and dismay, looking for the underwear that should have been there but so far she hadn't been able to find. She was oblivious to the brief knock on her door before Drax opened it and walked in.

The shock of seeing him brought her upright, but as she stood her foot caught in the trailing hem of the towel, causing it to slip from her body and leaving her completely naked.

For a heartbeat neither of them moved. Sadie couldn't even breathe, never mind retrieve the towel. But still her soft, pale-skinned rounded breasts lifted slightly, as though she had drawn in her breath, whilst her nipples, still damp from her shower and lightly gilded from the discreetly placed lighting, tightened subtly. But not so subtly that Drax's attention wasn't caught by their quick hardening—a hardening that was reciprocated far less subtly by his own body.

Without taking his gaze off her he pushed the door shut. Its soft click as it locked them together into the silent privacy of the bedroom made a small pulse jerk in Sadie's throat. She made a small sound, a protest that wasn't a protest at all, more a moan of female acknowledgement, her eyes widening as Drax took a step towards her.

It was almost as though she had been turned into two different people, Sadie thought. One of them, the Sadie she knew, was urging her frantically to pick up her towel and conceal her nakedness and her vulnerability with it. But the other Sadie, a Sadie who bemused and astonished her, wasn't listening. She was choosing to stay where she was; she felt only the pure female awareness of the power of her naked body and its right to accept the homage of the man who was subjecting its every curve and line with the look of a critic and a connoisseur.

Sadie had never stopped to think of her body as an object of artistic beauty before, and the Sadie she knew was horrified by the thought. But the other Sadie took pride in knowing that she could command the silent attention of such a man. *She* might as well have been a slave girl, commanded to stand before a man who would buy her for his pleasure, Sadie told herself, trying to goad this new, rebellious side of herself into submitting to angry shame. But instead *that* Sadie mocked her for her cowardice, and whispered to her that a slave girl could command the man who was her master if she had the courage to do so. She could give him such pleasure that *she* was the one who enslaved *him*—so that he was commanded by her pleasure to worship the sensuality she embodied. Such a woman knew how to tempt and torment a man until all he could think of was possessing her; until the slavery between them encompassed and held them both; until he was as shackled to her by the unseen chains of his own desire as surely as she was shackled in the market place for his inspection.

With every thought this unfamiliar Sadie had the old

Sadie could feel herself becoming her, so that her belly hollowed erotically, and her breathing deepened and quickened, and the tight thrust of her nipples hardened into flushed arousal.

He had come here to tell her about the clothes he had bought for her, but the truth was, Drax decided, she didn't need clothes. She was perfect the way she was. And the heavy, unsteady thud of his heartbeat echoed the potency of his thoughts.

The only covering such perfection should have was that of his hands, exploring every silken centimetre of her soft flesh, or his lips, paying her the homage of his male hunger. She would taste of the fruits of her own country, ripe summer berries salted with just enough sharpness before being dipped in honey-sweetened cream that would meld on the tongue, leaving behind the memory of its velvet softness and warm scent. Her skin was as pale as the desert sand in the moonlight, her nipples the rose-gold of the dawn shadows on the mountains beyond the plain, the cleft between her legs as delicately hidden as one of the secret valleys deep in those mountains, concealed from the eyes of men.

If she were his he would command that she always came to him unclothed. He would build her a house with a secluded courtyard, its floor covered in the softest, deepest rugs, so that she could walk upon them without damaging the tender flesh of her feet. He would plant it with thornless roses and scented plants, so that when he took her in its seclusion the scent of the petals crushed beneath her body would release their perfume all around them. She would be his to enjoy as and when he wished.

But she wasn't going to be his. He had chosen her for his brother.

With one swift movement he reached down and retrieved her towel, handing it to her. His curt, 'Cover yourself,' brought Sadie out of the spell her unfamiliar half had woven around her, snapping her back to reality and to the humiliating embarrassment of her nudity.

She snatched the towel from Drax, holding in front of herself, her face on fire. 'You should have knocked,' she told him fiercely.

'I did. When you didn't answer I assumed… wrongly…' His eyes narrowed. 'Or perhaps the assumption I made was the right one? At least as far as *you* are concerned.'

It took several seconds for his meaning to reach her. When it did, the embarrassed pink of her face changed to an angry red.

'If you're trying to suggest that I *wanted* you to come in… Well, I didn't,' she told him flatly, when he didn't say anything. 'And now I'd like you to leave, please, whilst I get dressed.' It struck her that she was in no position to order him around on his own plane, but there was no way she was going to have him making those sort of accusations against her.

'You will have to be quick. I came to warn you that we are about to take off. You will need to be seated in the lounge area and wearing a seatbelt.'

'Fine. I'll only be two minutes.'

'You were looking for something when I came in?'

'It wasn't anything important,' Sadie said quickly. There was no way she could tell him that Monika's maid had omitted to pack her underwear in the case. And not just some of it. All of it.

'We can't waste any more time. There will be a robe in the bathroom—put that on.'

He obviously wasn't going to leave the bedroom without her, Sadie realised. She hesitated, and then, seeing the irritated look he was giving her, wrapped the towel tightly around herself and hurried into the bathroom to retrieve the robe she knew she ought to have put on in the first place.

While she was gone Drax looked at the bed. If he had followed his instincts right now she would be lying on it, her eyes closed in pleasure, her heart beating against the delicacy of her flesh, whilst he kissed and caressed her until she opened herself to him and begged him to possess her. But she wasn't his to possess. That pleasure would belong to Vere—if he chose to take it.

When Sadie emerged from the bathroom, securely wrapped in the bathrobe, Drax was standing beside the bedroom door—holding it open. His face was grim.

Was he going to tell her that he had changed his mind and there was no job for her after all? It frightened her to acknowledge how little she wanted to hear him say that.

CHAPTER FIVE

'CHAMPAGNE?' Drax asked curtly.

How decadent that would be—drinking champagne, dressed in a bathrobe, reclining in an expensive leather seat, in the company of a dangerously handsome and very wealthy man—and how completely opposite to her normal way of life.

'No, thank you,' Sadie said primly. She had already noticed the glossy carrier bags which seemed to fill almost half the floor space of the cabin, and her eyes darkened with an emotion she didn't want to admit to as she contemplated the woman they were destined for and her probable role in Drax's life. The role no doubt her unfamiliar self had been so busily and eagerly promoting for her!

Sadie could feel a hot wash of guilt burning through her body. Of *course* Drax would have a mistress. And more than one, to judge from the number of designer bags in the cabin. What did he do? Summon each one to spend the night with him in a strictly observed rota? Did they all live together, housed in opulent luxury in an old-fashioned-style seraglio, their beauty only ever seen by one man, the whole focus of their lives that of pleasing him and only him? What must that be like? To give oneself over totally and completely to one man's pleasure? To make it and him the whole purpose of one's life? To spend hour upon hour preparing your body for his possession in every way there was? She wasn't prepared for the fierce shudder that gripped her, convulsing her in a series of small physical pangs so intimate and betraying that they made her gasp softly in embarrassed shock.

Immediately Drax focused on her.

'You are afraid of flying?' he demanded sharply.

Well, that was one way of putting it, Sadie thought ruefully, but she shook her head. 'Afraid' wasn't exactly the way she would have described the emotion that had gripped her. Raging jealousy was closer to the mark.

Raging jealousy? Of the women in this man's harem? Had she gone completely mad?

'Then please fasten your seatbelt; we are about to take off.'

They certainly were. Almost before she had done as he'd instructed, she felt the power surge of the jet's engines as it raced down the runway and then lifted into the darkening blue of the early-evening sky. Below them Sadie could see the airport buildings, and then the city itself, and then they were banking and turning out into the Gulf itself, before soaring up into the starry sky.

'You can remove your seatbelt now. Ali will be serving us with a light meal shortly, but first there is something I want to discuss with you.'

This was it. He was going to tell her that he had changed his mind.

'It occurred to me that Monika might not only have retained your wages but also some of your personal possessions, including your clothes, and for that reason I have decided that it is both necessary and appropriate that a replacement wardrobe should be provided to you as part of your salary package. You will understand that, since you are to be working so closely with both myself and my brother on the preparatory work for our country's future as a new financial centre, your appearance must be commensurate with the status of this project. In my country a man is valued for what he is within himself, but nevertheless it is expected that his outer appearance is one that commands the respect of those around him. The poor beggar in the street will never be ignored or refused alms, but neither will he be invited to sit at the side of his ruler.

'I appreciate that in your own country it is not always considered acceptable for a male employer to provide a female employee with a new wardrobe, but here we live by different rules. Therefore, I hope you will understand and accept the necessity for me to provide you with clothing which I consider to be essential to your role.' She wouldn't, of course, grasp the hidden meaning within his words, Drax knew, since she had no idea what his real plans for her were.

'Are you saying that you're providing me with special working clothes?' Sadie queried uncertainly.

'Yes. Although the clothes I have acquired are yours to wear at all times—indeed, I wish to make it clear that you will be required to do so. It is important that you create the right impression even when you are not working.'

Sadie knew that clients in this part of the world could be very demanding, and very specific about their demands, and she was relieved that he was not telling her, as she had feared, that he had changed his mind.

'I expect the cost will be deducted from my salary, will it?' she asked him.

'No. That is not my intention. While we are having dinner Ali will take everything and pack it for you, but I shall require you to select one outfit to wear when we land and I introduce you to my brother. I would suggest the cream suit is probably a good choice.'

As he spoke Drax nodded his head in he direction of the massed carriers, causing Sadie to stare first at them and then at him, before demanding uncertainly, 'You aren't…? I mean, all those…? You can't mean that *all* those are for me!' But she could see from his expression that he did.

He gave a small dismissive shrug. 'We don't know how many formal events you will be called upon to attend. Naturally we shall require you to be appropriately dressed for every occasion.'

She couldn't believe this was happening—and neither could she remove her awed gaze from the glossy carrier bags as Ali served them the meal Drax had mentioned. Then, while Sadie ate food that wouldn't have been out of place in a Michelin-starred restaurant, Ali started to remove the bags to the bedroom.

'I've bought you a couple of cases to hold everything,'

Drax told her. 'I appreciate that you won't want the embarrassment of arriving clutching an untidy array of carrier bags. My brother is an extremely fastidious man who prizes efficiency and neatness above all things.'

'I'll remember that,' Sadie answered dutifully, even as her mind went into overdrive. A designer-brand suit? She had never so much as possessed a designer lipstick, never mind a suit.

If any other man but this one had been offering her a designer wardrobe her suspicions would have been immediately aroused. But not only had Drax shown her that even if he wanted to have a physically intimate relationship with her he was ignoring it, she also knew from Monika that wealthy men here thought nothing of spending obscene amounts of money in ways that were not experienced at home. She had heard of employers handing out solid gold watches to employees for no better reason than that they felt like doing so, or ordering uniforms for their staff and then changing them on a whim because they had seen something else they liked better.

Even so... Sadie looked at the logos on the few remaining bags and swallowed. A cream suit wasn't going to be the only designer item in her new wardrobe. She just hoped that her new clothes were going to fit her.

As Sadie waited to descend the stairs from the now stationary jet, she smoothed the delicate silk skirt of the cream suit. It fitted her perfectly. And, from what she had seen of the rest of the new wardrobe she had been supplied with, the clothes were all in colours that were perfect for her—subtle creams and taupes, cool

white linens, gorgeous chocolate-brown silks, and
thankfully none of the prissy fussy pinks or patterns
she had dreaded.

This suit, highlighted with gold thread and trimmed
with antique lace, was simply cut, and yet had such a
stunning elegance that it had her walking tall. She was
glad she had taken the time to apply a little of the makeup she had found stacked with meticulous neatness into
its own leather travelling case.

Her new luggage alone must have cost a small
fortune, Sadie recognised. It was certainly far more exclusive than anything she could ever have afforded. She
looked down at her strappy high-heeled shoes and
wondered apprehensively if Drax's brother was going
to approve of her being employed by him. She looked
hesitantly at Drax, who was standing a few yards away
from her, talking to the Captain of the jet.

So far he hadn't said a word about her transformed
appearance, or the suit—though he had flicked an assessing glance over her when she'd stepped uncertainly
into the main cabin, having changed into her new
clothes. Did that mean that he was satisfied with her appearance or that he wasn't? She wasn't going to admit
to herself that his lack of response had disappointed her.
He was her employer, nothing more, and there was no
reason why he should comment and no reason why she
should wish him to do so.

'Ready?'

She had been so busy refusing to admit to wanting
his approval that she hadn't noticed that he had stopped
talking to the Captain and was now coming over to her.

'Yes. I... I put on the cream suit, as you suggested. I hope your brother...'

'It looks fine.'

She was wearing her hair up, and several fine tendrils had escaped from the knot at the nape of her neck and were starting to curl softly round her face. The silk stroked lovingly against her body, hinting sensuously at what it concealed as though it were a lover. The fabric itself possessed a quality that made him want to reach out and touch it—and her. He had been aware of that need from the moment she had stepped into the cabin, looking at him with eyes that held both uncertainty and a shy appeal. For what? For him to tell her that she was a highly desirable woman? He couldn't do that. But he wanted to do it. He wanted to tell her to show her just how sexy he found her.

No! He had chosen her for Vere. But that suit was perhaps not the best choice for his brother to see her for the first time. Its soft sensuality underlined her own equally soft sensuality, and would not appeal to Vere. He should have chosen something more tailored, more conservative, Drax told himself as he waited for Ali to open the cabin door.

'When you said you'd bought some luggage for the clothes, I didn't realise...that is...'

They were in the back of a leather-upholstered Bentley, being driven to the palace down a wide straight road, with the sea on one side and the lights of Dhurahn city on the other. The road was lined with palm trees, their trunks decorated with tiny fairy lights, and the overhead street lighting revealed immaculate flower-beds set into green verges. Theirs wasn't the only car on the road, but the Royal pennant fluttering from the bonnet ensured that other traffic gave way so their progress was speedy and stately.

Drax had hardly spoken to her since they had landed, and she still wasn't over the shock of seeing over half a dozen brand-new cream leather suitcases being loaded into the car and realising they contained her new clothes.

'I've already explained the situation with regard to my decision to provide you with a new wardrobe. The matter is now closed.'

Drax didn't even look at her as he spoke, and it was obvious to Sadie that he did not wish to engage in conversation with her, but nevertheless there were questions she needed to ask him.

'We haven't discussed where I am to stay while I am working for you. If it is to be a government-owned apartment, will the rent—?'

'You will be staying in the palace and there will be no rent.'

'In the palace? You mean with you?' The moment the words had left her lips Sadie realised how gauche they sounded, and wished she could recall them, but it was too late. Drax was turning to look at her. In the dark interior of the car his face was highlighted by the streetlights so that she could see its aquiline arrogance. Sadie felt a fierce need to reach out and trace the harshly etched strength. His skin would feel warm beneath her fingertips, the savagely sensual shape of his mouth smooth to her touch...

'I mean that you will be accommodated in the women's quarters within the palace complex.'

'The women's quarters? You mean I'll be staying in a harem?'

Was she imagining that the green gaze had ignited with dark fire?

'The men of my family have for many generations been monogamous and faithful to their single chosen wife. It might excite your imagination to believe otherwise, but that is not the case. There is no harem as such within the walls of the palace. Nevertheless, we are a free society here in Dhurahn. Our people can worship as they please, and we are bound to respect their religious beliefs. Thus we adhere to the tradition of maintaining a separate women's quarter within the palace complex. Our visiting female guests feel more comfortable knowing that their traditions will be respected.'

'But I am not a guest. I am an employee—'

'You have worked in Zuran, so you will be aware that the Ruler there conducts administrative business from within the palace, which is also his private residence and that of his extended family. It is the same for us here in Dhurahn. The palace is our home, but it is also the centre from which our country is run. Members of our extended family as well as some senior officials and their families live and work in the palace. There will be nothing untoward in you residing within the complex. In fact it might be considered rather unusual if you did not. Here, there is normally only one reason a man sets a woman up in her own apartment—and, though it might be a business arrangement, I do not think it is one you would wish to be associated with.'

Sadie's face had begun to burn as she listened to him. He had managed to make her feel both naïve and ignorant of the region's customs.

While they had been talking the car had slowed to a halt outside a pair of huge, beautifully decorated wrought-iron gates depicting a pair of peacocks, their tails spread and studded with richly coloured stones— not *real* jewels? Sadie wondered faintly as the gates swung open and the uniformed guards beyond saluted and then salaamed.

Inside the gates there was a large courtyard, beyond which a flight of cream marble steps led up to a columned portico and a pair of tall wooden doors.

The moment the car stopped alongside the steps the wooden doors opened and a line of household staff appeared, all of them wearing the same livery.

It was like stepping into something out of history, Sadie decided. The kind of gilded luxury she had never imagined experiencing. It should have at worst appalled her and at best overwhelmed her, but as she stood next to Drax, listening to him greeting each man in turn and seeing the way they smiled back at him, she recognised that she was witnessing genuine respect and affection between the co-Ruler of Dhurahn and those who served him.

'My brother?' Sadie heard Drax ask.

'Highness, His Highness sends his apologies for not being here to welcome you home. He is in his private rooms and has asked that you go to him there as soon as you are able.'

Drax frowned. It would be a grave breach of court protocol for him to take Sadie to Vere's private rooms, and he was disappointed that Vere wasn't here to greet them so he could see his brother's amazement when he saw her.

'Please take Ms Murray to the women's quarters and see that she is made comfortable while I speak with my brother,' he instructed one of the waiting men, before turning to Sadie. She looked calm and at ease, her manner towards the palace staff as she inclined her head and smiled both warm and yet just distant enough to command respect. Vere would appreciate that in her, Drax approved, and he went to her and touched her lightly on her arm.

Sadie was amazed at how intensely she could feel the virile warmth of Drax's touch through the soft fabric of her jacket. It jerked her out of the tiredness that had come to seep through her and made her whole body stiffen slightly.

'I have to go and see my brother. Nasim will escort you to the women's quarters. They will make you comfortable there. Please feel free to ask for anything you might need. '

He was turning away from her before she could respond, taking the long flight of marble stairs that led upward to a balcony enclosed by fretted shutters that could conceal anyone watching from above. As she looked upwards Sadie gave a small shudder, suddenly feeling very alone and very alien, as though she were in fact being studied by unseen watchers hidden away from her view.

'This way, please, lady.' Nasim bowed low to her before guiding her towards a door that led off the hallway.

It was foolish in the extreme for her to wish that Drax had not left her, to wish that she could run after him and beg him to stay with her. Foolish and very dangerous—she was going to pretend she hadn't thought it.

'Drax. I have missed you.'

'I have been gone less than a week.' Drax smiled as he and Vere embraced.

'The palace seems quiet when you are gone, my brother,' Vere told him ruefully. 'I am sorry I was not able to welcome you back, but I am preparing to leave for London now. My main meeting has been brought forward, and at this stage in the negotiations I didn't feel that I could object.'

'I was disappointed not to see your reaction to the bride I have found you.'

'I saw her in the hallway.'

'Yes,' Drax agreed, his suspicion that his brother had been looking down on them confirmed. 'She is most suitable for our purpose, Vere. Educated, intelligent enough to be groomed as your bride, of good moral character, and naïve too; you only have to persuade her to fall in love with you, and—'

'She is neither blonde enough nor tall enough for my taste, Drax. You know I prefer the cool elegance of a soignée blonde.'

'You will be marrying her, Vere. Not taking her to bed.'

'If I am to persuade her to fall in love with me surely there will come a time when I shall be obliged to at least initiate *some* intimacy between us?'

Drax could sense that Vere was watching him very closely, but it still stunned him when Vere suggested quietly, 'Perhaps you should think of marrying her yourself?'

'No. I brought her here for you. I promised I would find you a wife first. We can discuss it further on your return. Is there anything you need me to brief you on before you leave for London?'

'You mentioned Sir Edward Reeves and his opposition to our proposals. You said that you thought the best way to handle that would be via a personal meeting with him?'

'Yes. I spoke to his people whilst I was in London, and I've set things in motion for you to meet with him. He's one of the old school of diplomats. He fears that a financial exchange here might not operate with the probity he considers necessary.'

'I shall endeavour to convince him otherwise. And now I must go.'

'I'll walk you to your car.'

'To persuade me to reconsider the charms of Ms Murray?' Vere asked lightly.

'No. When you return, you will witness them for yourself—and then you will need no persuading,' Drax told him suavely.

Sadie was so tired she was almost falling asleep sitting upright on the slightly uncomfortable low chair—obviously designed for women who were more used to sitting elegantly cross-legged.

Nasim had handed her over to a plump, smiling woman wearing a feminine version of his own livery.

She had introduced herself as Alama and then shown her into a large, luxuriously carpeted and furnished salon before disappearing. Several minutes later a shy young girl who'd introduced herself as Hakeem had appeared, to ask her in uncertain English if she would like coffee. Sadie had refused, knowing that drinking the strong local coffee would keep her awake. Now, though, she was beginning to regret her refusal, and longed for a drink of water.

How long would she have to stay here for? Until she was summoned before Drax and his brother to be inspected?

The door to the salon opened and Alama came in, accompanied by Nasim.

'His Highness wishes to speak with you,' Alama informed her. 'Nasim will escort you to him, and then, when you return, Hakeem will be waiting for you, to take you to your rooms.'

Nasim escorted her back down the passageway he had brought her along earlier, taking her through the hallway and into a room off it that was obviously some kind of office. Drax was there, seated behind a large desk, frowning as he studied a computer screen.

'Regrettably, my brother has had to leave without meeting you,' he told her as he waved her into the chair opposite his own. 'It will be several days before he returns from London, and during that time...'

Sadie could hardly believe what she was hearing. She was tired, and her head was aching. In the last twenty-four hours she had lost one job, been denied her rightful wages and then been virtually thrown out in the street. She had been bemused, bullied and virtually blackmailed into accepting a job in another country, and then told that it was necessary for her to dress in designer label clothes in order to gain the approval of a man who now apparently had disappeared and was not likely to return any time soon. That was if he had ever existed in the first place.

She had, she decided, had enough. In fact, she had had *more* than enough! She pushed back her chair and stood up, then drew herself up to her full height and told Drax fiercely, 'During that time I shall have returned to London. You virtually kidnapped me, and then black-mailed me into coming here with you. You said that you had a job for me, and that your reasons for wanting to bring me were are all completely above board. Then you demanded that I wear clothes that you bought for me so I would gain the approval of your brother—even though when you offered me the job you didn't mention his approval was necessary. And now you tell me that this brother of yours isn't here. Well, do you know what I think?' Sadie challenged him angrily. 'I think that this brother of yours and the job you've offered me have a great deal in common. In that neither of them has any existence outside your imagination.'

She shook her head bitterly. 'It's my own fault, I know. I made it all so easy for you, didn't I? You'd have thought that after what I'd experienced with Monika al Sawar I'd have had more sense than to believe you.'

While she had been talking, letting her wild angry words tumble hotly into the silence, Drax's expression had undergone a subtle change which, now that he too was pushing back his chair and standing up, made him look every inch the kind of haughty, autocratic male who held the power of life and death over those he ruled. But it was too late to wish she had been more circumspect—and besides, why *shouldn't* she tell him what she thought?

'If you are trying to say that you believe I have *lied* to you—'

'I'm not *trying* to say that. I *am* saying it,' Sadie said, standing her ground. And then felt her knees tremble when he let out his breath in a hiss of suppressed fury.

'There is no job, is there? Just like there is no brother,' she challenged him. 'And you have brought me here—'

'For what purpose?' Drax stopped her even while he reflected inwardly that it was just as well Vere wasn't here to witness her outburst. Vere was emotionally controlled, often remote, and very much aware of his position and what was owed to him. Sadie's emotional fury would only have added to his brother's conviction that she was not a suitable candidate to become his temporary wife. Sadie, on the other hand, obviously thought it was a very different role Drax had in mind for her.

When she didn't answer him, but instead compressed her mouth and gave a mute shake of her head, he spoke softly, deliberately spacing out each and every word. 'I thought I had already made it clear to you that I have no sexual interest in you. It is well known that there is a certain type of over-excitable foreign woman who seems to assume that men of my country are unable to resist her charms. It is a subject of some amusement for

us.' He gave a small dismissive shrug. 'One sees it in
their eyes. There is hunger and stupidity… It takes no
great intelligence to know that such women come here
already fantasising about having sex with a robed lover.'

He gave another shrug. 'There are, of course, some
young men who amuse themselves by encouraging
these women's fantasies while laughing at them when
their backs are turned. It occurs to me that in repeatedly
accusing me of having sexual designs on you, you may
be concealing your own sexual curiosity.'

Sadie gasped in outrage. 'That is not true! There is
only one reason I came here with you. And that is
because you virtually forced me.'

'I offered you a job, which you accepted.'

'Because you virtually blackmailed me into it! You
refused to return my passport, and you still have it.'

'Indeed I do, and I intend to keep it until you have
completed the probationary period we agreed on. And
let me warn you—this is the second time you have made
the kind of accusations against me that no man bears un-
punished. Just remember that, if you should be tempted
to repeat them a third time. My brother, as I said, has
been called away on urgent business. However, I have
spoken of you to him, and he agrees with me that you
will be perfect for the position we have in mind.'

It was the truth, after all—even if Vere had rejected
her and proposed that Drax should be the one to have
her. He was almost tempted to take on the challenge and
tame the wild cat she had just proved herself to be—in
his bed, where he would make sure she purred with
pleasure for him instead of hissing and spitting as she

was doing now. She had certainly angered and aroused him enough for him to want to punish her for her audacity. There was unexpected spice beneath the outer meek blandness of her manner, Drax acknowledged, and, having exposed it, like any man worthy of the name he naturally wanted to explore it. And to conquer it, and her?

Drax mentally shrugged aside the sly thought that had somehow insinuated itself into his mind. He could find himself the necessary temporary wife easily enough, but Vere was not like him. Vere had a tendency to withdraw and hold himself aloof, which meant that he did not always find it easy to forge relationships with those outside the rarefied atmosphere in which they lived. The truth was that the kind of arranged inter-Royal family marriage their fellow rulers were proposing for them was probably the kind that *would* best suit his brother—although Vere himself was not likely to admit to that, Drax knew. Neither of them liked having his hand forced—they both had a fierce determination to be masters of their own fate—but Vere, once he had set his mind to something, could not be swayed and would not compromise.

He had said that he did not want to be inveigled into a diplomatic marriage, and that suited *him,* Drax admitted, because at the moment he did not want to marry full-stop. While he knew that his way of life and his method of doing things seemed unorthodox, compared to Vere's rigid adherence to protocol, Drax had his own strong sense of where his loyalties lay and how he felt about them.

For all that Vere was the firstborn, and carried about a certain sternness and an air of discipline, as if it was his duty to take on board more of the sometimes onerous weight of their shared responsibility, Drax often felt as though he was the more senior. He was the one who was more in touch with the realities of modern life and who had lived out in the world. He also knew that sometimes he protected his brother. But it was, to Drax, part of what their twinship meant that he should give this service of care to his brother without remarking on it.

In deciding that Sadie would make an ideal temporary wife for Vere, Drax had been doing what he had done all his life—he had seen Vere's need and potential vulnerability and had stepped in to ensure that his brother was protected. He did not want to acknowledge, never mind accept, that there was something about Sadie that was making him physically aware of her—and not just aware, but hungry for her. Sadie was merely a woman who fitted a specific purpose, and she would be adequately recompensed once it came to an end. As far as Drax was concerned there was very little difference in paying off a no longer wanted mistress and a no longer wanted temporary wife. Both should be removed from one's life with speed and efficiency and the minimum of fuss. Other men might indulge in the folly of 'falling in love', but Drax knew that he would never allow that to happen to him.

Their parents' death, especially the loss of their mother, had left both Vere and Drax exposed to the old-fashioned mindset of their father's well-meaning but rather traditional royal advisers. With no women playing a prominent role in the country's government over the past decade, they had been encouraged to develop a somewhat dismissive attitude towards romantic love.

Drax flicked another assessing look over Sadie, frowning as he saw her trying to smother a tell-tale yawn.

'It has been a long day for you, and it is late. I shall summon Nasim and instruct him to escort you back to the women's quarters. Tomorrow will be time enough for me to discuss my plans for our new venture with you in more detail.'

CHAPTER SIX

SADIE came up through the heavy layers of her deep sleep slowly and reluctantly on hearing the soft sounds of padding feet and the chink of china. When she opened her eyes it confused her at first not to see the bare discomfort of her small room high up under the roof of the al Sawar house.

And then she remembered. She wasn't in Zuran any more; she was in the Royal Palace of Dhurahn.

She sat up quickly in the comfortable wide bed, thankful that she had taken the trouble to slip on a clean tee shirt before going to bed. Was that because she had feared that her sleep might be interrupted not by the shyly smiling Hakeem, who had just brought her a breakfast tray, but by the man who had brought her here?

Drax. Prince al Drac'ar al Karim bin Hakar. Just thinking about him was enough not only to raise the heat of her body, but to make her sensually aware of the cool stroke of the undoubtedly expensive bedlinen against her suddenly sensitised skin. She could feel the pulse of her own body, and the ache it sent radiated out all over her, making her nipples tighten and her toes want to curl.

She must not think like this, Sadie warned herself, shocked by the waywardness of her thoughts. She made herself focus on Hakeem, who was telling her softly, 'I have brought you your breakfast, *sheikha*. If there is anything else you should wish?'

Sheikha? Surely she had no right to such an elevated form of address? Or was the girl simply being polite? It frustrated Sadie that her knowledge of Dhurahni customs was so limited. That was something she would have to address if she was to stay and work here.

Her thoughts suddenly busy, Sadie refused to admit to herself that she might be keeping them that way to resist giving in to the temptation of thinking about her new employer.

She smiled at the waiting girl and shook her head. 'No. This is lovely. Thank you.'

'I am to return in one hour to escort you to the public rooms of the palace, where you will be met by of one His Highness's assistants,' she told Sadie carefully, as though she had been rehearsing the words.

Sadie gave her another smile. She was glad she'd have someone to show her the way along the corridors. She had been too tired to take much note when she was whisked down them last night.

With Hakeem gone, Sadie got out of bed, tempted by the shafts of sunlight coming in through the open shutters of the windows to see what lay outside them. She had also been too tired to explore the suite of rooms she had been given, but this morning she could see just how luxurious her bedroom was. Its décor was an eye-pleasing mixture of traditional and modern. The bed was wide and low, a beautiful silk rug hung on the wall opposite the bed, and several more equally beautiful rugs were scattered over the tiled floor. Two sets of double doors opened off the bedroom on opposite walls adjacent to the windows. One set led into an elegantly furnished sitting room-cum-office, and the other into a wardrobe-lined dressing room which opened up into a large, modern bathroom with limestone floors and a huge free-standing 'infinity' bath.

Pulling on the towelling robe she had left at the end of the bed the night before, Sadie went over to the windows. As she looked out her eyes widened in delight when she saw the enclosed courtyard garden that lay beyond them. A pair of French windows opened out onto a tiled area, protected from the sunlight by a deep veranda. Beyond that were mosaic pathways and raised flowerbeds filled with a variety of hosta-like wide-leaved plants and neatly clipped topiary balls of white roses. The beds were finished off with a border of frothing white flowers Sadie didn't recognise. In the middle of the enclosed area water splashed down from a fountain into a basin which overflowed into an ornamental stone-edged pond. As she watched, a large, sleek, beautifully-coloured fish rose from the water to snap at a hovering fly before subsiding back into the water.

Even from inside the room Sadie could smell the scent of the roses. Beyond the enclosed area was a miraculously green hedge, no doubt watered by some under-soil watering system. In the hedge was a 'doorway', which led to yet another garden—this one, so far as she could see from the window, containing more roses and topiary.

Sadie had never ever stayed anywhere so luxurious—made all the more sensual because it was so discreetly understated. She picked up the cup of coffee Hakeem had poured for her and drank it quickly. It was hot and sweet, although a bit strong for her taste. There was also a basket filled with small, sweet, sticky pastries, a selection of fruit and a bottle of water. But Sadie wasn't hungry. In fact her stomach had started to churn with apprehension as she remembered the interview she'd had with Drax the previous evening.

Telling herself that it wouldn't be a good idea to be late for her meeting with him, she poured herself another cup of coffee and drank it quickly, before hurrying into the bathroom.

Now, *this* was the kind of luxury she could easily get used to, she admitted as she paused to admire the infinity bath. There was no time for lingering this morning, though. A shower would be quicker, and probably far more therapeutic as it wouldn't encourage her to indulge in thinking about Drax.

Half an hour later she was ready—her hair washed, blown dry and neatly secured, her body clothed in what seemed to be the plainest of her new clothes—a neutral-coloured linen-mix skirt with a white short-sleeved, softly fitting top embellished with decorative natural-coloured 'stone' buttons at the shoulders and on the small V-shaped neckline. His Highness, it seemed, had thought of everything—including, as she had just discovered, two pairs of designer sunglasses.

She had no idea what on earth she would do with all these things when she returned to the UK. She certainly hoped he didn't expect her to want to keep them and then pay for them out of her wages. She would be paying for them for the rest of her working life, judging by the labels. But then perhaps to a man as obviously wealthy as Drax the cost of supplying an employee with a wardrobe bulging with designer labels was an insignificant perk. And the clothes weren't for her; they were for an employee. She was a visual attachment to a very important venture, and as such she had to project the right image.

Sadie could hear the outer door of her suite opening. It was Hakeem, coming to collect her. Quickly slipping her feet into a pair of pretty shell-decorated summer mules, she hurried out of the dressing room, smiling at the young girl patiently waiting for her.

'Heavens, I'll never get used to all these corridors,' she told Hakeem ten minutes later, envying the other girl's elegant, straight-backed walk as she led her down a series of interconnecting white-walled corridors. She would have loved to have had time to stop and study the paintings and artwork, with their rich, vivid colours and sculptured lines, but Hakeem obviously didn't want to linger. Like the domestic staff employed by the wealthy in Zuran, Hakeem was Indian, and so delicately beautiful that Sadie felt clumsy and awkward beside her despite her new clothes.

'It was kind of you to bring me my breakfast this morning, Hakeem,' Sadie said, and thanked her.

'You like?' Hakeem gave her another shy smile. 'And you like the bedroom of the Royal Princesses? It is very beautiful, is it not?' she asked proudly. 'We have had only the ladies of the Royal Household of Zuran to stay in it before, when the Sheikha, who was the mother of our Rulers, was alive. But that was a long time ago—before I was here. It was before I was here too that Their Highnesses' mother and father were killed and the whole of Dhurahn mourned their loss. It was very sad for such a dreadful thing to happen.'

'Their parents were killed?'

'It was in a car,' Hakeem told her solemnly. 'But not here,' she assured Sadie hastily. 'And it was a long time ago.'

'How dreadful.' Sadie couldn't help shivering a little as she contemplated how awful it must have been for Drax and Vere to learn that such a terrible thing had happened to both their parents.

'It was very sad,' Hakeem repeated. 'Everyone loved the Sheikha, even though she was not Dhurahni and, like you, came from a land far away. Ireland.'

Another time it would have made Sadie smile gently to see how carefully Hakeem pronounced the unfamiliar word. But how could she smile when she had just heard about such a tragedy?

'It is unusual to hear of a Dhurahni prince marrying a European girl,' she told Hakeem, guessing that she was expected to make some comment on her story.

'Not so here. Here it is tradition,' Hakeem corrected her firmly.

Before Sadie could question her any further, she indicated a pair of heavily carved dark, polished doors in front of them, and said, 'Ahmed will be waiting for you outside the doors to the women's quarters to escort you to His Highness, *sheikha.*' She then salaamed gracefully and backed away from Sadie.

'Hakeem—' Sadie began, about to question the maid's manner of addressing her. But it was too late. The double doors were opening and Ahmed was now salaaming to her.

He led her not back to the room, where she had seen Drax last night, but down a corridor and then through a large room ornately decorated, its furniture heavily gilded and its low sofas piled high with richly jewelled silk cushions.

At one end there was a raised dais with two throne-like chairs on it, and Sadie guessed that the room must be the audience chamber where the brothers held their formal *divan*—the event at which any subject could present his petition to his rulers and be heard.

However, they still had to negotiate another long corridor before finally Ahmed led her across a square hallway so plain in its architectural design and furnishings that the contrast between it and the rooms she had just seen was like receiving a glass of cold pure water after the stickiness of spiced wine.

The floor of the hallway was tiled with matt black tiles. A stairway led to an upper gallery, its banister carved out of some ebony-coloured wood, the symmetry of its curves so perfect and plain that it made Sadie catch her breath.

After knocking briefly on the closed double doors, and then opening them for her, indicating that she was to step through, Ahmed salaamed again and then backed away.

A little hesitantly, Sadie walked through the doors.

The room beyond them was as modern and breathtaking as the hallway, and three times the size. It was a combination of a living area and an office, its furniture made from the same dark wood as the stairs, the seating streamlined and stylish.

A huge plate glass window looked out onto a courtyard, enclosed on three sides by the modern architecture of the building, with a large swimming pool at the far end.

Awed, she stared at the pool—and then realised it was occupied. Her heart thumped heavily into her ribs as she watched Drax place his hands on the walkway, his flesh hard and tanned, the water running off his shoulders and chest, and spring lithely out of the water, completely naked, before turning his back towards her as he reached for the robe on a recliner. Her heart was racing so frantically she had to breathe faster to keep up with it. *Had* he been naked? Or had she just thought that he was? Had that brief glimpse of male nudity before he turned his back on her been the product of her imagination? Surely he wouldn't have swum naked knowing that he might be seen? Why not? an inner voice challenged her. He was one of the ruling Princes of a rich Arab kingdom, and so arrogant that he probably did exactly what he felt like when he felt like it. Who was there to stop or question him after all?

He had disappeared out of sight, but her heartbeat still hadn't returned to normal.

'You were admiring the view?'

The sound of his voice behind her had her swinging around, her face burning. While she had been staring out into the courtyard like an awestruck virgin, he had entered the room and was now walking towards her, still wearing his robe and making a very subtle and mocking reference to the fact that she had seen him getting out of the pool.

Well, two could play at that game, Sadie decided angrily.

'It's a very clever effect,' she answered him coolly. 'Very pared down and sparse. I like the clean lines and the sense of space—although of course we all know that it is merely a trick of the design that makes less look more.'

She was quick—and clever, Drax acknowledged. He had embarrassed her, he knew that, but she still had the wit to parry words with him. But how long would she be able to keep it up? Drax decided to put her to the test.

'And, like most of your sex, you always opt for *more*—is that it?'

She was getting into deep water now, Sadie admitted uncomfortably, all too aware of the double meaning behind the mocking words.

'It surprised me to see such modern architecture…' She had meant to bring the subtle *double entendre* element to their conversation to an end with her reply, but when she saw the way he was looking at her, her expression gave her away. 'I mean, all of this…' she amended hastily, waving her hand in the direction of the entire room. 'It is lovely but…not what I expected.'

'So that is twice this morning you have witnessed something you weren't expecting, then?'

Sadie opened her mouth and then closed it again. Her whole body was burning now.

'Such embarrassment—and all over a glimpse of a

naked male body,' he taunted her softly. 'You surprise me, Sadie. I had thought you would be rather more so-phisticated.' He gave a dismissive shrug. 'I'm sorry if you were embarrassed, but I didn't realise Ahmed had shown you in here until it was too late.'

Inwardly Drax was thinking that Vere would be pleased that she was so easily embarrassed. It pointed to a genuine lack of experience that would please his fastidious brother. As it pleased *him?* He frowned. Why should *he* have any personal opinions on the matter of her experience or lack of it?

'He did knock on the door.' Sadie didn't want him thinking she had come in of her own accord, or that she had *wanted* to catch sight of him levering himself out of the pool.

Drax gave another small shrug. 'It isn't important. As I've already said, I'm sorry you were embarrassed. Now, I shall ring for Ahmed to bring you some coffee, and I'll go and get dressed. I want to show you the building we intend to use as the headquarters for our new financial sector. We've put aside a hundred acres of land which will be used exclusively to house the fi-nancial business sector. The main building has already been constructed and is finished, ready for use.' And, as Vere had already said, they would be left with it on their hands if their meetings failed and they did not get approval to go ahead.

Although Drax was covered from his throat to below his knees by his robe, Sadie was acutely aware that beneath it he was naked—and male. Very male indeed, if her brief glimpse of him had been accurate. Not that she had seen enough nude men in the flesh to compare. But it had been obvious to her that Drax was boldly 'endowed', as the saying went.

Drax knew that he was embarrassing her, Sadie recognised.

'I hadn't expected that the palace would look so modern,' she confessed, determined to change the subject before it got too out of hand.

Was he actually giving her a small smile—too mocking and knowing for her peace of mind—or was she just imagining it?

'Not all of it does. Only this new wing, which I have had added as my own private quarters. My brother is a traditionalist at heart, and he prefers the design and décor of our forebears. He did not altogether approve initially when I told him what I planned to do.'

'But it looks wonderful,' Sadie assured him quickly, and then, worried that she might have sounded horribly sycophantic, added lamely, 'I've always preferred modern architecture and design.'

'It has its benefits,' Drax agreed.

For some reason she was thinking about the swimming pool and his naked body again, Sadie realised guiltily, and rushed to ask, 'As I won't be meeting your brother, presumably I don't have to wear the Chanel suit today?'

'Not whilst you are alone with me, no,' Drax allowed.

What was it about those words 'alone' and 'with me' that set her heart rocketing into her chest wall? Did she really need to ask herself that question? Wasn't the answer openly obvious in the way her body was reacting? And did that small smile Drax was giving her mean that he had guessed what she was thinking? Oh, please not, Sadie prayed inwardly. The last thing she wanted was for this arrogant and sexually potent man to know that she had unconsciously filed the mental image she had of his powerful male physique to review again when she was on her own. Heavens, it shocked her enough to have to admit to *herself* what she had done, never mind have him know about it as well.

'However,' Drax continued, forcing her to abandon her frantic inner thoughts and listen, 'Dhurahn is a very small state. It will soon become common knowledge why you are here. There are already several independent European financial services people resident in Dhurahn city. They refer to themselves as entrepreneurs—although I am aware that the financial press often prefer to refer to them as predators.'

'You invited them here?' Sadie asked.

'No, they are not here at our invitation. These are not the sort of people we would want.' His mouth curled in disdainful dislike. 'They are vultures. Like all their kind, they possess an early-warning system that alerts them to the scent of fresh blood. However, you may rest assured that they will not be allowed to get rich on the backs of citizens of this country. I must warn you that everything that is discussed between us is privileged and confidential information, and must remain as such.'

'Are you saying that my contract of employment will contain penalty clauses for breach of confidence?'

Drax eyed her thoughtfully. She had, of course, no

idea what her ultimate 'employment' was going to be, nor how apt her question was. Certainly when Vere married her she would be signing a pre-nuptial agreement. It was a great pity that Vere couldn't see her now. The top she was wearing hinted at the softness of her breasts, her skin showed the beginnings of a faint tan, and Drax was pleased to see that she was wearing only minimal make-up. It had amused him earlier to see the shocked expression on her face when he had leapt naked out of the pool, but his amusement had rebounded on him when his body had reacted to the knowledge that she was watching him. He had had to turn his back on her very quickly to conceal his reaction from her. He should not, of course, have allowed such a situation to arise at all. *Arise* being the operative word, he admitted grimly. Because he certainly had been aroused. Extremely aroused. So much so that even now...

She was going to marry his brother, he reminded himself. He was determined about that. So determined that he had already given the household a subtle indication of her future role as a Royal wife by installing her in the Royal suite of the women's quarters.

'Your quarters are satisfactory?' he asked her now, remembering his duties as a host. 'You have everything you need?'

'The suite is magnificent,' Sadie answered him truthfully. 'But...'

'But?' Drax demanded.

'Hakeem, the little maid, keeps addressing me as *sheikha,* even though I have tried to tell her that I do not hold such a title.'

Drax tensed momentarily. It would not do for Sadie to get wind of what he was planning before she had had the chance to meet Vere and he had put his plan into action by encouraging her to fall for him.

He gave a deliberately dismissive shrug. 'It is merely a formal mode of address. She no doubt means simply to be polite to you. However, if you would rather have someone else to attend you…?'

'No…no. She is lovely. She…she has been telling me about the palace and your family, and—' Sadie could see him tensing and stopped, but it was too late.

'And?' he probed.

'She also told me about your parents,' Sadie admitted, adding quietly, 'What a dreadful thing to have happened.'

'Yes, it was.' Drax's answer was so terse that Sadie wished she hadn't said anything. Had she inadvertently touched a still raw wound? Didn't it make sense that the loss of one's parents in such a horrific accident would *always* leave a raw wound?

She had been tactless, she decided guiltily. 'I'm sorry. I shouldn't have mentioned it.'

Both her guilt and her apology were so genuine that they made Drax frown. He wasn't used to people treating him as though he was vulnerable and could be emotionally hurt. To be aware of her compassion touched a nerve within him that produced the echo of an old and deep pain.

'My mother didn't have to go that day. But she always went everywhere with my father. Theirs was a true love match. She used to say that I had inherited personality traits from her side of the family—she was Irish.'

'Yes, Hakeem told me. That explains why you have green eyes, of course—' Sadie stopped speaking abruptly, and put her hand to her lips in consternation.

'Yes, Vere and I share her eyes. But Vere inherited the preferences of our paternal ancestors. It is traditional for scholarly men to take an interest in our literature and to write classical poetry; it is as much a part of being a Dhurahni prince as is the love of falconry and the desert, and Vere has already won renown for his skill in the writing of poetic verse. I, on the other hand, while I too love the desert and honour our traditions, have inherited my mother's grandfather's love of architecture and design. Our parents valued both aspects of our dual inheritance because they reflected what they each saw and loved in each other.'

What was happening to him? Drax challenged himself angrily. He couldn't believe he had just spoken so intimately to Sadie. He never talked about his parents to anyone other than Vere. He comforted himself that at least their conversation had given him an opportunity to bring Vere's virtues to her attention. If his brother wasn't here to encourage Sadie to fall in love with him then he would just have to do his best to help her to do so in his absence. The fact that earlier she had aroused him meant nothing, less than nothing, he assured himself, and if it did happen again... If it did? It wouldn't. He intended to make sure of that.

'To lose them both must have been unbearable,' he could hear Sadie saying.

Was she right in thinking that his words of praise for his brother masked an unacknowledged feeling that his brother had been their parents' favourite because he was the elder son? Sadie wondered compassionately. If so, how foolish of his parents not to value him as he so obviously deserved to be valued.

Sadie felt angrily protective on his behalf. Was the arrogance she had seen in him simply a means of protecting himself? Like these rooms, pared down and clinically bare of any softening personal things? Her compassion for him grew, startling her when she realised that it was making her feel almost tenderly protective of him. What on earth was happening to her? He was her employer. That was all. She had no need to feel protective of him and he was hardly likely to want it.

Without Vere, the loss of their parents would have been unbearable, Drax admitted to himself. But he had no intention of telling Sadie that. Instead, he said distantly, 'It had to be borne. That was our duty to Dhurahn and to them.'

His cold sharpness speedily dissipated Sadie's compassionate concern. She was a fool to feel sorry for him—a fool to feel *anything* for him, she warned herself firmly, as Ahmed arrived with the coffee.

To Sadie's relief, if the manservant thought it oddly intimate that his master should be talking to his new employee dressed only in a towelling robe he was too tactful to betray it, simply obeying Drax's instruction to pour Sadie a cup of coffee while Drax went to get dressed.

As soon as she had emptied the small cup Ahmed lifted the coffee pot to refill it, but Sadie shook her head and hastily covered her empty cup with her hand, to indicate to him that she didn't want any more. If she kept on drinking such a strong brew she would be on a caffeine-induced high for the rest of the day. But at least thinking about how dreadful it must have been for Drax and his brother to cope with the deaths of their parents gave her something to help her stop focusing on the memory of his nakedness. She was not the kind of woman who wasted her time mentally dwelling on naked male flesh. Or was she? Wouldn't it be more honest to admit that she hadn't *previously* been that kind of woman?

She was aware, so much aware, that those tiny tingling shudders of 'being aware' were still pulsing dangerously inside her—like a kettle simmering just off the boil, just waiting for that touch to turn up the heat, and then... She could feel the beading of sweat breaking out at her hairline.

This was crazy. She couldn't be obsessing sexually about a man she had only just met. A man who spoke so glowingly to her about his brother that she could be forgiven for thinking that he was actually trying encourage her to fall for *him,* if such a scenario wasn't totally unlikely. A man more unlikely to become her lover it was possible to imagine.

Her lover? She *was* crazy. She had to be. Who had said anything about her wanting a lover? She didn't do lovers. She never had. And she certainly didn't go around fantasising about arrogant ruling princes taking her to bed and making love to her. But just thinking about Drax's tanned, naked body spread against the whiteness of her sheets set her mind racing. What would it feel like to straddle him and keep him there on her bed while she slowly explored the muscular contours of his shoulders and torso? Would he allow her to dominate him like that and take her visual pleasure of him without seeking to master her? Would he let her slowly stroke her way along the byways of his body?

She made a small choking sound of rejection and disbelief in her throat as she tried to disown her thoughts.

'You would perhaps like water?' Ahmed offered her solicitously.

'What? No. Oh, yes, please,' Sadie answered with a quick smile. Perhaps a glass of water might cool her overheated thoughts as it soothed her throat.

Walking through his bedroom, which was as elegantly minimalist as the rest of his quarters, Drax paused in his dressing room to remove clean clothes and then walked into his bathroom, shrugging off his towelling robe as he did so.

He showered quickly, almost brusquely, refusing to focus on his body in any way as he put up a mental barrier to stop himself from thinking about Sadie and the effect she had had on him earlier. But, while he could control his thoughts, he couldn't hide from himself the knowledge that both the ache and its urgency were still there, and that were she to come to him now...

Were she to *what?* Angrily he reached for a towel, jerking it off the heated towel rail. What the hell was he letting himself think that for? She was nothing to him—less than nothing. She was just someone he could use to solve his brother's current problem.

So he wasn't going to mind when Vere took her to

bed? Vere probably *wouldn't be* taking her to bed; all his brother needed to do was persuade her to marry him. He didn't have to consummate the marriage. In fact it would be better if he didn't.

Better for whom? For him? Because he couldn't control the white-hot surge of male blood-lust that possessed him at the thought of his twin touching Sadie? Why should he think something like that? He dropped the towel and strode into his dressing room, pulling on clean clothes—not the white tee shirt and the stone-coloured chinos he had originally intended to wear, but traditional Arab dress instead. Because wearing it would reinforce the barrier he needed to create between him and Sadie?

CHAPTER SEVEN

'AND this, as you may remember from the plans I showed you earlier, is the main building of the complex.'

Sadie nodded her head, glad that she was wearing her sunglasses and had covered her head against the strong sun as she stood next to Drax, looking towards the gleaming, mirror-fronted building that rose up in front of her from the desert floor and was so many storeys high it seemed as though it was trying to reach the sky.

Apart from being able to recognise the central completed building, Sadie couldn't pick out any of the other distinguishing features she had seen on the plans in the vast construction site all around them.

Drax had driven them both here himself, not for the first time surprising Sadie with his preference for informality—or at least what passed for informality for him. Sadie hadn't missed the way people turned to look at him, obviously well aware of who he was.

'This new four-lane highway you see under construction runs from the complex to the airport, with this spur, which they are currently working on, going into Dhurahn city. Dhurahn Financial, as we intend to call the new development, will in effect be a city within a city. It will operate under English mercantile law and have its own judiciary system and buildings. Those who work here will have the option of living within its environs in apartment blocks or of moving out to the coast. We find that many overseas nationals prefer to live by the sea if they can, and so we plan to construct another four-lane highway to a sleeper township on the coast.

'The official language within Dhurahn Financial will be English, but naturally translation services will be provided in much the same way as they are in Brussels. Although *our* system will be rather more state-of-the-art.

'The new city is being constructed on a circle plan. The central building will be ringed with roads and additional rings of buildings, which will be divided into segments of quarters, eighths, then sixteenths and so on as the circles widen. Each segment will have its own national flavour with regard to facilities and food outlets, as we intend to become a global financial meeting point.'

Sadie listened in awe. The sheer scale of the plan was breathtaking now that she was here at its centre.

'No one will ever have seen anything like it,' she said.

'No,' Drax agreed calmly. 'That is our plan: that it shall be unique and remain unique. In order to maintain security we intend to operate a chip and pin pass system for everyone who works here. No one will be allowed to enter Dhurahn Financial without the correct authority. Now, let me show you inside the main building.'

As they walked towards it Sadie could see a fleet of immaculate mini-coaches parked outside the main entrance.

'We have been inviting certain financial sector personnel to come to Dhurahn for inspection tours,' Drax explained.

'You've done so much already. I can't see why you would need to employ someone like me,' Sadie told him impetuously, turning to him as she spoke, and then giving a small gasp as her foot slipped on the rubble underfoot.

Drax reacted immediately, reaching out to take hold of her bare arm to steady her.

She was so close to him that she was convinced he must be able to hear the frantic thudding of her heart, never mind see the swift rise and fall of her breasts as she gulped in air. She was suddenly aware that her fingers were clutching at his forearm. The white cotton of his robe felt crisp and fresh beneath the hot stickiness of her hand. She could smell the elusive but sensual scent of male skin and sunshine, and some subtly pleasant cologne; it enticed her to move closer to him so that she could breathe it in. She had taken a step towards him before she could stop herself.

The hand he had placed on her arm moved up to her shoulder, to accommodate her move forward. She could feel its warmth cupping the rounded ball of her shoulder joint where her bare skin met the cotton edge of her top's short sleeve—only his hand wasn't on her sleeve, it was on her bare flesh, as though he had slid his fingers beneath the edge of her sleeve. Just thinking of that kind of intimacy made her tremble as though a fine thread inside her linking every erogenous zone she possessed had been pulled tighter. She could see the dark column of his throat, its skin taut and golden. If she lifted her gaze a little higher she would be able to see his mouth.

Her heart missed one beat and then another as she did exactly that. She couldn't remember ever studying a man's mouth so closely before, or wanting to do so. If she had, the moment was completely overwhelmed now by the experience of absorbing every tiny detail of Drax's mouth. His bottom lip was full and curved, indenting sharply into the corners. She wanted to touch it, to draw her fingertip slowly along it. She wanted... She wanted to lean forward and press her own mouth against his. She wanted...

Did she know what she was doing, looking at him like that? Looking at his mouth with those big eyes, their gaze drowned in open desire? Drax's fingers tightened on the warm, bare flesh of her shoulder, where he had slipped his hand beneath her sleeve, kneading and caressing its curve. He looked down at her body and saw how her nipples were pressing against the fabric of her top, signalling her arousal. It would be the easiest thing in the world to lift his free hand to shape them and then pluck erotically at the boldly aroused flesh, to whisper to her how he would kiss and caress its nakedness before taking it into his mouth to unite them in fierce physical pleasure.

The easiest thing, and the most dangerous. The erection he had controlled earlier throbbed urgently with aching need. He could take her back to his car now. They would be back within the palace and the privacy of his own quarters within half an hour, and then he could take his pleasure of her in all the ways his body was demanding.

Except that he had vowed that she would be Vere's. *Vere's*—not his!

He released her so swiftly that Sadie wasn't sure if what she was feeling was relief or disappointment. What had possessed her to simply stand there like that? she wondered uncomfortably as she tried to keep pace with Drax's long stride. Was it possible that somewhere deep inside every sensible woman there was a throwback gene to a more primitive age, with a secret desire to be claimed by a man strong enough, daring enough and powerful enough, to snatch her up and make her his own?

'It is a pity that my brother isn't here to show you round the building. I am sure that when he returns he will wish to do so. This venture is very close to his heart.'

'But the design concept for the overall plan is yours?' Sadie guessed intuitively, as they reached the entrance to the building.

She didn't want Drax to bring his brother into the conversation. Somehow it broke the intimacy between them, almost as though he was actually physically standing between them. The sharp stab of jealousy she felt shocked her. What kind of foolishness was this? Surely only a woman teetering on the verge of falling wildly and passionately in love with a man could feel jealous of a brother she had yet to meet?

Drax was holding the door to the building open for her. Relieved to have an excuse not to pursue her unwanted line of thought, Sadie stepped through it, shivering a little at the chill of the air-conditioning.

As she gazed upwards from the spacious ground floor with its inner atrium, Sadie couldn't help but be impressed. She knew from the plans Drax had shown her earlier that the building had its own state-of-the-art health club complex, complete with a gym, a swimming pool, treatment rooms, and a restaurant. It also had a cinema that could be used for conferences as well as to show the latest films, several bars and restaurants, and off-duty meeting rooms for the use of those who worked in it. And this was only one of the planned buildings that would form the whole complex.

'What do you think?'

Sadie was astonished that Drax felt he needed to ask her opinion.

'With a set-up like this you're bound to be able to attract top-quality personnel,' she told him honestly. 'I can't imagine anyone turning down the opportunity to work here and be part of such an exciting new venture.'

'We've tried to plan for all contingencies. Some of the more senior personnel will be older, with families, so we're planning to open schools in the new complex on the coast. Dhurahn already has a university, originally endowed and established by our grandfather, but my brother has taken on its expansion as a personal project. He is the philanthropist, while I am more the hard-headed businessman. I think when you meet him that you will find Vere is very much more on your wavelength than I.'

Sadie tensed. For some reason she was beginning to feel almost hostile at Drax's frequent references to his brother's virtues—although she knew there was no logical reason why she should feel that way.

As they waited for a lift to take them to the upper floors Drax's mobile rang. He turned aside to answer it at the same time as the lift doors opened to disgorge a group of European men in business suits, all of them young and, to Sadie, very obviously what she privately termed 'trading floor types'. They exuded the male confidence, arrogance and street cred that epitomised the City boy, and Sadie wasn't surprised to find herself being openly inspected.

That didn't bother her particularly, but she felt far less sanguine when one of them suddenly detached himself from the others and came over to her, saying loudly in an over-familiar way that infuriated her, 'Well, if it isn't Sadie! Prim little Sadie, who doesn't do sex. What brings you here? You can't be up for a job. They only want the top graduates—although Lord knows you must need the money since you got the push from the bank.'

To Sadie's relief Drax, still speaking into his mobile, was standing too far away to hear what was being said, although he had turned round to face them.

'Actually, I already have a job, thank you, Jack,' Sadie answered as calmly as she could.

Jack Logan. Jack the Lad, as the other men in the office had admiringly nick-named him. Sadie had disliked him from the moment they had been introduced—and she had ended up disliking him even more after he had trapped her in an empty office and tried to coerce her into having sex with him. Luckily she had managed to escape before he had tried to force her, but Sadie knew that he hadn't forgiven her for rejecting him. His comments now were, she acknowledged, a form of payback.

Drax had finished his conversation and was looking enquiringly at her. Sadie wriggled past her unpleasant former colleague and hurried over to rejoin him.

'An old friend?' Drax asked her coolly.

'We used to work together,' Sadie answered shortly, wondering what Jack the Lad would make of the deference being shown to Drax by his guide as he salaamed with deep reverence and Drax responded with a small inclination of his head.

'And this, of course, is the main dealing room.'

Sadie nodded her head in acknowledgement as they completed their tour of the building. As yet the vast room did not reek of male hormones and the sharp scent of bullish aggression, like the dealing rooms she was used to, but no doubt they soon would.

'That young man you were talking to earlier,' Drax demanded abruptly. 'What exactly is your relationship?'

If the question had come from anyone else, Sadie knew she would have refused to answer it. But she was becoming used to Drax's autocratic belief that he had a right to have even his most intimate questions answered. Either that or her emotions were becoming so entrapped by him that she wanted him to know everything about her and her past. Though of course she wasn't silly enough to let herself get emotionally involved with a man who had shown no signs of wanting an involvement, was she?

'As I've already told you, we worked together.'

'His body language suggested that his relationship with you was more than that of a mere work colleague,' Drax said.

Sadie shook her head. 'The young men from the trading floor always behave like that. It's part of their macho image; it doesn't mean anything.'

'So you weren't involved in a sexual relationship with him?' Drax persisted.

He wasn't asking these questions on his own account, he assured himself. Why should he be? After all it was of no interest to him how many men had taken her to bed. No, he was thinking of his brother.

He knew Vere would never accept as his wife a woman whose ex-lover was the kind of man he had seen talking to Sadie—even as his temporary wife. It was unrealistic, of course, to expect her not to have had a sexual partner—even more than one—but the people of Dhurahn would have certain expectations about the wives of their rulers, and those expectations would have to be met—even if its rulers knew the marriage was only going to be temporary.

'No, I wasn't,' Sadie reaffirmed, almost fiercely. Was her face burning as much as she thought? Betraying how uncomfortable she felt? It wasn't that she had anything to hide, or at least not the kind of thing that her employer seemed to think she might have to hide, but she was acutely sensitive about the fact that for a woman of her age and situation she was lacking the kind of sexual experience she might be expected to have. There probably never had been an age when a woman in her twenties was proud to say openly that she was still a virgin; in earlier times, when female virginity had been prized, girls had been married in their teens, and unmarried virgins past that age would probably have been looked upon as objects of pity—rejects, unable to find a husband and bringing shame on her family.

Now, while it was laughable that any woman should feel rejected because she wasn't married, there was a certain stigma—a certain sniggering kind of unkindness, especially from men—attached to a woman who remained a virgin.

Sadie could well imagine how someone like Jack Logan would react if he knew the truth about her. Which was, of course, why she had made sure that no one did know, keeping her secret to herself.

It wasn't as if she had made some kind of vow to cling to celibacy—far from it. It was just that the right partner had never come along at the right time, and then, when she had begun to realise that she might have left it later than normal to lose her virginity, she had started to worry about how any potential partner might react to the knowledge that he was to be her first lover. That in turn had caused her to keep the men she did date at arm's length, so that the whole situation had grown steadily more burdensome—rather like compound interest, she told herself with grim humour.

Drax watched her, wondering what it was causing the defensive and almost secretive look to darken her eyes, and what it was she was so obviously withholding from him. There could, of course, be only one thing. She was lying to him about her relationship with the man he had seen talking to her. Normally the knowledge that a woman was lying to him about her sexual past would have caused him to feel merely cynically amused. But, as he was slowly being forced to recognise, nothing that had happened to him since he had first set eyes on Sadie came anywhere near being close to his 'normal' reaction. That alone was enough to infuriate him, without the added thought of Sadie with another man. He could see her now, giving herself to that man with wanton abandon, inciting him with her soft full mouth and her sweetly curved body to take them to the savage erotic heights he himself so ached to show her.

Drax fought desperately to ignore what he was feeling and thinking. But it was too late. As surely as any genie let loose from its imprisoning bottle, the reality of his desire for her had been exposed.

'We need to return to the palace,' he told her curtly. 'I have a meeting I need to attend.'

There wasn't any meeting, but he didn't trust himself to remain alone with her in his present mood, and at least if they returned to the palace he could distance himself from her.

Sadie was too relieved that he had stopped questioning her about her non-existent sex-life to worry about his brusque manner.

They were waiting for the lift when the man who had been escorting Jack Logan's group came hurrying towards them, salaaming to Drax and then saying something urgently to him in Arabic.

'Go downstairs and wait for me in the foyer,' Drax told Sadie after he had listened to the older man. 'There is something I have to attend to. I won't be very long.'

Nodding her head, Sadie got in the lift.

The foyer really was magnificent, she acknowledged, as she stepped out of the lift on the ground floor. Drax and his brother were bound to make a success of their venture, and she admitted that she hoped there might be a real future for her here.

Although Dhurahn, like Zuran, was a modern city, there was still that awareness of the proximity of the desert and its mystery, and she had learned while she was in Zuran that there was something about it that enthralled her. She had taken a couple of organised trips out to the *wadis,* and had marvelled at everything she had seen, gaining respect for the strength and pride of those who had lived for so many centuries in this hostile but strangely beautiful environment. If she were allowed to stay on she would try to explore the desert a little more, get to know more about it, she told herself, letting her thoughts drift as she waited patiently for Drax.

When she at last heard the hum of the descending lift she waited expectantly for the doors to open—only to stiffen with shock when it wasn't Drax who got out, but Jack Logan. He was grinning wolfishly at her in the almost obscenely vain way he had that she had always found so threatening.

'I saw you get in the lift, so I thought I'd come down and keep you company,' he said mockingly. 'How did you manage to get involved with the top man, by the way? Not via his bed, I'll bet... You wouldn't have lasted two seconds there once he'd sussed out how sexless you are...'

Sadie swung round, turning her back on him, praying that Drax would appear and unwittingly rescue her from her tormentor.

'Sadie, Sadie…' Jack Logan was singing softly. 'Who won't open her legs for anyone. What's it like being so uptight? Tell you what I'll do, seeing as I'm feeling generous, I'll show you what it's like to have a man…'

If she just ignored him he'd get tired of harassing her and leave her alone, Sadie reasoned. If she just stood here and avoided eye contact— She gave a shocked protest when Jack suddenly grabbed hold of her and swung her round. He was considered good-looking, she knew, but he had mean eyes, and the cruel look in them made her shudder.

'You thought you were so clever, making a fool of me in London—didn't you? Well, now it's your turn. Now it's payback time, Sadie.'

This couldn't be happening to her. Not in broad daylight, here in this beautiful building. But it was. Jack Logan was laughing at her as he held on to her, and then he reached out and squeezed her breast. When she shuddered with loathing and closed her eyes he laughed even more.

Sadie didn't hear the lift door opening. Nor did she see the look on Drax's face when he saw her standing with her back to him in another man's embrace, another man touching her. But Jack saw Drax, and he saw the look in his eyes, so he bent his head and kissed Sadie fiercely and unkindly on her tightly closed lips, before releasing her and saying softly, 'Like I said, it's payback time,' then sauntering off, leaving her to take a deep breath and wipe her hand across her mouth in an attempt to wipe the taste and the feel of him from her memory.

'If you're ready?'

The icy coldness in Drax's voice made her turn towards him, her eyes still dark with shocked distress.

She felt too numb to say anything, much less attempt to explain what had happened as she fell into step beside him, struggling to match his long, impatient stride as he hurried her back to his car.

It wasn't on his own account that he was filled with such ferocious and all-consuming anger, Drax assured himself. No, it was because her behaviour, as he had just witnessed it, had proved her to be a liar and a sexual adventuress—and thus totally unfit to become Vere's wife. That meant bringing her here to Dhurahn had been a complete waste of his time, and time wasn't something Drax liked to waste.

He strode ahead of Sadie without bothering to turn and check that she was able to negotiate the rubble safely. Not because his anger had wiped out his good manners, but because he simply did not trust himself to speak to her, never mind touch her right now. How could she have allowed that oaf to maul her like that? And in public. Where he could see them. In *his* country, where such displays of sexual intimacy were an offence in the eyes of some of his more devout people. She had behaved with a complete lack of respect—for his country, for him, and for herself. Normally that would have been enough to thoroughly disgust him. Normally?

He *was* disgusted, Drax assured himself as he yanked open the driver's door to his car. Disgusted and bitterly, dangerously angry. So angry, in fact, that... That what? he challenged himself as Sadie slid into the passenger seat of the car. He could smell the scent of her skin, and with it her fear. Her *fear?* Surely she should have smelled of her boyfriend and the intimacy they had been sharing?

Drax didn't trust himself to look at her. Because he was jealous of the fact that she had given herself to another man?

No!

Sadie sat rigidly in her seat, trying to focus on the view ahead and stop herself from giving in to her emotions. Inwardly she felt nauseous and shivery, shaking with loathing and horror from Jack's touch. And sickeningly aware of just how much he had enjoyed humiliating her in the way that he had.

Thank goodness Drax had come along when he did—because if he hadn't... She tried to tell herself that she was over-dramatising what had happened, and that Jack had simply been tormenting her. He surely wouldn't have gone as far as actually...raping her? She shuddered violently, gritting her teeth against the whimper of horror bubbling inside her.

Drax saw her small shiver and automatically turned down the air-conditioning. He could see the goose-bumps on her arms. She was staring into the distance, no doubt wishing she was still with her lover, imagining what they could be doing. He cursed savagely under his breath. He couldn't believe the extent of his own misjudgement. He, who had always prided himself on his swift and accurate assessment of a person's true character. She hadn't even had the grace to attempt to make an excuse for herself, never mind apologise for the lies she had told him.

They had reached the palace, and the guards

salaamed them in through the heavy gates. What was she thinking now? Did she imagine he was simply going to ignore her conduct—and her lies? If so, she was speedily going to discover her error.

He brought the car to a halt and switched off the engine, saying curtly, 'Come with me. There is something I wish to discuss with you.'

Numbly, Sadie nodded her head. She had no idea what Drax wanted to say to her, but she hoped that whatever it was it would be compelling enough to help her stop reliving what had happened with Jack Logan. Her breast actually felt slightly sore where he had squeezed it. Sore and dirty… Everything felt dirty… Every bit of her, inside and out, and not just her body, but her thoughts as well—as though somehow he had contaminated all of her with his disgusting behaviour.

CHAPTER EIGHT

IT FELT as though days rather than hours had passed since she had last stood in this room, Sadie reflected as she stood in the middle of Drax's private sitting room, looking out towards the swimming pool.

Drax had brought her here and then told her to wait, disappearing in the direction of what she assumed must be his bedroom.

This time he hadn't asked her if she wanted anything to eat or drink, and the truth was that she felt desperately in need of a reviving caffeine boost. Instead she had to make do with what water was left in the bottle she had taken out with her earlier. Now lukewarm, it tasted slightly brackish.

Drax would have to tell Sadie that she was dismissed. He had no other option now, knowing that she had made contact with what was obviously a past lover here in Dhurahn. There was no way that Vere could be allowed to marry her. It was unthinkable. His only option was to pay her off and put her on the first flight back to London, her lover with her.

The supposedly calming, cool shower he'd just had had done nothing to lessen the boiling heat of his emotions. He reached for a towel to dry himself and then changed his mind, instead pulling on the fresh towelling robe that his manservant had left ready for him. He headed barefoot into the room where he had left Sadie.

Sadie was standing facing the window, her now empty water bottle clasped tightly in her hands. Drax didn't want his body to react the way it did when he looked at her, but he seemed powerless to stop it. He made a small harsh sound of self-disgust beneath his breath that caused Sadie to turn and look at him, her eyes darkening and her face heating with colour for all the world as though she were remembering seeing him naked and was embarrassed that he might know. Drax could taste the bitterness of his own raw emotions.

'You really had me fooled, you know,' he told her with forced calm as he walked towards her. 'When you put on that act for me, pretending to be shocked by Monika's suggestion that you seduce her clients, I fell for it completely. When you told me that the grinning ape you were encouraging was merely a business acquaintance, I believed you.'

'I told you the truth,' Sadie said. This was not what she had expected to hear him say, and she couldn't conceal her shock.

'Liar! I saw the way you were letting him touch you.'

Her emotional radar registered his banked-down fury, but she couldn't understand what had caused it.

'I saw the intimacy between you,' he continued

harshly, adding savagely as he caught hold of her, '*This* kind of intimacy.'

He was holding her as he had done earlier, his hands sliding beneath the capped sleeves of her top to grip the rounded curve of her shoulders. But this time he wasn't just holding her, he was kissing her as well—possessing her mouth, forcing her lips to part for the demanding thrust of his tongue. She knew she ought to stop him, to push him away and insist that he listen to her, to demand an apology and a retraction of his accusation, but the need inside her was powering through her, obliterating reason and conscience, ruthlessly silencing every warning voice that would have spoken against it, filling her until there was nothing else—nothing else but his kiss and no one else but him.

What was happening to him? Somehow Sadie had taken the kiss he had begun as a savage indictment of her duplicity, allowing a safe escape for his own anger, and turned it into something different—something so sensually sweet and magical that his desire for her was drawing him under like a swimmer caught in a powerful undertow. He could neither resist it nor escape it. It called out to him with a siren song that lured him into waters so treacherous that he was already lost.

When he let go of her she reached for him and drew him closer, encircling him with her arms around his neck, tangling her tongue with his in a slow dance of rebirth from which they would emerge not as two separate people but as one. He slid his hand beneath her shirt, spanning her back and then letting his fingertips trace the narrow sharpness of her collarbone. She felt so fragile, as though he could crush her in his hands, and yet she was so strong—strong enough to overpower him with her sensuality. Her tongue-tip touched his mouth quickly and delicately, retreating as though shocked by its own boldness, and then returned to taste him again, almost compulsively. His hands slid to her breasts. Inside his head he could see himself touching them whilst she arched back in his hold, her throat tightly corded with desire, the heels of her palms pushing on his shoulders. Another minute and he would be pushing her top out of the way to taste her willing flesh…

Sadie quivered with emotion as Drax's hands tightened on her breasts. It felt so good to have him holding her like this, to feel his touch burning away the loathsome memory of Jack Logan. She wanted to beg him to take away all the barriers between them, to hold her so that from now on when she closed her eyes and thought of today all she would be able to remember was him. She didn't know how they had got to this level of intimacy so swiftly, and she didn't want to know. All she wanted was to be burned clean and purified by the fierce heat of their mutual passion. Her ability to think logically was wholly suspended, overridden by the demands of a new command centre. All she wanted was for Drax to take her to bed… No, all she wanted was for Drax to simply take her, she amended dizzily. To take her completely and totally—here, now, at once. Eagerly she pressed herself into his hands and his body, lifting her own hands to hold his head while she kissed him over and over again, whispering to him how much she wanted him.

This was madness, Drax knew. But why should he

not have her? She was offering herself to him, he wanted
her, and with what he knew about her now she could
never marry Vere. Why shouldn't he have her? Why
shouldn't he take her as she was begging him to do?

There were a thousand reasons why he shouldn't—
but they weren't enough to outweigh the one compelling, compulsive reason why he must. So he lifted his
hands from her breasts, swung her up into his arms and
carried her into his bedroom. Sadie wrapped her arms
around his neck and kissed his jawline and his throat,
then pushed aside the neck of his robe to kiss his collarbone, so that by the time he had reached the bed she
was so high on his scent and taste that no power on earth
could have matched the intensity of her desire for him.

Drax lowered her onto the bed, pausing only to shrug
off his robe, and Sadie gazed up at him, marvelling at
his male beauty as he arched over her. With her fingertip she traced the corded sinews of his arms, wondering at their male strength beneath the satin heat of his
skin. His chest was dark with fine hair which arrowed
downwards, causing her heart to leap high inside her
chest and then beat unsteadily and too fast as she remembered the way she had felt that morning when she
had watched him emerging from the pool. The water
had run from his chest straight down that dark line, and
she had followed its journey and seen, as she could see
now, the base of the stiffening evidence of his desire for
her. Sadie trembled as she leaned forward and kissed
the base of his throat.

Drax arched against the caress of her mouth, not
knowing why that kiss and this woman should affect

him so immediately and so fiercely that he could feel his reaction right down to his toes.

As she kissed him he undressed her, feeling her slip eagerly and easily from her clothes and into his hands. Even now her mouth was still pressed against his skin. She had fantasised about this, Sadie acknowledged dizzily, and now somehow Drax was lying on his back and she was above him, instinctively straddling him. The reality was a hundred—no, a thousand times more erotic than her imaginings, and if she closed her eyes how much more intense would the sensation of Drax's hands on her body be? But she couldn't bear not to see him, not to watch him as he touched her and she touched him. And she wanted so much to touch him…so desperately *had* to touch him.

She leaned forward until her hair swung down to shield her face and stroke Drax's body. But he could still see her expression. She touched him in a way that no woman had ever touched him before, eagerly and yet unknowingly, as though everything about what she was doing was new to her, as though she was following her instincts rather than her experience. When her fingers touched him and then curled around him he felt her hesitate. She looked at him as though seeking reassurance, and then, when he gave it, he could see her confidence grow—and with it her need. It was as though she hungered desperately for him—as though the touching filled her with intense delight and yet fed her need for more of him.

In her eyes was a look of wondering and amazed delight. It curved her mouth and somehow filled the air between them, so that he could almost taste it himself. Nothing he had done before had been like this. Or like her... Whatever magic spell she had cast it had pulled him under its influence, he admitted, as he caught hold of her free hand and lifted it to his mouth, kissing each finger in turn and then licking her soft palm. He watched as her nipples tightened and her belly quivered, and beneath her closed eyelids welled tears of intense arousal.

He reached for her, his hands on her waist, lifting her and steadying her, his fingers digging into her flesh when he felt her hesitation.

She moistened her lips with the tip of her tongue, her voice husky and uncertain as she said, 'I'm not... I don't... Oughtn't we to...?'

He was tight and hot and hard with a surging need that didn't want to wait.

'Oughtn't we to what?' he demanded.

'You know...use something. For...for safe sex and...' She was blushing now. She could feel the heat burning her skin. 'And to make sure that I don't... I mean... I'm sorry,' she told him simply, 'but I haven't done this before.'

How could he feel such anger and yet still want her? He pushed her away and sat up in the large bed,

'What on earth are you saying? We both know that is a lie,' he said savagely. 'No woman your age hasn't "done this before",' he told her scornfully, mimicking the soft uncertainty of her voice. 'I wouldn't believe it even if I *hadn't* seen you letting your lover maul you with my own eyes.'

'Letting him... I wasn't letting him do anything!'

Sadie said, filled with shocked disbelief that he should speak to her that way after the intimacy they had been sharing. 'For your information—not that you're going to believe me, and it's obvious that you don't *want* to believe me—'

Her voice had started to tremble poignantly, and she had to fight to control it. 'He grabbed hold of me and wouldn't let me go. And he *isn't* my lover. He never has been. *That's* why he did it. For revenge. He told me that.'

Even now, having heard the antagonism and rejection in Drax's voice, seen it in his eyes, she still couldn't fully take on board what was happening. She had heard the emotion and felt the tears threatening to break through into her voice as she'd tried to deal with Drax's verbal attack. How could things have changed so quickly? Was this what men did when they took you to bed and then changed their minds about wanting you? Did they seize on some imagined shortcoming instead of being honest? He had left behind their shared intimacy, abandoning it as speedily as he had abandoned her; she was still struggling to release herself from it. Her mind and her emotions might be trying to deal with the hurt Drax had caused her, but her body was still aching for satisfaction. Her pain was still mercifully at the brutally numbing stage, when she knew that it was going to hurt but the shock of it was still too great for her to feel it.

Sadie couldn't be what she was claiming to be. It just wasn't possible. But there was something about the look in her eyes that shamed him. And his body was reminding him of how innocent and untutored her touch had been.

Innocent? he taunted himself. After the intimacy she had shown him? Intimacy, yes, but an intimacy full of desire and longing—the kind of intimacy that was devoid of skilled experience but which reached right to the heart of the man being shown it. And wasn't that why he was feeling the way he was? Torn apart by a toxic mix of anger, rejection of what his heart was telling him, and the fear of having gone too far in a direction he couldn't afford to take?

Why didn't Drax say something? Anything to show that he was listening to her, really listening to her and absorbing what she was saying.

In desperation Sadie said fiercely, 'Jack Logan is the kind of man who thinks that every women he meets ought to find him attractive. When I made it plain to him that I didn't he started to see me as some kind of challenge.'

She had tugged free some of the bedding and was now holding it protectively in front of her, to hide herself from him. The shame inside him drove deeper. For some reason her need to cover herself touched something sharply painful inside him. He wanted to go to her, and hold her, take the look of bleak pain and hurt pride from her eyes. He wanted to take *her* back in his arms and tell her how precious and rare what they shared was.

He wanted to finish what they had started. But how could he now? Her reminder about the need for them to practise safe sex had brought him back to reality. If she wasn't lying, if she was as untouched as she was claiming, then that meant...

That meant she was Vere's.

The choice was his. He could take her back to bed, find out for himself if she was speaking the truth and then face the consequences. Or he could question her companion before he left the country. There was a sour, bitter taste in his mouth. His pride jerked against the thought of humbling himself enough to do such a thing. But he had to do it. He had to know. Not for his own sake, and not even for hers, but for Vere's. The loyalty he owed his brother came before anything and anyone else.

'Get dressed and go back to your quarters,' he told Sadie curtly. 'We'll discuss this further later.'

CHAPTER NINE

Was she really so weak that she was actually allowing Drax to treat her like this? Sadie derided herself angrily an hour later, as she sat alone in what should have been the tranquillity of the private gardens of the women's quarters. Why hadn't she objected when he had virtually ordered her to come here? Why hadn't she refused and told him that she wanted to leave Dhurahn immediately? What was wrong with her?

Did she really need to ask herself that? What was wrong with her was the same thing that afflicted every woman who had ever fallen in love with the wrong man for the wrong reasons.

Fallen in love? Where had those words come from? She hadn't fallen in love with Drax! No? Then what was the motivation behind her current driving compulsive need to be with him, to hold him and touch him, to talk with him and learn all about him, to open her heart and mind to him, to take his hand and cling to it while they walked together though the shadows of her past, to give him the intimacy of herself and to be given the same intimacy back from him? What was all that if not love?

How could she deny to herself that this was how she felt? But how could she love him when she knew that he did not feel the same way? And how was she going to deal with that and protect herself from its pain?

It had been a simple enough matter for Drax to delay the return flight to Heathrow carrying the young bankers and MBAs who had leapt so eagerly at the chance to come to Dhurahn. He was actually in the terminal building when the Royal flight bringing his twin home a day ahead of schedule touched down— although he was not aware of Vere's arrival.

Jack Logan wasn't at all concerned at the delay in their flight's departure—the only thing that hadn't run to schedule in the whole of their superbly organised and tightly packed trip. He was quite happy to while away the time demanding more of the vintage champagne being served by the pretty hostesses, at the same time subjecting them to some heavily explicit flirtation. Nor was he too concerned when an immaculately dressed middle-aged official came to escort him off the plane. To the cat-calls, whoops and cheers of his companions, the older man explained to him that there was a small irregularity that needed to be dealt with.

'Small, is it, Jack?' one of his friends called out coarsely. 'And there's you always boasting that it's six inches and rising.'

'Nah—six inches *without* rising,' Jack quipped back over his shoulder, grinning at the pretty hostess standing by the exit.

By the time he was actually shown into Drax's

presence ten minutes later he was swaggering boast-fully, and blustering out an arrogant demand to be told what the hell was going on.

'Forgive me for the inconvenience,' Drax apologised calmly. 'I assure you that you will soon be free to rejoin your flight. You know Ms Sadie Murray?'

Since Drax was now in western dress, and speaking very calmly, Jack had no sense of being in any danger. Nor did he make the association between the tradi-tionally dressed man he had seen with Sadie and the urbane authority of this man seated in front of him. He immediately leapt to the conclusion that Sadie had lodged a complaint against him. The better part of a bottle of champagne had dulled his normally sharp awareness of how to protect his interests, and led him now to laugh and say unkindly, 'Yes, I know her. She's the type that acts like she's wearing a chastity belt and enjoying it. As sexless as it's possible for a woman to be.'

'You saw her earlier on today, I believe?' Drax continued, outwardly ignoring Jack's swaggering manner but inwardly registering every betraying word and look.

'Yeah, I saw her. Ms Don't-touch-me,' he told Drax mockingly, and then swore crudely before con-tinuing, 'God, but I really hate her smugness. If anyone has it coming to her, she does. Acting like she's too good for me.'

There was an ugly look in his eyes, and Drax had to swallow hard against the sour taste in his mouth as he realised the danger Sadie had been in. 'You wanted to show her who was boss? Scare her a bit...punish her?' he suggested.

'Yeah, right.' Jack was warming more and more to his interrogator by the second. 'She deserved it. Turning me down like she did. I'd have been a fool not to take the opportunity to pay her back.'

'So you slipped away from the others and followed her?'

'Yeah. She's complained about me, has she? That's typical of her. Just because I gave her a bit of a scare. If I'd been that desperate I'd have found myself a woman who knows what it's all about—not some prim, innocent virgin-type like her.' He gave a contemptuous shrug. 'Man, what a turn-off she is. But she owed me, and she had it coming to her.'

How could he not have believed Sadie? Drax was torn between a need to walk—no, *run* from the small enclosed room and go straight to her, and a savage urge to grab Jack by the throat and tell him what he thought of him. Instead he had to conceal what he was actually thinking and ask pleasantly, 'What do you mean, she had it coming to her?'

Jack Logan grimaced. 'She turned me down and made me look a fool, so it was payback time. Come on, mate, *you* must know what it's all about when a woman acts that way.'

'What way do you mean?' Drax asked.

'You know. She made out that I was some kind of pervert just because I made a bit of a play for her, and threatened to complain if I did it again. So I thought I'd pay her back for it.'

'Frighten her, you mean?' It was an effort for Drax to keep his voice empty of emotion and to offer Jack a small, man-to-man conspiratorial smile.

Jack was starting to relax. This was a man's man, he could tell—the type who understood what life was all about.

'Yeah, that's right. Okay, so I grabbed hold of her and touched her up a bit. If she's fool enough to make a big deal of it then that's her problem. Anyway, don't you have a law out here about women being guilty as hell if they get themselves raped?'

Drax decided he would very much like to tear Jack Logan limb from limb and throw his body to the desert vultures to pick clean. But of course he could do no such thing.

'Thank you for your time, Mr Logan,' he said distantly. 'You will now be escorted back to your plane.'

Jack stood up and gave him a lewd grin.

'Great—I've got one of those pretty little trolley dollies all set up, ready and waiting to go.'

Drax made a mental note to make sure that the cabin crew were warned to keep a close watch on him on the return flight—but his thoughts were really on Sadie and how fast he could get back to her and apologise.

Sadie hadn't realised that there was another entrance into the garden until she saw Drax walking towards her from the opposite end to her own quarters. He was wearing traditional robes, the sunlight falling across his arrogantly handsome face.

Her heart leapt and then abruptly stopped leaping, and

then did nothing except beat in its normal way. Even when Drax was standing within a few feet of her, looking at her with that small, half curling twist of his lips that normally sent her heart-rate into overdrive and turned her weak with longing, she didn't want him. She felt like pinching herself, just to make sure she could feel something and hadn't somehow gone completely numb. How could she not feel *anything?* But she didn't. Not a single throb of desire or an ache of longing, not a single inclination to run to him, not even the anger she had every right to feel after the way he had treated her. Which meant... Which meant that she didn't love him after all. She was safe; she no longer needed to worry. And yet...

'If you've come to apologise—' she said fiercely.

'I do owe you an apology, it is true.' He was inclining his head slightly, his voice cool and remote, almost as though...

'You aren't Drax,' she accused, not knowing really why she should say it or how it could be true, and yet at the same time utterly convinced that she was right.

'No,' he agreed. 'I'm not Drax. I'm his brother—Vere. And you, of course, are Ms Sadie Murray?'

'Yes,' Sadie said, suddenly feeling rather self-conscious.

'I must congratulate you, Ms Murray. Very few people can tell Drax and I apart, even though they may have known us for years. You, on the other hand, perceived almost instantly that I was not my brother.'

'I don't know why I said that,' Sadie admitted. 'You look like him.'

'Actually, *he* looks like *me,* since I am older. But,

yes, we are identical.' He smiled at her. 'You will forgive me, I hope, if—having introduced myself to you and bade you welcome to our country and our home—I make my excuses?'

'Yes. Yes of course.'

The wonder wasn't that she had realised he wasn't Drax, but that she had ever imagined he might be, Sadie reflected as she watched him leave. They might look identical, but in character and manner they were very different. Vere was so much more formal than Drax, so much more reserved and withdrawn. Just as arrogant, no doubt, but stiffer, more wary and 'ruler-like'. And, of course, not anywhere near so desirable as Drax. But she had already warned herself that she must not love him.

How much more easy her life would be if Drax was more like his twin and she didn't want him, Sadie reflected ruefully, as she watched the goldfish swimming lazily amongst the water lilies in the pond.

On his way back to the palace all Drax could think about was Sadie. He had been wrong in refusing to believe her, but right in recognising that the real motivation for his anger hadn't been so much that he had thought she was lying as the fact that he had begun to realise his true feelings for her.

Vere, no doubt, would be highly amused when Drax informed him that he intended to take his advice and marry Sadie himself. But, instead of her being a temporary wife, he wanted her to be his permanent wife—his one and only wife, the wife of his heart.

He drove faster than normal, anxious to get back

to Sadie, and the first thing he did when he reached the palace was to make his way straight to the women's quarters.

Sadie had come inside, out of the heat of the sun, to have a cooling shower and drink the glass of mint tea Hakeem had brought for her. When she heard the faint tap on the door to her suite, she thought at first it must be the maid—until the door opened and Drax strode in, closing it firmly behind him.

This time her heart knew exactly who he was. She longed to throw herself into his arms. But she hadn't forgotten the cruel things he had said to her, so she stood tensely, watching him as he came towards her.

'I've come to apologise,' he said simply.

Just the scent of his skin was enough to send her dizzy with longing and to reactivate the unsatisfied ache he had left deep within her body.

'I've spoken to Jack Logan.' Sadie watched as his mouth tightened and anger flashed darkly in the depths of his eyes. 'He's scum.'

'But you were prepared to believe him when you wouldn't believe me?' Sadie pointed out quietly.

'I was jealous,' Drax said quietly. 'I'm not trying to make excuses for myself, Sadie, but it maddened me to see you in his arms and to think— Jealous men do stupid things; they think stupid things as well. I was wrong, and I should have believed you. Can you forgive me?'

Could she? She already knew the answer to that, and she saw from the way he was looking at her that Drax knew it too.

He was walking very purposefully and determinedly

towards her, and there was a gleam in his eyes that warned her of what he was going to do.

'Well?' he whispered huskily as he took her in his arms. 'You haven't answered me yet.'

'I don't know,' Sadie whispered. She couldn't stop looking at him, even though she knew he would read in her eyes how much she loved him. He was going to kiss her...

'Drax—' she began, but she knew she wanted her denial to be too late and ignored.

He was still holding her, and he could feel the unsteady thudding of her heart. 'Are you feeling what I'm feeling?' he asked softly.

'What...what do you mean?'

'You know what I mean. I mean *this*.' He pushed back the sleeve of her robe, stroking his fingertips the length of her inner arm until they rested on the furious race of her pulse.

Sadie could feel her body yearning towards his, wanting him, wanting everything he had denied her earlier.

'And this,' he continued gently, as he raised his hand to brush his fingertips across her throat. 'You love me, don't you?' he demanded.

He was so self-assured, so arrogant, that part of her wanted to be able to deny his words, to shake her head and tell him that he was wrong. But she couldn't. Not when he was teasing tender little kisses along the length of her collarbone, pushing back the neckline of her robe so that it slid off her shoulder, offering up the creamy swell of her naked breasts to his touch, showing him the eager dark flush of her nipples. No wonder he was cupping her breast and teasing her nipple into an even harder peak, tugging it gently with his thumb and forefinger so that it stiffened even more, when her longing arched through her from where he was touching her to the heat of her sex.

'What happens if I say yes?' Sadie asked huskily, made bold by the look in his eyes. A heady euphoria was taking possession of her, encouraging her to dare to tease him in response to that look. It was like learning to dance, Sadie decided a little breathlessly, and suddenly discovering that by some kind of magical empathy your steps were fitting together so well that you moved as one, without hesitation or awkwardness.

'This,' Drax answered her softly, cupping her face in his hands and then stringing tiny kisses along the line of her lips, alternating kisses with the words, 'I love you, Sadie Murray,' so that they became a paean of loving sensuality and desire that dissolved her doubts and melted her resistance.

'In that case, perhaps I should say it,' Sadie whispered back to him. 'I like to hear you telling me that you love me.'

'I think you'd like it even more if I showed you as well as told you,' Drax murmured.

Sadie barely felt the robe being slipped from her shoulders. It was all she could do to respond unsteadily, 'You do?'

'I do,' Drax said, and then he gathered her up in his arms, almost crushing her to him as he kissed her with all the fierce passion she'd been longing for.

The time for teasing and flirting was over.

Could there be anything more heart-soaringly beautiful and meaningful than this? Sadie marvelled as she lay on her bed in Drax's arms while he kissed and caressed her and whispered to her how much he loved her and how sorry he was for ever doubting her.

'I love you so much,' Sadie whispered back. 'I want you so much,' she added truthfully. 'Take off your clothes, Drax, so that I can see you and touch you.'

'You do it,' he urged, taking hold of her hands and placing them on his body. 'While I do this…'

How was she supposed to concentrate on fabrics and fastenings when Drax was kissing his way down the slope of her breast and then sensitising the dark aroused flesh of her nipple to the point of such exquisite and unbearable pleasure that it made her cry out his name? Wildly Sadie arched up to his mouth, her fingers digging into the hard muscles of his arms as she shuddered in the vortex of the surges of erotic need induced by the sensation of his lips closing round her aroused flesh. She was lost, taken over, filled by the intensity of her own fierce desire. She wanted to hold his head against her breast; she wanted to arch up against him, naked flesh to naked flesh; she wanted to wrap her legs tightly around him and draw him down to her so that he was within her and she was holding him, possessing him, drawing him deeper into that place where she ached for him.

But Drax wasn't responding to her passionate non-verbal pleas. Instead he was smoothing her gently onto the bed and then kissing his way down her body, his hands on her hips, his tongue circling her navel. Shivers of the most exciting and erotic sensation radiated out from where Drax was caressing her. He stroked his fingertips slowly and gently over the tops of her thighs, brushing her skin so lightly and delicately that she immediately yearned for more, for a stronger, more intimate touch. Of their own free will her legs softened and parted, inviting the movement of his hand to cup her sex whilst she closed her eyes to absorb the warm intimacy of his touch.

The pulse of her own need was hot and heavy, so fast and urgent that it was consuming her, making her arch up against his hand, small sounds of longing escaping from her lips until Drax took them from her in a possessive kiss. The tip of his tongue probed gently between her lips, almost mirroring the movement of his fingertip, stroking apart the swollen heaviness of the soft lips that protected her sex. First one and then the other parted in eager welcome, urging him to deeper intimacies. Whilst his tongue meshed and danced with hers, weaving a pattern of erotic enticement, his fingertip stroked the same message of promised delight along the wetness of her sex, until it reached the tight, excited centre of her pleasure.

She cried out, a muffled, almost disbelieving sound, riding the rhythmic storm of her pleasure as it possessed her, leaving her quivering in awed delight in the shelter of his arms.

'I want you, Drax,' she whispered passionately to him. 'I want you inside me. Now...'

His arms tightened around her. She could feel the

hard urgent throb of his erection, and her fingers reached eagerly for it so that she could stroke and caress him. But even though she could feel him growing ready beneath her touch, even though she moved invitingly against him, he did not cover her and take possession of her. Instead, he kissed her tenderly and told her softly, 'Not yet. I love you, Sadie, and I want our first time to be a special pleasure. I want you to marry me, Sadie.'

'Oh, Drax.'

'Is that a yes?' Drax demanded.

When Sadie nodded her head, Drax kissed her tenderly.

'You never told me your brother was your twin,' she accused him as he released her, suddenly remembering that she hadn't yet told him about seeing his brother. 'At first when he walked into the garden I thought he was you. He looks like you. But I knew somehow that he wasn't you—even before he spoke to me.'

'Most people can't tell us apart even when they've known us for a long time.'

'Maybe it's because I love *you* that I can?' Sadie suggested softly. 'Not that it wasn't a bit of a shock to discover that you hadn't warned me that there are two of you.'

'Vere is so much a part of me that I tend to take it for granted, I suppose.'

'You're very close, then?'

Sadie was guiltily aware that a part of her almost wished that Drax wasn't a twin. Why? Was it because knowing he shared such a close relationship with someone else who had been there for him all his life somehow threatened her own relationship with him? How could that happen? She was looking for problems where none existed, she told herself firmly. After all, hadn't Drax just told her that he loved her and wanted to marry her?

'I don't want to leave you, but I'd better go and find Vere.'

'To tell him about us? Me?' Why was she asking that? Did she feel some kind of need to test Drax?

'To tell him about you, yes,' Drax agreed. After all, it was the truth.

CHAPTER TEN

'VERE! I didn't realise you were back until Sadie told me she'd seen you. I wasn't expecting you until tomorrow.'

Drax embraced his twin warmly. Vere would be amused when he told him that he had taken his advice and that he was going to marry Sadie himself, Drax admitted. Not that he intended to tell him yet. For the first time in his life Drax was experiencing an emotional need to separate himself slightly from his twin and keep the discovery of his love for Sadie within the special circle of intimacy that belonged to those newly in love. Yes, part of him wanted to tell not just Vere but the whole kingdom how he felt—that he had found the woman with whom he wanted to send the rest of his life—but another part of him wanted to hold Sadie close while they got used to the sensation of the world rocking slightly beneath their feet, reaching for mutual support at the awesome mystery of loving and being loved. The truth was that a part of him was so jealously protective of Sadie and their love that at the moment he didn't want to share its existence with anyone other than Sadie herself.

Because he wasn't entirely sure of that love? *No*. He was sure beyond any kind of doubt about his own feelings. But not Sadie's? Sadie loved him. He knew that.

'Drax, I was just about to come and find you. I want to talk to you about Sadie, and to offer you my apologies for not listening to you when you first spoke of her to me. She is charming. Quite irresistible. Delightfully so,' Vere emphasised softly, with a gleam in his eyes that turned Drax's stomach and filled him with an unfamiliar and furious jealousy.

Vere found Sadie attractive? He *wanted* her? He hadn't let himself think that this might happen, that Vere might want Sadie. But why not? Why shouldn't Vere recognise how wonderful she was, just as he had done?

'A beautiful young woman,' Vere continued approvingly. 'You were right to bring her to Dhurahn, and I was wrong. She is indeed perfect wife material.'

Vere was smiling expectantly at him, but the last thing Drax felt like doing was smiling. *Murderous* probably came closer to describing his feelings, he admitted bitterly. But he couldn't blame his twin for recognising, now that he had spoken with Sadie, just how lovable and wonderful she was, and acting to stake a claim on her. After all, *he* had been the one who had been stupid enough to suggest that Vere should marry her. And he was the one who had refused to accept his own reaction to her within minutes of having blackmailed her into getting into his car. He should have acted then, instead of being too proud to admit that he had fallen head over heels in love with her. He should have told Vere then. Not that he had found the perfect temporary wife for him, but that he had found the perfect, the only, permanent love for *himself*.

'Drax?'

He could hear the concern in his brother's voice, as well as see it in his eyes.

'What's wrong?'

'Nothing,' Drax said shortly. 'As you say, she will make a perfect wife.'

'You don't look very pleased that I'm agreeing with you. I expected you to be more enthusiastic than this,' Vere told him lightly.

Was there a subtle warning in Vere's words? A hint, perhaps, that he was on the verge of guessing his feelings? A reminder that Vere, as the elder twin, had the right to 'first choice'? Drax could taste the acid bitterness of his own jealousy. He could feel its burning heat and its savaging pain. He had never imagined he could harbour such feelings toward his twin, nor had he imagined that there would come a day when his love for a woman would be so intense and so total that she and it would eclipse the bond he had with Vere.

But he was, Drax reminded himself, a man of principle. It wasn't, after all, Vere's fault that he too had fallen for Sadie. They shared the same genes, so why shouldn't they love the same woman? But only one of them could have her. And he had already promised her to Vere.

Why didn't he tell his twin that he had changed his mind? That he had already declared his feelings to Sadie and that she, in turn, returned them? an inner voice urged him. He was tempted to listen to it and take its advice—but how could he? He was a man of honour, a man of his word, and he had already given Vere a promise that he should have Sadie. How could he tell him that he had changed his mind and now wanted her for himself? How could he force his twin to suffer the dark bitterness of the emotions now gripping him?

So he was prepared to sacrifice his love for his twin, and he was prepared to sacrifice Sadie as well, was he? After she had told him she loved him? Was that fair to her? No, Sadie might believe she loved him, but Vere was more worthy of her love, Drax decided bleakly. Vere's were the shoulders that carried the greater burden of responsibility for their country. How could he, his twin, who knew him better than anyone else, see him denied the love and companionship of a woman as unique as Sadie? And she would learn to love Vere. How could she not do so? She would love him, and bear his children, and in time he—

The savagery of the pain that gripped him almost made him cry out. These were thoughts of a future he could not and would not endure. Sadie was *his*! Less than an hour ago he had only just stopped himself from making her his. If he hadn't done so, right now within her there could have been the life force that would create their child…

The darkest of thoughts stormed through his mind, both tempting and threatening his loyalty to his twin. The Drax who was so deeply in love with Sadie wanted to destroy anything and anyone who might come between them and take her from him. But the Drax who was Vere's twin fought against the dark pull of those feelings.

As he struggled to overcome them, Vere watched his

twin with a small frown. Drax's reaction wasn't what he had been expecting.

'Drax, if there's a problem you want to discuss with me…?' he began.

This was Drax's opportunity to confide in his twin, to ask him to step back and allow him to claim Sadie, but a mixture of loyalty and pride refused to let him do so. Even if Vere agreed that he should have Sadie, how could he ever be sure that Vere might not regret his decision and…and what? Blame him for taking Sadie from him? Try to steal her away from him? How could he ever feel the same way about his twin? How could there be that bond of absolute trust and loyalty between them there had always been? How could he trust himself not to betray it? Drax wondered bitterly. And yet that knowledge couldn't make him regret what he and Sadie had already shared. He would carry the memory of that sweetness locked away within himself until his dying day.

'No, there isn't a problem. Why should there be?' he asked Vere flatly.

Drax was withholding something from him, Vere sensed, but his pride would not allow him to press the point and insist on an explanation. They were grown men now, after all, not children and each was entitled to his privacy.

As always when he was hurt Vere retreated into the austere aloofness that Drax normally coaxed him out of.

For once Drax was too caught up in his own feelings to notice Vere's deliberate emotional withdrawal from him.

'The Minister of State wishes to remind us that it is

the anniversary of the creation of our country as an independent state next week.' Vere's clipped voice broke the heavy tension of their shared silence. 'He has made arrangements for the normal celebratory visit to the Oasis of the Two Doves. I take it you will be going?'

'Yes.' Drax's voice was as terse as Vere's.

'And Sadie will also be attending, I hope?'

Just hearing his twin say Sadie's name was like having a knife twisted in his gut.

'If that is your wish,' Drax replied woodenly.

'Given the circumstances, it certainly seems appropriate to me that she should be there,' Vere told him quietly. Couldn't Drax see how much he was hurting him by shutting him out like this? Or was it that he simply didn't care? Vere had never felt more isolated and alone. 'Indeed, I don't think it merely appropriate, I consider it very necessary that she should be a recognised part of the Royal party,' he added.

'If you say so,' Drax agreed curtly.

'I do.'

They were almost on the verge of falling out—and over a woman. Not just *a* woman, Drax told himself, but *the* woman... *his* woman. The woman he must now give up. How was he going to bear it? And Sadie? What of her feelings? She had, after all, given *him* her love. She was sexually innocent, yearning to be loved and to give her love in return. If she could love him after the way he had initially behaved towards her then surely she could and would love Vere? Would she close her eyes in Vere's bed and think of him? The torturous images that sprang to life fully formed inside his head shocked him. He must not allow them to take root there. He must put Vere first. He *must!*

Sadie looked uncertainly towards Drax. It hadn't been until the early hours of the morning that she had finally given up hoping that he would come to her and had gone to bed. As a consequence, even though it was now mid-morning, she was heavy-eyed with lack of sleep and the weight of a growing certainty that something was wrong.

For a start, Drax was ignoring all her desperate attempts to make eye contact with him. For another thing, the only contact of any kind she had had with him since he had told her he loved her had been the arrival of the maid this morning to tell her that she was to be formally presented to Vere and that she should dress accordingly. Nothing else. Not a word nor a gesture. Nothing.

She couldn't remember a time when she had felt more emotionally insecure and abandoned, Sadie admitted. She actually felt worse than she had done when her parents had divorced. In the space of a few hours she had gone from feeling so high on happiness and love that she couldn't imagine her life being any more perfect, to feeling so insecure and anxious that it was hard for her to believe that Drax had actually told her he loved her. Even worse, she was beginning to find it all too easy to imagine that Drax, having almost taken her to bed, was now regretting whatever it was that had driven him to desire her. If he *did* love her, as he had claimed, then as far as she was concerned there was no way he wouldn't have made at least some effort to make sure that she knew he meant what he had said. If he *did* love her then surely he would want to let her know how much he longed to be with her instead of virtually ignoring her?

Was he behaving like this because he was afraid that his twin might not approve of their relationship? Sadie frowned. She didn't want to think of the man she loved being someone who needed to have the approval of someone else to validate his love. However, she was trying to be logical, and to accept that Drax and Vere were twins and that twins had a special relationship. Which was why she was here right now, wearing the cream suit Drax had told her he wanted her to wear for her first meeting with his brother. She looked longingly towards Drax, but he still wasn't looking at her. Deliberately?

His twin, on the other hand, was most certainly looking at her. Studying her silently, his expression withdrawn and austere.

Being treated like this by Drax wasn't just humiliating, it was also unbearably painful. When he had left her the previous day she had been on an emotional and sexual high. Then it had been easy to believe that he had meant what he'd said—that he did indeed love her. After all, she loved him. She had even got as far as wondering about names for their first baby before she had begun to feel the chill wind of her own anxiety. Then she had sat in her room, counting the minutes, aching to see Drax and to be reassured that she had not simply imagined what had happened between them. But Drax hadn't appeared. And so eventually she had gone to sleep, hugging to herself the memory of the precious time they had shared instead of hugging Drax.

Now, of course, it was abundantly plain to her what that happened. Drax had got carried away by sexual desire and had said things to her that he had later regretted. The distance he was deliberately creating between them now was his way of making sure that she realised how he felt— or rather how he didn't feel. Mingling with her pain was anger. Was he keeping his back towards her because he was afraid that if he looked at her she would behave like a complete fool and fling herself into his arms, begging him to tell her he loved her? Well, she might *feel* like doing that, but she had some pride. Certainly enough to make it plain to him that he had nothing to fear from her.

Determinedly Sadie kept her own back towards him as she answered the questions Vere was asking her. He was so different from Drax. Being with him, looking at him, listening to him and talking with him, did not cause her heart to pound with the force of the love-induced adrenalin surging through her veins. There was no sense of breathless awareness, no stomach-clenching tension, no fevered and tormented longing to rip off Vere's clothes and greedily satisfy her need to possess him. Vere was just a very pleasant man, with a kind smile, who looked like the man she loved. There was no chemistry between them—nothing other than a curiosity about him because he was Drax's twin.

She already knew without having to turn round that Drax had moved and was standing closer to her. She could feel the heat coming off her body and she yearned to step back into him, to turn around so that she could touch him, kiss him. The pain of not being able to was so savage that it contorted her body and stopped her breath.

Drax took a step towards Sadie. She wasn't looking at him. She was too busy smiling at Vere. He knew that she *had* looked at him when she had been escorted into the Presence Chamber, but he had not allowed himself to look back at her, knowing that if he did so he would not be able to stop himself from claiming her. He couldn't bear to give her up, but at the same time he couldn't allow himself to break his vow to give his first and total loyalty to his twin. The fault was his own. If he had not made that boast to Vere that he would find him a wife, if he had not offered Sadie to Vere... But he *had* done those things, and it was not Vere's fault that he too had recognised how special she was. Just listening to the soft warmth in her voice as she answered Vere's questions filled Drax with such a surge of murderous jealousy that when it subsided he felt physically sick with self-disgust. He loved her. How could he endure not just a future without her but seeing her happy with his twin?

CHAPTER ELEVEN

'SO THIS oasis is where the agreement was signed?' Sadie was forcing herself to smile and appear light-hearted as she waited for Vere to answer her.

It had been Hakeem who had come to her, two days after Drax had told her he loved her and then turned his back on her, to tell her excitedly that she was to join the Royal party at the traditional annual celebration to mark the original signing of the agreement when Dhurahn had become part of the newly formed union of independent Arab states at the Oasis of the Two Doves, on the edge of the desert's empty quarter.

They had arrived at the oasis late the previous afternoon to find a small but very luxurious encampment of traditional black pavilions erected close to the oasis, and smiling staff on hand to attend to their every need.

Once inside the large pavilion assigned to her, Sadie had been awed by its luxury and comfort. She even had her own private bathroom, complete with a shower.

But what she didn't have was Drax. The oasis was beautiful, but her misery was making it impossible for her to enjoy and appreciate it. She hadn't been able to eat the breakfast she had been served, and she had come here, to this quiet part of the oasis away from the tents, to hide her confusion and misery from everyone else and to try to decide what she should do.

And now here was Vere, who had been so charming to her, and so kind, but who just wasn't the man she wanted and loved. While Drax, whom she did love and want, was behaving as though she did not exist. No wonder she felt so sick at heart.

'Has Drax told you that we are having to cut short our stay at the oasis?' Vere asked.

Sadie shook her head, unable to bring herself to admit that Drax hadn't said a word to her since they had arrived the previous evening.

'We have received a warning that a sandstorm is veering this way, far more severe than first expected, so regrettably we cannot remain.'

'The oasis is lovely,' Sadie told him listlessly. She had seen how much Vere loved the desert, and his own obvious disappointment made her feel that she should offer some kind of sympathetic response.

'Indeed—but the desert can be fatally cruel to those who treat her lightly. Did you enjoy last night's ceremony?' he asked her.

'Yes. It's a heartwarming tradition.' Sadie tried to sound enthusiastic.

'We certainly think so,' Vere replied. 'Our family had always ruled Dhurahn, of course, but we celebrate the signing of the agreement because it signifies Dhurahn's new era of peace between what were previously warring warrior tribes. When the agreement was

signed, two doves were released as a symbol of peace
and hope for the future. Drax and I have always celebrated the occasion at the oasis. As boys, it was something we looked forward to. To those born of the desert
there is always that sense of homecoming and completion about living as our forebears did, in harmony with
the desert, respecting its power over us. 'You look
unhappy,' he added suddenly, in a quieter tone, catching
Sadie off guard.

She could feel her emotions tightening her throat.
She bowed her head, not wanting to shame herself by
letting Vere see her tears. But to her surprise Vere leaned
forward and took hold of her hand, raising it to his lips.
His kiss was kind, but meaningless to her, Sadie
admitted wearily. Just as every man's kiss would be to
her from now on. Because he wouldn't be Drax.

Vere watched Sadie in silence. He could see how
upset she was, and he didn't want to upset her further.
A little to his own surprise, Vere had discovered that the
more he got to know Sadie, the deeper his feelings with
regard to her had become. She would make a perfect
royal consort as far as he was concerned. But now it
seemed, from his behaviour towards her, that Drax no
longer shared that view. It was, he decided, time that he
spoke to Drax and found out exactly what was going on.
He had held off questioning his twin directly in the
hope that Drax would come to him and speak openly,
and it saddened and hurt him that Drax hadn't done so.

Drax frowned as he watched Vere and Sadie. He could
feel the now-familiar sensation of unbearable emotional

agony ripping into him. He wanted to go to them and physically push his twin aside, then take hold of Sadie so that Vere couldn't touch her. He knew that Sadie herself didn't understand what was happening. He could see it in her eyes. But how could he explain to her that Vere was claiming her?

Vere had just left her when some instinct made Sadie turn her head just in time to see Drax disappearing inside his pavilion. Her heart felt as though it was being torn apart. She couldn't endure any more of this torture. She had to know the truth; she had to know if Drax had ever loved her or if he had simply been cold-bloodedly lying to her. And if so, why? Not because he had hoped to trick her into his bed, obviously! She would go and have it out with him now, before she lost her courage, she decided. And she would demand that he return her passport to her so that she could leave Dhurahn. Her mind made up, Sadie made her way back through the busy bustle of men working to break up the camp and prepare for their return journey.

Already the hot bright glare of the sun had become slightly dimmed, the sky taking on an ominous, sulphurous tinge. But it was the storm inside herself that concerned Sadie more than the sandstorm threatening the oasis as she headed for the black tent she knew to be Drax's.

The tents had already been erected when they'd arrived, and Sadie had been bemused to discover just how luxurious the drab black structures crouched on the sand were on the inside. Her own was carpeted with beautiful Persian rugs and divided into a bedroom and a sitting area, both of which were furnished with luxurious fabrics, rich silks and velvets strewn over low divans, and a wide, lonely bed in which she had been unable to sleep because of her longing for Drax. She had tortured herself with imagining Drax in his own bed. How she had longed to be sharing the scented darkness of his pavilion and its privacy with Drax. In her mind's eye she had seen herself going to him, as secretly as though she were a favoured slave girl summoned to her master, crouching at the foot of his bed, waiting his permission to slowly caress and kiss her way up his naked body. But Drax did not want her kisses. He did not want *her*. He had made that plain enough.

A group of men were working outside Drax's pavilion, causing Sadie to hesitate, wary of just walking inside in full view of them, knowing the strict moral conventions Vere and Drax's subjects followed. There was another, smaller side entrance, though, just as there was in her own tent, and she headed for that

Drax was working on his computer when Vere walked into his tent. He frowned, pushing back his chair and standing up.

'The storm is getting worse,' Vere told him.

Drax watched him grimly. Vere hadn't come here to tell him that.

'I want to talk to you about Sadie,' Vere said quietly. 'You're in love with her, aren't you?'

Drax couldn't make himself deny it. 'What if I am? It doesn't affect you.'

'Of course it does. We've always shared every-thing, Drax.'

Sadie had managed to slip unnoticed into Drax's tent, but now, as she heard the two brothers' voices, she panicked and turned to leave. When she tried she dis-covered that the exit had been blocked by the men working outside, their four-wheel drive now parked close by. What on earth was she to do? She couldn't leave, but she certainly couldn't brazenly walk in on the two brothers either. She would just have to stay here until either Vere or both of them left.

She heard Vere saying something, but as always it was Drax's voice her senses registered more clearly, clinging to it with all the desperation of the lover who was unloved. She was pathetic, she derided herself. But the sound of her own name had Sadie stiffening and creeping closer to the fabric wall separating her from the brothers.

'So we share her, do we? How? In bed?' Drax could hear the emotion he couldn't control cracking his voice. 'Turn and turn about? Until she's so dizzy she can't tell the difference between us?'

Sadie went icy cold with shock, and then hot with fear. Nausea cramped her stomach and rose sourly in her throat.

In the semi-light of the richly furnished tent, Vere waited to let the bitterness and anger spew out of his twin before he spoke. But Sadie could not wait. Driven by revulsion and horror, she stumbled back towards the narrow exit she had used to enter the tent and pushed her way through the workmen, no longer caring how it would look.

She was out of hearing range when Vere stepped

towards Drax and placed his hands on his shoulders, ignoring Drax's attempts to push him off. 'Why are you saying these things?' he asked him. 'I like Sadie, yes. But I do not desire her. When I think of her, I think of her as the woman you love.'

Outside, the wind had picked up dramatically, making Sadie stagger as she felt its full force. They would soon be returning to the city, but she couldn't wait that long for her escape or for oblivion.

A Land Rover had pulled up almost in front of her, its driver getting out and leaving the engine running as he hurried to help two other men who were staggering under the weight of what they were carrying. Without giving herself time to rationalise what she was doing, Sadie ran to it, ignoring the grains of sand tearing at her exposed skin and burning her eyes and mouth as she climbed into the vehicle and pulled the door closed after her. In front of her was a barely discernible track. She released the brake and put her foot on the accelerator.

Immediately the powerful off-roader surged forward into the seething storm. Sadie didn't care that she might be putting herself in danger. What was physical danger to her now, after what she had just heard? Her heart lurched against her ribs. She had thought that the worst pain she would ever have to bear was knowing that Drax didn't love her. But she had been wrong and naïve. So stupidly naïve. How many other women had been used by Drax and his brother as they had planned to use her? She knew there were those who might boast that they would enjoy such an experience, but she was not one of them. The thought of the two men touching her

intimately, using her body for their pleasure, excited by
the knowledge that they were sharing her, filled her
with disgust and loathing.

Vere held Drax's bitter gaze as he waited for his twin
to respond. The silence seemed to go on for ever, but
finally Drax exhaled and said thickly, 'Vere, you are just
saying that for my sake, because you know that I love
her too. But you forget that you have already told me
that she will make a perfect wife.'

'Yes,' Vere agreed. 'But for *you,* not for me. I had
hoped my words would encourage you to confide in me
and confirm what I had already guessed—that despite
the fact that you had insisted you were bringing Sadie
to Dhurahn for me you had fallen in love with her
yourself. Do you really think I am so blind, so insensi-
tive to your feelings, that I wouldn't know immediately
how you felt about her? Although I have to say, after
the way you have been treating her these last few days,
I wouldn't blame Sadie for doubting how you feel about
her. You've practically ignored her, and—'

'I did that for *your* sake! Because I thought that you
too had fallen in love with her.'

'And it was for *your* sake that I didn't ask what was
going on.' There was a hint of self-reproach as well as
compassion in Vere's voice. 'I should have spoken more
openly to you. But you know that I am not as comfortable in my emotional skin as you are in yours. I told
myself that were I in your shoes I would want to choose
the moment to tell you of my feelings rather than have
you confront me with them. I knew something was

wrong, but I had no idea what you were thinking. I should have guessed.'

'How could you?' Drax told him, sensing that this twin was blaming himself for what that happened. 'It is a well-known fact that when a man falls passionately and deeply in love he is lost to all reason. I assumed that because I love Sadie you must do the same. I was jealous, bitterly so, but I felt I had to stick to my statement to you that I was bringing Sadie back to Dhurahn for *you.*'

'Have you told Sadie any of this?'

'No. I couldn't bring myself to do so.'

'She is very distressed by your behaviour towards her,' Vere told him gently.

'She told you that?'

Now Vere could smile, as he heard and recognised the reason for the hostility in his twin's voice. 'Not as such. But it is plain to me that she is unhappy.'

While they had been speaking the noise of the wind had been increasing, to the point where now they had to talk loudly to make themselves heard above it.

'We need to return to the city,' Vere said. 'We don't want to be caught out here in the storm.'

'I'll drive Sadie back myself,' Drax said. 'And the first thing I shall want to do when we get back is set in hand the arrangements for my marriage—after I have apologised to her.'

Suddenly they were both laughing, embracing one another with genuine understanding and mutual happiness.

As they stepped back, one of the workmen suddenly

burst into the tent, exclaiming, 'Highness! The English girl has just driven out of the camp in one of the Land Rovers.'

Drax released Vere and turned to look at the anxious man who had come hurrying into the tent.

'What?'

It couldn't be possible that Sadie had done something so dangerous. But the look on the workman's face confirmed that it was.

The two brothers ran for the exit.

Outside, men were battling against the strong winds to pack everything up, some of them bent almost double against the force. A thick veil of storm-driven sand was turning the landscape into a yellow fog.

'Which way did she go?' Drax yelled at the workman above the keening howl of the wind.

The man pointed in the direction of the eye of the storm. Drax and Vere exchanged grim looks.

'I'm going after her,' Drax said.

'You can't—you won't—' Vere began, and then stopped when he saw the expression in his twin's eyes. 'I'm coming with you,' he said instead.

Drax shook his head, but the look he gave his twin was filled with love and gratitude.

'No, Vere,' he told him gruffly. 'We both know that I *have* to go after her, even though we also know the danger. My life is nothing without her.'

'As is mine without you, my brother,' Vere said simply.

Tears burned the backs of Drax's eyes. 'You will go on because you must—because our people and our country need you. But I cannot go on without Sadie. Before I met her I would have sworn that there could be no bond, no love that could ever be as strong as what I share with you. But Sadie has shown me that I was wrong. I have to find her.'

'And if you don't?'

'I won't rest until I do. I won't come back until I find her. And I *will* find her. Even if I have to search the desert through this life and eternity for her.'

Vere gave a small nod of his head.

'Go, then, my brother,' he said softly. 'And my prayers go with you. We will leave the generator and one of the tents, just in case you should need it.'

Drax nodded his own head. They embraced again, and Vere stood and watched as Drax ducked under the ferocity of the wind and climbed into his four-wheel drive.

'Excellency, we must leave soon,' one of the workmen begged Vere urgently.

Vere nodded, but didn't move until the whirling sand had swallowed up Drax's vehicle and he could see him no longer.

Outside the windows the sand whirled and the wind howled, battering the vehicle from all directions. Sadie had long ago lost sight of the track she had been following, but she didn't care. She didn't care about anything. She only wanted oblivion.

A sob tore at her throat, her emotions shaking her body in much the same way as the storm shook the vehicle. Both she and the vehicle were in the grip of a force so powerful that they could not escape from it. The storm was threatening to pluck up the heavy car and mercilessly destroy it, but it wasn't that that was making

the dry sobs tear at Sadie's throat. Drax! How could he
have planned to subject her to such degradation? She
couldn't bear to think of the fate he had been willing to
inflict on her, and she couldn't bear to know that she had
loved him. She wanted to tear his memory from her
heart and her mind.

The vehicle's engine started to race as it struggled to
climb a steep, invisible incline—so steep that it must
almost be perpendicular, Sadie realised, as the wheels
spun and the vehicle rocked. Without warning it
suddenly started to plunge downwards at great speed.

Sadie tried to brake, but it was no use. The vehicle
was out of control. She cried out in the seconds before
the vehicle lurched to an abrupt halt, causing her to
bang her head on the window, and through the pain she
was aware that she had cried out Drax's name. And the
pain of knowing *that* was far greater than the injury to
her throbbing head. Her forehead felt wet and sticky.
She lifted her hand to it and saw that she was bleeding.
Already she could barely see through the windscreen
because of the sand. She knew she ought to be afraid,
but somehow she wasn't. What was the point? Right
now dying felt easier than living with the knowledge of
Drax's cruelty.

Sadie couldn't have got very far, Drax tried to reassure
himself. She had driven off down a well-used track, ac-
cording to the driver of the off-roader she had taken. But
she had also driven right into the path of the oncoming
storm—which was why he had refused Vere's offer to
come with him.

That he would find Sadie was not in doubt. Whether they would survive the fury of the storm was a different matter. Like all modern vehicles in use in Dhurahn for desert travel, both were fitted with a special tracking system that ensured a driver could not become lost in the desert. His mobile phone might not work in the ferocity of the storm, but the tracking device would. Which was just as well, Drax thought, well aware of how easily a sandstorm could change the landscape, wiping out its existing features and creating new ones. It was impossible for him to see very much through his windscreen, but unlike Sadie he knew exactly what to do when he suddenly started to climb a steep sandhill.

Even though he knew approximately where the other vehicle was, it still took Drax several precious minutes to locate it, half buried beneath the sand. When he wrenched open the door and saw Sadie slumped over the driving wheel he felt as though his heart was being forcibly ripped out of his chest. But the moment he touched her she jerked upward, her eyes opening and darkening with horror as she saw him.

'No! Not you… No…' She was crying and half hysterical as she tried to push him away, to stop him from lifting her out of the car, but Drax persevered, dragging her free as she collapsed against him. Bent almost double under her weight, he struggled back to his own vehicle. Already sand was drifting against it, driven there by the unrelenting wind. Drax knew there was no chance of them making it back to Dhurahn ahead of the storm, but if they stayed here it would overwhelm them. The oasis was their best chance of survival—if they could get there.

Somehow he managed to manhandle Sadie into the passenger seat. He had left the engine running, and as he put the vehicle in gear Sadie started to come round.

She was with Drax. Sadie shuddered. Why had he come after her? Why hadn't he just left her in peace? Was he so perverted that he would risk death rather than be denied his sick pleasure?

Tears filled her eyes and spilled down on her cheeks.

Drax reached out his hand to touch her, and immediately she cowered away from him, her eyes bleak with pain.

'What are you doing here? Why did you come after me?'

'Because I had no choice. I love you, Sadie. You are my life and—'

'No.' How dared he lie to her like this when she knew the truth? How dared he look at her with a pain in his gaze that said she was more precious to him than life itself?

She started to laugh, almost hysterically.

'Yes!' he insisted. But Sadie shook her head.

'You're lying. You don't love me. I heard you, Drax; I heard everything you said about me to Vere. About the two of you sharing me.' She made herself say the horrible words and endure the poison of their taste. 'I won't let you do that to me, Drax. I'd rather die,' she said wildly. 'I won't let you abuse me like that.'

'Was that why you left the camp?' Drax demanded.

'You didn't think I'd stay, did you, after hearing something like that?'

Sadie gasped as the wind howled and screamed, buffeting the four-wheel drive and causing it to rock from side to side.

'Sadie, it isn't as it seems.'

'How can it *not* be? I heard you.'

'I know you did, but...' Drax cursed under his breath as he fought to control the vehicle. 'I love you, Sadie.'

'Don't say that! You're lying.'

'No, I'm not. What you heard me saying to Vere was—'

His explanations would have to wait until they got back to the oasis, Drax realised, as the wind died abruptly and suddenly there was complete silence.

'What—?' Sadie began uncertainly, sensing that the unnatural calm had a dangerous malevolence about it.

'The eye of the storm,' Drax told her grimly. 'If we're lucky, very lucky, we might make it to the oasis before all hell breaks loose. There it is up ahead—see?'

Sadie could. The camp had an abandoned, empty air about it; several of the palm trees had been uprooted, one of them having crashed down into the oasis itself. Drax brought the vehicle to a halt alongside the one remaining tent—Drax's tent, Sadie saw.

'Where are the others? Vere?' Sadie asked, almost stammering over his twin's name as she remembered what she had heard him saying.

'Back in Dhurahn by now. You drove straight into the path of the storm. Quick,' he commanded her, unbuckling his seatbelt and turning to unfasten hers. Sadie shook her head. She wanted to refuse to get out of the Land Rover, but the eerie silence was somehow more frightening than the thought of being with him. At least she knew that only he was here.

She wouldn't let him touch her, though, not even as she struggled through a deep drift of sand to cross the few feet that separated the vehicle from the entrance to the tent.

'We are lucky that the generator is still working,' Drax said once they were both inside. 'At least for now.'

'Maybe the storm is over and we don't need to stay here? Maybe we should try to get back to the city?' Sadie suggested. 'And when we do get there I want my passport back, Drax. I won't stay and be…abused.' She lifted her chin and said fiercely, 'If you and Vere want to play those sort of perverted games then you will have to find someone else to play them with.' Her face was burring with shame and disgust.

'Sadie—' Drax groaned, but he stopped speaking abruptly as suddenly, out of nowhere, the silence was torn apart by an unearthly sound as the wind returned to howl and scream its fury whilst tearing at the fabric of the pavilion as though it were an alien life force.

It was impossible to speak above its fury, but Sadie could see from Drax's expression the danger they were in. 'We're going to die, aren't we?' she whispered.

Drax must have read her lips, because he shook his head and mouthed back, 'If we do it will be together. And I would rather die with you, Sadie, than live without you.'

What was he saying? He couldn't possibly mean those words. To her disbelief, she saw that he was coming towards her. She tried to evade him, but it was too late. His arms closed round her and his mouth came down on hers in a fierce, possessive kiss.

She shouldn't be letting this happen. But somehow she couldn't stop herself from lifting her own arms to hold him close. Perhaps it was the knowledge that they might not survive that was fanning the embers of her need into such an urgent heat, making her return his kiss with equal hunger, urging her to take what there was before the darkness came down on them.

Outside the wind shrieked, but all Sadie could hear was the frantic thud of her own heartbeat and the voice inside her that said nothing mattered but this need within her. Her body ached and yearned for Drax's touch—and not just his touch, but his possession. She could feel her flesh heating, seeking a complete union with his, wanting at its most intimate level to draw him in and keep him there, to make him so much a part of her that there were no boundaries left between them and they were one perfect whole. This was all that mattered; it was all that she wanted to communicate to Drax.

She pressed her body up against his, willing him to respond to her need, to answer her impatient hunger, to have him destroy the barriers between them, to answer the storm inside her and tear away everything that separated them so that they could be truly together, flesh on flesh, heart on heart, until she possessed him deep within her.

Somewhere a small part of her registered that she was being driven by a form of madness, but her need scorned it. What was madness but a delicious form of intense reality? And nothing could be more real than this. She could feel Drax's hands moving urgently over her body. She moaned with hot, hungry pleasure, sliding her own hand down his back and then over the curve of his buttock, and then between their bodies so that she could touch him intimately. She felt him shudder when her flingers closed over him, and she shuddered herself in response, lost mindlessly in the storm of her need for him.

'Take me to bed, Drax,' she begged fiercely. 'Here and now, when it's just the two of us. I want you so much…'

'No.' His denial was low and raw, the aching, tormented sound of a man refusing what he wanted most. 'No, Sadie,' he repeated, releasing her. 'Not until I have talked with you. Explained everything to you.'

'We might not live that long,' Sadie said. 'And if we don't, I want my last moments with you to be in your arms, Drax. Not—'

Drax gave her a small shake. You mustn't say that. We are going to live. Now, let me explain—'

'Not here.' Sadie was being driven by an instinct she didn't understand but could no longer fight. 'Tell me in bed, Drax, while you're holding me.' What she meant was that a part of her didn't want to see his face because she didn't want to see that he was lying to her.

'Very well,' Drax agreed. 'In bed, in my arms, you shall hear the truth and know my heart, Sadie.'

CHAPTER TWELVE

THEY undressed quickly, feverishly almost, aware not only of their intense desire for one another and the unresolved issues between them, but also of the threat of the storm and its power to destroy them. The fine grains of sand brushed easily from Sadie's skin as she stood staring at Drax's naked body, unable to stop greedily absorbing the sight of him. She could feel the fine tremble of his hands when he reached for her, holding her so tightly in his arms that she could feel the rapid beating of his heart as though it were her own. She wanted him so badly, and to judge from his state of arousal his need matched hers. Would he think about his twin later, when he possessed her? Would he imagine that Vere was with them? Would he—?

He touched her face gently and kissed her forehead. 'Don't look like that, Sadie. What you overheard wasn't what you thought, although I can understand how damning it would sound.'

'You can't magic away the words you spoke, Drax.'

'No, I can't. But I can explain where they came from. The truth is that I spoke those words out of blind, driving jealousy and bitterness, Sadie. All our lives Vere and I have put our loyalty to one another and our relationship first. When I fell in love with you I discovered for the first time what it meant to hate my brother, to feel murderously jealous of him.'

'Why should you feel like that? You *knew* how I felt about you.'

'Yes, but the situation is more complicated that that. You see, I had promised you to Vere.' Drax felt her stiffen and try to pull away from him. But he had anticipated her reaction and held her tightly, keeping her close to him.

'You mean that you acted as a pimp for your brother?' Sadie challenged him savagely.

'No. Let me explain.'

Quietly and openly Drax started to tell her about the potential problems that might have arisen from the desire of the rulers of their neighbouring states to tie them to their families via marriage.

Sadie winced when she heard Drax repeating his mocking comment about virginal women falling in love with sheikhs, but Drax laughed softly and said, 'What I hadn't bargained for was that this sheikh was going to be the one falling in love, and that he would be so overwhelmed by the experience that he'd try to pretend that it wasn't happening.

'Vere guessed the truth, though. My brother isn't like me. He is more reserved. He finds it less easy to talk of what he feels, even to me, and he guards his emotional privacy fiercely. So he waited for me to come forward and tell him of my feelings. He tried to encourage me by commenting that you would make a perfect wife, and in my jealousy I imagined that he was telling me that he too had fallen in love with you and wanted you as his wife. How could he not love you when you're so loveable? How could I have so stupid as to not see that for myself the moment I set eyes on you?

'Because he is my twin, and because of the vow I had made to find him a temporary wife first, I felt obliged to step out of your life. I had no idea that when he talked about you being perfect wife material he was referring not to himself but to me. It was the jealous outburst you overheard that enabled him to learn how I had misunderstood him. What you heard me saying to him was not, my darling, a description of what I wanted, but the anger of a bitterly jealous man. I hated the thought of Vere so much as looking at you, never mind touching you.'

'But you were still willing to give me up to Vere, even though you knew I loved you?'

'I reasoned that since Vere is the better of the two of us you would love him more. You have to understand, Sadie, that because of our obligations to our country Vere and I have always put our loyalty to one another ahead of everything else. But now both he and I know that our relationship can never be the same again, because my love for you means that *you* will now be the most important person in my life.'

Sadie could hear the sincerity and truth in his voice.

'I couldn't bear what I thought I'd heard you say. I'd wanted to talk to you. To tell you that I wanted to return to England.' She shuddered. 'I shouldn't have taken the vehicle like that, but I had to get away.'

'And I had to find you.'

'Oh, Drax, we could both die here, and it will be my fault.'

He shook his head and smiled at her. 'We aren't going to die. Listen.'

Sadie looked at him and frowned.

'I can't hear anything.'

'Exactly,' Drax said. 'While you and I were battling our own personal storm, the one outside the tent blew itself out.'

'We'll be able to leave here and return to Dhurahn?' Would he sense her disappointment and guess how reluctant she was to give up the chance of this precious time alone with him?

'We could,' he agreed. 'But not tonight.'

'Not tonight?' Sadie repeated.

'No, tonight.' Drax repeated firmly. 'Because tonight I want you to myself, so that I can prove to you just how much I love you.'

'I'd like that. And I'd like it too if our child was conceived here tonight, Drax,' Sadie told him softly. 'Here, tonight, in the aftermath of the storm which could have destroyed us.'

She could see from the smouldering look in his eyes just how much her words were affecting him. She leaned towards him, reaching out her hand to enclose him, trembling with anticipation and desire when her fingers encircled his hardness. His flesh felt hot, tempting her caress.

'You know what's going to happen if you keep on doing that, don't you?' Drax said thickly.

'Show me,' Sadie said, catching her breath as he lifted her hand from his body.

He kissed her fiercely as his own hands mapped *her* body. When his hands cupped her breasts her nipples rose eagerly, seeking the touch of his flesh. His lips were against her throat, feeling the vibration of her moans of delight at the soft tug of his fingers and thumbs on her nipples. Sadie lifted her hands to his shoulders, pushing his head further down her body, wanting the erotic stimulation of his mouth against her breast. But when he obeyed her unspoken command the pleasure was shockingly sharper than she had anticipated. Drax slipped his hand between her legs as he drew her nipple into his mouth, the knowing stroke of his fingertip probing the folded outer lips of her sex mirroring the rhythmic tug of his mouth of her nipple.

Sadie thought she would die from the pleasure building so intensely inside her—or explode, its tension was so unbearably arousing. She opened her legs and pressed up against his hand, hotly eager for him to probe deeper and more intimately at the slickness of her aroused flesh. He had found the source of her female pleasure and was caressing it, drawing it to its full desire-swollen sensitivity, so that every shallow breath she took seemed to rock her on the edge of the orgasm she longed to engulf her. But each time she reached for it Drax withdrew from her, until she reached for him in a frenzy of need, telling him fiercely, 'Now, Drax. Now, please now.'

It was heaven to feel the weight of him against her, to spread her legs and then wrap them around him tightly, arching up against him. He thrust carefully into her, but his care frustrated her.

'Deeper, Drax, harder,' she begged him, her eyes darkening with feral pleasure when he obeyed her and she felt her body accommodate the sensation of him within it. Experimentally she tightened her muscles around him, and heard him groan with pleasure.

'How can you know how to do that?' he demanded in between kisses.

'How can I not?' Sadie whispered back against his lips. 'When it's what I want to do...when I want to feel you and hold you...when I want...'

'This?' he suggested, thrusting rawly, rhythmically, faster and deeper, while she clung to him and gave herself up to the pleasure of his possession. His rhythm was taking her, driving her, towards the pinnacle that was now so enticingly within reach.

'Drax...' she appealed.

He drove harder, filling her, making her move urgently against him, and she stiffened as the pleasure exploded inside her, surge after surge of it, in waves of exquisite pulsing sensation as her body gripped and caressed his and she felt the liquid warmth of him spilling into her.

'Drax,' she whispered, lifting her hand to touch his face.

He captured it, pressing his lips to the palm of her hand and then saying rawly, 'You are mine now. Mine for ever. My love and soon, I hope, my wife. You will marry me, won't you, Sadie?'

She was too overwhelmed by her own emotions to

do anything more than nod her head and let him hold her close while her body still quivered with small aftershocks of pleasure.

'Shouldn't you let Vere know that the storm is over and that you are safe?' Sadie asked drowsily. 'He's bound to be worrying.'

'There's no mobile signal out here, but don't worry. Vere will know that we are safe.'

'Because he's your twin and he will sense it?' Sadie asked him

'Yes.'

'But that doesn't mean he'll know you've found me.'

She could hear the love in his voice when he told her softly, 'Yes, it does. Because I told him when I left that I didn't intend to return from the desert without you.'

They were married three weeks later—first in a civil ceremony, and then in the traditional manner of Dhurahn's people, handfasted to one another by the tying of a silk scarf around their wrists as Drax held Sadie's hand firmly in the grasp of his own, their fingers interlinked.

It was Vere who officiated at the ceremony, as Leader of his people, and Vere too who welcomed Sadie with the kindest of reassuring speeches—a public reiteration of the private assurance he had already given her that he was happy to welcome her as Drax's wife.

It was a long day, with feasting and traditional dancing and singing, but finally they were alone.

'I love you,' Drax whispered as he took her in his arms in the privacy of their own quarters.

Beyond the large window moonlight glinted on the pool from which she had seen him emerging naked and had wanted him so fiercely. She wanted him just as fiercely now. But now she was free to tell him so—and to show him. She looked up at him, her feelings illuminating her expression.

'When you look at me like that, I know that I am the most fortunate man on earth,' Drax told her softly. 'If I have one hope left now it is that Vere will find someone to love and be loved, as I love and am loved by you, Sadie.'

And then there was only silence, punctuated by the softness of Sadie's long sighs of pleasure as he celebrated with her their commitment to one another.

THE SULTAN'S BED

LAURA WRIGHT

Laura Wright has spent most of her life immersed in the worlds of acting, singing and competitive ballroom dancing. But when she started writing, she knew she'd found the true desire of her heart! Although born and raised in Minneapolis, Minn., Laura has also lived in New York, Milwaukee, and Columbus, Ohio. Currently, she is happy to have set down her bags and made Los Angeles her home. And a blissful home it is – one that she shares with her theatrical production manager husband, Daniel, and three spoiled dogs. During those few hours of downtime from her beloved writing, Laura enjoys going to art galleries and movies, cooking for her hubby, walking in the woods, lazing around lakes, pottering in the kitchen and frolicking with her animals.

To a wonderful friend, amazing writer, brilliant
critique partner – and all around fabulous woman:
Jennifer Apodaca

Prologue

"**O**ur father sired another child."

With those words Zayad Al-Nayhal, Sultan of Emand, executed a perfect rotation and plunged his sword into his imaginary target's chest. When he pulled back, he fought to keep his footing on the smooth stones of the large terrace that spanned the entire third floor of his palace. His arms were tight, his body exhausted and he could plainly see that his right hand bled.

It was no wonder after three and one-half hours of exercise.

Correction—of diversion.

Last night he had received a letter from his father's aide, a man who had passed away quietly just one week ago. The letter had been delivered by the aide's son and had contained a confession of such emotional intensity,

Zayad immediately had called his brother and asked him to come home. Knowing nothing but the agitation in his brother's voice, Sakir had agreed and been en route within the hour.

Through the night, Zayad had attempted to sleep. But that had been a fool's endeavor. At two-thirty in the morning he had escaped his empty bed and his cold silk sheets and made his way to the terrace, prepared to wield his sword, to sweat and to await his brother.

Zayad returned to the present, heard the palace bustle with activity on the floors below, and nodded at the four servants who stood in readiness at opposite ends of the terrace. Beyond the palace walls the sun was slowly creeping its way across the desert, eager to plant itself firmly on the horizon.

It was daybreak, and his brother was finally here.

Swathed in a backdrop of stone balconies, terracotta silk curtains and golden domes that stretched high into the blue sky, Sakir Al-Nayhal stood tall, his arms crossed at his chest, a frown tugging at his full mouth. "You have done many things to get me back to Emand, but creating this story—"

His sword at his side, Zayad shook his head. "This is no story, brother."

"I do not believe you," Sakir returned. "I have left a beautiful pregnant wife because you sounded as though—"

"As though there were an emergency?" Zayad lifted his eyebrow.

"Yes. And I find you here trifling with your sword."

His eyes fixed on his brother, Zayad steered the tip of his blade toward a small round table situated beside a man-made waterfall and a hundred flowering plants. On the table was a gold tray containing Zayad's uneaten breakfast. And beside the plate sat a two-page letter, its thin edges flickering in the warm breeze. "Draka wrote that letter to me before he died. What he has to say is quite extraordinary and of such import that I thought it wise to take you from Rita."

Sakir stared at the letter but made no move to pick it up. "What does it say?"

"It states that twenty-six years ago our father traveled to America to meet with the two senators of California on modern oil-drilling practices." His lips thinned with irritation. "There he met a woman."

Sakir's brows knit together. "A woman?"

"She was a young aide who worked for one of the senators. It seems that our father was instantly captivated by her beauty and spirit. He asked her to take a meal with him that night, and she accepted. After dinner they took a long drive up the coast—" he paused, inhaled deeply "—then she invited him to her home."

It was a moment before Sakir spoke, but his eyes glittered with bewilderment. "This is very hard for me to believe. Our father detested Americans."

"I thought so, as well, but Draka says that the sultan told him that this woman was different."

For the second time in twenty-four hours, anger inched its way into Zayad's blood, and he hated himself for it. He was no romantic. He did not believe in true love, at least for himself. He understood the ways of men in his position—even married men. But his father had been different. Or so Zayad had thought. The Sultan had never taken another woman to his bed. Only his wife. He had always claimed his love for Zayad's mother was true and without competition and that the old ways had not, and would not, claim him.

"How long was our father in America?" Sakir asked.

"Three days."

"And his nights were spent with this woman?"

"It would appear so."

"You spoke of a child," Sakir said, his jaw tight.

"One month after the sultan returned to Emand, the woman contacted Draka."

"And?" Sakir prompted when Zayad paused.

"She claimed she was with child. She claimed the sultan was her child's father. She wished to speak with him, to tell him of this news."

"And what did our father say to her?"

Zayad walked to the balcony, searched for calm in the rugged landscape, the desert floor and the mountains beyond. "Draka did not tell our father of her call or her news."

"What?" Sakir fairly snapped.

"Draka did not believe that the woman was speaking the truth."

"Yes, but an investigation should have been made."

"Of course it should have." Zayad's gaze fell to the acres of lush garden that held fruit trees and herbs, but more importantly, held the grave of his youngest brother, Hassan. The boy had died many years ago in a military training accident, and for Zayad, grief still spread through his bones every time he thought about losing his brother.

Butterflies flew and fed at the red and purple flowers by Hassan's grave-site. A reminder that his spirit re-

mained, yet would always be able to fly free. Zayad
knew in that moment that even if there was the smallest possibility that he and Sakir had another sibling, he
had to pursue it.

"What are you thinking, brother?" Sakir asked.

Zayad turned, his back to his beloved land. "This is
a personal matter, a family matter, but one that needs
to be addressed. I am thinking that at long last an
investigation will be made."

Sakir nodded. "Yes. We will find this child."

"*I* will find the child."

"But—"

"As you said, brother, you have a beautiful pregnant
wife at home who needs you. You cannot be away from
her for longer than a few days. I feel selfish in taking
you away for that long, but I was convinced a phone call
would not do here."

"You were right."

"And I am right about you going home and staying
there with your Rita."

Sakir's mouth formed a grim line, but he nodded.
"The child's DNA must be tested."

"It will be. But, Sakir, you understand that this is no
child. Not anymore."

"Of course. He must be a full-grown man by now."

With a quick flick of his wrist Zayad stabbed at the
letter with the tip of his sword, piercing the paper. He
thrust it at his brother. "Read the last paragraph."

Sakir slipped the paper from the blade and read.

With curious eyes Zayad watched his brother,
watched as his face turned from interest to unease to
shock.

When Sakir finally looked up, his green eyes were wide. "A girl?"

"Yes." Zayad had been just as stunned when he had read this. After three men of Al-Nayhal, the thought of a girl child born to his father hadn't occurred to Zayad.

"Where is she?" Sakir asked.

Walking over to the table, Zayad grasped the glass of plum juice from his tray and drained it. "She lives in a town one hour from Los Angeles, California. It is called Ventura."

"When do you leave?"

"Tomorrow morning. My investigation is already under way. I must have more information on this woman and her life before I leave, before I attempt to get close to her. I will fly with you to the States, then continue on to California."

"Then what?"

"I will live as an American, get to know this Jane Hefner, see if she is truly an Al-Nayhal, see if she is capable of knowing and accepting her truth."

"You will keep me updated, yes?"

"Of course." Zayad motioned for a servant to come and remove his breakfast tray and for another to take his sword. They were swift in their tasks, and soon Zayad and Sakir were heading inside the palace.

Sakir stopped at the doorway to the ballroom, turned to Zayad and grinned. "We could have a sister."

Not sharing his brother's enthusiasm, Zayad continued walking down the marble hallway. "Do not get your hopes up just yet, Sakir. We could have a sister. But we also could have an impostor."

One

*A*re all men jerks, or what?

Mariah Kennedy stepped out of her '92 Escort—sans air-conditioning—and into the ninety-degree California weather.

Gorgeous, brilliant, charming—ten million dollars to his name—and yet he refuses to pay child support for his three-year-old twins.

She slammed the car door shut.

Sweat beaded at the base of her tight blond bun and threatened to drop down the back of her faux Chanel suit as she stalked up the stone pathway to her ancient—though still very charming—duplex. The early summer wind whipped off the ocean's surface just a half a mile away, trying to cool her skin as well as her I'm-so-going-to-lose-this-case mood.

No. All men can't be jerks. Dad was a real stand-up guy. It must be all the gorgeous, overly successful and far too irresistible ones that earn that label.

Mariah reached the front door and, in her usual style, fumbled around in her purse for her keys while simultaneously bending down to snatch up the newspaper she never had time to read until she returned home from work at five.

Normally she accomplished both tasks without a problem.

But today was all about problems.

The headline, Sun Exposure Blamed For Weight Gain, screamed up at her, and she hesitated a second too long in picking it up.

Something rustled behind her. Without a thought she straightened and whirled around—all at the same time.

Not a good combo.

In that same inept, awkward and very humiliating style that had plagued her all morning in the judge's chambers, she ran smack-dab into a heavily muscled chest.

A strange cross between a hiccup and a gasp erupted from her throat, and she dropped her purse. The contents spilled out all over the walkway, except for a red pen and an extra pair of nylons, which sailed west into the hydrangea bushes.

"Dammit!" Mariah dropped to her knees.

In seconds the man was beside her.

"Don't worry about it," she said, shoving lipstick and iron pills into her purse as quickly as she could. "I've got everything under control here."

"All signs would point to the contrary."

Mariah stopped her manic sidewalk cleanup for a moment. In the seconds before, when she'd been off balance, smashing headfirst into strangers and letting her purse travel south, she'd barely glimpsed the man beside her.

Dark…tall—that's about it.

She glanced up.

Heat, and not from the sun this time, oozed into her bones. Never in her life had she seen the cover of *GQ* magazine live and in person. Yet here he was. Dark, soulful eyes that assessed her; short, well-groomed black hair; sharp, angular features that screamed exquisite breeding; and a full mouth that she was sure had driven far too many sane females mad with desire.

He was the kind of man who could easily utter in your ear as he was nibbling on your neck, "I'm female poison. Beware."

She forced her pulse to slow, but it did little good as the man sat back on his haunches and gave her an amused look.

He was probably midthirties, she guessed, and ridiculously handsome. He had that look of supreme confidence in his manner and expression, the kind that usually made such a stellar impression in court—both on the men and the women. Though this man was not dressed in lawyerly garb. No suit and tie. No, he wore a simple black T-shirt under an exquisitely tailored white shirt. Of course, on that lean, hard body they looked anything but simple.

Mariah hated herself for feeling weak-kneed and ultra feminine. And she wanted to laugh. This impossibly beautiful man was no doubt the new tenant Mrs. Gill had told her about yesterday.

The tenant Mrs. Gill had referred to as "a sweet young man."

The "sweet, young man" raised an eyebrow at her. "I did not mean to insult you. It is just that you seem quite out of sorts."

A husky baritone accompanied by a sexy accent. She mentally rolled her eyes. *Perfect.* "I'm not out of sorts at all."

He picked up her ratty copy of *Women Who Love Men Are Morons,* glanced at it for a moment, then held it out to her. "If I could offer a suggestion…"

She snatched up the book. "What? That maybe next time I should look where I'm going?"

"There is this, yes." He stood, offered her a hand. "Slowing one's pace is also good."

She took his hand, let him pull her to her feet. "I've never been any good at slow."

He didn't acknowledge her comment but continued with his advice. "And I also find that apologizing for situations you have caused is a very admirable trait."

At that she gave him a half smile. Maybe she was wrong about all gorgeous, smart and charming men being jerks. "It *is* admirable, and I appreciate the apology. You did scare the heck out of—"

"No. I was speaking of you."

Maybe not.

"Excuse me?" she said.

"It was you who ran into me, was it not?"

"Yes, but it was an accident."

"I do not believe in accidents. But even so, an apology is in order."

Everything in her lawyerly bones urged her to argue the subject, but after a day like today—when every question, every word had been challenged—she just wasn't up for it.

Yet she wasn't in the mood to apologize, either.

So she went halfsies.

"I feel deep regret for plowing into you." She brightened. "How's that?"

He didn't look appeased. "I suppose it will have to do, Miss..." His dark gaze traveled over her.

"Mariah Kennedy," she said, through a severe case of the belly flips.

"I am Zayad Fandal. I live beside you."

Of course he did. Her guess had been right on target. After all, it was her destiny to live beside, work beside, be divorced from and argue against tall, dark and irritatingly gorgeous men.

Remember...look but don't touch, M.

"Nice to meet you, Mr. Fandal. Welcome to the neighborhood. And again, deep regret about the head in the chest thing." She turned to her door and shoved the key in the lock.

"Wait a moment, Miss Kennedy."

She glanced over her shoulder just in time to catch him checking out her backside. "Yes?"

"I wonder if I might ask you something?"

She mentally shook her head. *Not interested, playboy. But thanks.* After the hellish divorce that had claimed her life for nearly four years, then seeing the daily nightmares that her female clients went through with guys just like this one, she had sworn to only date men under five-seven with unhypnotic eyes and thin lips. Men who neither dazzled her brain nor her body.

Stupid idea? Yes, probably. But safe. Very, very safe. And she was all about safety now.

"What is it, Mr. Fandal?" she asked with a patient smile.

"I wish to know if your roommate, Jane Hefner, is at home."

What a loser!

Waves of embarrassment moved over Mariah as she took in the tender look in this guy's eyes. Here she was thinking Mr. Next Door was coming on to her when he was clearly interested in Jane. And who could blame him? Her beautiful, raven-haired roommate had men drooling night and day. Mariah's dirty-blond hair and short, curvy figure were no match for Jane's slender, long legs and bright green eyes. No doubt Zayad had met Jane this morning—without the sweat, the acerbic lawyerspeak and the head-on collision—and wanted to ask her out.

What a total idiot.

"Jane's working right now, but she'll be back later."

"Thank you." He grinned. "Goodbye, Miss Kennedy."

He inclined his head, then walked past her down the steps before disappearing into a shiny black SUV. Her hand on the doorknob, Mariah stared after him thinking about how great he looked, both from the front and from the back.

Mariah released a weighty breath. More than anything in the world she'd love to delve into a nice sum-

mer romance. She had been pretty lonely lately. No
dates, even with the under-five-seven crowd. A summer
fling with Mr. Tall, Dark and Handsome could be fun.
But fantasies needed to remain just that. Men like that
one cheated and lied and jumped ship when the going
got rough.

For a moment Mariah just stood there mulling over
her thoughts, her beliefs and theories. It wasn't a pretty
picture. If truth be told, she hated how bitter she'd become. Sure, it had made her a better lawyer, but what
had it done to her as a woman?

She couldn't help but remember a time, long ago and
oh-so far away, when she'd lived in an eternal spring-
time. Love had bitten her and sent her reeling. Like
some Disney cartoon. But a man had stripped her raw
of that feeling and taken her trust and hope along with
it.

Her faux leather briefcase felt like a bag of rocks as
she headed into the house to her beloved Little Debbie
snack cakes and later a long, hot bath.

The sultan had taken a risk in coming to America
with only a handful of security. But he refused to be
under guard. He had brought just three men, and all
were under strict orders to protect only when commanded.

With a quick glance in the rearview mirror at the
beautiful and highly spirited woman who lived next
door, Zayad pulled away from the curb and headed
down the street. Behind him another car also moved
from the curb. Zayad had an almost irresistible urge to
floor the black Escalade and give his men something

to chase, but as always, he would resist impulses and desires that did not serve his country's purposes.

His cell phone rang. He took his time in answering. "Yes, Harin?"

"Where are you going, sir?"

"To the beach." His body was tight. He needed exercise, something to calm his nerves. His sword lay in the backseat, ready for work.

"If I may suggest Dove Cove, sir. It is deserted at this time. You will not be disturbed."

"Very good, but I will go alone."

"Sir—"

"Take the next exit and return home. I will let you know when I have need of you again." Zayad snapped the phone shut. He was only going to the beach. Surely he could protect himself if the need arose. He was, after all, a master swordsman. A man who had studied under the great warrior, Ohanda. All knew that at the age of twelve the young sultan had been able to hear a predator—animal or otherwise—ten feet away and easily take him down.

But as an adult Zayad also understood that in certain situations it was wise to have protection. His people must have him back safe and sound. As must his son, who was young yet, just thirteen, and not ready to take his father's place as ruler if something were to happen.

The thought of his son sent Zayad's mind racing toward another child. A female. One who could be his father's daughter. A young girl who might never have known she was of royal blood. A girl who might never have known she had two brothers who would give much to know her.

Zayad glanced to the seat beside him and flipped open a file folder. A photograph stared up at him. A beautiful young woman with the late sultan's cheekbones and Sakir's green eyes. Zayad did not need a DNA test. This woman felt like family even in her photograph. But he knew it would be necessary for others. So, while his doctor performed the test, he would get to know her. Tonight.

A child's excitement moved through him. He had been born to rule. To remain impassive. He had been taught to live well, think great thoughts and be lenient when the time arose and severe when it was demanded. And like his brother, Sakir, understand that wishes and dreams were for others and death came too quickly with little mercy. But then there was the rare occasion, like the birth of his son, when the purest of joy had threatened to overtake him. Meeting his sister for the first time certainly would be one of those moments. He would allow himself the pang of excitement.

Zayad swung left at the farm stand and headed toward Dove Cove. He would only take a few hours of exercise on the warm sand, as he needed to return to the duplex. He had much to accomplish, including keeping his true mission a secret to those around him. His council, like the men he had brought with him—save Fandal—believed his purpose here to be one of rest and relaxation. Of course, they did not question his living quarters or his interest in his neighbor. They dared not. And Zayad expected that they would remain devoted servants for his two-week stay.

Ah, yes, he thought. Two weeks with no questions, no interruptions and no diversions.

A pretty blond attorney with a voluptuous body and angry eyes the color of the hot Emand sand at sunset flashed into his mind. His sister's roommate was tough and spirited, and if he had more time, he might consider pursuing an affair with her.

His hands tightened on the steering wheel.

His father had once said, "A man is not a man without restraint. Especially in matters of the state."

Sea air blew in through his window, but Zayad did not calm in its caress. The irony was too plain. His father, the great sultan, had overlooked his own counsel when coming to America.

Should he expect any less from his son?

Two

Jane Hefner was to food what Manolo Blahnik was to shoes.

Perfection.

Mariah took another bite of the sublimely delicious, strangely refreshing basil ice cream and sighed. "Tell me again why you have to leave?"

Jane folded a pale yellow shirt with faultless precision and gently placed it between two pieces of parchment in her suitcase. "The restaurant wants publicity, so it's me to the rescue. And teaching some pampered movie star how to make veal piccata and garlic mashed potatoes for her next film might sound like a chore to some people, but to me it's—"

"A dream come true?"

Jane laughed. "Hey, it's Cameron Reynolds."

"Right." Mariah sat on the bed, folded a pair of jeans for Jane. "You understand that you're forcing me to eat a week's worth of frozen dinners?"

Jane eased the jeans from Mariah and refolded them. "Dry fish sticks, watery mashed potatoes, mushy pea-and-carrot medley and fig compote?" She shrugged. "I don't see the problem."

"You may be a genius in the kitchen, but you have absolutely no compassion on my poor stomach."

"I know. But I'll be back before you know it."

Mariah paused, realized how pathetic she sounded with all the Miss Lonely Hearts prattle. Seemed she relied on her friend too much. After her divorce from Alan, she'd clung to Jane as a sister, as a friend—the way she had when they were kids, when her parents had died and her feeble grandmother had given her a home but little else.

Mariah fell back on the bed. "Can I just say that your boss is pretty ballsy for making you go on such short notice?"

"It's cash, M."

Jane's sudden serious tone and slight grimace made Mariah pause, ease up on the semiphony guilt trip. She knew Jane was saving up to open her own restaurant. It was her dream. And as her friend, Mariah wasn't about to be anything but all-the-way supportive. "All right, but if your boss doesn't compensate you big time for this, you know I can always sue him. Or, hey, I have a friend down at the board of health and he's really into closing down Italian restaurants." Mariah leaned on her elbows. "I think his brother was taken out by the mob or something."

Jane laughed, shut her suitcase. "Thanks, M. I'll think about it."

"No you won't. You're too damn nice to think about it."

She grinned. "So, I hear our new neighbor's moved in. Have you met him yet?"

Mariah rolled her eyes. "Have I met him? You could say that."

"What happened?"

"Let's just say I was in rare form—there were bruises and razor-sharp banter on the menu."

Jane laughed, sat down beside her. "Is he good-looking, or a toad like the last one?"

"Why are you asking me all this? You've met him, too."

"No, I haven't."

"Sure you have."

Jane shook her head.

Mariah blinked at her. "Maybe you said hi in passing or something, because he knows you."

"He knows me? What are you talking about?"

"He asked about you when he bumped into me—well, when I bumped into him. He wanted to know when you'd be home. It was like you'd met and talked and he was more than ready to ask you out."

Jane sniffed. "That's bizarre. Maybe Mrs. Gill told him about us, and after he met you he wanted to meet me…some neighborly, friendly kind of thing?"

"I dunno." Mariah shrugged. "But whatever his story is, be careful. He's trouble."

"Why?" Jane slid her feet into a pair of pink flip-flops that were placed neatly by the foot of the bed. "Because he's tall, dark and handsome?"

"For a start."

All humor dropped away from Jane's pretty face. She put a hand on Mariah's shoulder and took a breath. "Listen, M, someday you're going to have to see the world and every man in it with fresh eyes."

Mariah bristled, looked away. "I don't know what you mean."

"Yes, you do."

"Yeah, all right, I do. But that day's not today."

"Okay." Jane gave her a huge hug and said, "I'll call you," then stood, grabbed her suitcase and left the room.

After she had gone, Mariah headed into the kitchen to make herself one of the aforementioned TV dinners and contemplate her next move in the custody case she was working on. Her client's ex was smart and had hidden his affairs well. It was going to take some serious digging to find anything she could use.

When the breaded fish and compote were ready, she went outside and sat at the pretty picnic bench Jane had set up on the brick patio. The backyard looked lovely bathed in the night's light. Moon, stars, a few clouds...and soggy carrot-and-pea medley.

Ah, did it get any better than this?

"May I join you?"

Mariah gave a tiny jump, then glanced over her shoulder. Her new neighbor was walking through his patio doors toward her. He looked unbelievably handsome in the moonlight, with that dark-eyes-dark-hair-dark-tailored-clothes thing happening. He was also clean shaven, and it made all the sharp angles in his face look harder and sexier.

Her heart kicked to life in her chest, but she held fast

to a calm exterior. "I have some square fish and a few peas left, if you're interested."

His mouth curved into a smile as he sat opposite her at the picnic table. "I am not very hungry, but thank you."

"Just checking out the backyard? Or were you looking for someone?"

"Perhaps a little of both."

"Jane's not here."

His gaze went thoughtful. "I did not say I was looking for Jane."

"You didn't have to." Her tone sounded dry and acerbic, but he didn't seem to notice.

He said, "Perhaps I was looking for you."

Her heart literally fluttered. Foolish, foolish girl. "And why would that be?"

"Perhaps I wish to know more about this—" he studied her with a lazy, hooded gaze "—fiery woman who lives beside me."

Fiery! She nearly blushed.

Nearly.

"Well, there's not much to tell," she said, running her fork back and forth through the fig compote.

"I doubt that."

Lord, he had extraordinary eyes—so black, but flecked with gold. A woman could get lost in those eyes if she wasn't careful. Good thing Mariah was careful.

"Listen," she said with more regret in her tone than she would have liked. "I've got a ton of work to get to, so I'll say good—"

"What kind of work do you do?"

"I'm a lawyer."

His brow lifted a fraction.

"I help women who've been treated badly in their marriages get what they deserve."

"Interesting. And what do they deserve?"

"It depends. But first and foremost, respect. If they've given up their careers to take care of the home, I help them gain financial stability. If they've been cheated on during their marriage, their self-esteem robbed from them, I help them find a new life. Which is just like the case I'm working on now—"

Mariah came to a screeching halt. What was she doing? This man was no friend, no confidant, and here she was about to tell him the ins and outs of her case.

"What were you about to say, Miss Kennedy?"

She stood and grabbed the remains of her dinner. "Nothing, just that I'm working on a case and I'd better get inside and get to it."

She started to walk away, but he stopped her. "Miss Kennedy?"

She turned. "Yes?"

"You do not like men, do you?"

Walls shot up around her like steel plates. "Excuse me?"

He shrugged nonchalantly. "You make them sound like the enemy."

She lifted her chin. "In court, they are." And in life, her life, she thought, they weren't terribly far from that. She gave him a little wave. "Good night, Mr. Fandal," she said and headed into the house, where she could think and breathe again.

Moments later she had rid herself of "dinner" and

was walking into the bathroom. What she needed was a long, hot bath, to get that man's questions, comments and deliciously probing gaze out of her mind.

Hate men! What a notion.

Sure, she didn't trust men, she thought as she turned on the hot-water tap and let the tub fill up. There was a big difference.

Peeling off her clothes, she spotted her reflection in the mirror and took a moment to look herself over. The view surprised her a little. Under those bargain power suits of hers lay a pretty nice figure.

Her hands found their way to her flat stomach, up her rib cage to her large breasts. Her skin was pale and so sensitive, and as she ran her fingers over her nipples, she wanted to cry. She hadn't been touched in four years, and even then it had been seldom, as Alan had been far too busy making his mistress happy to help his wife find some pleasure.

She bit her lip. The truth was, she didn't hate men at all. In fact, if the right one came along, she was ready to go crazy with desire. But the fear in her heart was stronger than her need, and she couldn't imagine that changing anytime soon.

She turned away from the mirror and stepped into the hot bath.

Zayad cursed and pitched the bag of microwave popcorn across the room. The corn was black as night and had thoroughly stunk up the two-bedroom duplex he would be calling home for the next two weeks.

"I could hire a staff, Your Royal Highness."

Zayad turned, his back to the kitchen counter, and

eyed his aide and the closest thing he had to a friend—
the man from whom he had borrowed his last name.
"No, Fandal. I have told you there can be no show of
wealth and consequence. And do not call me 'Your
Highness.'"

"Yes, Your—" Fandal lifted his chin. "Yes, sir."

Zayad turned around, opened the cupboards, found
nothing as simple as the popcorn was purported to be
and moved on to the refrigerator. "I was hoping to
bring something with me when I meet with my sister this evening. An offering, a meal. But alas, I am
without."

"Flowers are usually well received, sir."

"I am to meet my sister, Fandal, not court the lovely
Miss Kennedy."

"Of course, sir." With a quick bow of understanding,
Fandal went to the bag of ruined popcorn and began to
clean up the mess.

Court the lovely Miss Kennedy? Zayad sniffed. His
mouth was without restraint. Perhaps because he could
not get the woman out of his head after their little discussion in the yard. It was most irritating. She had looked
so soft, so appealing, as she verbally annihilated her
client's ex-husband.

"May I say that the golden-haired woman seems unlike the women in our country," Fandal remarked with
just a hint of warning in his tone.

"She is at that." Blond, fair, a lioness with claws
outstretched. But something warned him that once
tamed, once her anger was released and desire ruled her
body, Mariah Kennedy would not let go those claws.
"Not that I would pursue it, but I imagine an affair

would not be casual with her. I fear that most American women want far more than a lover."

"Is it not true for all women, sir?"

"Not the women of my acquaintance."

"There was one."

The words had slipped from Fandal's lips far too easily. Zayad stopped short, his blood thundering in his ears at the memory of the woman who had left his company and that of her son with little regret. Turning around, he stood over a sheepish Fandal. "As you know, Meyaan did not want a true marriage. She did not want to share my life—or her son's, for that matter. She wanted to benefit from my power and the comfort allowed by the riches of a sultan." His chin lifted, though his ire sank deeper into his belly. "And she received both. But in the end I was the victor. I received the far more precious gift."

His face still ashen from his foolish remark, Fandal had the good sense to turn the subject to Zayad's child. "And how is His Highness?"

"Redet is well, happy at school." Getting far too mature at thirteen. Zayad missed his little boy.

Just then a loud thud reverberated off the walls. Zayad and Fandal ceased talking. Glancing around, they listened for a clue to its origin. When none came, Zayad uttered, "What the hell was that?"

Fandal shook his head. "I know not."

A woman's cry came next.

"Stay here," Zayad commanded. "I will go."

"Your Royal Highness, it could be dangerous."

"It is from next door. It could be my sister."

"I will go with you."

But Zayad was already at the door. "Do not leave this

house, Fandal, or you will find yourself swimming back to Emand. Are we clear?"

"Yes, sir."

"And say nothing to the others." Zayad was out of his house and at Jane and Mariah's door within seconds. He knocked swiftly, but there was no response. He gripped the door handle, but it was locked.

His chest constricted and he did not think, only reacted. He stepped back and lunged at the door with all of his strength. The lock pitched but remained intact. He tried again. Then again. Finally the lock collapsed and he was inside.

Three

"**...I** know I should have photographs of him with that other woman, but I can't find a thing, Miss Kennedy. Please call me back, okay?"

Through the pain in her wrist and ankle, Mariah listened to the end of her client's message, then the beep of her answering machine.

Nude, angry and lying in quasifetal position on the bathroom floor, Mariah sincerely wished she'd installed a telephone next to the bathtub. Such luxury had just proven itself a necessity, as she'd slipped trying to get out of the tub and into Jane's room for the phone.

Wondering if she could roll over, get her weight on her good leg, she rose slightly and made the effort. But when sharp pain whipped up and around like a tornado in her ankle, she collapsed.

What the hell was she going to do? Lie here all night like a fish? Maybe inch her way across the bathroom floor, down the hall and into—

Just then Mariah heard something. A crash. Downstairs. Wood splitting. She sucked air, and her pulse jumped in her blood. Not good. Robbery and incapacitated naked girl did not go well together.

She tried to work herself up into a sitting position, but her wrist and ankle hurt like hell, and she was slow.

There were footsteps on the stairs, a rustle outside the bathroom door. A thought poked into Mariah's brain—one she clung to for dear life. Jane. Maybe she'd forgotten something.

She called out, "Jane!" *I can't believe I'm about to say this.* "I've fallen and I can't get up."

"Do not be alarmed. I am here to help you."

Sick, gut-tight fear gripped Mariah, made her forget the pain screaming up her ankle.

Not Jane.

Had she locked the bathroom door?

"I have a knife and a baseball bat in here," she shouted, scanning the room for anything that resembled those two items. Emery board, toilet plunger… "And I'm not afraid to use them."

"I am sure that you could do great damage if provoked, but I am not here to hurt you, Miss Kennedy."

Was it Mr. Sexy Accent?

Mr. Next Door?

Oh my God.

"Don't come in here," she warned, more afraid of him seeing her naked than she was of him attacking her.

She was such an idiot.

"Miss Kennedy, I heard you scream." He was right outside the door now and probably unstoppable.

"I'm fine." She sounded embarrassingly hysterical. "Nothing's wrong. I just saw a mouse and—"

"I do not believe you."

The door squeaked open.

"Oh my God, don't come in here—"

He didn't listen. "Perhaps you need a doc—"

"Dammit!" Completely nude and in a most unflattering position, she tried to roll into the bath mat. "Get out. Get out."

"You are hurt."

"I'm also naked. Get out."

He went to her, knelt beside her. "I would never take advantage of such a situation."

She glared up at him. "I don't believe that for a minute."

A glimmer of humor lit his eyes. "Smart girl." He grabbed a towel and draped it over her. "But I give you my word this is no attempt at seduction, merely a rescue."

"I don't need to be rescued."

"I beg to differ."

"Listen, Mr. Fandal, this is my house and I want you to leave."

"Who will help you if I leave?"

"I'll think of someone or I'll get out of here myself."

"Crawling around on the floor like a lame pup?"

"Did you just call me a dog?"

Zayad gave an impatient groan, flashed his gaze to the ceiling. Never had he known a woman like this one—obstinate, headstrong, ready to injure herself fur-

ther in the name of pride. He was not used to following the orders of others, but with her he felt it would be
far more productive. "If you prefer to wallow in your
mulishness, I shall stand behind the door in case you
have need of me."

"No. Thank you. Seriously I appreciate the gesture,
but you can leave. I'm fine."

He stood up, walked out of the bathroom and waited
behind the door. "I shall stand behind the door until you
realize you need my assistance."

She snorted. "Well, you'll be waiting all night for
that, buddy."

Moments later he heard her groan with pain.

"Miss Kennedy?"

"I'm fine. Just fine."

Seconds later there was another cry of pain and a
soft thud.

"Still fine, Miss Kennedy?"

"Yes."

He shook his head, walked back into the bathroom.
"I do not enjoy playing games. You will not send me
away again, and I will help you until more suitable
help arrives."

"There is no suitable help."

"Your roommate is not home yet?"

"No."

"But she is returning soon, yes?"

"She's actually going to be out of town for a week
teaching some Hollywood bimbo how to cook."

Alarm moved through Zayad. He had not heard her
correctly. Jane gone for one week. Impossible. He had
but two weeks to know her, make her understand her

past, her family's history, see if she was ready to return to her homeland and take up her duties as princess. How could this happen? How could he have allowed his plan to be thwarted?

Frustration swam in his blood. What was he to do now? Follow her? Rent another home in Los Angeles for one week, then return to Ventura with her?

He glanced down at the woman who needed his assistance. With great care he eased her into his arms. He had to take care of this situation first and quickly, then find a solution to his woes with Jane.

Head against his chest, Mariah groaned. "This is so humiliating."

"What is? Falling down or being nude?"

"Oh, of course the naked part."

A grin tugged at his lips. "Miss Kennedy, you have nothing to feel ashamed of. Your body is beautiful, lush, and your skin is softer than silk. It took great effort to tear my gaze from you, but as you were hurt, I felt compelled to do so."

He watched her eyes widen and her lips part.

Chuckling, he lifted her up, bath mat and all, and headed out of the steamy room. "Praise be. I have found a way to keep you quiet."

Four

The pounding in her ankle aside, Mariah was still reeling from Mr. Next Door's compliment as he carried her down the stairs. She knew she shouldn't be reeling. In fact, she should have told him that his cheesy lines about her lushness and soft skin sucked and then given him a good slap.

But the thing was, she didn't want to think that what he'd said was a line. He'd looked at her with such devilishness, such sincerity, it had nearly had her wrapping her arms around his neck and demanding a kiss. And not just any kiss. From him she wanted open mouth, a little sweep of the tongue and maybe a nibble or two on her bottom lip.

Oh, it had been too long. She felt like an old, ratty plum on a tree, desperate to be picked, saved from a pruney future. Dangerous waters…

"Where are you taking me?" she asked him.

"To bed."

There it was—the deep end of those dangerous waters. "Mr. Fandal—"

"I think it is now appropriate for you to call me Zayad."

"And I'm thinking, after the whole bare-butt incident, it might be best to preserve some boundaries."

"And you think formality is the way to do this?"

Not a clue. "Let's not get off track here. We were talking about you taking me to bed."

"That's correct. Not to get undressed and join you, but so you may rest as I call the doctor."

She wilted—just slightly. "Oh." Not that she would allow herself to contemplate such a thing, but it sure would be nice to be wanted.

When he reached her bedroom, Zayad whipped back her white cotton sheets and placed her gently on the bed. "I will only be a moment," he informed her. "I must make a phone call to the doctor, then I will return."

"My doctor doesn't make house calls."

"No. But mine does."

"Yours?" She stared up into that rough, intense and highly sensual face and wondered just who this new neighbor of hers was. Had his own doctor on call—and at eight o'clock at night, no less—had a fancy accent, worldly expression, tailored clothes, highly intelligent eyes and was impressively quick with a comeback.

A stab of pain the size of New Jersey suddenly invaded her ankle. She dropped her cheek to the pillow, closed her eyes and moaned. When she opened her eyes again, Zayad was halfway out the door.

"Hey, Zayad?"

He turned. "Yes?"

"How did you know this was my room?"

A slow, almost fiendish smile drifted to his lips. "Careful deduction. You do not seem a risk taker to me, so the first-floor bedroom seemed correct."

Sad but true.

"And then there was your computer, law books and yellow legal pads." He pointed to her many Hockney posters littering the white walls. "The artwork. This is you."

The law books and such, she understood, but the artwork—that startled her. In all the time they were married, Alan had never even asked her about her love of Hockney, much less noticed if she had a connection to it. "Why is the art me?"

His gaze swept the room and he took a thoughtful breath. "Firstly, you live in a town that boasts a beach-like feel, as many of Hockney's paintings do. You are also very colorful, Mariah, and there is an interesting humor about you, as well."

She just stared at him. *He got all that in two meetings? Oh, yeah, this guy was dangerous all right.* "That was some pretty swift deducing from doorstep to back-yard to bathroom to bedroom."

He grinned, haughtiness filling his black gaze. "I am said to be intuitive as well as highly intelligent."

"And maybe just a bit arrogant, too?" she added with a pained smirk.

"Oh, no, Mariah," he said without humor this time. "I am far more than a bit." And with that he turned and left.

Thirty minutes later, after a complete examination of her wrist and incredibly swollen ankle, the doctor—

who was so young Mariah wondered if he'd had his first shave yet—told her in the same accent as her neighbor's that her wrist was badly bruised. But her ankle?

"I am afraid it is a serious sprain," he said, his dark eyes on her. "I will prescribe a mild painkiller and bring you a brace and crutches. You may want an X-ray as well. In the meantime, you must rest. You will need to remain off your foot for a few days."

Mariah shook her head. "I can't stay in bed. I have a ton of work to do."

"Work that will have to be done from bed, young lady."

She had to bite her tongue to keep from laughing. The twelve-year-old doctor had actually called her "young lady." "I'm an attorney and I have a huge case to prepare. Lives are at stake and all that," she said, trying to appeal to him in a way he'd understand. "If I can't get up and get to work, I can forget about court in three weeks, and getting a wonderful mother of two custody and child support."

The doctor tried to look sympathetic. "I understand, Miss Kennedy. But if you want your ankle to heal, you will do as I say. And you will need someone to help you."

Zayad turned to her. "Your roommate is returning—"

"In a week."

His lips thinned. "Do you have a friend to help you?"

"Not really." Jane was her best friend. She'd allowed no one to get close to her since Alan. Of course, she had her work colleagues, but no one who she'd feel comfortable asking for help.

"Family?" Zayad asked.

Mariah shook her head.

"A man?" asked the doctor.

Heat rushed Mariah's cheeks. "No. No man."

Zayad felt relieved at the news, though he did not wish to examine why. He had more important matters to see to than his attraction to this woman, such as seeing to his sister.

Beside him Mariah shifted on the bed. She looked so beautiful, so soft and needful, lying there still draped in her large white towel, her legs exposed. It took all he had to force his mind to shut down, to remind his body that it would be foolish to climb in beside her, remove that towel and explore.

She was injured, and he had to think of his mission.

Right now he should be following his sister to Los Angeles, finding out about her passions and pursuits, as he should have done so many years ago. He should be telling her the truth. But he had given it much thought on the way to get the doctor and he knew that wouldn't be wise. He would look like a stalker, following her from Los Angeles back to Ventura, and he would never get the answers he needed.

Mariah looked up, found his gaze.

Answers Jane Hefner's best friend might be able to reveal as she recovered from her injury.

Zayad paused, his mind circling a new path.

He was no nursemaid, but his need to uncover the truth about his sister and her past and present could force his hand—could draw him in to Mariah Kennedy's world for a few days.

An interesting, though risky prospect.

He turned to Dr. Adair, the son of his physician in Emand. "I will care for the girl myself."

Adair's eyes went wide. "Your— Sir, I do not think…"

"It is done," Zayad said swiftly.

"Excuse me?" Mariah fairly sputtered.

Zayad continued speaking to Adair. "I live next door. I will cook for her, bathe her—"

"Are you certain that is wise, sir?"

"I am." His answer was firm, unmovable, and the doctor nodded.

"Excuse me." Mariah actually sat up, her anger evident in those beautiful tiger's eyes and irritated tone. "First of all, I'm not a girl. And second of all, there'll be no bathing by anyone other than me."

Zayad began, "I was merely suggesting that I remain on hand to assist—"

"I don't need any extra hands," she uttered through pain.

"I am afraid you do, Miss Kennedy." The doctor eased a brown brace that resembled a boot over her foot and ankle and set the Velcro straps in place. "As I said, you must remain in bed, off that ankle for at least two days. If Mr. Fandal does not help, who will?"

She opened her mouth, then promptly shut it. What a question. And one that made her feel like a gigantic loser. Seriously, Jane was gone and Mariah couldn't ask her to come home—not with that kind of money at stake.

Mariah frowned, winced. Her ankle hurt. Dammit! There really was no one who could come to her rescue. Except…she lifted her lids, found his black gaze, and her belly softened and warmed.

"Why in the world would you want to do this?" she asked him. "You hardly know me."

Zayad sat beside her on the bed. Behind him Dr. Adolescence discreetly left the room.

"Have you never felt compelled to help a stranger in need, Mariah?" he asked.

Every day of her life since she'd climbed out of the depression-coma her ex had sent her reeling into after he'd not only cheated on her with his fitness instructor but also had announced he wanted to marry the woman. From that day on she'd felt compelled to help others in similar situations—hopeless and alone and without much in the way of funds. She'd gone back to school, passed the bar with flying colors and opened up her own practice a few months later.

She dropped back against the pillows and sighed. "After our conversation tonight in the yard, I think you know I fight for the underdog. And I bet you can also guess that it's become a passion of mine."

A passion Mariah had hoped would help her heal a little with each case she took and won. Sad thing was, she didn't think she *had* healed all that much.

"I will see the doctor to the door," Zayad told her. "And when I return, we will talk about dinner, yes?"

"Listen," she said as he stood up. "I'm sorry if this seems ungrateful, because I really do appreciate what you're trying to do—"

"But?"

"But I don't trust you."

"I understand."

She lifted herself up on her elbows. "You do?"

"It is your nature."

"It's my past," she corrected.

He nodded.

She said, "You're clearly after something here, and I don't know if it's me or Jane or if it's a way of repenting for some horrible sin you've committed, but know this—I'll be watching you like a hawk."

Sensuality fairly dripped from his smile. "I would expect nothing less from you, Mariah."

She swallowed thickly. "Good."

"Incidentally, the only sin I cannot seem to shake is continually wanting the one thing I definitely should not have." His grin widened as his gaze flickered to the white towel she held firmly to her breasts. "But I will never repent."

Lust ripped through Mariah's core at his words. The pain in her ankle was nothing to it.

She watched him walk out her bedroom door, leaving an aura of irrepressible and highly erotic male in his wake. For the past four years she'd often wondered if she might be dead from the waist down. But now she knew the truth. She was alive and well and tingling and hot and she wanted to feel a man on her skin again.

But not just any man.

She closed her eyes and inhaled.

That man.

And the knowledge scared her to death.

Five

"**Y**ou have done what?"

Standing at the kitchen counter, a can of soup in his hand, a cell phone tucked between his ear and shoulder, Zayad tried to explain to his brother the realities of this strange situation he had found himself in tonight. "I have agreed to care for our sister's roommate until she is back on her feet."

Sakir snorted. "This is madness. You know nothing about care. You cannot cook, clean, make small talk. She will see through you in an instant."

"Perhaps, but she has little choice in the matter. She has no other help. Her family is deceased, her friend is gone and...she has no man."

"No man?" Sakir said all too slowly, a reminder that he still lived most of the year in Texas. "You say this as though it pleases you."

"I having no feeling either way."

"I do not believe you, brother. Seduction is on your brain, I sense it. Is she pleasing to look at?"

A flash of heat moved through Zayad. He found the feeling most disconcerting. "She is blond and small with heavenly curves. Her eyes are the color of Emand's softest sand and her lips the color of wine. She is far more than pleasing, my brother. But—"

"But? There should be no reason for you not to—"

"She is an American and I am Sultan. That is reason enough, but I will give you more. She is angry at something or someone, and I feel in no mood to soften her." He opened a cabinet and grabbed a blue bowl. "No matter how strong my desire might be, I am only staying here to gather information—"

"Staying there? In her home?" Sakir roared with laughter.

The bowl dropped from Zayad's hand into the sink with a loud crash. He barked at his brother. "It is the only way to ensure that my mission is successful. I must be around her to acquire information. I have but two weeks to learn all I can about our sister, and then I must return to Emand."

"The mission, yes. It must be the most important thing." Sakir switched gears for a moment. "You will not return to Emand without another stop in Texas, as promised?"

"Of course. But it is only to see your beautiful wife."

"Rita is looking forward to it, although she is a bit under the weather."

"Your son or daughter is already causing their mother trouble, yes?"

Sakir chuckled, light and familiar. The sound bore into Zayad's hardened heart. He missed his brother greatly. Their friendship. Their battles, both verbal and with sword. And now, with the talk of family so prevalent as of late—his sister, his son and Sakir's child on the way—Zayad wanted nothing more than to have his entire clan together, safe, under one roof. If that were only possible.

"Do you want me to come to California?"

Zayad smiled at his brother's offer while he grabbed something Fandal had called a "can's opener" from the drawer. "No. You should not leave your wife just now. You will meet our sister soon enough. And besides, two sheikhs would surely stand out in this small town."

Sakir laughed. "Indeed."

Zayad cursed as large droplets of chicken broth hit the floor.

"What is it?" Sakir asked.

"I am attempting to open a can of something called 'chicken and stars soup.' It's my patient's favorite."

"You are not actually cooking?"

"I am," Zayad replied indignantly.

"Why not get one of the servants to see to the meal?"

Zayad leaned over the sink and turned on the faucet. Water shot into the sink. "I must act as a normal man."

"A normal man would have called a pizzeria by now."

Again Zayad cursed. "I must go. I have added too much water to this mess."

Zayad ignored his brother's laughter and hung up the phone. He had battled lions, six warriors at one time and the fiercest of swordsmen, he could see to one simple meal. He only had to concentrate.

Ten minutes later he walked into Mariah's bedroom. The clock on the wall chimed nine. A little late for dinner, but she had claimed she had not eaten a thing since noon and had looked very pale when he had left her.

On a tray he had found under the kitchen sink Zayad had placed the watery soup, some cheese, a slice of anemic-looking bread, a second pain pill, a glass of water and a glass of wine for himself.

He stopped just before the bed, tray still in hand, and took in the sight before him. She was sitting up, white blanket tucked in at her waist. She looked young, her face free of makeup and frustration. Her long, blond hair hung loose. She had put on the robe he had brought her, and at first glance he thought it very prim and proper. But at second glance he noticed that its white fabric was fairly thin. He could see the outline of her breasts through the cotton.

An invisible vise gripped his chest as he stared. She was no practiced seductress, sitting there in her virginal white world, but to him she could not be more disturbingly sexy.

He placed the tray on her lap, and fought his roguish impulse to catch a closer look at what lay beneath that flimsy robe.

He lost the fight.

The robe gaped slightly at the chest, and he could not help but see one slope of full breast, one rise of pink nipple.

His groin tightened painfully and he moved away, fell back into a chair beside the bed. He was surprised by his lack of restraint. Surprised and bothered.

"Thank you for this," she said, placing the napkin in

her lap. "I may not show it, but I really appreciate your help."

He crossed his arms over his chest. "Wait until after you have tasted the soup before thanking me. I am afraid I am not much of a chef."

"I'm sure it's great. I can't cook, either. I can barely nuke a hot dog without incident." She picked up her spoon. "The cooking is Jane's department. She's a genius."

"Is she in food preparation?" As if he did not know.

"She's a professional chef. Works downtown at an Italian restaurant. She should have her own restaurant already, but, you know, money is always an issue."

He did not know, but he nodded anyway.

She took a bite of cheese and asked, "What is it you do, Zayad?"

It was the answer he had always longed to give. Impractical and unbecoming a sultan. But quite right here. "I am in art. Collecting, preserving, then selling if the buyer is right."

"Really? Well, that explains the Hockney thing. Do you collect paintings? Sculpture?"

"Swords, actually."

"Swords." Her bite of cheese fell back on the plate. "As in slice and dice, battles, *Braveheart*—those kinds of swords?"

An amused smile played on his lips. "In my country swords are revered. Even swordplay is considered an art form, a sport. Like fencing. Boys as young as five are taught the art of swordplay."

She picked up her spoon, looking a little uneasy.

"And to think, LEGOs and monster trucks are as far as most American five-year-old boys get with play and sport. What country are you from?"

"A little place you probably have never heard of."

"Try me."

"It is called Emand."

"Nope, never heard of it." She smiled—a smile wide and open and just a little teasing—and it was the first time Zayad had seen her without a mask of acerbity. With the mask she was beautiful, but without it she was stunning, irresistible.

Would she fight him if he kissed her?

He imagined she would.

"What is your country like?" she asked.

He sighed, his mind falling away from seduction to his homeland. "It is magical, beautiful, yet still a little wild."

"Wild, huh? The deserts or the people?" She looked down her nose at him. "The men don't drag the women around by their hair or anything, do they?"

"The ruler of Emand abolished the ways of the caveman long ago." When she smiled, he did, too. "The truth is while some choose to follow the ancient, more traditional ways, most of the women in my country are educated, feministic and have no qualms about telling their men what is on their mind."

"I like this ruler of yours."

And he likes you.

Aloud he said, "And what of you? I know that you are an attorney. What I do not know is why you seem so on edge, full of tension."

"You mean stressed out?"

"This sounds appropriate, yes."

She paused, stared at him, then sighed and shook her head. "I have a case that's not going very well. I tried to get the parties to settle out of court, resolve their issues without involving a long legal battle, but the ex-husband won't agree. Now I'm trying to find information that will help my client win." She gestured to her ankle. "And look what I have to contend with."

"What is the case?"

"Child custody."

"In specifics, Miss Kennedy," he said with a grin.

"Do you really want to know?"

"I would not ask if I was not interested."

In between small sips of soup, she explained. "The woman I'm defending was a wonderful wife and mother for fourteen years. Her husband was verbally abusive, had numerous affairs. He didn't want to spend time with his kids. They've been divorced for about a month now, and she got custody of the kids. A few weeks ago she met a man and has been dating him. Well, the ex-husband heard about this and flipped out—though he has a girl-friend." She sighed, put down her spoon. "He's suing for full custody of the kids. Kids he couldn't care less about. My client never asked for alimony. She didn't want any-thing from him for herself, just child support for the kids. But the husband's pride has been nicked. His affairs never came up in court, and now he's claiming he was a faithful, devoted husband and father and she was the slut and that his kids shouldn't be around a mother like that."

Zayad's jaw was rigid. He detested men like this one—cowards. "He wants to use the children as re-venge."

"Exactly. This guy is rich and powerful and has no trail for his affairs that his ex-wife or I could find. The women aren't talking. His friends and business associates aren't talking. The hotel and flower receipts my client had found have suddenly vanished."

"There is always a way to recover these things."

"I've tried. She's tried. Nothing." She nibbled on the bread. "I don't want to lose this case."

The male protector inside Zayad sprang to life, and he made an imprudent vow. "You will not lose."

"I have a killer sprain and no way to do any legwork on this case."

"We will find this man's trail."

Her eyes narrowed with surprise. "We?"

He moved from the chair to her bedside. "This case reminds me of my own struggles. I, too, had to fight to reclaim a child from a parent who only wished to use him."

"What are you talking about? What child?"

"Mine. I have a son."

Mariah's mouth dropped open. "You do?"

"You do not see me as parental?"

"Well, no." She shook her head, felt cruel for saying something like that. "What I mean is that, well, you're so…"

"What?"

"I don't know." *Gorgeous, charming, cultured.* The men she knew with those traits were usually the kind of men she fought in court. The kind of men who wanted to get rid of their baggage—wife, kids—and start fresh. Her mind whirled. This man had a child? This man had fought for his child? "I don't know what to make of you, Zayad."

He leaned toward her, brushed a stray lock of hair behind her ear. "It was falling in the soup."

He didn't move away. He stayed close, his mouth just inches from hers. She felt his warmth, and her heart jumped her in chest. "It's really bad soup, by the way," she whispered.

His gaze moved over her face, pausing at her lips. "I did warn you."

Mariah paused, let those words sink in, cool her heated skin. She couldn't believe herself. She actually had been ready to kiss him, throw her arms around his neck and go for it. This man she hardly knew. This man who represented everything that terrified her in a lover.

She swallowed hard. "I'd better get some sleep. That last pain pill is starting to wear off."

For a moment he remained, deliciously close and still tempting. Then his gaze flickered and he pulled back, a vein in his temple pulsating. "If you need anything, I will be in the living area."

Her heart dropped into her belly. "*My* living room?"

He nodded. "On the couch."

"The couch." Just outside her bedroom door? Him in his boxers, or whatever he wore to bed, on her couch, in her living room?

"This is all right, yes?" he asked, standing. "If you need assistance in the night."

"Yes, of course," she sputtered.

"Good night then."

"'Night," she called after him. "And again, thanks."

When he left, she fell back on the pillow and sighed. Oh, what she had to be missing right now. The feeling of his face so close to her own had been heaven. She could just imagine that a kiss would be absolute magic.

Just the thought had her body glowing, had her senses high and heady with a feeling she hadn't wanted to feel ever again—a feeling that made her vulnerable.

Pure, unadulterated lust.

"Well, I'm here," Jane said over the phone ten minutes later. "The house is enormous and the actress is anorexic, but she seems pretty into the cooking lessons so—" She paused. "Wait, what's wrong?"

"What makes you think something's wrong?" Mariah asked, kicking off her covers with her good leg and reaching for the wine Zayad hadn't touched.

"You haven't interjected or snorted when I said the anorexic thing. What's going on?"

After a healthy swallow of wine, she admitted, "Well, there is something."

"I knew it. Spill."

"Funny you should say that word, because after you left today, I took a bath. And, well, I sort of had a spill when I tried to get out."

"Oh my God, are you okay?"

She thought about telling Jane the truth, but didn't want her running home to help. "It's just a sprain. I'm fine—if you don't count the fifteen minutes of humiliation I had to endure."

"What's there to be humiliated about? You fell—"

"Naked. I fell naked. And I was lying on our ratty bath mat totally naked when Mr. Gorgeous from next door heard me scream and busted in like a superhero to help me."

"You're lying!"

"Do I sound like I'm lying?"

"Wow. So then what?"

Another swallow of wine. "So, then he picked me up and put me in my bed, called his doctor and then proceeded to tell me that he's staying with me until you get back."

"I'll be home in two hours." Panic dripped in Jane's voice.

"No," Mariah said firmly. "Me and my bum ankle are not coming between you and your restaurant money."

"Forget that. You've got a stranger taking care of you."

"No. It's fine. He's fine. He's actually…" Mariah set the empty wineglass on her bedside table and reveled in the decadent relaxation she felt.

"Actually what, M?" Jane asked.

"A pretty nice guy if you ignore the killer looks, arrogant and opinionated attitude and irresistible mouth."

"Oh, really?" Jane said, a wide grin in her tone. "Well, good for you. It's about time."

"No, no, no. Nothing like that. If anything, he's into you. Whenever we have a conversation, the subject always seems to come back to you."

"I don't know why. I've never met the guy." Jane paused, then said, "So, are you sure I shouldn't come home?"

"You stay with the stick-figure actress and make a ton of money. I'll be good."

"Oh, for once I hope not."

Mariah grimaced, feeling tired and ready to crash. "'Night, Jane."

"'Night."

Mariah hung up the phone and without much thought popped a pain pill. Her mind was on her new roomie and his sexy bod on her old, plaid couch.

Sigh.

Maybe Jane should have come home, if only to protect Mariah against her own messed-up feelings. But Jane had been doing that for four years now. Wasn't it time Mariah protected herself?

Without an answer Mariah turned off the light and settled into the pillows, hoping sleep would soon seize her mind.

Zayad heard her get up and checked his watch.

Twenty minutes past one in the morning.

He hadn't been to sleep yet. Could not sleep, in fact. As he tried to maintain a semicomfortable position on the thin and frustratingly short couch, his mind rumbled with activity. Though not on the subject it should be on. No, he was thinking about the softness of his patient's cheek, the scent of her skin, the hunger in her eyes. She had made him weak with just a look, and he would wrestle a king snake for another moment such as that one.

How was he to stop himself from making love to her? How was he to remember his mission here if the one woman who held the key to that mission also held the key to a new and boundless pleasure?

Behind him he heard her shuffle in, the roughness of the boot brace apparent on the wood floors.

He sat up, turned to look at her. "Miss Kennedy?"

She gasped. Her hand flew to her throat and she said a little too loudly, "You scared the life out of me."

"I apologize."

She gripped the window ledge to hold herself steady as she stared at him. She looked like a beautiful phantom in the pale yellow light of the street lamp outside, and Zayad had to force himself to stay on the couch instead of going to her and pulling her into his arms. "What are you doing out of bed?"

She shook her head. "Nothing."

"Then let me help you back." He knew it was a mistake to go to her, but there was nothing for it. She needed his help.

She sagged against the window, her thin robe gaping at the chest, her eyes and head hanging down.

"Are you all right?" he asked.

"I don't really know. I'm kinda out of it."

He tilted her chin up, made her gaze meet his. "Did you take more than one pain pill?"

She shook her head vigorously. "Nope. But I did have your wine."

"That was not a wise decision."

She gave him a mock frown, perhaps mimicking his own, then she pushed away from the window and leaned into him. "I wouldn't normally say this, but I find you very attractive."

He smiled, could not help himself. "Thank you, Miss Kennedy. I find you very attractive, as well."

"No 'Miss Kennedy.' I'm not a schoolteacher, for heaven's sake." She let her head fall against his chest. "But I think I've become a nun. Maybe you should call me Sister Mariah."

"I do not think so."

She looked up, her tiger's eyes warm and vulnerable. "What would you call me, then?"

He touched her face, his thumb moving over her cheekbone. "I would call you alive and desirable and filled with a hunger that needs to be satiated or—"

"Or I'll wilt."

"It is possible."

She sighed. "I know. I know. I've been celibate for too long."

"You need sleep, Mariah. Let me take you back to bed."

"No." Her eyes on his, she grazed her lower lip with her teeth and said, "I think I'm going to kiss you."

Zayad said nothing, just held her as she looked completely ready for his mouth on hers. He could not allow this, not in her state of mind. After all, he was no scoundrel. At least, he tried hard not to be.

No, he should not allow this.

But he did not have a choice as she fell against him, her arms wrapping around his neck, her fingers threading in his hair. With just a wisp of a smile she pressed his head down to hers and kissed him. It was unlike him, but he let her lead him, let her take the control and the pleasure that her body needed.

She sighed and tilted her head to reach him better as her fingers fisted in his hair. Zayad tried to slow his heart, ease the tightness in his chest, but it was not easy. Her kiss was slow and sensual, wet lips and soft tongue. He could not restrain himself. He nipped at her bottom lip, pressed his groin into her belly.

With great effort, Mariah eased back for a moment. Her eyes were liquid as she said, "I haven't done that in years."

Zayad stilled, his arms around her. Years? That could

not be true. It was not possible that this striking female could go years without being kissed by a man.

Her eyes drifted closed, then opened, then closed, and Zayad knew she was starting to fade. Shifting his position, he gathered her in his arms and lifted her up.

Her head promptly fell against his shoulder as he carried her into the bedroom. "You will sleep late tomorrow, Mariah."

"No," she murmured. "Tomorrow I have to visit Mama Tara."

"Your mother?" Zayad said, confused. "I thought you said you had no relatives to care for you—"

"She's not my real mother."

Zayad thought it best not to ask her any more questions. She was exhausted and on a combination of pain medication and wine. It was time for her to sleep.

He laid her on the bed and tucked the covers under her chin. But she did not fall asleep immediately. She looked up at him, gave him a melancholy smile.

"You see, my parents died when I was twelve. My grandma raised me until I was eighteen, then she died, too. While she was alive, she wasn't all that active, so my best friend's mother—Tara—took me under her wing. She treated me like a daughter and she was every bit the mother to me."

Shock bit him, made him feel slow and detached from time and the room. "Your best friend?"

"Jane."

His gut clenched with tension. Could she be speaking of the same Tara? "Where is this woman now?"

Mariah closed her eyes, let her head drift to the side. "She lives in Ojai, at a beautiful facility there."

LAURA WRIGHT

"Facility. She is not ill?" He asked questions he knew the answers to. But he had to be certain.

"No. She's blind."

Zayad's throat went dry. Yes, this was Tara.

Before he had seen the pictures that his investigators had supplied, he had built up an image of his father's American lover—wild and interested only in power and a rich lover. He had thought her like his son's mother. But in those photographs her face had shown none of these traits. Though he would see for himself.

"You will visit Tara tomorrow," he told Mariah.

Mariah's lashes lifted and she stared at him, groggy and very beautiful in the moon's light. "But how? That infant doctor of yours—"

"I will take you myself."

"He said I have to stay in bed for two days."

"He wanted you off your foot. You will be off your foot."

Her eyes narrowed lazily. "You're taking care of me, helping me with my next case and driving me to Tara's. What is it you want from me?"

He did not answer her query, but on his way out of the room said, "Get some rest. We will leave at nine."

Six

Her pride hurt as much as her ankle the next morning.

Mariah sat in the passenger side of Zayad's black SUV as they raced up the 101 freeway. Her seat was slightly reclined and her booted ankle rested on a stack of pillows. Zayad had meant for her to be comfortable, but it was a lost cause. All she wanted to do was fade into the gray leather seats. She remembered everything that had happened last night, from her wine-induced rest on the window ledge to Zayad putting a gentlemanly arm around her waist to his not-so-gentlemanly kiss a moment later.

That last bit made her smile, so she turned to look out the window at the orange groves. Who was she trying to kid? Zayad may have kissed her back with double the heat and intensity of any man she'd ever known, but she'd been the instigator. She'd told him he looked mighty fine with her eyes, then gone in for the kill.

Damn that wine and pain medicine. They'd totally messed her up. She shouldn't be acting like a teenager anymore. She glanced over at Zayad, took in his chiseled features and those amazing, teasing, oh-so-full lips she'd felt last night. What did he think of her? He hadn't mentioned their make-out session last night or when he'd seen her this morning, and she couldn't read his eyes. With looks like that, maybe he was used to forward women.

Or, on the opposite end of the spectrum, maybe he hadn't really wanted to kiss her last night. Maybe he'd just been laying on the pity for the poor drugged-up cripple girl.

She mentally groaned.

Can I get any more pathetic?

Her gaze slipped from his face down to his neck, then lower still. Along with those amazing lips, she'd felt his chest and arms. Hard as steel and corded with muscle. Too bad he'd covered them up today, she thought, giving in to the thoughts of her wanton-woman alter ego. But his clothes did flatter what he had in spades. Tan pants that showed off his tight backside to perfection and a crisp white shirt open at the nape. If she wasn't so reclined, she mused, she could probably have a nice look at that muscle.

She frowned and shifted in the leather bucket seat. She needed to get her mind out of the proverbial gutter and onto something safer.

Casually she glanced around. "This is a nice car."

"Thank you."

"You must sell a lot of those swords."

A muscle twitched in his jaw. "They are very popular."

"I'm sure they are."

"There are many who enjoy a beautiful blade."

"Of course. So, why come to Ventura to work, then? Wouldn't Los Angeles be a better—"

"A better what?"

"Well, not better but a more lucrative place to collect pieces and sell them? Lots of stars and eccentric people who would be interested in adding a sword to their eclectic art collections?"

He glanced over at her, haughtiness in his gaze. "Do you feel life is only about gain, about money?"

The question made her laugh. This was the first time in her life she'd been accused of such a thing. "Of course not. Look at the work that I do."

He shrugged. "Perhaps you do such work for more than just altruistic reasons."

"What do you mean by that?"

"I do not know. I do not know your past or what drives your decisions now, but the way you speak of men, of winning for your clients, it is—"

"It's personal, Mr. Fandal," she interrupted, her words sounding far too tight.

Zayad said nothing to this and she stared past him to the ocean. Wild and inviting yet a bit intimidating at times. And the sand, soft and steady. Zayad had seen her soft last night, had seen the woman in her and not just the acerbic machine-for-hire she was at work. Perhaps he'd liked what he'd seen. Now the severe woman he'd met on the doorstep had returned. Normally at a moment like this, with an encounter that had nothing to do with work, she'd tuck her tail between her legs and retreat.

Her gaze flickered toward him. "Look, I didn't mean to jump on you—"

He turned, eyes suddenly filled with humor.

She laughed, a little shyly at first. "You know what I mean." She paused, then lifted her hands in mock surrender. "The thing is, you're right. I have some stuff in my past that drives most of my decisions today. But honestly I believe my reasons for doing what I do are altruistic in nature." *At least I hope so.* The afterthought alarmed her, so she decided not to examine it. She chose to return to a familiar subject.

"So, back to the beginning of this conversation. Ventura, California. Why?"

"Would it be too poetic to say that the ocean is a welcome tonic to my wearied senses?"

She followed along. "And that the glitz and glamour of Hollywood would bore you to tears, make you long for the simpler life?"

"Exactly." He grinned, gave her a wink. "I think you understand me, Miss Kennedy."

"Oh, for heaven's sake, let's drop the 'Miss.' I'm Mariah and you're—"

"Yes? Who am I?"

You're too gorgeous, too generous, too interesting and way too irresistible. "I think I'll save that answer until I know you better."

"And you are planning on knowing me better?"

There was a racehorse inside her chest thump, thump, thumping along, but she managed to say, "Well, since we're sort of stuck together, I don't know what choice I have…"

The corners of his mouth lifted in one sexy smile. "I like this…stuck together."

God help her, so did she. She turned and faced forward. She could hardly feel the ache in her ankle anymore. The ache in her heart, breasts and core had drowned out the pain.

This Ojai…

Around and around they drove, up the mountain and through the towns, with no security trailing behind— as he had instructed.

Zayad could not help but feel drawn to this spot. There were shades of Emand here, particularly the sultan's palace gardens. Fruit trees, perfect lawns and a sky so intense a blue, he wondered for a moment if he were at home.

He grinned. All that was missing were the golden sands.

He did not glance to his right, but knew he had his golden sands beside him. They dwelled in Mariah's eyes. Eyes that had haunted him through a painfully sleepless night. Eyes that had drawn him to that soft mouth, that pink tongue, that taste of wine and mystery.

"I love coming up here," Mariah said, ripping Zayad from his thoughts. "It's so different than the beachy areas, you know?"

Zayad pulled onto Main Street. "The mountains are beautiful, as are the pear and walnut trees."

"It's really peaceful. I'd love to move my practice up here sometime. Maybe get a horse."

"You like to ride?"

"I do. I'm not great at it, but I love the feeling of animal and person being one."

Horse and rider—one being. Zayad had said this many times. His gaze swept over her fitted white sundress. Yes, she would love his country.

"And of course," she continued, "I would love being closer to Tara."

Ah, yes, Zayad mused, his mood darkening slightly. The reason he had come here today. Tara. "What of Jane? Does she want to be near her mother, as well?"

The mention of Jane brought a slight frown to Mariah's lips. "Of course she does. She's tried to get a chef's job here, but the competition is stiff and the money's worse. That's why she's working so hard. She's trying to save enough cash to open her own restaurant up here."

Not if he had anything to say on the matter. Jane was an Emand princess. She need not work if she did not want to. And if she did, no door would be closed to her, and money would be no object. But she would be in Emand, not Ojai.

He turned back to Mariah. "If Jane moved here, where would that leave you?"

"What?"

"She is your closest friend, yes?"

Mariah paused, felt a sudden tug at her heart. She swallowed hard. "She's my best friend."

"And you have no lover, correct?"

"We've already covered this, haven't we?"

He chuckled. "We have."

"And that's by choice, by the way."

"Yes, of course. But my point is this—if your friend moves, where does that leave you?"

She shrugged and fastened on her ol' reliable tough-cookie attitude—the one that was complete BS but made her feel in control and less like a loser. "That leaves me alone, I guess."

"And this is good for you?"

"I don't see you with a wife and a boatload of friends by your side. Must be good for you, too."

He took a moment in answering. "Yes, but alas…"

"Alas what?"

"A man can do very well—"

"Don't even go there, buddy." She pointed her finger at him. "Don't even say that a man is programmed to wander the earth alone, never needing to fully bond with one person. And that a woman requires a mate to be happy and fulfilled."

He shrugged. "All right, I will not say it—but only because I could not say the words as well as you just have." He grinned.

She wanted to toss him a huge frown, maybe a little sneer if she could muster it, but nothing negative sprouted from her heart. And even more annoying, she couldn't stop the smile that tugged at her lips. The guy was clever and drop-dead handsome and he made her weak—in more ways than one. She shook her head. "I think I'm not meant to find true happiness with someone. I don't believe in happily ever after anymore and I don't believe in soul mates."

"Neither do I. I have always been happiest when I am alone."

Why did that admission sadden her so much when her own had filled her with confidence?

He continued to say, "But I have never met a woman who also felt this way."

"Surprises you, huh?"

"Very much." His gaze moved over her. "You have been nothing but surprising to me, Mariah."

Her belly twisted and warmed under his gaze, and she turned to face the road. They were only about a block away from Tara's place. Good thing, too. If Mariah didn't watch her step, instead of telling him she was going to kiss him, she'd be coaxing him into the backseat of this truck.

She took a deep breath and said, "Turn at the next light."

The apartment the assisted-living coordinator showed them into was painted in bright, bold colors, and Zayad thought it interesting that a woman without sight lived in such a vivid atmosphere. The furniture was more of the same—a menagerie of red and gold and blue pieces, though all looked comfortable and at home in the rather small space.

Zayad's gaze shifted and he noticed a potter's wheel was set up in one corner of the room, facing a set of charming French doors, where a cool breeze floated in.

When the aide left, Zayad gestured to the wheel and asked Mariah, now ensconced on the red couch, "Who is the artist?"

"Tara is."

"She does not share this room with another?"

"Nope."

"But how would she work…?"

"She is an amazing woman." Mariah smiled at Zayad with eyes that read, "Just wait until you meet her." "She lets nothing stop her—especially when she wants something badly enough."

He wanted to remark that Tara sounded like a wonderful, brave and interesting woman, but he felt he would wait to meet the woman first.

"I have guests."

The cheerful, husky tone came from the doorway. Zayad looked up in time to see a tall, slim, long-legged woman in her midfifties with short blond hair streaked with an attractive pale gray. She wore a flowing orange dress with beaded earrings to match. She was very beautiful, but there was far more to her than her looks. This was a woman who was overflowing with life, happiness and an open spirit. Zayad understood at once why his father had been drawn to this woman.

Tara thrust her hands to her hips. "Where's my lovely Mariah? Why isn't she running over here to greet me?"

"I would run over to you, Tara," said Mariah, her eyes bright with the warmth one felt for someone they loved greatly. "I hurt my ankle last night."

Hearing her voice brought Tara straight to Mariah. She sat beside Mariah on the couch, fumbled just a bit for her hand. "It is of no importance. You came, my little one, that's what matters. Now, what's wrong with your ankle?"

"It's just a little bruise." Mariah glanced up at Zayad and smiled. "No worries."

Tara feigned gruffness. "It is my right to worry about you."

Mariah laughed. "I know."

"So, you didn't drive yourself up here, did you?" Tara turned, tilted her chin and faced Zayad. "Who have you brought with you?"

Zayad stepped back, feeling strange and slightly uncomfortable at how easily she had found him.

"How did you…?" Mariah laughed. "Of course."

Of course? What, of course? He had made no sound, no movement, no indication that he was in the room. He wanted to know what the mystery was.

"This is my neighbor," Mariah explained. "And… well, friend. He graciously offered to bring me up here even though I've been a real pain in the neck to him."

"Ah, my girl, your spirit is your charm." Tara stood, walked straight to Zayad and extended her hand. "Is it not?"

Zayad took her hand. "It is."

Her brows drew together. "Does this friend have a name?"

Zayad bent and kissed her hand. "My name is Zayad."

Confusion, then an unmistakable shadow of alarm moved across Tara's features and she eased her hand from his. All warmth, confidence and animation seemed to melt away from her expression, and Zayad wondered how well she had known her lover. Had she known of his family? His children's names?

It seemed she did.

"Are you two hungry?" Tara asked, recovering quickly and turning away from him.

"A little," Mariah said.

"Good. I'll go and get our lunch, then we can have a nice chat. I can't wait to hear what's been going on with you. And of course, finding out more about your new neighbor and what he's doing so far from home."

"Can I help you, Mrs. Hefner?" Zayad asked.

She headed into the other room. "No, thank you."

When they were alone again, Mariah turned to him. "That was a nice offer. But she likes to do these things herself. Oh, and it's not 'Mrs.' She was never married. Actually I think she was over-the-top in love with Jane's dad and couldn't bear to think of another man after he left her."

In love. Zayad bristled.

"What's wrong?" Mariah asked, watching him.

He shook his head. "I was thinking about this man leaving her."

"Yeah. What a jerk, huh?"

"How is it you know this?"

"Jane told me."

Black fury ignited in Zayad's belly at his father's foolish aide. For his sister to think that her own father did not want her—it was despicable. Even though Zayad's son came from a mother who only wanted to see gold, Zayad had only told him good things about Meyaan and that she did not come to see him because she was not well, but that she loved him a great deal.

"To not even want to know your own child." Mariah shook her head. "Horrible."

"Perhaps he did not know he had a child."

Mariah's face contorted with dismay. "What makes you say that?"

He could not answer, nor did he want to, as Tara rejoined them. She carried a platter laden with food. "My cold lemon chicken, potato salad and biscuits."

Zayad helped her with the platter and the serving until they were ready to eat. As they sat around a small iron table in a tiny though peaceful yard overlooking the mountainside, Tara spoke mostly to Mariah. She wanted to know all about her upcoming case and what her strategy was. When Mariah mentioned that Zayad was going to help her, Tara put down her uneaten biscuit on her plate full of uneaten food and faced him. "So, where are you from, Zayad?"

She knew exactly—he could see it on her face—but he replied anyway. "From a small country called Emand."

Sadness etched her features. "And is it a beautiful place? Ripe with olive groves and fig trees? Scented with spice and the warm sand at sunset?"

"It is." His father had told her much, and he almost felt badly for her.

"Sounds like you've been there, Tara," Mariah remarked, using the table to get herself into a standing position and grab her crutches.

"Perhaps in my mind," Tara said softly.

"Where are you going?" Zayad asked Mariah.

"The little girls' room to freshen up." She grinned. "Wanna come?"

"I will help you there, of course."

After Zayad had helped Mariah to the bathroom and told her to call for him when she was ready, he returned to the table and to Tara.

"Could you pass me a lump of that sugar, Zayad," she said. "As you have probably surmised by now, I cannot see well."

He did as she requested, watched as she placed the sugar in her glass of lemonade. "I think you see very well, madam."

"Thank you. I work very hard for normalcy." She smiled in his direction. "As Mariah has probably told you, I wasn't always blind. The furnishings you see around you have been with me for ages, and five years ago, when my sight began to wane, the comfort of being able to still detect color helped me for the rough months to come."

"It must have been very difficult for you."

"It was at first. But like all things, I grew accustomed to the darkness. I looked for the light in other things—and other people."

That made him think of Mariah. Under her mask of ire she was all light, all heat, fire and female. "I must return for Mariah." He stood, then paused. "Perhaps we can talk another time."

She sipped her lemonade. "I will see if my schedule—"

"We must talk, Tara."

She did not answer him. Her lips thinned and she placed her glass on the table with a little too much force. "I know why you've come."

"Do you?"

"Yes. Jane. She's a good girl, Zayad. She doesn't need to know the truth. Not now. Not yet. She doesn't need this kind of attention paid to her."

"I understand the wish for anonymity, believe me. But the truth remains—Jane is a princess." And whether her mother agreed with him or not, Jane deserved to know of her birthright.

A blanket of anguish seemed to encompass Tara as she thought about what he had said. Finally she gave him a nod. "Come back on Friday, then."

"I will be here."

"And you will not deny a semiaged woman her chance to explain?"

"Of course not."

An explanation, a true and full story, was the last thing—and the first thing—he wanted. He asked her to excuse him, then left the table to catch his breath and to help Mariah.

Seven

As they drove along the 101 freeway toward home, Mariah kept stealing glances at Zayad. Though he remained gorgeous and sexier than silk, he was also as stiff as a poker and incredibly pensive. She wondered at his mood, wanted to know if something had happened at Tara's, if the woman had said something to him while Mariah had been in the bathroom. But what? What would make him so rigid and thoughtful?

Her heart dropped a foot. She sure hoped it wasn't something about matchmaking. A quick setup was right up Tara's alley.

"Get the girl back on the horse" was her motto.

"A good ride will wipe that frown off your face, Mariah."

Ugh.

Maybe Mariah needed to set Zayad's mind at ease about her intentions to procure a date or a wild night of sex. "Say, Zayad, why don't you take the night off tonight?"

A semitruck passed them on the left, and he waited a moment before saying, "Pardon me?"

"Take a night off. From your 'duties.'"

"My duties?" He glanced over at her. "Do you mean *you*?"

"Yes. See, the thing is, I'm really jonesing for a pizza, and that's easy enough to order and have delivered. I'll make a place for myself on the couch, watch some TV—maybe an old black-and-white movie—and if I'm really feeling adventurous, dip into my work. Something tells me you need to get back to your work, too."

He sniffed almost regally. "There is plenty of time for my work."

"But isn't that little house you rented in the backyard calling you? I'm assuming it's an office space?"

"How did you know about that?"

"I've coveted that place for as long as I've lived here. I actually thought I might make it *my* office."

"What happened?"

"It's not in my budget."

"Ah."

"Anyway, the point is you've done enough for me." *And* to *me,* she mused, her skin warming at the memory of his arms around her and his mouth on hers. "Take some time for yourself."

His brow lifted. "Are you trying to get rid of me, Mariah?"

Just trying to keep myself a born-again virgin.
No.
Just trying to save myself the embarrassment of your rejection when I fling myself at you—and totally sober this time.

"Zayad, the truth is that you deserve a break. You've been amazing looking after me, making me meals, driving me to see Tara."

"I appreciate the thought, but I feel responsible for you and your well-being now."

"That's very gallant, but the knight-in-shining-armor routine is…" *Well, actually, it's so great I want to melt.*

"My mind will not be changed."

"But—"

"Like you, Mariah, I am a highly skilled debater."

"Yeah, I see that." She smiled.

He shifted into fourth gear, then third as he came off the highway and onto the main drag. When he turned onto their street, he asked, "Do you know much about swords?"

"Not much. But I find antiques and artwork very interesting." Actually she found it so interesting that she'd looked on the Internet this morning when Zayad had gone over to his apartment to change his clothes.

He pulled into the driveway with just a little too much speed, brought the SUV to a halt, then flicked off the ignition. "If you would like, we could share our worlds for the evening."

Fingers gripping the door handle, Mariah turned. "What do you mean?"

"You will come to my home for the pizza and, if it

amuses you—if you are truly interested—you could see some of my collection."

Her insides went tingly and raw. Weekend nights for old-maid Mariah Kennedy usually consisted of frozen food or takeout—because Jane was working—and a movie, just as she'd said she was going to do earlier. But this—this addition of a sexy man showing her his passion for antique weaponry... Well, strange as it may seem, that just couldn't sound any more fabulous.

But she smiled with only mild enthusiasm. After all, he didn't need to know how interested she was. "Maybe I could give you a fresh opinion on the pieces? Which ones you should sell and to whom? That kind of thing?"

A flash of humor crossed his face. "We will see."

Oh, he was so arrogant.

He got out of the car, came around to her side and helped her out. For a second he stood there, easing her arm about his shoulders, placing his hand unnecessarily on her hip. "We will see where the night takes us, yes?"

Heat snaked through Mariah and she found herself nodding as he lifted her into his arms.

"The man's name is Charles Waydon."

Thirty minutes later Zayad stood in his sparsely furnished living room, surrounded by yellow shag carpeting and badly stuccoed walls, and gave one of his most trusted aides the address of Mariah's client's unscrupulous husband. "He is to be watched twenty-four hours a day. I want to know where he goes, who he sees. I want photographs, Fandal. Even his refuse should be checked."

"Yes, sir."

"This is very important."

"I understand, sir."

Zayad turned his back on the man, snatched up the phone book. He would serve Mariah this pizza himself, order it himself. And he would not question his motives for wanting to perform such an inane act, for wanting to be just an ordinary man for tonight and for the next two weeks.

Though his servant might.

"If I may ask, Your Royal—sir?"

"Yes, Fandal?"

"Why are you helping this woman?"

"I have given her my word."

"Yes, but why? She is not the woman you seek."

No, she was not. But she was intriguing and beautiful and angry at the world. Her fire made him want to stay close, even though the warmth was not a sweet one. Her need for more than physical help intrigued him, made him want to give. Yes, he was used to handing out monetary assistance, but never had a woman wanted his friendship, needed his kindness of spirit.

It was somehow addicting.

But he could not allow his aide to know this. "She is the key to what I want. She is my sister's closest confidante. I am convinced that to know her is to know Jane." Zayad flipped through the Yellow Pages, looking for a pizzeria that sounded remotely distinctive. "Mariah Kennedy must be appeased, must be given all that she requires."

"I understand, sir."

"You may go, Fandal."

The man bowed and left the room.

Zayad grabbed his cell phone. What he did not understand was the intensity of his attraction to Mariah. His sympathy, yes. But gut-wrenching need?

In Emand when a woman caught his interest, he would offer her a night of pleasure, then anything she desired—anything but his heart. There had never been any mystery or deep ache of want with any of those women. Both he and his lover had always had their needs fulfilled and both had left content.

Mariah Kennedy was somehow different. With her caustic humor and the shadow of a deeply pained heart behind her eyes, Zayad felt he knew her. She had once said she did not believe in soul mates and he had concurred. If he was ever to believe in such a foolish notion, he might entertain the thought that this woman was his.

And he had only tasted her once.

His finger stabbed the keypad of his phone, dialing the number of Harrison's Pizza Shack. He could hold on to his desire for only a short time longer. If she were to kiss him again, he would not be stopped for something as irrelevant as honor.

He would have her.

"I'm a pepperoni kinda gal. Classic, a little spicy, but always satisfying." Booted foot propped up on a pillow, dressed in jeans and a black tank and bottom sunk into the same yellow shag that covered her own living room floor, Mariah grinned and slid a piece of the cheesy pizza into her mouth.

Across from her, leaning back against his tan couch,

Zayad ate his own slice of olive-and-mushroom. "Are you sure you are describing the pizza, Mariah?"

Mariah paused, ran the description back over in her head. "Sure, that could be me—but alas, only in the courtroom."

"Why is that?"

"In the courtroom I dress classically and am a pretty spicy litigator."

"And how are you satisfying?"

Now that is a question, Mariah thought, her pulse kicking. And asked with such a devilish twinkle in his eye, too. "Well, I hope in my victories."

"Of which there are many, I am sure."

Mariah took another bite of pizza, not wanting to correct his statement. In part because for the past year she'd rarely lost a case. Then, about a month ago, something had changed. Her attitude? Her drive? Something to do with confidence? She wasn't sure, but she'd lost her last three cases.

"What about you?" she asked, quickly deflecting.

"Me?"

"Yes, what kind of pizza are you?"

"I do not do well in describing myself."

"Well, give it a try. C'mon, we're being stupid and silly here—a rare thing for us both, I imagine."

He stared at her, grinned, and she wondered if he liked her quick, dry humor. Most men didn't seem to, or maybe they weren't sure how to respond.

"Green olives," he began thoughtfully. "Mushrooms and hot red pepper."

"Interesting. What's the description?"

"I have an acerbic nature, like the green olive.

Mushrooms tend to grow and mature in dark, remote places."

His expression looked pinched and he didn't elaborate on the mushroom thing. Something warned Mariah not to push him.

"And then there is the red pepper." He grinned, his eyes full of sin once again. "I, too, enjoy a little spice."

Thrill bubbled in Mariah's throat—the kind that comes from strange, arousing, nonspecific flirting.

It'd been a long time.

Zayad finished off his slice of pizza and the quarter of a beer left in his bottle. "I think it is time for my trip to the back house. If you would rather remain here and watch the television, I would not be offended. Looking over my work may be boring to anyone else but me."

Was he kidding? Three slices of pizza and a half-a-beer buzz. She was ready to see her sexy neighbor's swords and maybe even wrangle another kiss out of him. "No, I'd like to go."

"Very good." He stood. "The walk is not far but perhaps too much on your ankle—even with the support of your crutches. I will carry you, yes?"

She nodded and allowed him to lift her up once again. If truth be told, her ankle was feeling better, and using the crutches was easy and convenient. But Ms. Ultrafeminist was really starting to enjoy the comfort of this man's arms.

The cloudless night was generous with its stars, and the curve of moon shone brilliantly. Zayad carried her out the patio doors and onto the grass, wonderfully fragrant from just being cut that afternoon. The walk only took a few minutes, but the mood seemed to change with every step they took. From light to dim to deep in the backyard, very secluded and woodsy.

Mariah had always coveted the small gingerbread-like structure at the back of the property but had never seen inside it, as it always had been locked. Zayad pressed his code into the security keypad beside the door, and they entered. The first things Mariah saw were rough stone walls, beautiful hardwood floors and several hanging lights. A white couch and chair looked to have been pushed to one side of the room to make space for several large, black velvet cases.

Zayad carried Mariah to the couch, making certain her ankle was elevated and that she was comfortable. Then he went to his cases and opened them. Metal gleamed up at him, and with great reverence he lifted two from the case and brought them to Mariah.

"These will soon be going to the two sons of Sheikh Jaran. He rules the country to the south of Emand."

"Wow, you've sold these to a sheikh?"

He only smiled as he placed the long sword on her lap. "This one is Persian." He ran his fingers slowly up the blade and over the intricately chiseled floral pattern.

Heat fused into Mariah's belly at the sight. If she asked, would he give her his attention, give her those glorious, sensual strokes that he was now bestowing on a sword?

"Notice the engravings," he said, his black eyes meeting hers. "In English it reads, 'Fear not my heart.'"

He slipped the sword from her lap and placed another in its place. This one had a lion-shaped hilt, and the blade was engraved with intricate latticework.

"You hold the Rajput sword. Very old and very rare." He leaned toward her and grinned. "It is said that Rajput marriages often took place between warring clans. Holding this sword, the groom sent a message to all who might take issue with the match that this woman was his and he would fight for her if the need arose."

Mariah gazed into his eyes, her pulse racing. "That's pretty dramatic."

"I would say so." His gaze flickered to her mouth. "But when a man and woman give themselves to each other, no person has the right to part them, do you not think so?"

Despite her issues regarding marriage, she found herself nodding. Who was she to disagree with such a romantic notion when Zayad sat so close, his eyes to hers, his mouth looking so warm and inviting?

She fairly sighed. Never in her life had she been so on edge, her skin prickly with heat.

"And this is how our young sheikh feels about his bride to be," Zayad said, breaking the spell just slightly. "I thought it an appropriate gift."

"An appropriate sale, you mean," Mariah corrected.

"Yes, of course." Outside the crickets started their song as Zayad stretched the Rajput sword out before her like a sacred offering. "Feel this."

She reached out, brushed her fingers over the metal. "Sharp."

"But beautiful, yes?"

Yes, he was. She wanted to kiss him so badly, she almost grabbed the blade and pitched it so she could grab him.

"I will put these away. I think we are done for tonight."

His words made her frown. Cleanup meant carrying her into the house and putting her and her ankle to bed—and not in a good way.

But she was wrong. After he put his swords away, he came to sit with her on the couch. "How is your ankle?"

"Heavy and a little achy." *Just like the rest of me.*

"Would you like to go inside?"

"Not just yet."

He nodded. "You must keep your ankle up until then and stay warm." He reached for a blanket and draped it over her. "Better?" he asked.

She didn't nod, couldn't nod. She didn't feel better. She felt uptight and needy and a little bit desperate.

He leaned in, brushed a strand of hair out of her eyes. "What is wrong? Is the pain very bad?"

He smelled of male and metal, and it had been so long. "Zayad, last night when we kissed…"

"Yes?"

He looked casually amused and she felt crazy embarrassed. But then again, she had started this, had blurted out phrases and words such as *last night* and *kissed.* There was no turning back. "Did you kiss me because you felt sorry for me?"

"What?"

"Was it because I was a little out of it?"

Why didn't she just ask him to pick her last for dodgeball? Or maybe—

But Mariah didn't get the chance to say anything more, think anything more. Zayad's hands went to her face, his mouth closed in and he kissed her so deeply, her heart fairly leaped out of her chest.

Then he eased back, his gaze fierce. "I do nothing out of pity."

"I just had to know if—"

"Do not say it again. You insult me."

He slid his hands down her arms to her waist. Sensation followed him, but Mariah couldn't revel in the pleasure. She didn't have time. He was under her shirt, his palm raking up her hot skin, cupping her breast. Heat penetrated the skin beneath her thin bra, and her nipple beaded instantly.

"Your hands feel like heaven," Mariah uttered, her breathing labored.

"And you are full of life, Mariah." His free hand held her neck as he nibbled her lower lip, then crushed her mouth beneath his again.

When he pulled back, Mariah released a breath.

"Wow," she said, her gaze as limp and desperate as her body.

"I do not know this word, but somehow it sounds appropriate."

"You *are* attracted to me," she muttered stupidly.

"What?"

"Nothing," she said, shaking her head.

Solemnity lit his eyes and he gripped her chin, held her steady. "Look at me, Mariah."

She lifted her gaze, feeling girlish and completely vulnerable.

"Do you not see the way I look at you?"

Did she? She didn't know. It had been way too long since she'd allowed herself to see a man for a man and not as the enemy in a courtroom. "I don't think I could notice such a thing now," she said a little sadly. "My past relationship really did a number on me and on my confidence as a woman."

"You were hurt?"

"Pretty badly."

He held her tightly against him. "And it still stings, yes?"

"Yes."

He said nothing for a moment, just looked at her. Mariah tried to decipher what was going on behind those black eyes, but he was a well-kept secret.

Finally he released her. "I do not wish to hurt you further."

"What do you mean?" she asked, suddenly feeling empty and cold, her breast aching for his touch again.

"I will not be another man who stings you."

"Wait. That's not what I meant by this. I…" Her words faded out, and she felt foolish. Because of what she'd said, there'd be no more kisses. No more caresses. An end to a delightful flirtation. And just when she was starting to come back to life.

"You are right to be cautious, Mariah," he began. "I am a man who cannot make commitments."

Her heart pitched, but she held steady. "I'm not asking for that."

"But you should. You deserve a good life with everything you desire. When you are ready to take such a chance again, of course."

Frustration bit at her, sexual and otherwise. "Listen, I don't need anyone to tell me what I deserve or don't deserve. Believe me, I've spent enough hours on the subject to write a self-help book. I want this—fun, sex, feeling lighter than air for the first time in a long time— with no strings."

He looked unsure and unconvinced. "I think it is time for our night to end, yes?"

No! she wanted to yell at him. But she didn't speak up, and he took control. He lifted her and carried her to the house, to her room and to her bed. She fell asleep fifteen minutes later, alone and dreaming of swords and a beautiful, frustrating man atop her nothing wearing but a devilish smile.

Eight

"I am very proud of you, Redet."

"Thank you, Father."

It was close to seven in the morning in California, and Zayad had arisen early from his restless sleep on Mariah's ridiculously small sofa in hopes of speaking to his boy. Zayad missed the child and wanted to hear his voice, hear that he was well and tell him that he would see him soon.

Leaning back in one of the deck's patio chairs, gazing out at an amazing sunrise, Zayad warmed with care for his son. "I wish I had been as intelligent as you when I was in school."

"You were not?"

Redet sounded very surprised and Zayad chuckled. "No. I had no head for figures or for the sciences, although I did fairly well in history."

"What of sport?"

"My father—your grandfather—would only allow me sport if I did well on my exams."

"And what sport would you have chosen if your grades had permitted?" Redet fairly giggled, for of course he knew.

Zayad smiled. "The sword, my son."

In the background Zayad heard a bell ringing and the scuffle of what he assumed were children milling about between classes.

"I must go, Father. My second class is to begin."

Zayad's heart clenched. He was a man and yet this boy made him ache like a woman. "I love you, my son."

"And you, Father. When will I see you?"

"In just a few weeks. I come to you straight from America and we will ride together and—"

"Have swordplay?"

"I have found a special sword for you. I will bring it with me."

From the open patio door Mariah listened. Granted, she'd heard just one side of the conversation, but she couldn't help but feel that one side was all she needed to hear.

Damn Zayad Fandal!

Why couldn't he be like all the rest of the charming, intelligent, handsome megalomaniacs she knew? Why did he have to be different—why did he have to have the whole package? Sure, he was a tad arrogant. But strangely that attitude was tempered with a caring, loving and generous spirit.

She watched him as he played with his coffee cup, his thumb gently circling the rim. Her belly tingled. His fingers were so long and tapered, so warm and so strong. She wished his hands would move over her again.

Fat chance, she told herself. Zayad had made his position pretty apparent last night. Mr. Noble was staying clear of her to protect her bruised and battered heart—a heart that had once been so overgrown with weeds, she'd thought she'd never escape its captivity.

But she had. Somewhat. And this man had swung the ax.

"May you remain safe and protected, my son," Zayad said. Then he paused for a moment, and finally added, "Goodbye, Redet."

As he clicked off the phone, Mariah made a swift turn back into the house, but with her ankle she wasn't fast enough to avoid Zayad's gaze.

"Good morning, Mariah."

"Morning." She gave him a sheepish grin. "Sorry for eavesdropping."

"It is fine. You are walking on your ankle." His gaze swept her bare legs only partly covered with an oversize T-shirt. "Does it still pain you?"

"Only a little now. The boot keeps it pretty steady. I'm actually feeling pretty good today."

"How did you sleep?"

"Fine." *If tossing and turning while dreaming of you beside me is fine.*

"And what are your plans for today?"

"I have a lot of work to do."

"Well, sit down and have some breakfast first."

"Breakfast?" She saw nothing on the round mosaic table but his coffee cup.

"I will make eggs," he announced and stood, walked to her. "I am getting very good at eggs."

He looked like all the breakfast she needed, with his wet hair and black sweats, and she fought the urge to fake a pain in her ankle and fall. Maybe he'd lift her into his arms again, hold her close, his eyes penetrating hers as he said, "Let us go to bed...."

The shrill ringing of the telephone interrupted her idiotic fantasy and she turned to tug the receiver from the base on the wall.

"Hello?"

"Hey, it's me."

She glanced up at Zayad. "Hi, Jane, how's the teaching coming along?"

Zayad looked mildly interested, but didn't stay around to listen to her conversation. Instead he went to the kitchen and started on the eggs. Mariah went outside and sat in the chair he'd just occupied.

"I have the funniest story to tell you," Jane began with a devilish chuckle.

"Good. I could use a funny story right now."

After a night of sensual dreams and an early morning rise that consisted of only more thoughts of Zayad and his magical mouth, she needed something.

Jane laughed again, already three paces into her story about her student actress and a disastrous puff-pastry incident. "I warned her not to try it by herself, especially after a night of full-on partying, but you know, she's got a mind of her own. Needless to say, the fire department was called."

"Sounds great."

"Sounds great? What kind of medication are you

on? I just said—" Jane stopped short, sniffed. "Wait a minute. Where's Mr. Tall, Dark and Foreign right now?"

"Making breakfast," Mariah said sheepishly.

"Ohmigod, you slept with him."

"I did not."

"And he was supposed to be mine," she said dramatically.

"Oh, Jane. No. It's not—there's not—"

"Hon, I'm kidding. I never wanted the guy in the first place. I don't even know him or how gorgeous he is." She laughed. "C'mon, you so obviously have a crush. And that's wonderful."

"No, I do not have a crush," Mariah said sullenly as she picked up Zayad's coffee cup.

"Let yourself have a good time for once, Mariah. It's not going to kill you."

"How do you know?"

"You're such a cynic."

"Sad but true."

"Well, it's getting old and so are you."

"That not only rhymes, but it's a terrible thing to say."

"I'm not going to say I'm sorry," Jane said. "You're my best friend and I want you to be happy for once. I want you to go for it—for once."

Mariah mentally shook her head. How could she tell Jane that she was willing and able, but the man in question had integrity issues? "I'd better go. My eggs are getting cold."

Jane snorted. "Oh, sister, so are mine. We'd both better get going."

Mariah laughed and said goodbye to Jane. As she

hung up, Zayad walked through the patio door with two steaming plates of eggs.

"How is your friend?"

"She's good. A little irritated by her student, but otherwise good."

He didn't ask her why Jane was irritated, but asked instead, "Is she an impatient person?"

"Not at all."

"Perhaps she does not appreciate having to teach her skills to others?"

"No way. Last summer she spent an entire month teaching kids how to cook down at the community center." Why did she feel as though she were defending her friend? And why did Zayad make her feel as though she had to?

Mariah quickly finished off the last bite of her eggs. "Well, thanks for the breakfast, but I'd better get going on my work."

"Work?"

"I have a case to win, remember?"

"Ah. Yes." He wiped his mouth, tossed the napkin on his empty plate. "Did I tell you that I have a friend looking into this Charles Waydon."

Shock tore through her. "You do?"

"I said I would help you."

Yes, but she'd been thinking along the lines of brainstorming or something, not asking someone to do reconnaissance. She didn't get this guy. Didn't get him at all. Smart, sexy, helping her, taking care of her. What was he after? If he wasn't interested in Jane, why was he doing all this? Mariah took a deep breath. Could it even be possible that he liked her—really liked her—

but was a little freaked by his feelings and wanted to take things slow?

Oh, who was she kidding? What guy ever wanted to take things slow? "You did say you'd help me, but I didn't think—"

"You did not think I would follow through with my word?"

"No. Not in such an in-depth way."

He clucked his tongue. "Such cynicism, Miss Kennedy."

Her heart lurched. First Jane and now Zayad. She hadn't really listened to herself in the past few years, but she knew they were probably right on the money. She came across as cynical and very bitter. "The thing is, I don't expect you to help because you're honestly not obliged to—as in, you don't have to. If you want to stop right now, you're off the hook."

"I do not want to be off the hook."

Even biting her tongue couldn't stop her from asking. The question needed to be answered. "What is it you do want, Zayad?"

He leaned back in his chair, crossed his arms over his chest. "Let there be no work today. For either of us. I think you and I have seen too much work and not enough relaxation."

"I can't."

"You can. One day is not going to win or lose this case for you, but it actually might relax you enough to see your path better."

She sat up in her chair. "I can't afford to relax."

"When was the last time you were pampered, Mariah?"

"Pampered? You're joking, right?"

"I am not."

She thought back, frowned, then thought back even further. "Well, senior year of high school I had an eyebrow wax before prom. 'Course, the woman made me look like something out of a *Star Trek* episode, so I don't think I'd call it pampering exactly."

He shook his head. "Pathetic."

"I would say so."

"Well." He stood up, reached for her hand and eased her to her feet. "I thought we would return to Ojai. They have a spa that is purported to be very good."

"A spa?"

"Saltwater baths are good for the ankle, and hot-stone massages are simply...good."

Salt water and hot stones? It sounded exotic, sensual and wonderful—just like him. "I couldn't...."

"You will." He kept her hand in his, his thumb playing with her palm.

She swallowed hard. "And where will you be while I have stones and steam?"

"I will have a massage, as well. Perhaps we can experience a few of these treatments together, then have dinner?"

Mariah's heart beat wildly in her chest. Was it even possible that he'd changed his mind? That last night had been as tough on him as it had been on her? That he wanted to end the madness and just go for it?

He tipped her chin up. "Your mouth says little, but your eyes say yes."

"You're right, but..."

"But?"

"As wonderful as this sounds, it's too extravagant for both of us."

"I insist on taking you as my guest."

"No—"

"Yes. There will be no argument. I rarely participate in frivolity. I, like you, am committed to work. I wish to—what is this word you use?—spluge a little."

She laughed. "I think you mean *splurge*."

"Of course." His grin widened and he led her inside. "We will leave in one hour."

As Mariah readied herself for their day trip, Zayad finished up an important phone call. It had been short and to the point. Tara Hefner was expecting him at one o'clock today, and he would not be late.

A flash of guilt invaded his belly, but he pushed it aside. He had come to California for answers and he would have them.

Mariah gazed around the inn's sumptuous lobby and felt totally out of place in her jeans and white tank top. "Well if you wanted to *spluge* a little, this is how you do it."

"It is comfortable," Zayad said without enthusiasm.

Mariah snorted. "You must've really lived the high life before coming here, because this is way more than comfortable."

Grand in scale yet inviting and peaceful in its Mexican flavor, the Ojai Spa boasted beautiful yellow travertine tiles, overstuffed white couches, handmade rugs and a ton of exotic plants. She'd never seen anything like it. Heck, the only place her ex-husband had ever taken her was the Yellow Duckling Bed-and-Breakfast in Buelton—which also happened to be the pea-soup capital of the world.

"Welcome to the Ojai Spa." A fresh-faced young man and an exquisitely fit woman in her fifties, both dressed in white, sidled up to them with two cups of lemon-and-cucumber-scented water. "Sir, I will take you to your changing area, and Delilah will take you, Ms. Kennedy."

"Well, I guess this is goodbye," Mariah joked, giving Zayad a broad smile.

"Not for long, mi'nâr."

"What does that mean?"

He only grinned, then walked away from her, leaving the fresh-faced kid to run after him toward the locker room. For a moment Mariah just watched. He, too, wore casual attire—linen pants and a white shirt—and looked completely at home in the fancy surroundings.

Gotta be the attitude, she thought.

"Please come with me, Ms. Kennedy." Delilah led Mariah down a marble hallway and through a door marked Ladies. Once inside she found herself blanketed in the spa atmosphere. As she sipped her water, she took in the marble everything—the hot tub, steam shower and dry sauna. It was pure loveliness, and she was glad Zayad had talked her into coming here.

Delilah found Mariah a locker, then handed her a soft, white robe and one matching slipper. "I suggest you take your ankle brace off and enjoy a nice soak in the whirlpool before your massage, Ms. Kennedy. It's scented with rosemary and mint and is very relaxing."

"Okay, thank you."

Delilah nodded, then gave her a very coy smile. "Enjoy your stay and the massage." She pointed to a door at the far end of the locker room. "That will take you to your room. It's number five."

Mariah wasn't even going to try and figure out the woman's strange smile. Mariah was in paradise and she was going to enjoy every moment.

After a quick shower, she settled into the steamy, hot and deliciously scented whirlpool. Thirty minutes seemed like only seconds when she got out and slipped on her robe. *Must be the way of the spa,* she mused as she headed into massage room number five.

The lights in the room were dim and soft, and relaxing music played. The scent of vanilla permeated her nostrils and she breathed it in, smiling. In the center stood the luxurious massage table laden with towels and a note.

Curious, Mariah picked it up and read.

Please get undressed. Lie facedown. And prepare to be pampered.

Mariah shrugged out of her robe without a thought. After all, who was she to question the experts? With a decadent smile she climbed onto the table, slipped under the sheet and blanket coverlet and rested her head on the soft open circle.

The music, candle and dim lights did their job. She was just starting to drift off when the door opened and her therapist entered. The woman said nothing, merely folded down the blanket covering Mariah's back and got to work.

With one almost sensual stroke from her shoulders down to her lower back, Mariah came fully awake.

These were not feminine hands that massaged her—unless the woman had worked on a fisherman's boat for the past ten years. No, these were male hands, rough and strong.

She tried not to be prudish. After all, didn't people get massages from both sexes all the time? And she hadn't specified a preference at the front desk.

Maybe she should have.

Maybe this was why Delilah had been practically sniggering.

"Are you comfortable, Ms. Kennedy?"

Or maybe not.

Mariah's skin tightened, and all relaxation fell away. She lifted up and whirled around, the sheet covering her buttocks falling to one side. Standing above her in black drawstring pants, black T-shirt and magnetic black eyes was none other than Zayad.

He lifted a brow. "Too rough?"

Nine

She looked shocked and a little bit panicked, and Zayad wanted to put her mind at ease.

Along with several other areas on her beautiful body.

Acting the professional, he righted the loose sheet—though it pained him to do so, as her sweet backside was pure pleasure to behold. But he would start slowly, let her grow accustomed to his touch, ease her into relaxation.

He turned to a nearby table and applied some fragrant oil to his hands. "I apologize for startling you."

"What are you doing in here?"

"I thought perhaps you would feel more comfortable if I gave you a massage instead of a stranger."

In actuality he had been thinking about this all morning. He had nearly missed the exit for Ojai as the plan unfolded in his head. Mariah nude, her skin glowing with oils as he stroked her. Upon his arrival the spa had informed him that such a plan was out of the question, but as always, money had changed their minds. And it was a good thing, too, as there had been no female masseuses available today, and although Zayad hated to admit it, he did not want another man's hands on her.

"Instead of a stranger?" Mariah said with a stilted chuckle. "*You're* practically a stranger, Zayad."

He picked up her uninjured foot. "This is untrue. Have we not touched?" He began to knead her skin. "Have I not covered your mouth with mine? Is this the act of a stranger?"

Mariah felt as though she would melt right there. He did have a point. "No, not the act of a stranger."

He grinned, worked each toe with gentle yet firm strokes. "If I do not please you, tell me now and I will summon Larz."

"Larz?" Mariah laughed softly.

"One of the masseurs on duty. A large Swede with wild eyes."

"Is that so?"

"Yes." Zayad shook his head. "What a man like that could know about hot stone massage is nothing."

"And you do?"

"A common practice in my country." He took a stone from a small basket, held it up. "Shall I continue?"

"This is the strangest thing that's ever happened to me, but—"

"Yes?"

"All right." She turned, let her head fall back into the doughnut-hole thingy and let human nature take its course. "So, why did we have to come all the way here if you're such an expert?"

After a moment he said, "This massage is just one of many treatments—and the only one I will administer."

"No sugar rubs or deep-sea exfoliation back home?"

"No." He placed several stones on her back, then applied light pressure. "A woman's skin would not be fed sugar strictly for the purpose of beauty."

Heat fused into Mariah's belly, then quickly spread downward, between her thighs. "I'm almost too afraid to ask…"

"We use such things as…I think you call it foreplay."

"Foreplay?"

"It is not a common practice but a sensual game." He removed the stones, then massaged deep and wonderfully hard in the hot spots.

"A game," Mariah mumbled, feeling too good.

"Stimulating the skin for the woman while stimulating the tongue for the man."

Mariah fairly jumped with tension as his words hit her full force. Her mind took hold of an image and clung to it. An image she'd not allowed herself in years. A man's head between her thighs—this man's head between her thighs.

She inhaled deeply as her breasts tingled and her belly clenched.

And then hot stones were placed on the back of her neck and the soles of her feet.

She gave a startled gasp, or maybe it was a moan of pleasure—who could tell at this moment? She was hardly thinking straight.

"The heat will ebb," he told her soothingly. "Then fuse into your muscles."

As he spoke, the words he uttered turned to fact and she felt herself fall deeply into relaxation.

She let her mind drift, let her body go limp as he placed stones on her calves and her thighs. She didn't argue or feel embarrassed as he eased the towel from her and placed two hot stones on her bottom.

"How did you do it?" she asked, her voice as slow as her mind.

"Do what, Mariah?"

"This. This massage. The spa management would probably kick us out if they—"

"I have taken care of everything. There is no problem. Do not think of it."

"My mind should be a blank canvas, right?"

He chuckled. "No, you should be thinking of pleasure."

As if she could think of anything else at this moment. Well, besides Zayad on top of her, spreading her legs, entering her slowly as he nipped and kissed the back of her neck and the lobes of her ears.

"Please turn over."

Too lost in her fantasy, she muttered a raspy, "What?"

"Turn onto your back, Mariah."

"My back?"

"Yes."

The fantasy subsided and reality took over. Turning over meant she would be totally exposed—head to toe and everything in between.

The slow, rhythmic beats of her heart suddenly jumped and pounded. "Where's the towel?"

"You do not need it."

"I think I do."

She felt his face close to hers, his lips at her ear and his hands on her waist. "You have a beautiful body. Nothing to be ashamed of. If you could feel what simply looking at you has done to me, you would not fret as you do."

She turned her head, reveled for a moment in the feeling of his slightly stubbled jaw in that sensitive crevice between shoulder and ear. "Maybe I would like to feel what I have done to you, Zayad."

Maybe I desperately need to feel what I've done.

Maybe the thimbleful of self-regard I have left needs to feel it, too.

She felt him smile against her skin as he took her hand. "As you wish."

His lips remained by her ear while he put her hand on him. She took in a breath, felt suddenly dizzy. She'd never felt anything like him in her life. Rock-hard and very large. She wanted nothing more than to explore him, but Zayad didn't give her the time or the access.

He backed away. "Will you turn now?"

She slowly rolled to her back, trying to hide her satisfied smile. But it wasn't easy as his gaze moved over her, every hill, every valley.

His jaw looked tight with tension when he finally resumed his ministrations, taking her feet in his hands. "You would make a dead man come alive again, Mariah. And perhaps you already have."

His words tore into her, straight through her and into her heart. She suspected that this man was rarely vulnerable, rarely made such telling statements.

Up he moved to her calves, kneading the flesh with great care. Then to her knees and her quads. She felt so good, so on edge, so desirable. The closer his hands inched toward the pale curls at the apex of her thighs, the more her insides quaked with desperation, the more she imagined his fingers exploring and the steely hardness she'd felt a moment ago sliding slowly into her body.

He placed more stones on her hip bones, making her suck air through her teeth, sending heat to her core.

He placed warm stones at her breastbone and rib cage, arousing her belly, causing her breasts to tighten, her nipples to bead.

Her breath caught in her chest, then followed quick and slightly labored. She looked up, found him watching her, his nostrils flared, his lips thin.

"Do you enjoy?" he asked.

"Yes. Very much." *What a hell of an understatement.*

She wondered what he would do next. Remove the stones and finish the massage, then turn off the music and call it a day—leave her in a state of sexual panic and frustration?

But he didn't massage and he didn't leave. He leaned down and kissed her mouth. There was nothing soft or gentle about it. And she was glad. She wrapped her arms around his neck, pulled him on top of her, moaned as she felt the delicious weight of him.

He pressed openmouthed kisses down her neck, her collarbone, removing stones as he went—lapping at her hot skin with his tongue. Then he boldly took one full breast into his mouth.

Mariah whimpered, maybe even cursed—she wasn't sure. Zayad's tongue whipped over her jutting nipple, then he took her between his teeth. Squirming on the table, Mariah held his head in her hands.

But not for long.

He moved down, kissing her belly, grazing his teeth over her warm hip bones. Breath coming quickly, Mariah came up on her elbows to see him, watch him as he kissed and laved and nibbled her aching skin.

Lower he moved, clear on his target. But the awkwardness of the massage table had him leaving her for a moment. He stood, scooped his hands under her bottom and eased her forward. Her knees now bent, he pressed her legs apart and grinned.

Anticipation threatened to overwhelm her as he lowered his head and captured her with this mouth. She nearly screamed and muffled the sound with her hands.

He suckled her, let his tongue dance up the bundle of nerves at her core.

It had been too long, far too long.

She let her head fall back.

Heat built inside her and she knew she would orgasm quickly. She hated the fact but didn't want him to slow, didn't want herself to slow.

She arched her hips, pumped against his mouth. Then she stopped, stilled. Heat and pressure and tension all conspired, led her over the moon and into deep pleasure.

Over and over the waves hit, and she bucked and arched and moaned. Until finally the ebb came and she started to breathe again.

"Mariah..."

She reached out for him, but he stayed where he was, even bent to pick up her towel.

With supreme gentleness he placed the cotton over her. "I must leave you now."

"No." She sounded like a child, but she didn't care. She'd only gotten half of what she wanted.

"I must." He bent over her, kissed her mouth. "I will see you in two hours, yes?"

She sighed, knew it wasn't wise to take more right here, right now. "All right."

He went to the door, turned back. "You had much pleasure?"

"Yes."

He nodded, then left, and Mariah sat up. She felt tight and happy and sad and unsure. She was no longer the bitter, chaste divorcée. She was now a woman on the verge of intense desire for a man she hardly knew and didn't trust.

He had hated to leave her.

Zayad pulled into the assisted-living-center parking lot, found a space and cut the engine. Even though a sign marked Guest was directly in front of him, he saw only a dimly lit room, a massage table with white towels and one of the most beautiful women he had ever seen lying naked atop them, bucking and gasping with climax.

He inhaled, tried to rid his mind of her—for now, at least. But it was impossible. Her scent lingered, as did the feeling of her skin on his palms.

Damn his lack of control. He had come here to question Tara, not to find himself fantasizing—and certainly not to find himself feeling actual need for a woman he would never see again after his two weeks were through.

He ripped his keys from the ignition and got out of the car, walked across the lawn to Tara's bungalow door. He would have to fight his desire for Mariah Kennedy. He could not allow this kind of pull, this kind of distraction, when he had work to do here.

After two decisive raps on the door, it opened and the lovely older woman who had so captivated his late father stood before him.

"Good afternoon, Zayad."

"Ms. Hefner."

"Tara, please." She smiled, stepped aside so he could enter.

"Thank you for letting me come, Tara. I know you did not have to."

"I'll admit I'm just as curious as you are." She showed him into the same living area where they had begun their last visit. She had some lemonade and cookies set out on the coffee table. She took a glass and started for the pitcher of lemonade.

"Allow me," he said.

"Thank you."

He poured her a glass, then eased it into her hand. He also took a cookie and placed it on a napkin in front of her on the table.

"Thank you," she said with a grin.

Her ability to sense or hear the smallest of movements amazed him. "If I may ask, how did you lose your eyesight?"

"I have macular degeneration."

"I am sorry."

"I'm not."

"Really?"

"Well, that's not entirely true. I would love to see my work, my child's face, Mariah in the courtroom and your wicked grin—the same as your father's, I'll bet. But I can't have those things. I see in a different way and I came to realize that sometimes that is a good thing. I believe now that it was a precious gift to have my sight taken from me." She paused, smiled. "You're shocked by that, right?"

He took a cookie. "I am intrigued."

"Good answer." She also reached for her cookie. "When I lost my sight, it was slow. Darkness took over the light little by little. Before, I had lived a life of judgments, as I think we all do. What we see on the outside is, of course, what is on the inside. We hardly question this. But when you start losing the ability to see the outside of anything, you're forced to deal only with the heart, with the deeds, with the real stuff."

She took a breath, then smiled. "All judgments left me, and instead I had questions. No more anger or cynicism or 'why mes,' only curiosity and compassion." She looked at him, her eyes so blue, so kind, yet there was a little sadness there. "I say no regrets, true. But I'll admit I've always had a hole in my heart for a time that ended too shortly."

The cookie felt dry in his mouth. "The three days with my father?"

"Yes." She leaned back in her chair. "He was an amazing man. Our time together was magical. Morally right or wrong, it was the best three days of my life—except for Jane's arrival."

"You loved him?"

"Very much."

Zayad's chest tightened. Why had he asked that? He did not care for love. This was about Jane and her future. This was about wanting to know why his father had given so much of himself to this woman. Who she was. Perhaps it was also about knowing his father better.

She nibbled on the cookie and tucked her feet up under her. "I know this is probably the last thing you want to hear, but it's part of the story. I thought your father cared for me a great deal. When he left, he told me he loved me. But we both understood that we belonged to different worlds. And of course, he had a family."

"Yes," said Zayad with mild tension.

"And I would never have messed with that. But I just couldn't believe that what we shared was all a lie. That he didn't care for me at all. And it kills me to know that he didn't even care for the life growing inside of me."

Though Zayad hadn't come to ease the pain of his father's mistress, he knew he must say something. "I am certain he would have cared for Jane if he had known."

"Known?" For the first time since he had met Tara, she looked completely unsettled. "Of course he'd known, he just didn't—"

"My father did not know of your pregnancy, Tara."

Her brows knit together. "What?"

"He knew nothing."

"No, that's not possible." She shook her head. "His aide said—"

"The man did not inform my father of your calls or

of Jane's existence. He felt he was protecting my father and the royal family from—"

"Don't say it." She put her hand in the air as though to block all negativity from reaching her. Then she let it fall, and her face fell along with it. "Are you really telling me the truth? He never knew he had a daughter?"

"He did not."

"So, he didn't lie to me." It wasn't a question. A look of hope crossed her features, and she took a moment to just breathe. Then suddenly she looked pensive again. "Why have you come to America, Zayad? Why have you sought out Jane? To tell her about her heritage or to see if she's worthy enough to accept it?"

"Both."

She nodded, her lips thin. "You will not hurt my child."

"I have no intention of hurting her."

"She's innocent. I never wanted to burden her with stories of her father. She knows nothing of this."

"She must."

Tara paused, bit her lip, shook her head. "Yes. I suppose so."

"I want to talk with her when she returns from Los Angeles."

"No, I will tell her when she comes to me next week." She nibbled more on her cookie. "As much as it pains me, we all have to know our truths."

Zayad nodded, agreeing fully. Truth could be a bitter pill to swallow, but there was no way to escape it.

"And what of my other child?" Tara said.

Zayad's brows drew together. "Mariah?"

An almost sad smile hovered about her lips. "She's

growing fond of you. She hasn't looked twice at a man in ages. To be honest, it scares me to death."

"She has nothing to fear from me."

"You're going back to Emand, right? To your work and your life."

"Yes."

"And you're going to leave her here broken-hearted. I've been there, Zayad. In love and alone. It's not something I wish for Mariah."

"Mariah does not have such feeling for me."

"Maybe not right now but soon. I see it in her."

"You see—"

She smiled. "I sense it. Please be careful. With both of my girls, okay?"

"I will."

When Zayad pulled away from the center, he felt as confused as ever. He had wanted to hate this woman, to tell her that his father could not possibly have loved her, to laugh at her story and admissions of care for the sultan. But he could not and did not, as those were the reactions of an affronted child.

He took each curve of hill a little too dangerously. He was beginning to feel something new—an out-of-control feeling that worried him. He wished he could speak of his fears with Mariah. He did not know why, but he felt close to her, a friendship as well as desire. But it was unwise to engage her in emotion. If what Tara had said was true, he could only allow himself the closeness of skin and sweat and desire.

A shot of disappointment went through him, and he despised himself for feeling so. When had this soft side where women were concerned overtaken him?

The ocean came into view.

He knew exactly when. It had been early evening several days ago, and a frustrated but heavenly lawyer had run headfirst into his chest.

He had surprised her.

Mariah had been under the impression that after several awesome spa treatments they'd be heading back home. But no. After her last treatment, a wonderful woman had come for her, led her out of the spa building and into the hotel portion of the inn. With just a sentence or two of explanation she'd left Mariah in the most gorgeous of suites overlooking a small lake littered with ducks.

Zayad had arranged this, the woman had told her. He wished for Mariah to relax and he would be here in an hour for dinner.

Mariah wanted to feel shocked by his boldness and maybe muster up some pangs of anxiety about the whole thing, but she couldn't get herself to feel anything except excitement.

Well, that and a little frustration that she hadn't brought anything but the casual clothes she was wearing. She was going to have dinner in this magnificent suite overlooking a lovely lake during sunset and she had no fabulous outfit.

Of course, she didn't own all that many fabulous outfits to choose from. And what really went with a brown ankle boot?

But when she walked into the white bathroom, she saw that Zayad had further surprises in store. Her toiletries were set up on the counter, and the two prettiest dresses she owned hung on the shower rod, along with one she didn't recognize. It was a pale yellow silk slip dress, very beautiful and very expensive looking.

Without a thought she knew Zayad had bought it for her and she also knew she was going to wear it tonight.

After a quick shower, a long blow-dry and some light makeup application, she let the chef in, then reclined on the couch and waited for her date to arrive. As she sat there, her senses being pummeled by the scents of roasted lamb and fresh rosemary bread, she thought about the afternoon and specifically about the massage table. Shivers of desire rippled through her, but there were far more nerve-racking sensations to contend with. For the first time in years she'd allowed a man to touch her both emotionally and physically.

She was opening herself to getting hurt again.

Maybe if she didn't view this affair as she had her marriage, she could cast aside her fears about getting hurt. There is no commitment here, no words of love spoken, no promises made. She didn't have to have expectations of him, only pleasure for however long it lasted.

As the door opened and Zayad walked in, she wondered if that were possible.

Looking unbelievably handsome in a black suit and a crisp white shirt open at the collar, Zayad stopped in front of her. "You look beautiful, Mariah. The color of the sun is magnificent on you."

"Thank you, and thanks for the dress."

"It is nothing."

It was more than he could ever know. No man had ever bought her anything so personal.

"How was the rest of your day?" he asked.

"Wonderful."

"And your ankle?"

She lifted her booted foot so he could see. "Much better."

His gaze moved over her bare skin, from toes to midthigh. "Are you hungry?"

You have no idea. "I could eat."

"Our chef comes highly recommended." He helped her to her feet and led her over to the preset table in front of the French doors. "Can I pour you some wine?"

"That would be great, thanks."

The chef came out and placed the chicken, bread and salad between the white candles and red roses, then nodded at Zayad and left the suite.

When a curious Mariah turned to Zayad, he smiled. "I thought it best if we could dine alone. Is this all right?"

Alone with Zayad...

She smiled as much to herself as to him. "Of course." She took a sip of the white wine, then asked, "So, what did you do today while I was getting pampered?"

He offered her some bread. "I had some business to attend to. One of which was planning our dinner."

"Well, you did a great job. It's beautiful." *And you're beautiful.* She looked up at him. *And I don't know if I can pretend this means nothing more to me than sex.* "Everything's perfect."

Wineglass to his lips, he studied her. "Something is wrong."

"No."

His gaze bored into her. "Are you having regrets?"

"About what?" As if she didn't know.

"Allowing me to be your masseur instead of the Swede?" He reached across the table and took her hand. "For, you understand, I could not abide him touching you."

Delicious shivers crawled up her spine. "Why?"

"I would not like it."

She forced herself not to ask why again. "I don't think I would've liked it much, either."

"Then I was wrong? You have no regrets?"

She shook her head.

He played with her fingers. "There is something I must tell you, Mariah."

Oh, God, what? You're a woman? You have a woman? You want to bring a woman into our bed tonight?

She was going completely nuts.

He released a weighty breath. "I am only in California for a short time."

Not icky, not perverted, but definitely not good. "Okay."

"I want to be...as honest as I can with you."

"I appreciate that." *Sort of.*

"You see, my life is in Emand, my work, my son and—"

"Zayad, I understand. Really." She didn't want to hear any more. She knew now that this affair would end. Heart strings really wouldn't be attached. Knowing that, she simply could enjoy herself with no worries about the future. His honesty, though heartbreakingly disappointing, was refreshing. For once a man wasn't lying to her. She gave him a soft smile. "Let's talk about something else, okay?"

He took her hand and kissed it, then released her and reached for his wine. "What other treatments did you have, and were they as good as your massage?"

Flirting. Yes, this she could do, this she wanted. "The body exfoliation was pretty good."

"This is the one with sugar, yes?"

"Yep."

"To make the skin softer?"

Mariah laughed. "I hope so."

"I would be willing to judge this, if you would like."

"You'd be willing, huh?"

He flashed her a devilish grin, stood up and walked around behind her. He put his hands on her shoulders, let his palms rake down her arms. "Yes. Very soft."

She sighed, closed her eyes.

"But I feel I must explore further to make certain."

His hand slipped inside her dress. Her breath hitched as he palmed her bare breast, as he let his thumb move back and forth over her swollen nipple.

She released a moan. Forget food, forget talking and flirting and getting to know each other more. They had waited long enough, hadn't they? She needed this. Her body needed this. Clearly he did, too.

She stood, turned and faced him. "Take me to bed."

She waited for him to say no, not yet, after dinner. But he didn't. His eyes were black as ink and hot as hell as he nodded and said, "Yes?"

"Yes." She smiled, knew she looked desperate, on fire, totally ready and willing.

Zayad lifted her up, and she buried her head in his neck.

Ten

Mariah closed her eyes as Zayad laid her gently on the bed. She'd wanted this moment to happen, fantasized about it day and night, hoped against hope that Zayad was as into her as she was into him. But now that it was happening, she couldn't help but feel a bit self-conscious. After all, her last relationship had ended over sex. True, it had been her husband and another woman who had actually had the sex, but she'd always wondered if she'd driven him into that woman's arms— if she was a horrible lover.

But all thought died as Zayad lowered himself on top of her and claimed her mouth. The weight of him made her high, his chest smashed against her breasts, his erection pressed gloriously against her belly, the way he rubbed his lips back and forth over hers, swiped her upper lip with his tongue.

Mariah groaned with approval and arched her hips to meet him, her underwear feeling wet and confining. Her hands went around his neck, plunged into his hair.

"You want this, yes?" he uttered, tense.

"I want you," she answered breathlessly.

Zayad tugged at the thin straps at her shoulders, then pulled her dress down. She wore no bra, and he looked ready to feast. With one hand he explored the fullness of her breast, his thumb and forefinger torturing her stiff nipple. With the other he snuck under her dress, over her panties, and palmed the swollen V between her thighs.

"You feel too good, Mariah." He stroked her, quickly and lightly, then eased two fingers inside of her.

Her breath caught in her throat and her body quivered with the need to release. But she held on. She wanted to have him inside of her as she climaxed this time.

Zayad must have sensed her urgency or he simply couldn't wait. In seconds he had her dress off and his own clothing removed. And in mere moments his hands returned to her hot skin and his mouth found her nipple.

Heat pooled in her belly, and her hands raked down his broad back, down to his buttocks. She dug her fingers into his taut flesh, pressed him hard and rough against her. Desperation filled her. "Please, Zayad. I can't wait. I don't want to wait."

He lifted off her, reached over to the side table. With deft fingers he quickly protected her. "I am without control tonight. Forgive me."

She didn't understand him but didn't have time to ask as he rose up and positioned himself over her.

Her breath coming in gasps, Mariah spread her legs

wide. She was tight and he was large, but as he inched his way to paradise, she felt an all-consuming pleasure.

And then he was through and deep, and her breath caught in her throat.

He fit her perfectly.

Maybe this was different. Maybe this was the something real she'd never thought existed.

His eyes probed her soul as he dipped his head and kissed her hungrily. When he eased back from her mouth, he remained deep inside her, but his hand disappeared behind her head. He brought back a pillow, then easily slipped it under her hips without breaking their connection.

"What is this?" she asked.

"It will make your experience more fulfilling."

"I don't think that's possible."

His smile was soft, but his eyes were filled with intensity and heat. A heat she understood, and wanted to express. She squirmed beneath him. He grinned, this time with wicked intent, and he rose out of her, then pushed back in. His strokes were long and liquid as his pulse jumped in his temple.

Tension built like a rising dam inside her, and she knew she was close. She wanted to curse, wanted to cry. She wanted to stop and start again. But it was no use. And when he reached under her hips, lifted her higher, his rhythm changing, quickening, rising to a frantic pace, she leaped, then fell—sank into the waves and the quakes of pleasure, the heat and all of the beautiful electric pulses.

Zayad ground his hips against hers and called out in a husky male growl as his body quivered and shook. It was an amazing sight.

He dipped his head and kissed her again, a salty, searing kiss that sent another shudder through her. Then he sat up, brought her with him so they were both sitting, facing each other. It was an incredibly intimate gesture, and Mariah felt so connected to this man, she wanted to bury her head in his chest. But he wouldn't let her. He clearly had something to say.

"You have much passion, Mariah. But it has been buried deep, yes?"

Her throat went tight. "Yes."

His hands found her face. "You must release it."

Mariah stilled, not sure of what he was telling her. Was she not passionate enough? Her gaze fell. She felt as if she'd failed again. No wonder her husband had gone with another woman. Maybe she was frigid or something. "Am I a horrible lover?"

"No." He chuckled, tilted her chin up so she was forced to look at him. "This is not what I mean. You are wonderful. You are a woman filled with heat, with deep thought and a touch so extraordinary it makes me hard as stone."

"But—"

"There is no but." Zayad kissed her. "Your body gave like no other. You were wild and wonderful. I want not just the pleasure but the hurt behind your eyes, as well. I must release it. I must make you release it."

"Why?"

His gaze flickered, and he looked pained suddenly. "I do not know."

"I really don't think it can be released, Zayad. Or maybe I just don't want to show it to anyone ever again." The intimacy growing a little too tough to handle, she tried to move away from him. But Zayad wasn't about to let her feel her fear alone, much less let her leave.

"Tell me about this man who has made you question everything and everyone."

She shook her head. She didn't talk about him, about what happened, to anyone. Especially not now.

"Tell me," Zayad insisted.

He held her tightly and carefully, but held her to him until she finally said something. "He was handsome and charming and a great businessman—and one helluva good liar."

"And why is he no longer your husband?"

"He didn't want me." Tears threatened and she wanted to kick herself. "He wanted another woman instead."

"He was a fool."

She looked down.

He pulled her to him and lay back down on the soft pillows. "We must pity him. For he made many mistakes and they cost him the most amazing woman in the world."

Mariah put her head to his chest, feeling emotional and confused. She took a deep breath. "No more of him. Tell me about your homeland. Make me think beautiful thoughts."

"All right." He kissed the top of her head. "Ah, Emand. Nowhere in the world is there a better place. Dawn is my time. I love it." He played with her hair as he spoke. "The sun is just making its entrance. So slowly, you feel as if you have wasted many hours in its presence. Yet you feel no regret for it. The sand of the desert is cool, a dirty brown color, before the sun meets it. Then it turns copper. The gardens are fragrant and lush, the mountains and lakes pure and untouched. The people, though deep in their traditions, are generous and forgiving."

"Why would you leave such a place? Even for a short time. It sounds like paradise."

He pulled her to him, held her tightly. "Business can take you away from even the most wondrous of settings."

Neither one of them spoke after that. They cuddled and stroked until sleep took them both. Mariah went willingly into her dreams. It was the first time in four years she'd slept next to a man.

It was the first time in Zayad's life that he had slept beside a woman.

He had always appreciated being alone. There was a certain comfort in it, an understanding between himself and his lover that what had transpired between them in bed would not transcend his desire for solitude.

Zayad stood at the balcony window of their suite, watched the black sky being eaten up by the dusk that came an hour or so before dawn.

Last night he had consciously pulled Mariah into his arms and fallen asleep. He had wanted to wake up with her, wanted to make love to her again, wanted her open in both mind and spirit beside him. He wanted to rid her heart and mind of that bastard she had called her husband.

He closed his eyes for a moment, then opened them hoping he would see gardens and beyond, miles and miles of sand. He missed Emand. He felt like a boy for feeling that way, but it could not be helped. After all, he was acting as a child—forgetting why he was here, what he was after, all for the sake of a beautiful and enticing woman.

He heard her get out of bed, heard the rustle of a sheet as she walked. She came to stand beside him and he glanced her way. The washed moonlight illuminated the thin white sheet wrapped around her from breast to foot. Her skin looked soft from sleep. Her blond hair fell about her shoulders. She didn't say anything, just moved in front of him and splayed her fingers on his chest. He released a breath, and she let her fingers snake downward, over his belly, to the black hair below his navel.

He was hard before she fisted him.

Her eyes on his, she massaged him, stroked him, made him groan with need, then when he was ready to take her, she released him. Slowly she lowered to her knees, thrust his legs apart. His gut tight with anticipation, Zayad gripped the top of the doorway. Mariah cupped his buttocks with one hand and eased him into her mouth with the other.

Zayad nearly howled.

She let her fingers dig into his backside as she suckled him deep. Then she drew back and flicked the tip of him with her tongue. Zayad reached behind himself and took her hand, squeezed. He knew it was a sweet, sentimental gesture, but he could not help it. It was how he wanted her.

She pumped him slowly and deeply, and when he felt himself on the brink of release, he uttered a hoarse, "Mariah," and eased her back and to her feet.

"We will find pleasure together, yes?" he said, his tone gruff.

Her lips wet, her eyes brilliant with desire, she pushed him back against the bed. Zayad grinned, for he knew she was casting aside her fears and taking control, taking what she wanted for the first time in a long time. But that smile quickly waned as she said, "Lift me up, put me on top of you."

His mind near to exploding, Zayad forgot to think and did as she instructed. "Wrap your legs around me."

"Yes."

They were clumsy, awkward, but it didn't matter. He was sheathed and inside of her in seconds, thrusting furiously as Mariah held on for the ride. Her head fell back and he devoured her neck, his teeth raking down, his tongue smoothing up.

And when he slipped his arm to her waist and she fell farther back, he took her nipple into his mouth, pushed her into release, then followed her, exploding into the predawn air.

"We have photographs, sir."

Sitting at a small glass table on the balcony of his suite, Zayad took a swallow of orange juice, then switched his cell phone to his other ear. "Are they worthy, Fandal?"

"Oh, yes, sir."

With a quick glance to the door, Zayad grinned. When Mariah returned, she would be very pleased indeed. On his insistence, she had gone down to the spa to have a manicure and pedicure before they left for home. She had fought him on it, she wanted to stay in bed, make love again. But Zayad had wanted to spoil her in more ways than sexual. If he had his way, they would fly to Los Angeles this very afternoon and he would take her to the finest shops in Beverly Hills— clothing, diamonds, anything she wished.

Many women he had known, including Redet's mother, would be vastly contented with such a plan, but something told him that Mariah would want nothing more than a lazy day in bed with him, holding him as he kissed her mouth, neck, breasts.... She had once had a man of means and had found it unfulfilling.

The thought made his chest tighten. He was growing contrite. He knew he must tell Mariah the truth—and soon.

"I would like to see one photograph," he told Fandal.

"I can bring it to you, sir. As you know, we are just two floors down."

He had almost forgotten. Almost. "No. Fax it to me immediately. Your best one."

"Of course, sir."

Zayad gave his aide the room's fax number, then hung up. He went inside and waited by the phone. In under a minute a photograph ambled through the fax. Zayad had it in his hands in seconds and looked it over thoroughly.

He grinned. His men had done well, and had laid four separate pictures on one sheet of paper. The top two were of the man and woman kissing outside a motel room. One of the bottom ones, though perhaps a bit too voyeuristic, was of the couple making love inside the room. And the last one was of the couple having dinner in a restaurant, very close. Zayad did not want to know how his photographer had gotten these, nor did he care.

Suddenly the door to the suite burst open and Mariah entered.

"The manicurist had some bad Chinese and had to go—" Mariah paused, stared at the paper in Zayad's hand. "What's that? Work?"

He shook his head, held out the fax to her. "I told you I would help you. I have a man tailing your client's ex-husband at all times. These are photographs of him and his lover."

Brow furrowed, Mariah made a beeline for the fax. She studied it hard from every angle, then looked up. "They're good—and you're amazing for going to all the trouble of helping me. Thank you."

"There is a but, yes?"

She nodded, dropped the fax on the table. "I'm afraid they won't help my case."

Eleven

"Why not?"

Mariah gave Zayad a bleak smile. "They only show that he's messing around now, not that he did before. Sure, it'll help, showing that he's lied about seeing someone recently. But it's his past infidelities—the affair he had while they were married—that's going to bring around the justice, show him as the liar he is."

"I see."

He was clearly disappointed, and the sight filled Mariah with gratification as much as empathy. Never in her life had a man cared this much about her and her pursuits. Zayad Fandal was a great lover and he was an amazing friend. She was lucky to know someone like him.

Though a little cursed, as well.

She went to him, put her arms around him. "You've been wonderful. Thank you."

"I have not found you your answers."

"You've done the best you could."

"No, but I will."

"I'll figure this out."

"With my further assistance."

She looked up at him, melted in the heat of his dark gaze. "You've done too much already—"

"I will see this through, Mariah."

"Why is it so important to you?"

"Because it is important to you."

Her heart squeezed just then, and she let her head fall against his chest. He felt so solid, so strong, his heart beating against her cheek. He made her feel like a woman, feminine and cared for, and she couldn't deny it any longer—she was in love with him.

Maybe these feelings in such a short time were crazy and stupid, but she didn't care. She felt alive. Bitterness had gotten her through the pain, but now it was stopping her from not only loving, but living.

A thought snaked into her brain. A thought built on hope. If Zayad had fallen in love with her, too, or was on his way, would he stay?

"There is another reason I wish to help you."

His words vibrated against her cheek, their content sending spirals of nerves through her belly. Was he about to tell her how he felt? What he wanted? Or was this an admission of something outside of them?

"I also do this for Redet."

Her belly clenched. "Your son." Of course. Of course he couldn't stay. He had a child in his country. A child he loved above all others. And if he even contemplated leaving his son to be with her, he'd be no better than the jerks she fought against in court.

Irony sucked.

There was no way this could work, she realized, her heart plummeting into her shoes. Her life was here, and his life was in Emand.

Zayad stroked her hair. "This man you battle, this man who cheats and lies on the woman he is bound to, does not deserve his child."

Anger and disgust filled his tone. Two emotions Mariah felt, as well. But she detected more than anger. There was a thread of disappointment, maybe even fear, in his voice. She didn't know his history, what he and his family had been through. She couldn't help but wonder if it played a part in those hidden threads of emotion. Or if what she was hearing was just his feelings regarding Redet and his mother.

She tilted her head, stared up at him. So handsome, so chiseled—such the look of the warrior about him. He made her weak with desire, yet his conviction and spirit made her admire him so much.

"Kiss me?" she said.

Fire lit his eyes, and he bent and covered her mouth with his own. All thought of anything but love evaporated into the gentle morning breeze floating in from the suite's French doors.

There were ten messages on the answering machine when they got home at noon, and Mariah knew she was in big trouble. All but three were from Jane.

There were several "This actress is making me insane

and I need to vent," a few "Where the hell are you?" and one "Call me back or I swear I'm going to call the police."

After changing her clothes and telling Zayad she'd see him later, Mariah picked up the phone. She paused before dialing, a little shocked at herself. She hadn't told Jane where she was going and what she was doing. She'd completely forgotten her soul sister, her mind totally focused on Zayad. After allowing a man to rule her thoughts and actions for many wasted years, she wasn't entirely sure how she felt about that.

"I could kill you right now," Jane barked, sounding far more relieved than angry.

Opting for a lighter mood, Mariah teased, "If only you weren't a hundred miles a way."

"Right." She took a breath. "So, how's the ankle?"

"Much better," Mariah said. "Listen, sis, I'm sorry I didn't tell you where I was going. It was just so spur-of-the-moment, ya know?"

"No, because you haven't done anything spur-of-the-moment in I don't know how long. Especially with a guy."

"This guy," she almost sighed, "as difficult as it is for me to admit, makes me forget my name, my responsibilities, my—"

"Mind?" Jane asked, her mild irritation morphing into an affectionate chuckle.

"Yes, actually."

"I can't believe you've fallen for our neighbor." Jane snorted. "It's so *Peyton Place.*"

"He's not going to be our neighbor for very much longer."

"What do you mean? Where's he going?"

"Back to his country." The words felt like sandpaper on her tongue.

"What? He's leaving you after all this."

Mariah took a breath. For the four years that she and Jane had been roommates, she'd always thought that Jane was the one who had done the influencing—her great food, her positive attitude. Some of that stuff had actually rubbed off on Mariah—or the hope that it would have rubbed off, especially the cooking part. But the truth was, Mariah and her negative, supposedly realistic, views on life and love had rubbed off on Jane, and now she was spouting that fear-based crud back at Mariah.

Irony really did suck.

Mariah didn't want to be the poster girl for sad women anymore. She'd tasted love again, and even though it might not last, it was spicy and addicting and she wanted more, no matter what the consequences.

"Jane, the thing is, he has a son. He can't stay here because he wants to be close to him. You know how I feel about that."

Silence ate up a moment or two. "Sure. Jeez, of course I do. What about going with him?"

"He's never mentioned it, and I'm not going there."

"Why not?"

"I won't push him. That'll only make me look desperate and make him feel cornered."

"But maybe he needs—" Jane never finished her sentence as a shrill shout from the other end of the phone had her cursing.

"I gotta go, M," Jane said. "Cameron Reynolds calls. I'll see you in a couple of days, 'kay?"

"'Kay."

"And don't do anything you'll regret." She laughed, then stopped. "Wait. What am I saying? Go for it. Hang from the chandeliers, order up some whipped cream and kinky toys. You of all people deserve it."

Mariah was still laughing as she hung up. She wasn't into kinky, but a few more nights like last night would be fabulous.

She walked over to the window and looked out over the backyard to the little house where her man of the moment was working out.

When they had been in the suite, it had been all romance all the time. But now they were home. Would things be different? Awkward? After all, he wasn't caring for her anymore—the invalid Mariah, that is. No, now they were lovers, friends, sharing each other.

She pushed away from the window and went to her computer, switched it on. When emotions ran high, she looked to her work for focus and perspective. Sure, she had a love affair going on, but her client was counting on her for help.

She had to win this case. And though the pictures Zayad's friend had taken might not help her win it, perhaps there was something in there that might help or get her thinking.

She snatched up the fax Zayad had tossed on the counter next to her mail, and settled into a chair to study it.

Sweat dripped down Zayad's temple to his jaw as he wielded his sword. Slashing left, then right and right again as he moved across the hardwood floors. His breath coming heavily, he made a quick turn, shot the blade to the ceiling and thrust it back down, halting just centimeters from the curve of a ripe apple.

He grinned. Yes, his son would do well with this sword.

The thought of Redet brought on more thoughts of family, and as Zayad reached for a towel on a side table, he realized that just two days remained until his sister returned. He had found out much from Mariah and was ready to know Jane for himself, ready to tell her the truth and take her back home.

He had not left room for her to refuse him and her title. He could not. Duty remained above all else, and Jane must understand this fact, too.

He held up the Scottish sword, turned his wrist to see its lines.

He recalled something his father had once said. "The heart of every blade is the steel from which it is forged." This blade was a combination of iron and carbon, a perfect blend that allowed him power and flexibility. In the ancient days, power had been most important. But as times changed and people opened their minds to new ideas, a balance was needed. Zayad and his people also had changed to serve the times.

Zayad glanced out the bay window to his right. Afternoon had melded into sunset without his knowledge. It was always thus when he took his exercise.

In that moment, his mind left politics and focused on something far more pleasing. Mariah. He had only two days left with her and he wanted them to be as wonderful and as pleasurable for her as possible. Surely when she found out why he was here and why he had not been forthcoming about his identity, she would want nothing more to do with him.

His gut clenched. He was a fool, but he did not want her to know who he was. He wanted things to remain as they were.

For the first time in his life someone was not aware of his role, his fortune, his title. Mariah cared for him as a man, not as a prince. And for that he would always be in her debt. Starting with her court case.

"Dinnertime."

Zayad turned, and his body went rock hard, fast.

There she stood, moonlight at her back, draped in a thin white cotton tank and little white cotton shorts. She looked ready for bed, not for dinner.

But then again, he mused as he walked to her, he could always be persuaded to eat dessert first.

Twelve

"**I** was wondering where we'd end up," Mariah said, burrowing deeper into the warmth of his chest.

Last night they had forgotten all about dinner and had gone straight to bed, where they'd quickly stripped back the sheets, then stripped each other bare.

Two hours later they'd fallen asleep. Two hours after that Mariah had woken Zayad up with a kiss in a very sweet, very sensitive spot.

Needless to say, the rest of the night had pretty much followed this pattern.

Zayad kissed the top of Mariah's head. "What is this 'end up'?"

She laughed. "Between our two apartments. I wondered if we were going to end up in your bed or in mine."

"Ah, well, as long as we are in bed together, yes?"

"Oh, yes."

Dawn broke with resplendency outside her picture window, and Mariah sighed. She watched the morning's creamy yellow light creep in and hint at a beautiful day. A bright sunny day was always in favor, but for Mariah it really wouldn't matter if a hurricane blew in. She wasn't about to let anything bring her mood down. She was savoring the time she had left. She had just one day with her man until Jane returned and things got different and…well, back to normal. There would be questions asked—questions she didn't even want to look at, much less answer right now.

Since the day she'd smashed into this amazing man, she'd been having the time of her life. And as long as the fantasy kept rolling along in this perfect manner, she had a ticket to ride.

She let her hand trail down Zayad's chest to his belly, let her fingers brush over his navel. "I like sleeping in the same bed with you," she said, having no fear of how vulnerable she sounded. "I thought I'd never like sharing a bed. I've grown accustomed to being alone, sleeping alone, living alone."

"You do not live alone."

"I wasn't talking about sharing space. I meant inside my heart. I'm alone inside my heart. By choice, of course, but…"

"There is comfort in being alone at times. Even in the heart. Sometimes such detachment protects us, no?"

"You bet." She sighed, slid her knee across his thigh, the weight of her boot slowing the process a bit. "I spent four years protecting myself, maybe longer."

"And now?"

"I don't want to do it anymore."

"Even if that means being hurt again?"

"Even if that means getting my heart shredded to bits."

Zayad put a hand to her face and tilted her head, looked at her with complete bewilderment. "How can you say this after all you have been through?"

"Because I've been slowly dying these past four years. Sure, I was protecting myself all the while. But a life built out of fear is no life at all."

"I try not to think such thoughts."

"Why? Because you believe that things shouldn't change or because you're afraid of what will happen if they do?"

He stiffened, and the light, loving mood of a moment ago was lost.

"I'm sorry." She shook her head. "That was wrong and pushy of me. It's your life, your choice."

He gave her a dusty, glum smile. "We do what we must. And our changes come in our own time."

She nodded, then put her head back on his chest. He was right. Even though he had been the impetus to her change, her acceptance of life after a hideous divorce, maybe he wasn't ready to move away from his tricky history. Maybe, like her, he needed to fall in love to get there.

Her heart actually squeezed with pain, but she mentally shook it off. Zayad may not love her, but, unlike her ex and the losers in the courtroom, he had integrity. He'd never promised her anything, never told her he loved her, then snatched away her trust by cheating and lying.

No. He just wasn't ready.

She came up on her elbow, gave him a winning, playful smile. He had done so much for her, been a caretaker, a friend, a lover. If he was going back home in the next week or so, she wanted to make sure he wouldn't forget her—or the time they'd spent together.

"Any plans for today?" she asked.

"Yes."

Oh.

She looked away. Of course he had other things to do. Not every day could be a play day. And she could use the time to work and clean up the house and…

His hand was on her cheek, his thumb brushing over her lower lip. "After my physician takes a look at your beautiful ankle, I have plans with you, mi'nâr."

"Are you going to tell me what that means?"

"Perhaps one day." His sexy black eyes crinkled at the corners as he grinned. "I was thinking about the beach."

Her heart skipped and she smiled in return. "A picnic lunch?"

"Yes, with a little wine perhaps."

"And sand-castle making."

His brow furrowed. "What is this sand castle?"

"You don't know what a—" She waved her hands, tried to look aghast, but just ended up laughing. "I'll show you. You're gonna love it. After all, it's an artistic endeavor."

Zayad sat back in the warm sand and smiled. He was excessively proud of his work, but today that did not seem to be enough.

Curious.

He had never needed anyone's approval.

He glanced at Mariah, magnificent in a pale blue bikini, her curves making him tight with need, her smile making him wonder if true happiness might not be possible after all. She was different from any woman he had ever known. He would admit this much. He also would acknowledge that he wanted her opinion, her praise.

No. He needed it.

Gesturing toward the shape he had created in the sand, he asked, "How does my structure look?"

"Fabulous," she said, her hair whipping in the breeze like a golden sail. "It looks like something out of a Disney movie."

"Does it? Well, this is no imitation of a movie set, mi'nâr. This is the sultan's palace in Emand."

"Really?" She looked impressed.

"Without the wondrous gardens, swimming pools and other exterior additions."

"Of course." She laughed. "Well, it's pretty fancy, not too mention insanely enormous. The sultan must get lost just getting up to brush his teeth."

"I am sure he knows his way." Zayad's gut clenched. This charade had started out with purpose and understanding, but now it had turned into a lie. A cover-up. He was not proud of this. He did not want to continue deceiving Mariah. He cared for her too much now. He would tell her the truth. Tonight.

For a moment he wondered why he had not revealed himself sooner. He knew it was not because Mariah would tell Jane before he had his chance. Well, it might

have been initially. But over the past few days he had
wanted nothing to interfere with their affair. Nothing.
Not even his duty, not even his honor.

The knowledge clawed at him like a Feron scorpion.
He had deliberately cast aside the good of his country
for this woman, and his principles for their pleasure.
Perhaps it was good he was leaving soon.

"Is this a new palace," Mariah asked, tugging him
from his thoughts. "Or one of those ancient places you
read about in the history books?"

"To the people of Emand, it is timeless. The royal
family has lived in the palace for centuries."

"Do you know their history pretty well?"

"I do."

"The current sultan—is he old? Does he have several wives and many kids?"

"Actually he is unmarried. And in Emand, though
the old customs are still accepted, the royal family has
always taken just one spouse."

She smiled as a wave crashed behind her. "I like
that."

"Yes, most Americans do."

She laughed. "And I like you."

His chest went tight at the compliment. A simple
compliment. But it held great truth and significance.
This woman did not know that the man they spoke of,
the wealthy prince who lived in a golden palace, was
the very same man who had made love to her all
through the night, the same man who wanted more than
anything to make love to her again right here, right
now.

No.

She thought him an ordinary man and she liked him.

He took her hand and kissed the palm. "What else do you wish to know?"

"Have you seen this sultan up close?"

"I have."

"What's he like? Dictatorial, fierce, demanding?" Her eyes shined with intrigue.

"He has a country to watch over, Mariah. There are times when he must be all of those things."

She nodded. "Of course. It's funny, we make royalty sound so romantic, but it isn't always that."

"It is rarely that...I imagine."

"What an incredibly hard job. But I'm sure he has many advisors to help him."

"Many, but surprisingly they are not as competent as he would like." He knew he should stop at that, but he did not. It was glorious to speak of such matters with a true friend. "This can be a source of frustration for him. Emand has many social-rights issues he wishes to address. It is not easy to turn around centuries of fears and prejudices and foolish ideas. But things are slowly coming along."

She grabbed a bottle of suntan lotion and squeezed a bit out into her hand. "This sounds like one forward-thinking sultan."

Her admiration pleased him. "I am proud to say that he is."

She dabbed the sunscreen on her cheeks and nose. "To right many wrongs, to help closed-minded people see beyond their senseless fears—that's a great job." Suddenly her shoulders fell, and she sighed. "It was the job I set out to do."

"You have." He reached for her and pulled her into his arms. "And you will continue to do this."

"I hope so."

"Enough of these low spirits now." He helped her to her feet, grabbed her hand. "Come with me."

"Where?"

"Do you not like surprises, mi'nâr?"

Mariah warmed at this new and wonderful endearment Zayad kept calling her, and she squeezed his hand. "I never have liked surprises much, but the ones you keep cooking up are slowly changing my mind."

He turned to her and gave a little bow. "I hope that I may always grant you extraordinary surprises."

All thoughts of work and fears of failure were snatched away in the salty breeze. Mariah shivered with excitement as they walked away from the seaside and their castles and into the beach grass.

"I found this place the day after I moved here," Zayad told her as he led her down the side of a small-ish sandy hill.

The sound of the waves crashing against the shore still clung in the air, but no longer were they amongst the public. Zayad had found a private refuge, a lovely cave.

The hollowed-out rock before them beckoned for strangers to enter, and they did. Mariah had no clue what to expect—damp, smelly, dead fish…who knew?

But she couldn't have been more wrong.

All the seaweed and wet earth and rock she'd expected had been cleared away. In the center of the cave, sitting atop clean sand, was a large and very colorful carpet. And on top of the carpet was a picnic lunch.

Actually it was a feast. Meats and cheeses, salad and fruit and cake and wine. She could see this very well indeed, as there were several gashes in the rock wall where seductive little shards of sunlight peeked in.

She'd never seen anything like it and imagined she never would again.

Zayad urged her to sit on the carpet, a shaft of warm sunlight piercing her shoulder and thigh. "I thought we should have our privacy," he said, falling down beside her.

She took in his hard chest and sinewy thighs and fairly sighed with desire. "How did you do this? When did you do this?"

He grinned, took a piece of melon from a plate. "I asked a few...friends to assist me."

"Nice friends. This is incredible."

"I am glad it pleases you." He guided the sweet melon into her mouth.

Didn't he understand that he constantly pleased her? "You've spoiled me for other men, Zayad."

She hadn't meant to say that aloud. She'd been trying to be playful, complimentary—and maybe, in some crazy way, honest about how much she cared for him, how over-the-moon in love with him she was.

But there was nothing playful in those black eyes of his. No, they burned with ire.

"I do not want to think of you with another man," he said gravely.

"Neither do I." Hell, she didn't want to think about another guy for the rest of her life. "Or you with another woman."

"I want no other woman."

"I know. Not now, but—"

He put his hand on hers. "Please. Let us eat, yes? I despise this subject."

So did Mariah, but she couldn't stop herself from going there, from thinking about his future and hers without him in it. But she knew she must. If only to preserve their last day together. "This spread is something else. And I'm starved." She grinned, leaned in and kissed him, hoped that her gesture would inch them toward playful once again. "I've worked up an appetite building that palace."

He tossed her a wry grin. "Did you now?"

"Yep."

He raised an eyebrow.

"Fine, I wasn't actually involved in the building part, but I did haul all that sand and water. You got to give me that."

"Yes, I give you that." He looked as though he wanted to say more, but he didn't. He filled a plate with food and handed it to her. "Come. Let me serve you."

They ate their pretty picnic lunch. They talked about her case, his art and their shared penchant for raspberries. Time flew by and before they knew it, afternoon had appeared, taking away the pretty sunshine and replacing it with shady beams of gray and the drumming sounds of rain on the cave's roof.

Mariah cleared away the dishes and placed them at the entrance to the cave. When she returned to the carpet, she eyed Zayad, looking all too handsome with his black swim trunks, mussed black hair and fiery gaze. "Looks like we're not going anywhere for a while."

The left side of his mouth tipped up. "Are you content with this?"

"Being stuck with you, you mean?"

He nodded.

"I think so." She turned coy and flirtatious and sank to her knees at the edge of the carpet, her fingers playing with the straps of the modest bikini top she'd bought on her way to the beach this morning. "But what shall we do?"

With a full-fledged grin attached, he crawled toward her, an animal stalking its prey. "I can think of several things."

She scooted back playfully. "Like what?"

Quick as a cat, he had his arm about her. He flipped her to her back and rested his chin on her belly. "This."

He kissed her hot skin.

"That's nice," she said, her breath in her throat.

He tugged down her bathing suit bottom, grazed his teeth over her hip bone. "And this."

"Yes." It was more of a squeak than a word, but she didn't care. She loved when he nibbled and suckled and tasted, made her forget everything and just enjoy. Unable to stop herself, she squirmed beneath him, thrust her hips up.

And he answered her call.

His eyes on hers, he eased down her bathing suit. "And this."

"Yes, Zayad. Please." Never in her life had she begged for something, especially something so intimate. Maybe she'd always thought she didn't deserve this kind of love, that she wasn't sexy enough, desirable enough...

Zayad's gaze flickered to the tuft of soft curls between her legs. "Yes, this could keep me occupied for hours."

Mariah could say no more, think no more, as he eased her apart and slid his tongue inside her. Deep and deeper still, until she couldn't breathe. His hands slid under her buttocks and he squeezed.

She sucked in air.

He eased out of her and blew his warm breath over the tense bundle of nerves at her core. "You taste like heaven, mi'nâr."

She moaned, fisted sand.

Slowly, achingly slowly, he slid his tongue upward, between her wet folds. Back and forth so slowly, building her toward the most intense climax of her life.

"Zayad, please," she begged.

"What is it you need?"

"You...faster...please."

"I cannot." He swept his tongue back over her. "I must go slow."

The intensity burned inside her. Her nipples were hard beneath her bathing suit top. Wet heat leaked from her onto the carpet. And outside the cave the waves roared and crashed against the sand while the rain continued to fall.

And then Zayad raised the stakes.

His tongue on her, his breath on her, he took his hand from beneath her bottom and slipped three fingers inside her.

Mariah shook, shuddered, grabbed a fist full of his hair and rode him, bucked against him. Zayad pushed deeper and she couldn't hold on. With a cry she climaxed against his mouth.

In the glowing aftermath, Mariah reached for him, wanted him to slip inside her. But surprisingly and sadly he didn't. Instead he held her tightly against him, kissed her hair and followed her into sleep.

Thirteen

The road was puddle after puddle, and Zayad wished he were back in the cave beside, beneath or on top of Mariah.

But good things had to come to end, yes?

And as the afternoon had worn on and the rain had subsided, they both had known it was time to go. Once in the car, Zayad had secured Mariah in her seat with the seat belt, a blanket and a kiss, then headed away from the beach and toward home.

Now only the sound of the radio could be heard as they drove. He thought about what would happen when they got home, when Jane returned tomorrow. Mariah was doing a little work beside him. She scanned the photographs Zayad's man had taken of her client's cheating ex-husband. She looked contemplative and uneasy. Zayad felt suddenly protective of her and wished she would put the photos away and talk to him. There were issues they had yet to discuss—not amusing issues but important ones. For instance, she had not asked him why he'd pulled her into his arms after making love to her in the cave, instead of pulling her beneath him. He knew it was on her mind. It was certainly on his. If she did ask, he was prepared to say that he had no protection. Which was the truth.

But there was more.

Much more.

He *had* been ready to make love to her, with or without protection. He had wanted to feel her inside and out, with no barriers, and had been ready to damn the consequences.

This fact had scared the life out of him, and he had forced back his desire and given her all the pleasure he could afford.

If he were honest with himself, he would admit that Mariah Kennedy had captured his heart—or what remained of it—and that he did not want to leave California in one week's time.

"Ohmigod!"

The outburst had Zayad jerking to attention. He glanced her way. "What's wrong?"

She was holding up a photograph, staring intently at it. "I can't believe this."

"What is it?" Zayad asked.

"There is something here." She shook the photograph, grinned. "Something we missed before."

"What?"

"Or something I missed."

"Mariah, you make me crazy," Zayad said, exasperation threading his tone. "Suspense in such matters as these is cruel."

"Sorry." She grimaced. "What we've got here is a blue Tiffany's box and an engagement ring."

"I do not understand." Zayad pulled off the main road and shoved the truck into Park.

"Look at this." She pointed to the photograph of the cheating couple at dinner. "He's slipping a ring on her finger."

Zayad took a closer look. It was as she said. The man was placing a small diamond on the woman's left hand. "Yes, I see. But as you said before, this man's proposal happened in the present. He and your client are now divorced. It does not matter if he is with another woman."

Pure childlike excitement glistened in her tiger's eyes. "Unless he bought this for his mistress when he was still married."

Zayad paused, thought about this. "Go on."

"In the credit-card statements I went through during their marriage, there was a charge from Tiffany's. When I asked my client about it, she told me she knew all about it and that it was just a birthday present for herself and the twins—they all have the same birthday. And the amount didn't raise suspicion because he'd always given her and her children extravagant gifts." Mariah shrugged. "So I didn't check it out."

Zayad shook his head. "I do not understand. He obviously did purchase these gifts."

"Yes, but maybe he added a small engagement ring to the bill knowing his wife would never check a birthday gift charge."

Her meaning became clear as glass and Zayad grinned. "You are brilliant."

She blushed. "Nah."

He laughed, momentarily forgetting that he did not belong with this woman, and allowed himself the pleasure of basking in her happiness. "I knew you could do this." His gaze swept over her covetously. "My man is still digging. Perhaps he will find something more on this man's past, and with this new development you have unearthed, your client will have her children yet."

Mariah granted him the most beautiful of smiles. "Yes, I'm starting to think that could really happen."

"What did I tell you?"

"That I might just win this case."

"And you will listen to me more often, yes?"

She shrugged, said playfully, "Maybe."

"Maybe?" He pulled her into his arms and kissed her breathless as rain began to fall once again against the windshield. "I want you," he uttered.

"I want you, too, but—"

"But perhaps we should get home?"

She moved to his ear and nibbled gently. "Car sex always sounds like fun, but I can't think it actually would be."

He grinned. "Agreed," he said, though at this particular moment, with Mariah's breath and teeth against his ear, he did not care overmuch about where he yanked down his zipper and placed her atop him. But it was her wish that they wait, and until he left, she was his princess. He would do as she bid him. "We should both take a few hours of work, yes? Then find each other for dinner?"

She nodded, her eyes flashing almond fire. "And dessert?"

"Raspberries?"

"Yes." Her gaze moved over his face. At first she looked hungry for more than raspberries, but then a look of melancholy shuttered her eyes.

"What is it?" he asked.

She shook her head. "It's nothing."

"Tell me."

She took in a breath. "I don't know. I've just never known a man so unselfish."

Unselfish? She could not be speaking of him, especially not when it came to her. All his moments, his choices, had been based on what was best for him—for his country, though they were one and the same.

Turning from her, he pulled away from the curb and back onto the road.

"And so supportive," she continued.

His fingers gripped the steering wheel. "I am none of these things."

"You are. The men I've known would never be so supportive."

"Your ex-husband did not support your work?"

"No way."

"Why do you think this was?"

"He never liked competition, in work or out."

Zayad sniffed arrogantly. "He wished to feel all-powerful over you, over his life. This is sad. He was a fool."

"For a long time I thought this was just how men were." She put her hand on his and he shuddered. "But you don't need to feel all-powerful, do you?"

The question nearly forced a brittle laugh from him. He was ruler in his country. He *was* all-powerful. But did he need this from those he cared for, women who were talented and intelligent and could debate and prevail? He believed not. Not now… "Everyone wishes to feel strong and competent in their lives, and I will admit in my younger years I exerted my authority over others for personal gain. But this childishness has thankfully left me."

"I'm glad. It's no way to live." She squeezed his hand, played with his fingers, then asked, "When did it leave you?"

He could have tossed out an answer—ten, twelve, fifteen years of age. But that was not true. The woman who had borne his child had been the one to send him out of childhood and into manhood. This and Redet were his only reasons for wishing the woman well.

As he pulled into their driveway, he said, "At twenty-one I was forced to realize that love and respect could not be commanded, forced or cajoled. It was a good lesson and one I intend to teach my son."

Admiration and something fearfully close to love swam in her magnificent eyes. He wanted to look away, did not want to see how she felt, did not want to get lost in her.

But for a moment he could not help himself.

Thankfully she turned and grabbed the door handle. "I'd better get to work. See if my assumptions are correct."

He nodded. "I had a wonderful day."

"So did I. Thank you."

Without thought he leaned in, kissed her tenderly on the mouth, then let her go.

It was only after she had closed the front door of her side of the duplex that the irony of that gentle action hit him full force.

Later that night they dined at her small but cute kitchen table. It was no cave with carpets and ocean strains, but Mariah had made the setting as romantic as she could. Candles and flowers from the backyard, wine goblets and Tara's silver.

She was pretty sure she'd done a bang-up job until Zayad said, "You are the very worst cook, Mariah Kennedy. A wonderful legal brain with legs to make a man sweat, but a cook—sadly no."

Mariah laughed. "I know. I'm completely hopeless. You didn't think it was possible to screw up spaghetti, did you?"

He held up a piece of limp pasta with his fork. "How long was this pasta cooking?"

"I got distracted."

"With work?"

No, not work, she thought. With him. Her brain was all about him. But she couldn't tell him that. She couldn't tell him that she'd been sitting at the kitchen table contemplating the future—specifically the weeks after Zayad left. No, she'd already billed herself as head over heels for him. Her eyes fairly dripped with love. She sure didn't need to tell him about her future career as a salesgirl for the self-help tapes *Pining for the Perfect Man*.

She filled his wineglass, then gave him another piece of bread. "Yes, I was thinking about my case."

"Do not worry, Mariah. I have told you it will go

smoothly. Especially now that you have spotted the flaw."

"You're right. I know you're right."

"It is a rare occurrence, but it does happen." He grinned. "You have confirmed the Tiffany's receipt, yes?"

"Yep. It was just as I'd thought."

"Very good."

A sudden breeze shot in through the open kitchen windows, sending the candle flames into a wild dance. Here they were having dinner again, kind of like normal people. A couple. Yet they were anything but normal and they certainly weren't a couple.

Mariah's heart dipped and she decided to switch topics. "So, have you spoken to your son?"

"Just one hour ago, as a matter of fact."

"How is he?"

"He is well. But I will see for myself soon enough."

She nodded, swallowed hard. Maybe they needed to get this out in the open, say what was on both of their minds.

Obviously Zayad thought so, too. He reached across the table, took her hand. "I miss my son and my home, yet…"

"Yes?" she said, foolishly hopeful.

"The thought of leaving fills me with a deep sadness."

"So don't leave," she said with a light chuckle, though she felt anything but light.

"I must." He took a swallow of wine. "It is complicated, Mariah."

"It always is." She eased her hand from his and

started gathering up the plates still heavy with her droopy pasta.

He grabbed her wrist. "Do not revert back inside yourself."

"I'm not."

"You are. For days you have been free and easy and happy."

Didn't he get it? Free, easy, happy, sexy, desired— it all came with him.

"I want you to understand my position," he said, clearly unwilling to release her so she could pout and pretend his departure meant nothing.

"I do understand, Zayad. You have Redet and a life there—"

"I *must* be in Emand. You are right—my life is there." A struggle went on behind his eyes. "A responsibility that is unlike any other. Now, if you wished to come with me, that would be a different—" He stopped cold, his dark skin going ashen. "What I mean to say—"

"No, please." She stopped him right there. She couldn't hear him take that back. Not if she didn't want to cry herself to sleep for the next two months. "Let's not say anything more tonight, okay? I can't hear you backtrack and I can't hear myself help you do it."

"Mariah…"

"Please. Let's just enjoy tonight."

He nodded, then gently coaxed her from her dishes onto his lap and into his arms.

By the flickering light of a single bedside candle Zayad pushed into Mariah's body. Hot, tight and wet, she closed around him, embraced his erection.

He groaned, a deep muffled sound against her neck.

He took her mouth, made love to her lips, her tongue, as he raised his hips, then thrust into her again.

His body was weak tonight and he couldn't wait. As soon as he felt her shudder beneath him, he quickened his thrusts and let his head drop back. His body shook, the sweet headiness of orgasm taking him while he allowed his mind to fall wonderfully blank.

Fourteen

"**H**oney, I'm home."

A woman's cheerful voice rang through the duplex like a thousand bells. Zayad stirred beneath the sheets, trying to register the sound and where it had come from, but his mind was still muffled from the lack of sleep last night, as he had paid sweet penance for his slip in control the first time around.

Rolling to his side, he reached out for Mariah but snagged only cool sheets. On alert now, he looked up, bright sunlight accosting his vision. She was gone and he was alone. His chest felt heavy. For the first time in his life he did not like waking up alone. It was a dangerous admission, but sleeping beside Mariah had been wonderful, and he would not mind if such an occurrence happened every night.

He shuffled out of bed and reached for his clothes. He threw on his pants and yawned. He was still buttoning his shirt as he walked into the living room.

But it was not the woman he expected to see lounging on the couch, leafing through a pile of mail. It was a woman he had longed to see, a woman who shared Sakir's long, lean body and his youngest brother's full mouth.

The beautiful dark-haired young woman looked up, startled. "Oh, hello."

"Hello." Such intensity of feeling ran through his blood as he looked at her. "You must be Jane."

"Yep, but you're not Mariah."

Humor glistened in her eyes. In that, she was her mother's daughter. His heart squeezed. His baby sister stood before him, and he was practically speechless.

She inspected him. "So, you're the man who's making my roommate's heart go pittypat."

"Pittypat?" Confusion hit him and he shook his head. "I surely do not pity her?"

She laughed. "No, no. It's an expression of how a heart beats. I meant Mariah likes you, that's all."

"Ah. Sometimes the English slang is unintelligible."

"For me, too, sometimes." She glanced around. "So, where is Mariah?"

"I am not entirely sure, but if I had to guess, I would say she went to check on something for her case."

Jane sighed. "Always working. I hope the two of you did more than work while I was gone."

He sat in the chair opposite her. "There was much time spent on folly."

Her grin widened and she grabbed a picture of her

and Mariah off the side table. "Good. She needs folly, and by the look of it—" she glanced up "—so do you."

He returned her grin. She had humor and fire in her blood. She had the soul of an Al-Nayhal—wise, quick. His father would be proud. "Perhaps we can discuss something else? I do not wish to speak of my time with Mariah." The thought of leaving her was killing him, and the sooner he dealt with the reason for his coming in the first place, the better.

Jane shrugged. "Okay." Though in her eyes he saw a little unease.

"Let us talk of you." He sat forward in his chair, ready to hear the wishes and dreams straight from his sister's lips. "Tell me of your passions and your pursuits. How long have you been a chef?"

She looked uncomfortable now but did not evade the question. "Five years."

"I am sure you are very good at it."

"I don't know."

"I know," Zayad said with deep conviction. The Al-Nayhal family excelled at their pursuits. "And you wish to open a restaurant, I hear?"

"Yes, I do." She looked around, at the door, at the picture of her and her friend. "Who told you that? Mariah?"

"Mariah and your mother."

Her head popped back. "You met my mother?"

"On two occasions. She is wonderful."

"She is. The best parent a girl could have."

"As was your father—"

She shook her head almost vehemently. "I never knew the man. He died before I was born."

Zayad crossed his arms over his chest. "Is that so?"

* * *

Mariah stood at the open window and listened, her heart fading back into its protective, sullen and miserable shell.

"I do not wish to speak of my time with Mariah. Let us talk of you."

And said with such caring, such deep curiosity, no one could deny he was interested.

Mariah sagged against the faded white stucco and fought tears as she listened to him prattle on about what a great chef Jane had to be. Mariah didn't understand. She didn't get how this amazing man who had cared for her, spoiled her, made love to her, was now royally hitting on her roommate.

And yet she could understand.

Her life had been full of these guys, just no one as smooth as this one. And she'd actually thought herself in love with him. How could she have fallen for another player? A guy so obviously into conquest—*get this one all hot, bothered and head over heels, then drop her. The chase is over. Move on to the next one.*

Her heart thudded in her chest, and she wanted to run away. She hated this feeling, this jumpy sensation, that life was about to come crashing down into a jagged pile of reality.

But even though the instinct to bolt was strong, she'd changed. She wasn't the fearful, angry, bitchy lawyer anymore. She'd felt love again and liked it, regardless of the pain it was bringing on now. There was no way she could run away this time.

Her hand shook a bit as she opened the front door,

her smile, too, as she saw her roommate—who looked beyond uncomfortable and a just a bit pissed off.

"Welcome back, Jane."

A smile creased Jane's face, and she stood up, ran over to Mariah and gave her a hug. "Oh, M, it's good to see you."

"You, too." Mariah pulled back from her. "Listen, can I have a minute with Zayad?"

Complete understanding and support glittered in Jane's eyes and she nodded. "Sure, I'll go unpack. Pizza and a movie later?"

"You're on."

Jane didn't even wave at Zayad. She was up the stairs in an instant, her door closed.

When Mariah found Zayad's gaze, she wasn't surprised to see him grinning at her. Still as charming as ever. Heck, he even had the balls to look as if he had missed her.

He motioned for her to come to him. "You were out of bed early."

But she remained where she was. "I wanted to hit the library."

"Did you find what you were looking for?"

"I did." She took a deep breath. "I also found what I was looking for here at home."

Confusion stripped his features. "I am sorry."

"Yes, you are." Nervously, she crossed her arms over her chest, then released them to her sides. No barriers, no protection. Not this time. "Look, Zayad, I was listening outside the window. I heard you with Jane. I heard your compliments and I heard your come-ons." She laughed, but there was little humor there. "Jeez, I'm such an idiot. I suspected you wanted Jane from the beginning—I mean, who wouldn't with all those questions. But then when you showed interest in me, I thought maybe I'd imagined your interest in Jane. But obviously I was wrong. You were just making time with me until she was back, right? Until another woman came along, right?"

His black eyes went serious and he stood up, walked over to her. "What you are suggesting is impossible."

Oh, the arrogance. "I just heard you, Zayad. 'Let's not speak of Mariah. Let's talk about you, your passions.' Blah blah blah. That's pretty clear."

"It may seem that way, however this whole thing is anything but clear."

"Don't play word games with me."

"What you heard was only my concern."

"Concern? For what? You've just met her. You don't know her."

His gaze didn't flicker. He said, "This seems odd, I know. But if you will just trust me—"

"Trust you? C'mon, Zayad. You know me. You know what I've been through with my lying, cheating ex-husband. After what I just heard, you think trusting you is actually a practical request?"

The doorbell rang.

Then again.

Mariah didn't move.

Zayad raised a brow. "Shall I get that?"

"No. I'll go." She shook her head with frustration and embarrassment and plain old grief, then turned and went to the door. "I think we're pretty much done here."

Another coward, Mariah thought as she swung the

door wide. But her thoughts stopped there. Like a scene from a movie, what felt like a hundred flashbulbs erupted in her face.

Fifteen

"They have found me. Come at once."

Zayad pressed the off button on his cell phone. It was a disaster. First he had made the mistake of turning off the security cameras and commanding his men to back off, as he had wanted more privacy with Mariah. Second he had waited too long to tell Mariah and Jane the truth.

Now he had paparazzi at his door, a sister who thought he was after her and the woman he wanted above all else thinking him a devious rogue.

Though on that last account, she would not be far from the truth.

Jane came running downstairs.

Mariah looked completely incensed. "What the hell is going on here? The press 'found' you?" Total bewilderment etched her features. She gestured toward Jane. "One moment I was accusing you of hitting on—"

"My sister," Zayad said quickly.

"—Jane, and the next there's a bunch of report—" Mariah stopped cold. Her eyebrows smashed together. She swallowed hard, licked her lips. And she just stared at him. "What?"

Coming to stand beside Mariah, Jane fairly choked out, "What?"

A knock on the back door made the women jump. Zayad shook his head. "It is one of my men. If you will excuse me for one moment."

The women said nothing.

Zayad brought Fandal into the room. "This is my chief of security."

"Your chief of security?" Mariah fairly yelled. Then her voice went low and dangerous. "I'm only going to ask you this once more and then I'm letting all those reporters out there inside to have at you. What the hell is going on!"

He had not wanted it this way, but he had little choice. "My name is Zayad Al-Nayhal. I am the sultan of Emand."

He watched the blood drain from Mariah's face. Jane looked completely confused.

"Several weeks ago," he explained, "my father's aide made a deathbed confession." He wished he could hold Mariah close as he spoke, but she looked as though she had cactus thorns growing out of her. "He claimed my father, on a trip to California, met an American woman and spent three days in her company. He also claimed the woman became pregnant and unbeknownst to my father gave birth to a child."

Mariah shook her head. "I don't understand."

"I already knew who she was when I left Emand. But before I told her the truth, I wanted to know her, see who she was and what she stood for." He looked over at Jane, who seemed ready to collapse. "I wanted to see if she would take her rightful place beside her brothers."

Jane fairly whimpered. She shook her head over and over. "No, I'm not… It's not possible."

"It is fact, my sister," Zayad said.

"My father died—"

"He did pass on, but far after you were born."

"My mother would've told me this. She wouldn't have lied to me."

Zayad remembered Tara's face when she had explained her reasoning, her fears. "She protected you. The aide never told my father of you and he lied to Tara. He told her that my father wanted nothing to do with the baby or the mother. So, you see, your mother was acting under the assumption that your father had denounced you. She only lied to protect your heart."

Jane looked stricken and stunned. "And why did *you* lie, Zayad?"

"I thought it best not to disclose my identity. I felt it was important to see who you were before—"

"To see if I was worthy, right?"

His chin lifted. "Yes."

They continued to talk, argue, question and answer, but Mariah couldn't listen anymore. She was thoroughly confused and very hurt. She slipped from the room, went through the kitchen and into the backyard. The large security man saw her but didn't try to stop her. She pushed past him and ran. She didn't know how she got very far considering she couldn't breathe all that well. But she kept running until she reached the back house. Once there, she went inside, saw Zayad's swords—shiny, beautiful, impenetrable—and collapsed on the wood floor, head in hands.

It was all a lie. Sure, he hadn't wanted to date Jane, but he'd wanted her all the same and he'd used Mariah to get her. She remembered all the questions, the interest in Tara. He hadn't cared about Mariah's foot. He'd wanted to find out about Jane, get easy access to her from her mother and best friend.

Tears pricked her eyes and she felt sick to her stomach. She'd done it again. Allowed another wealthy, charming, irresistible man to win her over and screw her up.

What a loser she was.

The door to the house opened and light spilled into the room.

"I know what you must be thinking."

She sniffed. "Get out."

"I will be as honest as I can."

"Well, that'll be a first."

He sat down beside her on the floor.

"Should princes really be sitting on the floor?" she asked, ire in her tone.

"Please curb your hostility for one moment."

She glared at him.

He sighed. "Yes, it started out as a ruse to gain information about Jane. But you must believe that everything changed that day in Ojai. I felt strong feelings for you, and they have only gained in strength."

She hated the lift in her heart and quashed it instantly. "Yet you continued to lie to me."

"I did. I felt I could not reveal who I was and who Jane was until she returned."

"You told Tara, didn't you?"

"She guessed."

"I think this is all a load of garbage."

He touched her hand. "I know you are angry—"

"Angry?" She swatted him away. "I'm beyond angry. You knew what I went through with my ex-husband. You knew what I continue to go through with my work and yet you still kept lying."

"Mariah, I am sorry. I so desperately wanted to see my sister, regain my family, I did not think. No, that is not true. Actually I could not stop thinking about my dishonesty to you."

"And yet you continued."

He didn't say anything for a moment. His eyes went somber, his mouth drew into a thin line. "You are right. I was selfish. I did not want our time to end and knew if I told you the truth, you would walk away from me."

"Just like you would've done in one more week anyway."

He looked ashamed. She'd never seen that on a man. And on this man, who was far too proud for his own good, it was a little disturbing.

"Mariah, please." He took her hand. "Believe that I will never lie to you again."

"No, you won't, because I won't give you the chance."

"Mariah, I care for you deeply. I want you to come with me to Emand. I want you to be my wife."

She stilled, her heart smacking against her ribs. He wanted her to be his wife. Oh, how she wanted to fling herself at him and say yes, yes, yes. But there was one hitch. He'd said he cared for her. Was that the same as love? Her belly clenched with pain. Did it even matter at this point?

"Remember what we spoke of that day at the beach?" he said, inching closer to her. "How the sultan needs advisors who believe in the good and who will fight for the basic human rights of others."

"Yes," she uttered, her brain a complete mess.

"We could do so much together."

She stared at him. He was serious. His eyes swam with tenderness. He really did want her, want to marry her. If she forgave him, believed him, she could be this man's wife, love him, have Jane as her true sister. Lord, it all sounded wonderful. It sounded magical. But for a woman with her history, it sounded too good to be true.

"I can't." Tears spilled from her eyes as she eased her hand from his. The fear was too great. She loved this man too much to allow him to hurt her again. "I can't put myself in that position again. It hurts too much."

"You cannot forgive, mi'nâr? Knowing the circumstances?"

She shook her head.

It took him a moment, his jaw tight, but finally he nodded. "I understand. What I did was unforgivable." He laid a file folder down by her feet, then stood. "Fandal just gave these to me. I have not looked at them. I hope you find what you are looking for here."

Mariah stared at the folder. She didn't need to look

inside. She knew there was more than enough information to help her client gain custody of her children. "Thank you."

He nodded, turned to leave, then stopped. "Can you tell me you have no love for me, Mariah?"

Her heart dipped, her throat felt tight and dry. Everything inside her wanted him, wanted to forgive him, wanted to go with him to his beautiful country and have a real family of her own. Everything but her pride. "I'm sorry." She said the words as much to herself as to him.

He didn't turn back. "I cannot stay here any longer. I must leave tonight."

"I understand. Have a safe trip."

"I love you, Mariah Kennedy," were the last words she heard him say before the door to the back house closed and she was alone again with her pride intact but her heart bleeding.

Sixteen

The lights of Emand flickered on before his eyes.

He had hoped to feel a great sense of peace upon returning home, but instead he felt empty.

Mariah had refused him—rightly so after what he had done, but it was a bitter pill to swallow. And then there was Jane. His sister had said she wanted some time to think, to speak with her mother, then to think some more. There was a time when Zayad would have fought that, perhaps coaxed her into coming back with him. But he had not the will to fight her.

Either of them, in fact.

The city lights dimmed before him, and in the thick plastic of his window he saw Mariah's eyes. The image grabbed his gut and twisted. Her eyes were filled with betrayal and confusion and a hope that had gone so hopelessly astray. Zayad turned away from the window. He could not blame Mariah's rejection on anything but his own bad deeds, and for that he hoped he suffered long and hard.

A servant crept in and cleared his untouched dinner tray, then placed a small dish of raspberries and cream in front of him. "Your dessert, Your Royal Highness."

He stared at the red-and-white perfection and wanted to smash it with his fist. He had lost the best thing that had ever happened to him—a friend, a lover, a true companion for life. All in the name of fear.

If he had the power to turn this plane around right now, he would. But he knew that would be no smart move. She needed time to cool, a few weeks perhaps.

Weeks… Pure torture for a man who had fought love for so long, then found the right woman, the one person who filled him completely. His brother, Sakir, had seen Zayad's feelings for Mariah immediately on his short visit to Texas this morning and had tried to coax his brother into talking. But Zayad could only manage the bones of the matter and had left early.

His jaw went rigid, and he pushed the fruit aside. He would not lose her. When he went back for Jane, he would try again.

And again and again. Until Mariah forgave him, accepted him and let herself love him again.

"What's the verdict, Counselor?" Jane asked, simultaneously banging on the bathroom door.

In the two weeks since Zayad had gone, Mariah had experienced pure rage, total despair, unholy loneliness and deep regret, but never had she felt sublime happiness.

Until this moment.

Sitting on the edge of the bathtub, her heart pounding and her hands shaking, she held up the pregnancy test again and spied the results. Nothing had changed. Still two blue lines.

Still pregnant.

"Dammit, M. Let me in."

Mariah rose, felt the water in her legs as she wobbled to the door and opened it.

"So?" Jane said, her eyes bright with excitement.

"You're an auntie."

Jane squealed and hugged Mariah, then squealed again. "I can't believe it."

"I can't, either. We were so careful."

"Things can happen. Providence can take a hand when mere mortals are being stubborn."

Mariah prepared herself for another fight with Jane over her refusal of Zayad, then thought better of it and sat back down on the bathroom floor. "I'm not giving in."

"Fine."

"Seriously."

"Fine."

Mariah sighed. "The bottom line is, he lied to me."

"There is no bottom line in life."

"No fortune-cookie quotes right now, okay?" Mariah said on a heavy chuckle.

Jane sat on the toilet lid. "Okay, so yes. Yes, he lied to you. He made a mistake. But it isn't the end of the world." When Mariah opened her mouth, Jane waved a hand. "He didn't cheat on you, M. He didn't take your dignity and your pride. He's not Alan."

"I know he's not Alan."

"No, I don't think you do."

Mariah looked heavenward, sighed. "Okay. You're right. Maybe I am having a hard time separating them."

Reaching down, Jane put her hand on Mariah's belly. "You've got to now."

A shiver coursed through Mariah. Sitting here in the bathroom, pregnancy test in hand, it felt like one of those defining moments. One where you look back in ten years and say, "Damn, I made a mistake," or "It was the best decision of my life."

She fiddled with the edge of the bath mat. She knew she had some soul-searching to do and some forgiveness to find within her hardened heart. She owed it to herself and to her baby to get past a mistake. "By the way, Auntie Jane, you sound like you've already accepted this whole Al-Nayhal birthright-princess thing."

Jane shrugged. "It's my mother. She's very supportive. I think Zayad made a killer impression on her."

Get in line.

"Anyway," Jane continued, "she told me everything, explained everything, made me see that I am who I am and there's no point in trying to deny it."

"But a whole new family…" Mariah began warily.

"I know." Jane's eyes shined. "Isn't it wonderful? I spoke with Sakir yesterday afternoon. He's amazing and so is his wife."

After studying her friend for a moment, Mariah pointed a finger. "You're going to Emand, aren't you?"

Jane nodded.

"When?"

"Tara and I leave on Friday."

Mariah wilted. "Tara?"

"She wants to see Emand, too. Well, she wants to see it in her way. And it's about time, don't you think?"

Mariah's stomach clenched. Life as she knew it was ending. "And Zayad is okay with Tara coming—"

"It was his idea."

"You talked to him?" Her misery was like a steel weight.

"Last night."

"Did he say anything…?" Mariah shook her head. She wasn't about to ask if he missed her, still loved her, wanted her to come to Emand, too.

But Jane offered the information anyway. "He loves you so much, Mariah."

Mariah shook her head, as if that gesture would erase her friend's words.

Jane persisted, "But he doesn't want to push you."

"Maybe I need the push." Leaning back against the cool tub, Mariah sighed. "What am I going to do, Jane?"

"I can only speak from my own experience."

"Okay, have at it."

Tears welled in Jane's eyes as she knelt beside Mariah, took her hand. "Every child deserves to know their father."

Mariah's jaw dropped and stayed that way as Fandal drove her through the iron gates and up to the sultan's palace. It was just as Zayad had described. Golden towers, a spectacular garden, miles of tawny sand in the distance.

A fairy-tale palace worthy of a magic carpet, a boisterous genie and, of course, Aladdin.

But this was no fairy tale she was walking into with her heart in her throat. This was real life, and she was about to see for herself what kind of ending it would bring.

After thinking long and hard about her future and the future of her child, she knew there was no other home, no other life she wanted to share than Zayad's. If he'd still have her.

She'd decided to come before Jane and Tara, before their own family began. It was best to be rejected without too many witnesses, she thought, her nerves a wreck as Fandal guided her through several entrancing rooms in the palace.

Finally he held a door open and ushered her inside. "This way, madam."

"Thank you, Fandal," she said, her eyes widening as she stepped into the most beautiful of libraries.

The servant motioned for her to take a seat on a leather couch, and she did. Her gaze moved about the beautiful room, then stopped on a certain piece of artwork. She swallowed, her throat tight.

"Is that an original Hockney?" she asked Fandal.

"Yes, Miss Kennedy. The sultan purchased it when he returned from America. He looks at it often."

"Does he?"

He grinned, nodded. "I am glad you have come," he said. "It will make the sultan feel better."

Her chest went tight with concern. "Feel better? Is he ill?"

Shaking his head, Fandal said, "I should not speak

of it, but I have never seen him so… He works with his swords far too much. And he has lost weight."

She didn't want to hear any more, think any more. She just wanted Zayad. "Fandal, please go and get him."

The man smiled, bowed and left. Mariah leaned back on the couch feeling as though she couldn't breathe. She'd imagined this moment for the entire flight, but for the life of her she hadn't had a clue how it would end.

She heard footsteps in the hall, then Zayad saying, "I told you I did not want to be disturbed, emergency or no. What could possibly be so important—"

She sat up, turned just in time to see him enter the library. She held her breath, waited for a sign of either his love or rejection.

He stared at her. "Mariah?"

She stood up. "I had to come. I had to tell you something."

"What is it?" He looked as pensive as she felt.

She gave him a half smile. "Well, first of all, I won my case. Because of your help, a devoted mother now has her children."

It took him a moment, then a soft smile tugged at his mouth and he walked over to her. "I am glad for this."

With a grin of his own, Fandal left discreetly, shutting the door behind himself.

Zayad was before her, his gaze eating up her face, his eyes dark with unanswered questions and unfulfilled passion. "How did you get here?"

"I spoke with Fandal. He was wonderful. He arranged for me to come."

"He is a good man and will be promoted this very day for what he has done."

Mariah smiled, hope seeping into her pores with every word he uttered. "There's something else. Another reason for my being here."

He reached out, brushed his thumb over her cheek. "Tell me."

"I've brought the sword you left behind."

His gaze was pinned to hers. "Thank you."

"Fandal has it. I thought it was important. You bought it for your son, right?"

"I did."

Confidence sparked her and she took his hands, put them around her waist. "Would you find another, Zayad?"

He sighed, pulled her into his arms and hugged her tightly. "I would buy you anything you wish."

Her pulse jumped. "The sword wouldn't be for me."

"No?"

"No." She took a deep breath, eased herself away from him. Her gaze found his and she found her bold soul. "Do you love me, Zayad?"

His eyes filled with desperation. "More than my life."

Tears filled her eyes and she took his hand, placed it on her belly. "The sword is for our child."

His mouth dropped, his eyes widened. "What?"

"I'm pregnant."

She stared at him, then finally saw what she was so desperate to see, what she had felt for days. Pure joy.

Again he pulled her into his arms, rocked her back and forth, uttered words she didn't understand but could feel in her bones—prayer, thankfulness. "My love, mi'nâr."

"Please tell me what that means, Zayad."

"It means my sweet, my beauty."

She smiled and felt as light as air, felt happy and so in love.

"This is the way it should be," he said. "We are together, you and me and our child."

For several moments they just clung to each other. But Mariah knew there was so much more she needed to say before they could embrace a future together.

She pulled back, touched his face. "I want you to know that I understand why you did what you did."

"Mariah…" He looked so pained, so full of shame.

"I love you, Zayad. I want my child to know both of its parents. I want it to see us as we are now, in love, happy, devoted, able to forgive each other."

"Yes."

"A lifetime of love."

He cupped her face in his hands. "Can you trust me again?"

"Yes, my love. You made a mistake, and I got scared. But someday—probably soon—I'll screw up, too. And you know what?"

"What?" He ran his thumb over her lower lip.

"You'll forgive me, and we'll go on and we'll be a family and we'll love each other through it all."

He kissed her with passion and thanksgiving. "I love you so dearly, Mariah."

"And I love you."

"Marry me?"

"Yes."

"And you will be happy here?"

"I will be happy where you are and our child and Redet. Like you said, there's much work for me to do here, and I'm ready."

"Redet. He is anxious to meet you."

"And I him," she said with real warmth.

"Shall we go and tell my son of our plans, then?"

"Redet is here?" Mariah asked, thoroughly excited to meet the boy.

In Zayad's eyes Mariah saw a man who loved his child deeply and a man who wondered what the future would hold for her and Redet. "My son has always wanted a mother," he said tentatively.

She grinned, her heart so full, so happy. "Well, he's got one. I've always wanted a big family."

Tears pricked his eyes, but for this man of power, tears were not customary. He inhaled deeply. "I love you, dear one. I am the luckiest man in the world."

"I believe we both got lucky."

He kissed her. "Yes."

"I think someone knew that after what we've both been through, maybe we deserved a break. Maybe we deserved some real happiness."

"I do not know if I will ever deserve you." He kissed her again, tenderly this time, then took her hand. "But I will spend a lifetime trying."

Smiles on their faces, hands clasped tightly, they left the library. And with a pleased Fandal at their heels, Zayad led the woman he loved upstairs, into her new home, into a loving family and a wonderful, brave new life.

* * * * *

SHEIKH'S CASTAWAY

ALEXANDRA SELLERS

Alexandra Sellers is the author of over twenty-five novels and a feline language text published in 1997 and still selling. Born and raised in Canada, Alexandra first came to London as a drama student. Now she lives near Hampstead Heath with her husband, Nick. They share housekeeping with Monsieur, who jumped through the window one day and announced, as cats do, that he was moving in. What she would miss most on a desert island is shared laughter. Readers can write to Alexandra at PO Box 9449, London NW3 2WH.

Alexandra Sellers' fabulous new novel, *The Untamed Sheikh*, will be published in the *Summer Sheikhs* collection from M&B™ in August 2010.

I would like to thank the following for their
generously given expert advice and help

Peter Godwin, aviator
Mark Hofton, designer
Jennifer Nauss, friend and editor
Geoff Tetley, life raft specialist
Jo and Dennis Wallace, world sailors

and AVON LIFE RAFTS.
I couldn't have done it without you.

One

Princess Noor pushed the fold of her bridal veil away from her face with an impatient hand and blinked out the cockpit window, her mouth opening on a soundless breath.

Cloud. A thick, grey-white mass blanketing the distant mainland as far as she could see.

But she had no instrument rating. She couldn't fly in cloud.

"It *can't* be!" she whispered, aghast. Sunlight still glinted merrily from the rich turquoise of the Gulf of Barakat beneath her, but that offered no solution when she had had zero practice putting the little amphibian plane down on water.

Why hadn't she noticed the cloud building up? She should have taken evasive action long ago. Had the yards of billowing tulle on her head confused her vision? Or had the humiliation gnawing at her stomach distracted her?

As if waking out of a dream now, Noor shook her head and looked around.

What was she doing here?

She hadn't even stopped to remove her veil before taking off into the unknown. Hadn't checked the weather. Didn't have a destination. Her only thought had been to put as much distance as she could between herself and marriage to Sheikh Bari al Khalid.

She gazed out at the cloud again, her heart beating fast. She might have put a very permanent distance between them. If that cloud caught up with her, she wouldn't be marrying anyone. Ever.

It had begun—when had it begun? When her parents' families fled their beautiful country in the aftermath of Ghasib's coup thirty-odd years before and both chose Australia? When the two young expatriate Bagestanis who became her parents had fallen in love and married?

Or had it begun only months ago, when the royal family's long struggle to regain the throne had at last been successful, culminating in Sultan Ashraf's now-legendary ride to the gates of the Old Palace through streets crammed with cheering, delirious multitudes?

"We loff heem!" the populace had cried, dancing, singing, laughing and crying, and even a jaded television reporter had unashamedly wiped a tear from her cheek.

Yes, perhaps that was the real beginning. For that was when Noor Ashkani's comfortable, predictable life had been tumbled into a disorder so shocking and startling she seemed to herself to have become a different person.

That was when her father had made his world-shattering announcement. When the family, like so many other exiled Bagestanis around the world, were watching events unfold on television, weeping and hugging each other in a powerful combination of hope, fear and joy, her father had pointed at the image of the stern, noble face of Sultan Ashraf al Jawadi on the screen, and said, "Now it can be told. You are not what you think. He is your cousin."

Cousin! That man on the white horse soon to be crowned Sultan of Bagestan! And not a distant cousin, either. Noor's mother was the daughter of the deposed Sultan Hafzuddin and his second wife, the French-woman named Sonia. Her father was descended from the old Sultan's sister. They owned palaces and property, seized by Ghasib, which would now be returned to them. They were titled.

So no longer was she Noor Ashkani, daughter of a wealthy Bagestani exile who had made good in his adopted country. She was Sheikha Noor Yasmin al Jaw-adi Durrani, granddaughter of the deposed Sultan of Bagestan, cousin to the present Sultan-to-be, and related to the royal family of the neighbouring kingdom of Par-van, too.

And to prove it, not long after, the new Sultan's invitation to attend the coronation in Bagestan arrived, printed on heavy white paper, with the royal seal that hadn't been seen on official documents for over thirty years.

"More of a command than an invitation," her father had said in satisfaction.

Noor had never in her life seen a sight so moving as that of the royal couple, tall and severely beautiful, glittering with gold, pearls and diamonds, as they slowly paced the red carpet through the halls of the ancient palace past the hundreds of breathlessly silent guests to the throne room.

Sheikh Bari al Khalid had been one of the newly appointed Cup Companions who followed behind the Sultan. Later she learned that he was the grandson of her own grandfather's friend, both of whom, in a time long gone, had been Cup Companions to the old Sultan.

But then he was just one of the twelve most gorgeous men she had ever set eyes on.

Noor keyed the radio mike.

"Matar Filkoh, this is India Sierra Quebec two six."

"Indi...not reading...say again." The radio crackled and spat, giving more static than speech. She must be nearly out of range.

"This is India Sierra Quebec two six," she carefully recited. "Request your current weather, repeat weather."

"Runway in...two, surface wind one eight zero deg...teen gusting thirty-five knots. Bro...at five hundred, heavy...with nimbo...rain..."

The signal broke up completely. Her heart beating hard, Noor signed off and sat for a moment taking stock. If the airport had been clear, there might have been a case for running the risk of trying to get to it through the cloud. But the airport was in the mountains. And with cloud, rain and wind gusting to thirty-five when she got there—if she got there—!

The sky had been clear when she took off. The cloud must have been building in the mountains. Or maybe it had just suddenly formed while she wasn't looking. Cloud could do that, given the right conditions.

Nimbostratus, she was pretty sure he'd said. The really treacherous clouds were cumulonimbus, which carried turbulence, but any cloud was deadly when she had no instrument rating. She didn't even have minimal experience of flying on instruments. There hadn't seemed much point when she flew only recreationally.

Cloud was terrifying because in cloud a pilot could so easily become disorientated. She could simply spiral down out of the sky.

The best alternative was an immediate landing on water. But she had never landed on water.

She had watched an expert do it. That counted for something, Noor reminded herself.

Bari. Involuntarily she glanced down at the pearl-encrusted white silk and lace that covered her breasts. Oh, yes, Bari al Khalid was an expert pilot. An expert at many things, including seduction.

Also an expert liar. But thank God she had found that out in time. Her eyes searched the instrument panel and found the clock. An hour! Was that all it was? If she hadn't heard what she'd heard, hadn't run, Sheikh Bari al Khalid would now be her husband.

At the grand reception after the coronation, powerfully masculine and fierce in a maroon silk jacket, with a glittering jewelled sword at his hip and a thick rope of pearls draped across his chest, of course Bari al Khalid made his presence felt. You couldn't be in the vicinity of so much arrogant masculinity and not notice.

But what drew Noor's attention was the way he kept staring at her, an expression on his face that seemed half passion, half rage. And as if they were attached by an invisible thread that he could not break, he seemed to circle her, so that whenever she looked up, he was always there, at a distance.

Noor was a pretty young woman whose soft, rounded face only hinted at the beauty that would be hers in a few more years, but that day she was stunning. Her parents had called the sky the limit, and Princess Noor was wearing a fabulously expensive *Arabian Nights* dress in pastel green silk from Princess Zara's own favourite designer.

A semitransparent bodice with a high halter neck, glittering with pearls and emeralds, clung to her full breasts and neat waist. Beneath, a cloud of multitoned layers of green silk swathed her legs, half skirt, half harem pants. And in a seductive mockery of the traditional veil, transparent tulle cascaded from the back of her head to her feet, caught in as if haphazardly at her waist to cloak her bare arms.

Noor's makeup was flawless, her dark auburn hair burnished, waving back from her temples and forehead to show small, perfect ears and emphasize the softly rounded chin and smooth, slender neck.

And all around, people were calling her "Your Highness."

But still, she was a little overwhelmed to think that an oak of a man like Bari al Khalid had taken one look and come crashing to earth.

The shadow of the little plane danced over the bright waves below as Noor grappled with her dilemma. She had put this plane down on land, albeit with Bari in the copilot's seat. She knew how it handled. If she had to, she would give a liquid landing her best shot.

But if there was another way… She pulled out the chart and tried to estimate her position. With the cloud obliterating all landmarks except the tips of the mountains, it wasn't easy.

Should she try an immediate landing? It would mean a lot of empty sea for someone to search when she needed rescue afterwards. Should she risk flying closer to land—closer to the cloud bank—before landing? What if the cloud suddenly swept out and grabbed her while she was putting down?

There was another problem: Noor was used to landing only where she had good visual conditions. She would become disoriented with nothing but the altimeter to tell her how close the surface was.

The sea was so deceptive. She might hit the water when she thought she was a hundred feet up. Or the reverse—what she thought was a ripple on the surface might be a ten-foot swell.

Like Bari al Khalid, she thought. *I thought I was close to him, but all the time he was miles away.*

The Cup Companion was introduced to his lord's cousin as a matter of protocol. He bowed formally, one hand a fist at his breast, but his expression was anything but formal. The arrogant sexual confidence in his black eyes melted her where she stood.

"Come," Sheikh al Khalid had ordered, in fine autocratic command, as if she could have no wishes different from his own. "I will show you the gardens. You will admire the fountains."

Noor had never been swept off her feet before. And she knew it could never happen again with such thrilling panache, such heady excitement. During the weeks she stayed in Bagestan, discovering the homeland of her parents, Bari monopolized her time, and never before in her largely fun-filled life had she had so much fun.

Bari was expert at everything. He played demon tennis, his dark body so lithe and muscled she was watching him when she should have kept her eyes on the ball, took her sailing on the most beautiful and perfectly seaworthy little yacht she'd ever seen, allowed her to pilot his private plane, escorted her to fabulous parties with the rich and famous that until now had been out of her reach, kept her constantly laughing....

And made intoxicating love to her for the first time in that small sailing yacht at the height of a storm. Noor had been a virgin, but that moment had answered all her dreams. Oh, it had been worth waiting for!

"Of course you will marry me," he told Noor, his voice harsh with passion. "We will make our life and raise our children in Bagestan."

It was far too soon; of course it was. Her cousin Jalia said it, and Jalia was right. But Noor's head was whirling. Everything on her personal horizon seemed to have changed in one heartbeat. In the sea of confusion that had surrounded her since her father's announcement, she had one spar—that Bari wanted her. That Bari was sure, and knew what he was doing.

She had flown home only to make her arrangements and return to Bagestan for the huge wedding, organized with breathtaking speed, that practically all of Barakati and Bagestani society would be attending.

And then, with the ceremony only minutes away, her one spar had been torn from her. She had learned what a fool she was, what a fool he was making of her.

Bari knew what he was doing, all right, but he didn't love her. He wasn't marrying her for love. He didn't even want to marry her.

The islands! her brain suddenly shouted at her. *There are islands out here!* How could she have forgotten that? She had flown over the scattered group of islands with Bari. *Al Jeza'ir al Khaleej,* he had called them. The Gulf Islands.

"They have been uninhabited since the forced evacuation," he had told her. "Except the biggest, which has a luxury hotel complex. The Gulf Eden was one of the ways Ghasib drew foreign currency into his coffers. Built by a huge international hotel chain to cater to very wealthy foreigners."

His tone had been filled with contempt, and Noor had dropped her eyes and omitted to mention that she had almost gone there herself once. Only her father's absolute diktat had stopped her.

This looks like my chance at last, she told herself dryly. But where were the islands? How far away? Her eyes dropped to the chart again, searching. *Please, God, show me a way out of this.*

TWO

Sheikh Bari al Khalid lifted his head and watched his runaway bride over the back of the passenger seat separating the cockpit from the luggage space where he was hidden.

How dared she abandon their wedding in such a way? How dared she run away from him like this? Without a word—no announcement, no explanation, not even so much as a blink of apology!

What sort of man did she think he was, to put up with such insult?

The heady mix of fury, shock and disbelief—if that were all!—that had driven his actions was now, however, tinged with grim amusement. So the airport was clouded over. That was a dangerous situation: his bashful bride couldn't fly in cloud, and she couldn't land on water.

How richly she deserved this dilemma!

She was a fool to have chosen this method of escape.

The weather had been volatile and unpredictable ever since the ending of the drought a few weeks ago, a fact she knew well. As an inexperienced pilot she should never have risked coming up alone.

A sardonic smile stretched his mouth, making him aware of how his jaw was clenched. He would like to leave her longer in this predicament, teach her a sharp lesson. Hell, he'd like to hide here till she was on her last gallon of fuel and begging fate for release. How he would enjoy seeing her desperate with regret and remorse!

But he couldn't risk it. Her calm might give way to panic without warning. And a few seconds of that would be enough to kill them.

No, Noor clearly couldn't be trusted to keep her head in the face of adversity.

Her head? She couldn't even be trusted to keep her word!

Well, she would be made to keep it. Of that he was determined. She would not escape. She had promised herself to him, and she would keep her promise.

He stood up and moved forward between the rear seats. "Caught in your own trap," he snarled when he was behind her. "What did you expect?"

"Bari?!" Noor's gasp sounded like tearing silk against the hum of the engine. Her head snapped up and she blankly took in the glaring black eyes, the darkly handsome face, the imposing figure magnificently sheathed in purple silk and draped with pearls. His dress sword hung from his hip.

She frowned. "Damn! I'm hallucinating!"

"I wish you were!" he said between his teeth. "I wish we were both hallucinating! Insanity would be preferable to learning what kind of woman you are!"

He lifted the bundle of her veil that nestled in the

right-hand seat and tossed it onto the floor behind her with fierce contempt, as if this symbol of their wedding made his stomach heave. Noor felt its drag against the headdress of fresh white roses still pinned to her hair.

Then, expertly manoeuvring the jewel-encrusted scabbard, he edged into the space and sat. With a deliberation that somehow infuriated her, he buckled himself into the harness.

"I have control," he announced formally and, with unhurried grace, his actions completely distanced from his vengeful mood, he engaged the secondary controls. The plane responded to its master's touch with a purr.

"Are you real?" Noor asked, wondering, *Am I totally crazy?* She had resigned control to what might be only a phantom. Was this why planes fell from the sky without explanation? Because the man flying it existed only in someone's desperate imagination?

"You will see how real I am," Bari growled. She had never seen that generous, sensuous mouth so narrowed. He must be real. Why would her mind trouble to conjure up a vision that only terrified her further?

"I guess you're the answer to my prayer!" she realized with a jerky laugh. "Some sense of humour God has!"

"Do you call this scenario God's doing? You are fool enough to think that, in acting like a barbarian, you carry out God's will?"

His tone was scathing, and her flesh shivered as the first delicate tendrils of shame reached through her blind panic to touch Noor's soul.

Bari's eyes moved to the instrument panel. Since she was in the pilot's seat, he had to crane. She felt the plane alter course in a broad arc, out over the sparkling sea. There was no cloud in this direction, but even if it caught up with them, she knew Bari was fully rated on instruments.

"How did you get here? You just materialized?"

His voice whipped her. "Do you imagine it was difficult to trail a white limousine with a bridal veil streaming from the sunroof through the streets? Nor was it difficult to guess that you planned to take the plane."

He was wrong there. She hadn't planned it. She had driven to the plane only when she realized that in her panicked flight she had taken nothing with her, neither her handbag nor a change of clothes. She had to have cash, but she didn't dare go to the palace—it would be the first place they looked for her. And if they found her, they'd take her back to the wedding.

The thought of returning back among the wedding guests, having to explain herself when no explanation would be good enough, had appalled her. Then she had remembered that Bari kept emergency fuel money in a secret compartment in the plane. In the swamp into which she had cast herself, she had grabbed at that one frail straw.

She had discovered the plane fuelled and ready for their honeymoon journey. Only then had the thought of flying away from the impossible problems she'd created suddenly and crazily occurred to her.

"Only the why of such barbarian, uncivilized behaviour escaped me." The words came at her in sharp, broken shards, as if he chewed up glass as he spoke. "Even a child raised in the streets would hesitate to act as you have done!"

His contempt came out through lips that had practically disappeared. Noor flinched. She had never seen such an expression on his face before. She had never seen anyone so angry, and she had to admit he had some cause. But she couldn't accept such wholesale criticism, such overwhelming blame.

"You got to the plane ahead of me, and instead of talking to me you hid, and you're calling *me* childish?" she snapped.

"No doubt you would have relished a public confrontation, Noor, but I did not. We will return to the house and you will marry me without comment, or any public airing of your unforgivable actions."

"Return to the house?" Her voice climbed in startled objection as she suddenly realized he had been altering course to fly back to Bagestan. She straightened with a jerk. "What are you doing? Where are you going?"

"We will land at the dock and walk up to the house and apologize to our guests for the delay. Then we will take our vows," he said with the clarity that only the coldest fury can impart. "A little late. But the bride is allowed that, I believe."

She stared at him. What arrogance! Noor's doubts about her behaviour were conveniently swamped in outrage. "Maybe you didn't notice that the bride changed her mind, Bari! I'm not going to marry you!"

"You did not change your mind," he informed her contemptuously. "You would not be acting like this if you had ever intended to marry me, of course. But you chose the wrong man. I do not play these Western games, Noor. You said you would marry me. You will do so."

"It's no game! Turn this plane around!" she screeched. How dare he brush her off when he must know her reasons for what she did? At the very least, he suspected! Who did he think he was?

"Who do you think—"

"It will not take long. You may pass the time by telling me what it is, if not a game. And I will have the truth."

"The truth! Oh, that's good, that is! *I'm* not the one who's been lying from beginning to end of this whole affair! I'm not the one with zero conscience! Suppose *you* begin by telling—"

"Do *you* talk to *me* about conscience?" he shouted, as if suddenly losing his grip on a fierce control. Her heart gave a nervous kick; his temper was at white heat. "What has been your motive in pretending to agree to marry me and then playing such a terrible trick? Hundreds of people have come—"

"You must have a very good guess as to what motivated me! Your lies! You must have known I'd find out the truth soon—"

"—from all over the world to celebrate not just our wedding but their hopes for the rebirth of our country!"

"—er or later! I guess you were counting on later! Too bad!"

"Do you know you nearly ran into the Sultan's motorcade as you drove out the gates? He and the Sultana—"

"The Bagestani flags on the fenders gave me a hint," Noor admitted. "He hires good outriders, your boss. They nearly drove me off the road."

He turned on her a gaze so black with threat she cowered. "Do not speak slightingly to me of a man of whose courage and strength you are ignorant."

The plane had turned 130 degrees, and the expanse of cloud covering the mainland suddenly came into view again out the window behind her head.

Bari's eyes widened, and then narrowed. How had he let his anger suck him into argument when he should have been watching the sky?

Noor turned to follow the direction of his gaze and let out a breath of stunned surprise. Bari had made his appearance not a minute too soon. The cloud had built fast and was rushing towards them.

If I were alone now, I'd be saying my last prayers.

"Cumulonimbus," the dark-eyed Sheikh murmured softly. "I am a thousand fools."

She gasped hoarsely, her hand lifting to press against the window in protest as she stared out at the sinister mass that approached.

But Bari was right.

"The airport said nimbostratus!" she cried.

He made no reply, except to the threat they faced. He was throttling back.

Cumulonimbus clouds were dangerous even to the most experienced instrument-trained pilot. They could carry severe turbulence. Turbulence might easily cause the plane to break up.

The plane began to lose height, and she felt it alter course again, away from the coastline. Of course he would try to get under the cloud, Noor realized. If only he could...

"Not even the sense to remove your lace finery before taking off into cloud!" he said harshly, his eyes on the instrument panel. The acres of silk and tulle surrounding his ex-bride didn't make his task any easier. "In the water, it would drag you down to certain death. Get rid of it."

His air of cold command was completely new. Noor gnawed her lip at that *in the water,* for it seemed to make the danger real. While he tried fruitlessly to raise air traffic control, she lifted her hands and frantically began to pull out the first of dozens of pins fixing the wreath of white roses in her hair, though if the plane broke up in the air it wouldn't be her bride's finery that killed her.

Abruptly, sea and sky and sun disappeared, and the little plane entered a world all grey. Noor heard a strange, quiet shushing. Droplets of water appeared on the glass.

Her fingers trembled and hesitated, then went on with their task. What else was there to do? Bari was in command of the situation as far as that was possible, and to offer resistance—or even help—now would be ridiculous.

Bari leaned over to peer at an instrument, and she distantly noted how a dark curl gleamed in the reflected glow from the panel. What a powerfully handsome man he was! Noor thought involuntarily. Not conventional, Hollywood handsome—he wasn't even at handshaking distance with the bland, polished looks that passed for masculinity on a movie screen. No, Bari was one of Saladin's warriors. Fierce nobility was what shaped his jaw, not pineapple facials and a perfectly judged beard shadow. If only…

But now was not the moment for such thoughts.

At last the flowers and tulle began to come loose, and Noor ignored the remaining pins and dragged at the headdress, wincing at the pain as hair came away with it. She tossed it over her shoulder onto the floor behind, where it sank into the nest of itself.

A faint, delicate perfume floated to her nostrils from the bruised roses. Her senses, it seemed, were heightened. Her fingers unconsciously massaging her protesting scalp, Noor picked out the pins that were still caught, combing through her hair, trying not to remember the excited, happy moment when the hairdresser had set the wreath on her head.

Without warning, a fierce gust of wind smacked them. The plane rocked, and so did her heart.

"Ya Allah!" Bari exclaimed, and the grey all around them abruptly turned dark. Another sharp slap of wind.

Then, much more ominously, a low rumble.

Horror shivered down her spine. Noor's heart lurched in frantic denial and her mouth was suddenly dry as the desert. It wasn't possible! *Please, God, let it not...*

Another crack of thunder cut her off. A thunderstorm. And they were in it.

Three

There are few things more dangerous than a thunderstorm embedded in cloud, and Noor knew it. It is the pilot's nightmare.

She might have chosen death not only for herself, but for Bari. Her heart thudded with useless regret.

"Are you strapped in tight?"

His voice was so calm it shocked her, an incongruity her mind couldn't cope with. It had the effect of setting her building panic at bay.

"No. My dress—"

"Damn your dress." She could feel that the plane was still descending, but there seemed no bottom to the cloud. "Get your harness on. Fast."

Though a stubborn part of her resented his autocratic tone, she knew it would be insane to resist. Noor twisted in her seat, groping underneath the swathes of silk for the webbing of her harness.

The plane was still losing altitude.

"Are we landing?"

"We'll see," Bari said dryly as another crack of noise drowned him out. She thought she sensed him adjust his heading again, but how he had any idea where they were, she couldn't imagine.

She had never seen Bari operating under pressure before. It surprised her that such a passionate, hot-tempered man could be so cool under fire. For a brief moment the thought of her only experience of his—of any man's—passion flicked across her mind. He hadn't been cool then...or had he? That must have been faked, too.

Her fingers quickly found one buckle, but the other eluded her. Noor half stood in the confined space and groped the seat behind her.

Bari reached across and fielded the buckle of her harness, holding it for her in one strong, well-formed hand. *Well, at least I won't die a virgin!* The thought rose unbidden, and a breath of laughter—and something else—escaped her. Her eyes brushed up to his as she took the harness from him with a murmur of thanks, but the look she met was hard and ungiving, and the only passion was rejection.

"Even in the lion's mouth," he mocked her.

A jolt of turbulence wiped any retort from her mind. She tumbled back into her seat to the sound of tearing. Her arm hit painfully on something, but Noor suppressed the automatic grunt that rose in her throat and buckled herself in. The webbing abraded the delicate white silk across her breast, tearing the clustered pearl embroidery.

She was sorry about that—it was a beautiful creation.

A pearl fell like a teardrop. A second followed, landing in her palm. Noor's fingers involuntarily caught it,

massaged the cool little sphere between finger and
thumb. How completely her dreams were being destroyed. And yet…

If they had gone through with the wedding, there
would have come a point when they sat side by side in
the plane like this. The thought gave her a curious sensation of being in two lives at once. Was there a parallel universe in which they had been married? That other
life seemed so close. She could almost feel it, as if she
might blink and find everything the same, but different.

Would she have gone on believing Bari loved her, living her fool's dream? Would he have kept up the pretence
once he had what he wanted, or would she have learned
immediately that he had made a fool of her? Would she
ever have guessed if she hadn't overheard the truth…

"She's so spoiled! All she cares about is clothes and
jewellery and having a good time. She's just totally
frivolous!"

Noor had been standing at the mirror, layers of silk
and lace surrounding her, her tanned skin and auburn hair
gleaming like the rich heart of a white rose, when the
bitchy malice filtered through from the room beyond.

"And I don't believe she's in love with anyone but
herself!"

And just like a droplet of dew on the rose's heart was
the fabulous al Khalid diamond. Bari's grandfather's
wedding gift to her had simply taken her breath away.
Noor was used to wealth and all its pleasures, but Bari's
family fortune went beyond wealth. The diamond was
the biggest single stone Noor had ever seen, and it lay
against her hand with a dark fire that almost burned her—
like Bari's eyes, she thought with a delicious flutter.

"She is young yet."

"She's twenty-four. Why are you making excuses for her?"

Noor let it wash over her. She had heard it before, directly or implied. The women in Bari's family were not uniformly delighted with his choice of bride, but what should she care about that?

"She has been raised by overfond parents, it's true," said the more placid voice of Bari's aunt. "But she is an al Jawadi by blood. She has more depth than she knows yet."

Of course they didn't know she could hear. She was in the large, luxurious bathroom set between her bedroom and another. A moment ago Noor had been at the centre of buzzing activity, the hair stylist and the makeup artist competing with the dressmaker and her personal maid for her attention, but now, with the excuse of one last nervous visit to the toilet, she had stepped in here to be alone for a moment and catch her breath.

And she had heard voices murmuring together in bitchy comfort in the other bedroom.

"He's only known her a few weeks," the younger one was still protesting, and Noor wondered if this particular cousin, whoever it was, was in love with Bari herself.

"You are talking like a true Westerner. Why should a man know his bride? It is enough that his family knows her family."

In a moment she would go back into her bedroom to face the renewed onslaught of perfectionism from her dressers and wait for Jalia and her bridesmaids to tap on the door to tell her it was time. Time to be escorted to meet the richest, the handsomest, the sexiest man ever to have deserved the title "Cup Companion," the man who had known he wanted to marry Noor Ashkani—Princess Noor Yasmin al Jawadi Durrani—practically from the first glance.

"It's different when the marriage is arranged, though, isn't it?" The murmurs in the next room grew louder as the two women moved past the slightly open door, in complete ignorance of the fact that the subject under discussion was on the other side of it. "Then the families at least have—"

"How is it different? This marriage might not have been arranged in the traditional way, but it was your grandfather who chose the bride."

"Really?" The younger voice sounded both shocked and deliciously intrigued, and Noor's eyes widened with startled dismay. "You mean Bari isn't in love with her?"

She sounded thrilled, Noor noted. Cow.

"He was very bitter when his grandfather told him what was necessary." The voices faded again and she heard the opening of the door that led onto the broad, shady balcony.

"How—but why would Bari agree to something like that? He's so independent!"

"Bari has no choice." The other voice was matter-of-fact. "If he wants the right to the property in Bagestan and the money to restore it, he has to marry as he is instructed. Your grandfather wants an alliance with the Durranis. He will leave the property away from Bari if—"

The door shut, cutting the voices off, and leaving Noor stunned and as white as her veil among the broken pieces of her stupid, childish dreams....

A loud rumble brought her back into the here and now, with all its dangers. Oh, if only her father had never told them their history! If only she could return to her ordinary life, and never learn whose blood ran in her veins. *Princess!* They had been happy as they were! And now...her life had so changed that it might end here, miles from her home, in the next few minutes.

Another, louder crack of thunder, and she bit back a cry. She had seen flickering light within the roiling darkness. If lightning struck...

They hit turbulence and dropped for a few metres before landing with a sickening thud on a boiling air mass. Her stomach churned. *Oh, let me not throw up!* she begged feverishly.

Lightning danced perilously in the black cloud again, and the noise was deafening. They were at the heart of the storm.

Bari struggled against turbulence, hoping he had a heading towards the Gulf Islands as he came down, but he was far from certain. The instruments were jumping so much they were all but useless. And as a mere human he was in the maelstrom, archetypal Chaos, the place where the ordinary senses were powerless as guides.

Flying by the seat of your pants, they called it. *On a wing and a prayer.* The clichés recited themselves in his head, describing truths no one with sense wanted to discover for himself.

He had been acting like a fool for too long. His judgement had been faulty ever since hearing his grandfather's ultimatum, and what a pity he could only recognize that now!

But this wasn't the moment to fan the flames of his legitimate anger, either with his grandfather or with Noor. His mind needed to be clear of everything except the job at hand.

He could keep dropping lower to try to get below the cloud, but that was risky: some of the islands were high and rugged. And even at the coast the foothills were over a thousand feet high in places. So whether he was badly off course or right where he hoped he was, there was terrible risk involved in flying low.

But to continue to fly inside the storm invited even more certain disaster. He had to take the risk and try to put down, trusting that he would break out of cloud in time to see where he was and take evasive action if it wasn't where he hoped.

Noor's mouth was dry. Her heart beat with terror; the metallic taste of panic was on her tongue. She had never been afraid for her life before. They could be struck by lightning. Turbulence could break the plane apart. They could fall from the sky like a stone.

Or the earth could leap up in their path and smash them to atoms.

She wanted to lash out and hit something; her legs were tense with the need to run screaming from the scene. She wanted her heart to stop thundering in her chest and cheeks and temples. She wanted to wake up from this nightmare and find herself safe.

"Oh God!" she whimpered as a fist of sound punched the little plane and set it juddering. How was it possible one tiny act had set such a chain of events in motion? If she could have it to do over again...

"Pray for some common sense while you're at it," Bari advised with grim humour. He was fighting to hold the plane against the turbulence, and he seemed to have as good a grip on himself as on the controls.

The injustice of the comment infuriated her—or was it the justice of it?—and as if that fury somehow served as an antidote to the emotion that engulfed her, Noor gritted her teeth in sudden revulsion for her own fear. If this was death, she wasn't meeting it as a coward! She wasn't going to spend her last few minutes in a panic, pleading with fate or regretting her own stupidity or anything else.

The noise was deafening now—the shriek of wind,

the rain and thunder and the protesting engine all con-
spiring together to produce cacophony. Noor ran her
eyes over the instrument panel. Even if they hadn't
been leaping around like drops of water on a summer
pavement, the instruments would have told her exactly
nothing.

"There must be something I can do!" she cried over
the noise.

Bari's eyes were steady on her for a moment, clock-
ing the shift in her state of mind. He indicated the radio
with his chin.

"Try and raise air traffic control again," he shouted,
less because he thought it likely than to give her something to do. "Give them our stats. Height eleven hundred and descending. Bearing two two five. See if they
have us on radar and can confirm our position."

But the radio responded with static. They were out
of range, but that told them nothing with regard to their
own position—except that a mountain might be between them and the airport. In the distance she heard the
pilot of another plane saying he could hear her, but the
signal faded and he didn't respond to her call.

"Go to the distress channel," Bari ordered, and a
thrill of renewed fear zinged through her. Every pilot
knew the channel number, but not in the expectation of
ever needing it. Her mouth dry, Noor turned the dial to
read 121.5. She coughed.

"Mayday, May—" she began hoarsely.

Suddenly there was a flash of light all around them,
as though they had touched an electric grid. Then a curious silence, as if the rain were taking a breath, or her
heart had stopped beating. Then rippling, cracking,
booming thunder.

"Did that hit us?" Noor barely breathed the question.

Bari shrugged. "The electrics are still working." He pulled back on the throttle, slowing the engine further.

"I'm going to put down. The sea will be choppy, but better to break up on the surface than up here."

If the sea was beneath them.

Noor felt a sudden calm. *Mash'allah.* "All right. What should I do?"

"There's a life raft in the rear." He sounded doubtful. "Can you get it out?"

She set down the mike and unbuckled herself. "Right."

"Be prepared for more turbulence."

She hastily kicked off her shoes and got up, scrabbling her way between the two passenger seats behind and into the back of the aircraft as fast as she could, yanking at the voluminous skirt of her dress, clutching tightly to anything within reach. Meanwhile the plane leaped and bounced as the storm did its unholy best to knock her off balance.

Strange, she thought distantly, all this bucking wasn't making her queasy now. Maybe having nerves at a fever pitch had something to do with that.

Still the wind howled and shrieked around the little plane. Lightning crackled within the clouds, and the answering thunder pounded and banged them almost physically.

In the luggage space behind the passenger seats, she saw a suitcase-sized container fitted to the bulkhead on a mounting. There were very similar items on the yachts of friends, and in her carefree life Noor had been miles from imagining she would ever actually need one.

She knelt into the cloud of her dress and wrestled with the clasps holding the case in the cradle. She noted only distantly that the tip of one perfect peach-coloured fingernail snapped off in the process.

"LIFE RAFT, 4 PERSON. DO NOT INFLATE IN AN EN-CLOSED SPACE."

Bari swore as the plane bucked again, and Noor fell against the seat and then the bulkhead as she dragged the case awkwardly off its mounting. It was heavy and hard and had a mind of its own, but with curses and tears she at last manoeuvred it to a position behind Bari's seat. Two more fingernails tore in the process.

The sweat of struggle was on Bari's forehead, and his face was white with strain. A black curl fell over one eye. "Sit down," he called. "We'll break out of cloud soon and I may have to take it back up fast."

Fear rushed through her again at this stark statement of what she already knew—that they might be blindly flying towards a mountainside. Biting her lip, Noor struggled back into her seat and shoved her arms through the safety harness, clicking it home.

Rain pounded the metal body of the plane, and the wind screamed around them, in an intensity of sound she'd never heard before. Thunder rolled all around. She felt the noise in her skin, in her body, as if sound itself embraced her, a physical thing.

She picked up the mike again. *"Mayday, Mayday, this is India Sierra—"*

Suddenly they were out of cloud, driving through rain so heavy there was scarcely any improvement in visibility. But below she could see water, and she let her breath out on a long silent sigh. Thank God, thank God. *Alhamdolillah.* She glanced at Bari, but she saw no emotion other than fierce concentration on his face.

"Brace yourself," he said briefly. The water looked choppy and unforgiving. Noor pushed her free hand against the control panel, pressed her stockinged feet against the floor.

"This is India Sierra Quebec two six, we are—"

He slowed the engine, dropping lower, trying to gauge the height of the chop by what he knew of the sea as a sailor. It was rougher than he had hoped.

The belly of the plane touched down with a hollow thump, and then another and another as they hit the waves. Bari wrestled to keep the plane from nose-diving, the muscles of his arms bulging with the effort. As he slowed to a standstill, a bigger swell grabbed the starboard wing. With a sharp, terrifying scream of metal the plane slewed around, bounced up, smacked down, pitched forward and then dropped back.

Four

The high scream stopped. The propellers stopped. The pounding rain increased in ferocity, but still it sounded like silence to the two in the cockpit. Bari slapped his harness open.

"Are you hurt?" His voice was harsh.

"No," Noor said faintly. The truth was she was so shocked that if she did have broken bones she wouldn't have known.

"The hull is damaged," Bari said, flinging open his door onto driving rain and waves that slapped against the belly of the plane, stretching greedy fingers into the cockpit. "We've got a couple of minutes before it goes under."

Noor, dizzy and shaken, struggled out of the harness and her seat again.

Bari was in the open doorway, the rain slashing at him, staining his jacket dark, plastering it to his skin. He tied the cord from the life raft to a metal brace with quick expertise. Somehow he did not look incongruous in his wedding finery. The purple silk jacket that was dress uniform to a Cup Companion only emphasized his physical power and masculinity. Around his hips the jewelled belt of his sword glowed dully. He looked like an ancient painting of a noble warrior, ready for anything.

Lightning crackled behind his head, and thunder exploded around them like a small bomb.

"Take your dress off," he shouted.

Her hand went unconsciously to her throat. "But I'm—"

"Now!" His voice was harsh. "Do you want to drown?"

She was too stunned by events to argue. He was right. If she fell into the water, the dress would drag her down. Anyway, what did she have to hide from Bari? He had been so intimate with her body he practically owned it.

Bari didn't waste time watching to see her obey. He dragged the life raft through the opening and heaved it onto the water.

Noor reached up behind her neck and her fingers tugged at the first of the dozens of tiny silk-covered buttons that ran down her back. She managed to undo three or four, watching as Bari jerked at the cord of the plastic case now riding the waves a short distance away, but the dress was too tight for her to reach further.

"You'll have to undo me," she said hoarsely, and so quietly he didn't hear against the sudden hissing and snapping as the life raft opened. Noor coughed. Since trying to make the Mayday call she seemed to have no voice.

"You have to undo me!" she cried louder.

He looked at her. She was offering her back, her head turned to look over her shoulder into his face. Bari's eyes took in the lifted shoulder, the fall of glowing auburn hair, the partly opened neckline of the dress, the soft skin of her back as it disappeared under the delicate white silk.

Even now, with danger crackling all around, the thought of the might-have-been passed over them. Wordlessly his hands rose to the buttons, and moved against her back to undo her wedding dress...as he might have done in a hushed bedroom somewhere, their hearts beating not with fear but desire....

He undid two of the tiny, impossible buttons, and then muttered something she didn't hear. His hands clenched against her skin for a moment before he wrenched them apart. The fabric screamed its protest at the violation of the should-have-been, and he tore the dress open from neck to hip. Buttons flew like little pellets, landing all around with a sound that was curiously distinct against the noise of the storm.

They said not a word. Bari lifted his hands and turned back to his task with the raft. It was nearly fully inflated now, and he quickly picked up a small satchel as water began to seep into the plane, staining the carpet with a warning that time was short.

Noor dragged the dress off, down her arms and over her hips. Clutching hard on the seat back against the rocking of the waves, she let it drop with a swoosh to the floor and stepped out of it. Now she was wearing nothing but a teddy and stockings.

She dragged the heavy weight of the dress up and flung it over her arm, and then stood waiting for his signal.

There was a loud pop as the bright red canopy snapped into place over the raft. Bari held the raft close to the battered plane, and she watched him toss the sheathed sword and the satchel through the canopy entrance. The eyes that glanced over her were clinically impersonal. Not even by a tightening of his mouth did he seem to remember that the last time he had seen her like this lovemaking had followed.

Lightning crackled between earth and sky, and the black clouds roiled as thunder echoed across the water. A gust of wind smacked them, causing the plane to make a terrifying shift.

"Shoes?" Bari shouted.

"Off."

"Jump onto the canopy."

She clutched her dress and prepared to leap. "What the hell's that for?" he demanded harshly.

"It's all the clothes I have!" she screamed against the turmoil. Without waiting for his approval, she leaped out, and landed spread-eagled on the canopy. It collapsed under her, and she banged her knee painfully on something underneath.

Noor almost panicked then, but when she looked towards Bari he was unmoved by the accident. The life raft rose and fell on the waves for a few seconds while the drenching rain came down, and the heavens roared and flashed.

"Get over!" Bari called. Her dress was everywhere, and she feverishly grabbed at it, rolling it into a bundle with one arm as she clutched desperately to a rope with the other and tried to make room for him.

Her bundled wedding veil landed with a thump, so Bari had seen logic in her decision. A moment later, he landed beside her.

"Get through the entrance—we've got to get the canopy up!" he cried, and for a moment she stared at him in confusion.

Under his rapid-fire direction, dragging her dress

and veil with her, Noor slithered through the entrance hole and under the flattened canopy as if into a sleeping bag, while Bari clung on precariously. Rain poured unmercifully into her face where she lay looking up at the churning black sky. There was something hard and uncomfortable under her thigh.

Bari edged closer, then slid headfirst through the hole beside her. To Noor's amazement, the canopy popped back into place, and suddenly they were inside.

Bari instantly jackknifed up, grabbing at her butt, and choking the sigh of relief in her throat. "What—?" she began.

She saw him heft the sword in the scabbard. He shoved it out the entrance and drew out the sword, tossing the scabbard to fall inside.

The action, the speed of it, choked her.

"Bari!" she screamed hoarsely.

With his free hand he reached for the rope that tethered them to the downed plane, and lifted the sword over it.

A huge swell slapped against the plane without warning, shifting it violently, dragging the rope out of his hand. Bari, the sword held high, was suddenly hanging precariously over the water. A wave lifted the little raft.

"Bari!" Noor shrieked again, in a very different tone. She flung herself on him, grabbed the jewelled sword belt he still wore, and held on tight. The raft slipped dangerously down into the lee of the wave.

He twisted in her hold, his back arching out over the swollen sea, his sword upraised, with rain pouring over him, looking like some ancient painting of a blood-crazed warrior. He stared at her in disbelief as she clung shrieking to his hips. The rain was so drenching she could hardly see, but she got the outrage in his eyes.

"Get back! You'll overturn us!" he ordered furiously.

Noor lifted her hands as if the belt were hot, and slid back inside, wiping the rain and hair from her eyes, her heart beating in tumult as she watched him.

Bari cut the cord that tied them to the plane and moved back inside. He wiped the sword uselessly against his wet sleeve, sheathed it carefully in the confined space and set it down.

Something beside her head on the canopy caught her eye. Her eyes sparkling, she said, "There appears to be a little knife stuck to the canopy here, Bari. I suppose not everyone is expected to be carrying their own ceremonial sword."

She caught the glimmer of a smile, of the old, humorous Bari, but there was no time for laughter. The sea smashed over them, the little raft rose with a sickening swoop, and the moment was lost. With a loud, terrifying complaint from the torn wing, the plane shifted again. Would they be dragged with it?

A red polythene bag was tied to the floor. Bari wrestled the neck open, then drew out a small plastic scoop and fixed a metal handle to it. Everything he did was quick, with an air of urgency that only heightened her anxiety. A breath of nervous laughter escaped her.

"What's that for?"

Bari tossed it down.

"Never used a paddle before?" he asked. "You'd better learn fast."

With a neat economy of motion he pulled another one out of the sack and fitted that together.

"Shouldn't we close the entrance? We're getting a lot of water in here," Noor complained.

"There's work to be done first. Pick that up and come and help me."

All her life Noor had been pampered. The only girl,

and the youngest child, she had always been special. No one made real demands of her. Her needs were always met through someone else's work—servants, her parents, her brothers, even her cousin Jalia had all conspired to cushion her against the truth that life required effort. Any effort Noor made went in the direction of fun.

And no one—including Bari—had ever spoken to her in the tones he was using now.

"What's the point? Where are we trying to get to? We don't even know where we are!"

"We know we're too damned close to the plane, and it's sinking," he informed her flatly. "We have no time to argue. Try to spread your weight as much as possible. It's dangerous to have all the weight on one side, but we have no choice."

Bari pushed his head and shoulders out into the rain and began to paddle, fighting to get the raft away from the downed plane. It lay helpless in the water, with its ugly broken wing, and their position was dangerous— a wave could smash them against the hull. Or they might be caught by the wing, or hammered by the tail, as the plane went under.

Or simply sucked down with it when it went.

After a moment, to his surprise, Noor moved up behind him and put her head out, paddle at the ready.

"What do I do?" she shrieked against the storm.

His biceps bulged under the soaking-wet jacket. "We'll aim to get around the nose and out that way," he shouted.

Noor could hardly see, hardly breathe in the downpour, but he had challenged her and she wasn't going to give in. She wiped her hair out of her eyes and tried again.

"Watch my paddle," Bari ordered, and that made it easier. Looking down she could follow the direction of his paddling, and she got less rain in her eyes.

They paddled together, side by side, wordlessly battling the waves that tried to drag them towards the sinking plane. Then suddenly, pushed close and then swept on by a high swell, they were past it and out of danger.

"That's good enough," Bari said. They drew back inside, and he rolled up the door flap and sealed it, and now at last they were cocooned against the storm. Soaking wet, Noor reflected, and chilled, and in a tiny space that was awash with water and bouncing like forty miles of bad road, but suddenly it seemed like comfort. She slumped down against the rounded side of the raft, panting, her heart drumming in her ears, and realized what a relative thing comfort was.

For a minute or two they rested in silence as their breathing calmed. Then Bari opened the flap again and looked out, using the paddle to turn the raft around and get a wider view.

They had been carried well away from the plane, now half-submerged. It would disappear soon. Gazing past Bari's head into the grey seascape, Noor caught no sight of ship or land. Still, such heavy rain might easily disguise land that was quite close.

Bari closed the flap again.

"No sign of land?" Noor said, hoping to be contradicted.

"No, but with a little luck we're near the Gulf Islands." He reached for the emergency pack again and pulled out a plastic-covered sheet of paper whose bold title read "Immediate Emergency Procedures."

Lightning flashed and flashed again, throwing an eerie orange glow over the interior, and making it hard for Noor's eyes to acclimatize. Bari frowned down at the paper for a moment, then lifted a hand to the centre of the canopy and turned on a little light.

Noor, uncomfortably curled in one corner, her shoulders resting against the edge of the raft, felt light-headed with the constant motion. Water was trickling down her back from her soaked hair. Her lacy stay-up stockings were slipping on her wet thighs, and she lifted a hand to strip them off as Bari pulled some rope and a curiously shaped piece of plastic out of the red sack.

"What's that for?" she asked, but he only shook his head as if her question were a bothersome fly. After a moment, her eyes fell on the wedding dress damply scrunched up under the satchel. It was slowly absorbing the water sloshing around the floor of the raft, but it was better than nothing. Noor reached out and pulled at the hem.

She knew she was being foolish and stupidly sentimental as she avoided using the beautiful overskirt and instead lifted one of the flounced underskirts and bent to wipe her face and hair on the impeccably hand-stitched silk. It came away blotched with black, green and tan, so no doubt her face was a mess. She tried wiping her hair and her arms, because she was starting to feel chilled, but the dress was too soaked to make any difference.

For several minutes as Bari got his bearings there was silence between them. Noor sat straighter and tried not to feel sick. Normally she was a good sailor. The raft was stamped with the information that it was for four, but it was a small enough space even for two when one of them was a runaway bride and the other her furious ex-bridegroom, she told herself with grim humour.

It was moving up and down with the stormy swell, the waves slapping it, the water on the floor sloshing around to produce deep discomfort. Once they felt a heave and a toss and then water pounded down on them, pushing at the canopy, and she knew a wave had washed right over them. The incessant drumming rain and the silence within made the little space even more claustrophobic.

Noor shivered. She had never been so close to the elements, so profoundly at their mercy.

And in this mood, that included Bari himself.

"How long do you think it will be before they find us?" she asked nervously.

Bari lifted an eyebrow and looked up from what he was reading.

"Who do you imagine will be looking?"

Five

There was a heartbeat of shocked silence. Thunder cracked and rolled again, but now, *Alhamdolillah,* it was moving off.

"What?" she whispered.

"Who knows we were on the plane? Who knows it went down?"

"But—radar!"

Bari shook his head. "We were probably flying underneath radar most of the time."

He began to unravel the sea anchor rope. "Even when people do discover that we went off in the plane, will there be any reason to assume that we have not arrived safely at our destination, whatever that might be?"

She stared at him. Did he really mean this might go on?

"Unless, of course, someone is expecting *you* somewhere." His eyes were hard as he spoke.

She didn't know what that meant. "What about our

hotel booking? Won't they ask questions when we don't turn up?"

A crack of laughter escaped him. "Who will be expecting us to take a honeymoon when we didn't get married?"

He went on with his task, as if he could forget from moment to moment that she was there. She hated that. Bari had never ignored her before, and although now she knew his intense interest had been an act, still she missed it.

She suddenly began to wonder what had happened after she ran. When had the alarm been raised? The guards at the gate must have noticed as she went roaring past in the bridal limousine, but what had they actually seen?

"Did people know what happened? Did they…" She faded off.

"Did they know my bride had changed her mind?" Bari supplied in harsh mockery, and abruptly the cool veneer dropped and his raw anger surged up again. "I don't know what they knew," he growled. "What does it matter? Insulting our families, our friends and all our guests! No reason on God's earth could justify such behaviour!"

No one ever criticized Noor, and in her current fragile state the stinging rebuke hit her hard.

"*You* were my reason!" she flared. "Easy for you to feel you should be allowed to walk all over me, but it's a bit much to expect me to agree!"

She was all the angrier, perhaps, because now that events had overtaken her, she was suddenly feeling very guilty. In countries like Bagestan and Barakat, hospitality was taken very seriously. It was practically a religious duty. And she had grown up in a family of exiles determined to maintain such traditions. It was in her blood almost as much as his.

"Walk all over you? Easier to walk over a bed of nails!" he snorted.

"With a soul as calloused as yours, no problem!"

"Not so calloused that I don't know when I've been lucky."

"Oh, I don't think so!" Noor snapped furiously. "A few minutes ago you were all for forcing me to the altar! Anyway, you weren't marrying me for my sweetness and light in the first place, were you? You had other mo—"

"Not even for your self-control under stress," he agreed. "Do you never consider pulling your own weight, Noor? Whatever *you* want is right?"

That was so outrageously unfair she gasped. "What do you know about it?" she demanded. "You've only known me for a few weeks! Ask my real friends if you want to know!"

Bari only shook his head and opened the hatch again. As more rain drove inside, he pushed something down into the water, then began playing out a line. Noor watched in silence. Not even for ready money would she now have offered her help. It would seem like giving in to his opinion of her, trying to win his favour. Not for a world!

But it irked her that he seemed not to have any expectation that she would be of help in what he was doing. Maybe he really did believe that she couldn't pull her weight; in any case, it seemed he could dismiss her completely from his field of consciousness.

She wished she could return the insult. She could probably have shared the raft with anyone else without feeling so claustrophobic; it was Bari's presence that made her feel so stifled.

The raft slowed and steadied somewhat as the little sea anchor took hold, and Bari closed the entrance again.

"Is there a first aid kit?" Noor asked, and Bari's piercing gaze fixed her.

"Where are you injured?"

"I only want the scissors."

"What for?" he demanded suspiciously.

"Life's not exciting enough, Bari. I'm going to punch a hole in the raft and add a bit of drama!" she snapped sarcastically, then held up one hand. "I broke my nails."

"The manicure will have to wait."

"I need to cut them off! They'll catch on everything!"

"You haven't lifted a finger so far, so what are they catching on?"

"You know what I mean."

"Other things have priority right now," he said with cold precision.

"Like what! Rowing to Australia?"

"You can start bailing." He tossed her yet another implement made of red plastic. "Use the observation hatch to get rid of the water."

Anything was better than sitting in sloshing water getting chilled, she supposed, but the bailer wasn't easy to use, and every time she put an arm out the hatch, water trickled down into her armpit, something that quickly became a form of Chinese torture.

Bari began to attach a plastic pouch to a narrow sleeve in the canopy above his head.

"What's that?" she asked warily, because she thought she knew.

"It collects rainwater."

Noor shook her head. "You're worried about conserving water?"

"The storm will pass. What then?"

Noor bit her lip and went on bailing.

When it was a little more than half full, Bari removed

the bag and tied the neck, setting it down. Then he picked up a plastic cup and began to help her bail. They worked together in silence for a time, bailing out as much as they could. Then they began sponging the floor dry.

"Do you think a boat or a plane will see us when the storm clears?"

"Not necessarily immediately."

"How long?"

He looked up from his task, as if exasperated that she insisted on forcing herself on his notice.

"You are not a fool, Noor! You know as well as I do that it is possible to be lost at sea for a very long time."

"But this is the Gulf of Barakat, not the Pacific!"

He apparently didn't consider that worth answering. She wondered whether they risked being carried out of the gulf and into the broader sea.

Abruptly she began to shiver. Her teeth chattered, and she realized how cold she had become. She wrapped her arms around herself, trying to stop the convulsions as shock suddenly began to make itself felt in her.

"I'm scared," she admitted in a whisper. "I'm so cold. Bari, would you—hold me?"

She despised herself for this show of weakness even as she asked.

Bari turned. His eyes fell on her bare foot, her ankle, then moved slowly up her brown calf to her bent knee. Then to the thin silk clinging to her body as snugly as a bathing suit. The teddy was made almost transparent by the wet, so that the nest of hair between her thighs was sharply revealed.

Just for a moment his eyes registered something very different than the bored irritation he had been treating her to. For one electric second they flashed with the familiar black fire that had so seduced her, and with an immediacy that was almost physical, Noor was remembering that other time they had been enclosed together in a storm....

They had sailed down the coast one morning and dropped anchor in a ruggedly scenic turquoise bay just before lunch. They swam in the crystal sea, over the submerged ruins of an ancient settlement that was now no more than a few squares outlined in raised earth and some scattered potsherds in the serene white sand, evidence of their kinship with those who had been drawn to this pleasant bay aeons ago.

Overlooking the bay, above on the rocky finger that marked the last reach of the Noor mountain range, was a more recent house in traditional Bagestani style. Its once-white paint was grey and peeling, its domed roof badly weather-damaged. A wooden door sagged on its hinges.

There were many such estates in Bagestan, she knew—abandoned by those who had fled the country under Ghasib's rule—including her family's own. Closer to the cities, such properties had mostly been expropriated by the government, but in remote areas often they had been left to the elements.

Noor had gazed up at the house as she swam in the jewelled water.

"So tragic," she said, for the house fired her imagination. "It must have been so beautiful, and now it looks—lonely. I wonder who it belongs to, and whether they intend to come back now and restore it."

Bari hadn't answered. Their bodies gleaming, they climbed back aboard and rinsed the salt off under the freshwater shower hose at the stern. Bari, the nozzle held above his head, suddenly pointed up at the sky. Dark clouds were moving out from behind the mountains.

"More rain," he said, with deeply felt satisfaction.

Then they sat under the yacht's shady awning, opened the picnic and spread out the little dishes of *bulghur* salad, *imam bayaldi, houmous* and a dozen other enticing concoctions.

The scent of richly spiced succulence rose delicately on the soft wind that blew over them, bringing the welcome rain clouds closer. Noor sighed luxuriously. She felt a sense of perfect physical well-being, bathed in a sensual glow that was the product of the heat, the sea, the food…and Bari's long muscled body, Bari's eyes.

He wanted her.

He had wanted her from the moment they met; he'd never tried to conceal that. That was why she had told him she was a virgin right at the beginning. She always told the men she dated, sooner or later, but with Bari it had to be sooner. *Only with my husband, or my future husband,* she'd said, the very first time he kissed her.

He had nodded, but she'd seen the muscle clench in his cheek, and his black eyes had burned hot enough to scorch her. And for the first time in such a situation she had felt the coil of something that might have been regret. For the first time she considered whether her friends—who talked about sex as if it were a great adventure to be undertaken with any man who looked like a promising travel companion—might be right.

Maybe he'd seen that momentary doubt. Something had flickered in his eyes then, as if he'd known he was the man who had the power to change her mind. Noor steeled herself to resist an onslaught, but in the days that followed Bari had never tried to wear her down, verbally or physically.

Other men had tried to undermine her, taking her to the brink and then insisting on her passion and their rights, but that treatment only fuelled her determination. Bari kissed her once, the kiss that so shifted her inner certainty that it had provoked her instant declaration of her status. After that, he hadn't kissed her, hadn't caressed her, hadn't complained…only his gaze had been given the freedom of her body. His eyes, not his mouth, had tasted the curving lips that had been made for kissing; his eyes had pierced her, as intimately as any thrust of his body, leaving her melting for more. His eyes, not his voice, told her what desire was in his blood.

She couldn't argue with a smile that faded and turned to a look of almost angry possession. She couldn't argue with the tightening of the generous mouth, the clenching of his strong, dark fist as he struggled against passion. And she couldn't resist when he insisted on seeing her, day after day, though it was an unnamed torment to them both.

She told herself his self-control was a relief to her, that she was glad his powerful desire didn't lead him to try to undermine her resolve. But in the long, hot Eastern nights, when she awoke in her solitary bed remembering Bari's eyes in lamplight, or the touch of his hand as it guided her and then lifted from her skin, slowly, weighted by deep reluctance, when her body was filled with yearning and a betraying wish that he had not lifted his hand, but had tightened his hold, had insisted on possession, was here beside her in the bed, to reach for and embrace—then what she felt was something that was almost regret.

The breeze grew stronger under the shadow of the awning, and brushed her forehead with the cool promise of rain.

"Do you think the drought is really over?" she asked. It had already rained twice in two days, and the whole country was rejoicing as if this relief, too, could be laid at the new Sultan's door.

He looked at her. "Yes," he said, his voice creating another sensation on her skin. "The drought is over. It has been long, yes? Too long."

There was a silence as she pretended not to understand him.

"Are you hungry, Noor?"

Noor nodded wordlessly and reached out at random to spoon something luscious onto her plate. Bari tore a piece of bread from the small, tender loaf in front of him, dipped it in spiced olive oil, lifted his chin and slipped the melting morsel between his lips.

Hunger, not for food, whipped her with a ferocity born of the long days and nights of unsatisfied desire. Days and nights when he had given her everything to build her hunger, and nothing against which to sharpen her resistance.

A smudge of oil glazed his lower lip. His upper lip pressed down to suck it off, and his eyes caught her gaze as his lips relaxed again into sensual fullness.

He lowered his lids and reached for the bread. His palm cupped and accommodated to the breastlike roundness of the loaf with deeply sensual appreciation, his long, square fingers dark against the whiteness of the loaf, sure and competent. He offered Noor a torn chunk of bread.

Her fingertips brushed his knuckles, and she winced as her wrist went weak. The little chunk of bread fell on the table between them. Noor breathed in, her eyes rising irresistibly to meet his gaze. He knew. Of course he knew. She swallowed, licked her dry lips.

"Thank you," she murmured, reaching for the bread again.

There was cutlery in the picnic basket, but Bari ate using his fingers or bread as his only tools. Somehow, she didn't know how, this added to the sensual impact of the moment. Then she realized that it was because he was a sensualist. Bari ate with his hands because the sensation of touch added to his pleasure in the food.

Just so, a part of her whispered, would he take pleasure in her body, if she allowed it. Touch, taste, scent…he gloried in his senses, and his senses would glory in her flesh.

He lifted a piece of chicken and tore it apart, offering her a morsel from fingers slippery with melted butter and olive oil, then watched in appreciation as her white teeth closed on the tidbit. He grunted when her lips brushed his skin and, in half-involuntary mimicry of his sensual approach, she closed her lips around his fingertip and sucked the spiced oil from his slightly raspy skin.

A bolt of electricity shot through her, all the way to her toes. Her eyes lifted as if he forced them up to lock with his gaze.

She was on very dangerous ground, but a treacherous part of her, the part that wanted to give in, kept telling her that nothing had happened. He hadn't even kissed her, let alone got close to making love. They were only eating.

But another part of her knew that Bari wasn't like other men, and that this attraction was like nothing she'd ever felt before, and that the point of no return was almost upon her.

The hungry part, the part that was desperate to experience Bari's sensuality at the deepest level, won out, and in involuntary temptation she licked her lips and smiled.

His eyelids drooped, and a possessive gleam shot out from under the lowered lids to tell her that she was lost. He scooped up another morsel of food and fed it to her with one hand, while the other tenderly stroked her throat and chin.

Her skin ignited like dry brush at a lightning strike. Noor opened her eyes and her mouth, but though his face was so close, he did not kiss her.

A delicate assault on her senses began. Resting his elbows on the table, Bari leaned forward to murmur in her ear that she was beautiful, desirable, and that no man could see her and not want her. Then he made her drink from his glass. Like a child—but not like a child.

He stroked her neck, her shoulder above the pretty gauzy sarong she had tied over her bathing suit, her hand, her wrist. He poured wine into her cupped hand and sucked it out with a sexual need that she felt as a blow. He explored her palm with his tongue and lips as if she, too, were heady wine.

As they ate, one desire was sated, but another grew. She felt her body's need for him hammer its urgent message in her blood, her brain, her skin, her breasts, her abdomen. His need for her was in his lips, his tongue, his trembling hands, and in his dark, approving eyes.

Meanwhile, across the sky, dark clouds were massing and moving closer. A rumble of thunder breached the silence now and then, and warm wind whipped at the canvas canopy that protected them from the sun. She felt that her body was like the parched earth that had longed for the sky's blessing for long months and years, and now that he was near it would be sin and worse than sin to turn away into dryness and infertility again.

Down inside the cabin there was a stateroom, and a bed. After an endless time, Bari drew her up from her seat and led her there, pushing her down onto the soft cushions and following to stretch his hungry body out beside her. Then he took her ruthlessly into his arms and, for the first time, let slip the tight rein he had kept on his passion....

Something landed in her lap, bringing her out of her reverie. She blushed, as if Bari might have guessed her thoughts.

"And what's this?" She lifted the little plastic envelope. She was shivering in earnest now.

"A foil blanket. It is dangerous to attempt buddy warmth with only two people in a four-man raft," Bari said. "All the weight in one place could destabilize the raft."

His voice was so full of contemptuous dismissal that she burned with embarrassment, as if she *had* been offering him sex and been rejected.

She didn't believe what he had just said. He simply didn't want to touch her. The rage and hurt of this morning's discovery flooded her mind once more. She was in a ferment to shake him out of his damned supercilious contempt, his smug calm.

"What gives you the right to look at me as if—as if...I was asking for *comfort!*" she shouted. "When did I *ever* throw myself at you? You were the one! Right from the beginning—as if I were water in the desert!"

Tears stung her eyes, but she would *not* be so weak!

"Instead you were a mirage," Bari said harshly, as her emotions succeeded in igniting his own.

"Me?" she exclaimed, choking on the injustice. "*I* wasn't the mirage! *I* never lied!"

"What was it when you said you would marry me, if not a lie?"

His voice was cold with fury. In the red glow cast by the canopy he looked unfamiliar, an angry stranger.

And that was what he was. She didn't know him at all.

"What was it when *you* said you wanted to marry me?" she countered hotly, the pent-up words bursting from her. "You don't want to marry me, and never did! And before you deny it, I overheard your aunt and your cousin talking. You're only marrying me because your grandfather wants an alliance with his old friend's family. He ordered you to marry me, and you were furious about it. You have to marry me to inherit the family property, isn't that right? You don't love me!"

He watched her steadily, one eyebrow lifted.

"Do you!" she prodded. *"Do you!"*

"No, Noor," Bari replied in a slow, calm voice, not at all the voice of a man caught out. "No, I don't love you. Why are you pretending outrage when you have always known it?"

Six

Noor's mouth opened in slow, appalled disbelief, but Bari gave no quarter.

"I never told you I loved you. You didn't ask to hear it. What you wanted was a wealthy, socially connected man who would cater to your desire for a life of selfish pleasure. That was what I offered you. That was your price, Noor."

"My *price!*"

"So the discovery that you say you have now made—that love is not part of our bargain—will not serve as an excuse. I ask you again—why did you back out of the agreement that both of us understood from the beginning? And why did you choose such a moment, such a grotesque and offensive way to do it?"

His teeth and eyes flashed in an angry smile.

"It's not true!" she cried, but if he heard the dismay in her voice it left him unmoved.

"What is not true? What part of what I have said do you dispute?"

"If you didn't love me, why didn't you tell me that when you proposed?"

"You never asked. My reasons for wishing the marriage formed no part of our bargain. You could have made it so, but you did not choose to know."

"Only because I thought—I thought—"

"What did you think?" His eyes narrowed. "You thought I loved you?" Fierce laughter erupted from him. "You got it all, is that what you thought, Noor? I offered you wealth and social connections, and my family's honour, and now you say you thought you had my love, too—and what were you offering in exchange? Not love, for you love only yourself."

"That's not true!" she cried, stunned by this battering. "Anyway, I didn't need your wealth or social conn—"

"Your name, that was the sum total of what you brought to our agreement. That you are the descendant of a man my grandfather remembers with love and respect."

His voice dripped with bitterness, and she knew then without a doubt that what she had overheard his cousin and aunt saying was the truth. He had been brutally angry over his grandfather's decision.

"Why do you flinch from admitting it?"

She could feel tears burning her eyes, but not for the world would she let Bari see how affected she was, her skin crawling with humiliation and shame.

"You pretended!" she accused him, her voice hovering on a sob. "Try and deny that! Don't call me a fool when you know perfectly well you acted as if you were besotted with me!"

He lifted a hand, a shoulder, in an expressive shrug. "You are a sexually attractive woman. But if you had really wanted my love, Noor, you would have acted like a woman who wants to be loved, not like one who knows she can do no wrong. When did you concern yourself with my good opinion? With the regard of my mother and sisters? With anyone's well-being but your own? Nothing is as important to you as your own wishes, it seems. Whose opinion matters to you? Whose feelings do you consider?"

"That's a lie!"

"So sure are you of your worth that you didn't notice I never spoke of love! Yet—you tell me now—all the time you were assuming that I loved you passionately. Is that the attitude of a woman with a heart? To take love for granted?

"And if you had ever believed you loved me, you would have told me so. Even when there is nothing but sex a woman will say *I love you*. But not you. *Oh, Bari, isn't it wonderful!* That is what you said. But no word of love."

Anger and humiliation scorched her. She had never been so insulted, so bitterly condemned.

"I was a virgin! Why do you think I waited all that time, if not for love?"

He smiled. "You waited for a husband. You said to me, *only with my husband, or my future husband,* not *only with the man I love.*"

"It went without saying. Of course I expected to love the man I married!"

His black eyes fixed her, as if with pins to a board. "And did you love him, the man you nearly married?" Her heart fluttered a protest.

"I—" Her mind seemed to stumble.

"Go on, Noor. Tell me you love me," Bari challenged mockingly.

Was he right? Was it the image she had loved, and not the man at all? What was love? She hesitated, and he laughed outright.

"You can't expect me to say it *now!*" she cried.

"If you imagine love is so easily killed, then you know nothing of love. You are suffering from bruised pride, and you imagine you have been crossed in love!"

"That is so untrue!"

He eyed her coldly. "And is this truly why you ran from our wedding ceremony minutes before it was to begin, leaving all our guests, without a word of explanation to them or to our families or to me? Because of an insult to your pride? Because of a conversation you overheard?"

Noor could hardly take it in. How could he be throwing her accusation back in her face like this? She had been on a rock, and with a wave of words he had changed that into shifting sand.

This isn't really happening! her brain kept insisting. *This is a dream!*

How had she gone from being an excited, beautiful bride, wearing the most exquisite dress in the world and a diamond worth a sultan's ransom, waiting for her wedding to a man who was crazy for her, to this—having flown through a terrifying storm in fear for her life, and crash-landed at sea, she was now lying in a storm-tossed life raft waiting for rescue that might not come, her makeup streaked, her nails broken and torn, her hair in rat's tails, wet, naked and shivering, and squashed into a tiny space with that same man who now despised her?

But worst of all was what she was hearing about herself. Did she act like a woman so used to being loved she took it for granted?

It wasn't true. If she had believed Bari loved her it

was because of the way he had treated her, not because that was her first assumption.

"I don't take love for granted!" Noor felt another chill sweep through her and, suddenly reminded, she sat up and tore the plastic bag from the tiny packet he had thrown her. She unfurled a sheet of rustling gold foil that glowed and glittered even in the dimness.

"Silver side in for warmth," Bari said, and began working a small air pump.

She wrapped herself in it. Whatever the strange foil was, it had an immediate effect on her chill. But it offered poor protection against Bari's accusations. They had already hit home.

"It looks like the Sultana's robes at the coronation," she muttered, tweaking the folds around her, trying to dispel her own gloom, trying to prevent herself hearing what he had said, what he really thought of her.

Could it be true? People had always loved her. Everyone she knew loved her. And not just her mother and father and her brothers and Jalia and her friends. At school she had been popular with everyone—except for a few girls who were jealous, she amended carefully…but no one was loved by everybody in the world! You couldn't be human and not have *some* enemies! Some girls were jealous of her because her family spoiled her, she'd always known that. She'd had lots of spending money and the freedom to do what she liked, and of course people hated that….

Bari's family had been cool with her, some of them. But she couldn't have cared less what they thought of her. Why should she? Bari was right about that—she'd taken no trouble to make them like her, not Noor! If they didn't like her as she was, that was their problem. Anyway, she'd told herself, it was only jealousy because Bari had fallen for her so hard.

But if it turned out Bari hadn't fallen for her, and they knew it, what did that mean?

That they disliked her for herself?

What had she ever done to deserve dislike? When had she ever hurt anyone?

As if in answer, her brain suddenly conjured up the scene her flight must have created. Jalia and the bridesmaids coming to the door of her bedroom, one of the women going to the bathroom to call her...had they gone searching through the house? And when she was nowhere to be found—what would they have thought? Her parents—what had they imagined? What were they going through now?

She thought of the guests, and what bewilderment they must have felt—were probably still feeling. What she had done was a personal insult to them all. She had treated them as if they didn't matter in the least. Bari was right—she had thought her own concerns of overriding importance. Some of their guests had flown halfway around the world to celebrate with her, and she hadn't even done them the simple honour of telling them that she had changed her mind and the wedding wouldn't take place.

As if that understanding unlocked a door in her heart, a host of other visions suddenly flashed through her unwilling mind, one after the other. Moments in her past when she had acted selfishly, even cruelly. Girls at school whom she had cut, or insulted, or laughed at when they tried to be popular, or wore the wrong clothes. Friends she had dropped without explanation, a boy she had mocked when he asked her out...

All the time believing she was in the right. Noor

Ashkani could do no wrong. She brooked no criticism. Dare to doubt Noor's actions and you were out of the charmed circle before you took another breath.

All her life she had acted as if she were the person who mattered. She hadn't believed that consciously, but she could see with painful clarity now that it had been the unconscious basis of her actions.

The discovery that Bari didn't love her had cut to the quick her self-importance, and she had reacted with pure arrogance. She had hurt and insulted everyone.

Noor looked up. Bari's expression was grim, but even if it hadn't been, she couldn't tell him what thoughts and what painful self-realization poured through her. Not Bari, of all people, who sat in such harsh judgement and had never loved—probably didn't even like—her.

Bari watched his bride impassively, her chin trembling as she struggled against emotion. She sat with head bent, her hands hiding her face, tears trickling down her cheeks. He let her cry for a few minutes. It was probably no more than the shock of the crash being released, and he was angry enough to remain unmoved. But when the choked sobs began to become a wail, it was time to call a halt.

"That's enough," he ordered without apology, tossing another packet at her. It landed on the rustling gold blanket. "You can't afford to waste any more energy."

Noor's breathing shifted into a series of panting gasps, like a child, as she struggled to stifle her tears. She wiped her face and blew her nose on her beautiful dress, picked up the little plastic box and gazed at it stupidly.

"What is it?"

"First aid kit," he said.

Why had she asked for the kit? The mixture of shame

and misery kept her head bent, and she found relief in
wrestling with the plastic seal. She reached for the flashlight and shone it briefly on the contents. The first thing
her eyes fell on was a vial of seasickness pills.

As if there were a direct causal link, Noor's stomach
heaved. With a strangled cry she tossed the kit and the
flashlight aside and dived for the entrance, her gold foil
cloak rustling wildly. She ripped the flap down and,
thrusting her head out into the storm, clutched the side
of the raft, leaned over, and heaved up the shock and
grief and shame and the million other undefined things
she was feeling, until there seemed to be nothing left,
either in her stomach or in her heart.

When it was over at last, she reached her hand down
into the sea and scooped up handfuls of water to wash
her face and rinse her mouth. The salt stung her eyes and
tasted on her lips, but the coolness of the water seemed
to bring her back to herself.

When she was through she felt purged, cleansed. She
drew her head back inside and sealed the flap again. Bari
ignored her.

Well, she wasn't asking for his sympathy. She wasn't
asking for anything from him. She had learned something
about herself in the past half hour, and it had been a very
painful lesson. Some fundamental shift seemed to have
happened in her, and for the second time in a few months
she had the sensation of not knowing who she was.

But there was no way she was going to try to tell Bari
that. He would probably think she was making it up.

"The storm is passing," she said, wrapping herself
securely in the rustling golden foil again. "I think I
saw land."

He nodded without looking up. He was still working
the air pump, and the floor was slowly inflating.

"May I have a drink of water?"

He tossed her the little plastic cup he had been bailing with. "Catch some rainwater in that."

Noor bit back an indignant response. She supposed his caution was appropriate, even praiseworthy—if they were going to be lost for any length of time the water conservation started now, even if that was land she had seen.

But he could have been less rude about it.

"I see we aren't going to be bound by any silly code of polite conduct while we're stuck here," she rashly remarked.

Leaving herself wide open, of course, and she realized it as soon as it was too late to call the comment back. Bari lifted an eyebrow, and though his face was in shadow, she could guess the expression in his eyes.

"You are speaking, of course, as someone who isn't bound by any code of conduct at any time."

There was no winning that one. Noor lifted the cup up to the sleeve as she had seen him do, but he had pushed it inside out. She fiddled with it for a moment, without discovering the trick. She glanced over at Bari, but he was working the air pump, his head bent.

Fine! She wasn't nearly as helpless or stupid as he obviously believed, and she'd be *damned* if she would ask for his help!

After a few moments she was rewarded with the sound of water dripping into the cup. *Nyaaa,* she told him in her head, but not by so much as the tip of her tongue did she let him see her triumph.

The rain funnelled down more slowly than before, and she suddenly realized how the rain had slackened, and how far away the thunder was. She filled the cup three times and drank the curiously tasteless liquid, then glanced at Bari.

"Do you want a drink?"

He looked up, surprised. "Yes, thanks."

Noor bit back a resentful remark—did he really think she was incapable of putting herself out for someone else even in a situation like this?—and passed the filled cup to him without comment. He tossed off the water in one gulp and gave it back to her with a murmur of thanks. She filled it again, and he drank again.

The transaction felt strange and awkward to her, because she felt uncomfortable with him now. No doubt Bari would say it was because she was so unused to doing even the simplest things for other people. But what did he know about her?

"I suppose it has never occurred to you," she remarked to the cup as she filled it for him for the third time, "that you have seen me in a very limited set of circumstances—namely, when I was (a) effectively on holiday, (b) had just learned, among other things, that my family owned a *palace* and (c) was suddenly being treated as a princess by everyone around me? How many people you know would have kept their heads in a situation like mine?"

Her eyes met his as she passed him the cup again. "You think a person should not be judged by their behaviour when life is going well for them?"

"Welcome to The Kangaroo Courtroom of the Waves," Noor announced bitterly. "Forget I spoke."

Bari drank and handed her the empty cup, signalling that he didn't want any more. Noor filled the cup one last time and then picked up the pack of seasickness pills and pressed one out into her palm.

Her broken fingernail caught as she did so, and after swallowing the pill she reached for the first aid kit again, located the scissors, and cut the three torn nails off short, as neatly as she could. She spread out her hands. If her nails were going to keep on breaking at the current rate it would be smarter to cut them all down now. On the other hand, if rescue were near…

Something made her lift her eyes, and she found Bari watching her, a cynical gleam in his gaze.

"Look on the bright side—they may have time to regrow before you have to face your admiring public again," he said.

Gritting her teeth, Noor picked up the scissors again and one by one cut the rest of her nails short.

"I hope you aren't making a mistake. Nails like that might have come in handy. Who knows how many fish we may need to scale, for example?"

Noor gave him back look for look. "No worries. I'm sure your ceremonial sword will do the job. It'll be a comfort to you to know all that family history is useful for something."

And so the battle lines were drawn.

Seven

Noor cast a half-despairing look around as they approached land. The faint shape she had seen earlier had proved to be a small, isolated island, probably somewhere on the outer fringes of the Gulf Island group.

The clouds had given way to blazing sunshine, which quickly turned the life raft into a sauna. But the sun's heat was fading now as it neared the horizon, and Noor was wondering whether it was safe to emerge.

Bari was sitting out on the edge of the raft using one of the paddles as a makeshift rudder, keeping the raft on a heading towards the island. He was also trailing a fishing line.

He had stripped off the purple silk jacket and was wearing it on his head, the sleeves twisted into rope and tied around his forehead, to form a makeshift keffiyeh. Anyone else, Noor reflected bitterly, would have looked like a complete idiot. Bari looked like a genie in a fairy tale, skin bronzed, chest and arm muscles rippling, white silk *shalwar* enfolding his legs, bare feet. He seemed perfectly at home.

Noor, on the other hand, had been forced by the fierce sun to stay inside the stifling confines of the raft through the worst heat of the day, painstakingly cutting a sarong and a scarf from the wet skirt of her wedding dress with scissors that weren't up to the job. Without such protection she couldn't hope to face the sun. Her predicament hadn't been helped by Bari's insistence that they had had plenty of water to get them through the first twenty-four hours.

They were communicating in monosyllables.

The island itself was a relatively attractive prospect, with a small curving bay protected by a rocky outcrop at one end, and clustered palm trees that promised water. But Noor had stopped hoping some time ago that it might also hold the Gulf Eden Resort.

Deciding that the sun had lost its danger, she carefully slipped up through the canopy entrance with the wet scarf in her hand, and as she did so, she was struck by a sudden, unconnected thought.

"Wait a minute!" she exclaimed, breaking the hostile silence unthinkingly. "Isn't a radio beacon part of the emergency equipment of this raft? An EPIRB?"

Bari looked at her.

She urged excitedly, "I'm sure my friends all have it as part of their yacht emergency kit."

"It isn't a part of the standard raft emergency kit. There was one aboard the plane…." He pressed his lips together in mute resignation.

Noor moaned her despair. "Oh, God, you *forgot* it?"

As if to comfort her, Bari said, "We have flares. When it is dark we will set one off."

"Why don't we do it now? Flares are visible in day-light, aren't they?"

"Is it worth wasting a flare merely to ease the present tedium?"

Noor wasn't used to the feeling that someone was secretly laughing at her, and she didn't like it. She held up the damp silk, and felt cooler just watching it flap in the breeze.

"It would be nice to see some action around here, and you don't seem to be having much luck with the fish," she said waspishly. "Why do you talk of wasting them? How many are there?"

"Two."

"*Is that all?* What if no one sees them? Oh, my God, and it's such a small island, too! Don't you think it might be better to stay in the raft in the hopes of reaching an island where there's more chance of finding people?"

Bari looked up, and his breath caught on a hiss which she did not hear. Standing in the entrance opening opposite him, Noor was leaning lightly back on the canopy, one foot propped on the edge of the raft, the square of silk forgotten in her hand. Her head tilted back while she turned her face this way and that under the luxurious caress of the wind.

Just so had she moved under the stroking of his lips.

Her body was barely covered by the delicate garment she wore, which did nothing to hide that creamy skin, warm with a light tan everywhere except her breasts and abdomen, the paler-textured places he knew as well as his own hand, even after only one interlude of lovemaking.

Her hair was damp with sweat at her temples, as if he had just made love to her. Her breasts swelled with the movement of her arms, pressing against the soft, expensive lace that cupped them.

The top of her thighs, with the thin damp silk revealing the nest of hair, was right in his line of vision. All he had to do was bend forward to bury his mouth where his eyes were. Heavy sensual memory tugged at his limbs, asking to be repeated. The hard tension of his body urged him.

"Wouldn't it be better?" Noor's impatient voice brought him back to the question. More hope of finding other people, was that what she wanted? Bari's jaw tightened in a grim smile.

"Does the thought of being without your entourage so terrify you?"

"My *entourage?*"

"You are afraid that you can't live without the army of doting servants and friends and Jalia and your brothers—or at least someone who might be willing to replace them? You would prefer to remain in the raft, with whatever dangers that entails, than face the possibility that you will now have to fend for yourself?"

His tone suggested that another minute on the raft with her would drive him to suicide. His teeth flashed in the mocking smile that her lacerated spirit suddenly found too familiar. Had the smiles that had melted her bones always secretly mocked her?

Noor gritted her teeth.

"I would prefer to take the rational course of action, regardless of my more immediate feelings," she said, her jaw tight. "But I see that in a fifty-fifty disagreement between brains and brawn, brawn is always going to get its way!"

His smile didn't falter, though his eyes flashed a message that raised nervous goose bumps on her arms. "Alas, it is the story of your sex," he mocked. "Always right, and always powerless."

It was a relief to be speaking in whole sentences again, whatever the sentiments being expressed. Feeling had to come out somehow, Noor felt, or eat her alive.

"Not *always* powerless," she snapped. "The patriarchy has had a brief reign, really—a mere two or three thousand years. A hiccup of deviance in the natural order."

"And are you expecting the return of the all-wise matriarchy any time soon?"

"Well, it'll be either that or the complete destruction of the species, won't it?" Noor snapped.

"You think men are certain to lead the world to destruction?"

"I think men who fear and hate women and don't allow us a voice or listen to our wisdom have brought us to the brink of it already. Tell me I'm wrong!"

"And you include me in their numbers," Bari said flatly. "How typical of a woman who has heard criticism of herself, to expand that into a generalized misogyny in the soul of the speaker!"

She bent over, bringing her face on a level with his.

"I don't give a damn about your criticism or dislike of me!" she lied fiercely, feeling that his black eyes burned her more harshly than the sun. "What I do care about is your assumption that my query over whether we should land on this particular island should be mocked, rather than taken into rational consideration, because it disagrees with *your* all-seeing, all-knowing decision on the matter! What makes you such a bloody expert on shipwreck? Ever done it before? Neither have I! That makes us equals in this situation, I think. Except that I need your agreement to go on sailing, and you don't need mine to land. Or should I push you overboard and steer the thing myself?"

"By all means, if you think you can."

"So here we are back at brains and brawn again. See?" Noor held up her hands and smiled, as if a slow pupil had finally been led to the light. Her smile was bright and mocking, and she could see it got under his skin in spite of his intentions.

She tried not to feel that she was lighting a fuse on an unknown quantity of explosive.

"Don't be so quick to assign yourself *all* the brains. I've told you before that these islands are now uninhabited. Except for the Gulf Eden Resort. Even a woman, I think, should have doubts about her ability to find one particular island when she doesn't know its position or her own."

Noor gritted her teeth. "No wonder men are turning the world into such a hell!" she said feebly. It was the only riposte she could think of.

"And when women ruled the world, everyone lived in paradise?"

"You don't find any city walls in the ancient matriarchal societies, do you?" Noor pointed out. "Sumer—"

"I suppose you learned this nonsense in *Feminist Perspectives on History for Beginners!*" Bari interrupted with harsh irony. "You don't find any city walls around Persepolis, either. The capital of the Persian Empire, which was ruled by the Achaemenid *kings*. It spread to become the greatest empire in antiquity. Are you suggesting it was not militaristic?"

"Tell me, is it nonsense because it's feminist, or because the ideas expressed are not your own?" Noor asked sweetly.

But the mocking tone didn't disguise her real feelings from herself. She glared down into his face, and noted helplessly how the sinking sun melted in his dark eyes, glowed on the black curls that clustered over his head.

The sea, too, was glittering with its rich golden light. The sapphire and amethyst of the deeper sea had given way now to turquoise and emerald, with flashes of white gold. It was as if some celestial painter had brushed diamonds on the crest of every ripple of the sea, as on each coal-black curl, underlining Bari's vital connection with the rest of creation, and reminding her of that other time they had drifted on the waves as the sun set. Then his hand had never been far from her skin, stroking her in tender possession in the aftermath of their lovemaking—her breast, her arm, her flank.

Her heart beat hard. So he was handsome, so what? So he had made the kind of love to her you read about in books! How could she be so weak as to find him attractive now that she knew what she knew?

And he was perfectly right: she didn't love him, and never had.

Meanwhile, Bari damped down his anger, though it cost him a struggle. He knew it would be dangerous to allow anger—or any emotion—to overwhelm him in these circumstances.

"It is because such ideas are based on nothing," he replied levelly. "We can scarcely hope to understand our neighbours today. How do we dream that we know anything of how societies operated thousands of years ago?"

Under the water now a floor of white sand appeared, across which their shadow rose and fell with the waves. Noor watched a school of delicate, sinuous, silver-and-turquoise fish flee from the threatening shape as the raft approached.

Suddenly Bari's fishing line jerked tight, and their conversation, such as it was, dissolved. Bari picked up the bailer and thrust it at Noor with a brief "Hold that and try to get it under him!" Then his strong hands began to pull the line with slow careful pressure, drawing the struggling fish closer and closer, playing it a little, and then inexorably drawing it in again.

Their differences were forgotten as they worked together on the urgent task of bringing in tonight's dinner, and when the fish had been captured, they smiled at each other involuntarily, forgetting their conflict for the moment.

"I could almost eat it raw!" she cried.

"You might have to."

The raft was being carried at an angle away from the sandy part of the beach towards the rocks. Bari jumped out, landed in waist-deep water and, waving her to stay aboard, dragged the painter over his shoulder. His arm and back muscles rippled as he guided the little raft into the long shadow of a rugged outcrop of black rock that thrust up out of the smooth white sand, the sea splashing gently against it.

Noor watched in helpless fascination as he strode up the sloping beach, the water level dropping to reveal his slim waist, his muscled hips, strong thighs. The white cloth of his *shalwar,* stained dark by the water, clung to him, outlining every rippling fold of well-toned muscle. The inside of her own thighs unexpectedly melted at the sudden sense-memory of the firmness of his body against her in those pleasure-drugged minutes when her legs had clung to him and he moved inside her.

It had been painful and an utter delight all at once, as her body now insistently reminded her. The slap of the waves against the raft, its gentle rise and fall, the erotic swelling that lifted the raft and let it sink, all conspired to bring back her first experience of that primal motion, that fundamental rhythm underlying all creation.

Though she hadn't achieved the peak under the thrust of his body, the pain of lost virginity hadn't stopped her hunger for him, for more, more, more. His mouth and his hands had been what sent her over the edge into swooping pleasure, but it wasn't mouth and hands she remembered now. It was him deep inside her, pushing her towards some magical truth that had eluded her then but still magnetically beckoned and promised. The mere touch of him had given her a deep satisfaction, even without the soaring pleasure, and it was that which, to her horror, she was suddenly yearning and aching for.

The completion. The sense of connection at the deepest level. The oneness of it.

He was despising you all the time, Noor reminded herself fiercely. *It was an act to trick you. He was prostituting himself for his grandfather's money.*

The life raft ran aground, and she climbed out of it with a slight stagger. The waves bubbled and frothed against her shins, warm and inviting.

"We must carry it ashore. Take that side," Bari commanded, as if he expected to be obeyed, and Noor just couldn't think of a way to rebel that wouldn't end with her having to obey. When they had carried the raft above the high-tide mark and into the lee of the rock, he nodded approvingly, as if to a child.

"Very good."

He searched inside for the flashlight, and Noor turned away from the sight of him to watch the sun set underneath a perfect spectrum of colours: blood-red at the horizon, then glowing orange, golden yellow, soft green blending to blue, then through deeper and deeper blues to indigo and finally, overhead, to dark amethyst.

Underneath the sky the water reflected the sparkling,

deep velvet blackness, the surface glowing with dancing touches of red and gold.

"Princess!" The voice broke in to her reverie and she looked up to see the mocking grin she so hated.

"I thought so!" Bari said, grinning. "But there's no *princess* on this island, Princess. The title's temporarily suspended. Everybody pulls their own weight here."

Noor glared at him. "I was just watching the sunset for a moment!" She didn't add, *as a way of keeping my eyes off your butt.* It would be a cold day in hell before she said anything like that.

"Uh-huh," Bari said, as if he didn't believe a word of it. "Well, sunset is the last thing you have time for, Princess. If you want to eat, you're going to have to work for it."

"I don't think it's so urgent we can't take a moment to get our bearings!"

"The sun's setting fast. Get your bearings in the morning. You can start by collecting stones to circle the fire. Then gut the fish."

"And what will you be doing while I do all that?" Noor enquired gently.

"Gathering firewood, Princess," he informed her, as if he'd been hoping she would ask. "Unless you were serious about eating your dinner raw."

He lifted his hand and dropped it again, and with a tiny chunk of sound, a knife embedded itself in the sand at her feet.

In the gathering darkness, Noor collected stones and laid them in a circle to contain their fire. Then she stood and looked around. In among the trees the beam of Bari's flashlight flicked up and down.

Strange places could be frightening at the best of times. She shivered, and felt how naked and unpro-

tected she was with only the homemade sarong to cover
her. She was glad he meant to make a fire.

If she had never gutted a fish before, at least she had
seen it done often enough to make a reasonable stab at
the process. Bari was probably hoping she would balk
at the task, and she was determined to disappoint him.
So Noor took a deep breath, picked up the knife, and
with a little moue slit the still-graceful silver-grey body
and cleaned it. She was laying the fish on a palm leaf
when Bari returned with his arms full.

"Good girl, Princess!" he applauded, eyeing her
preparations.

Noor gritted her teeth. "Good boy, Sheikh!" she said.

His eyelids drooped.

"Who started it?" she demanded, preempting any
complaint.

Bari laughed. Noor went down to the sea to rinse her
hands. When she returned, Bari had laid a fire and was
carefully lighting it. At his command, she went to get
the bag of water and the little plastic cup out of the raft.
She picked up the foil sheet and dragged it around her
shoulders, then opened another and laid it down as a picnic blanket—but there the comparison ended. There
was nothing else to set out, no other preparation she
could make. They had no utensils, no plates, no salt,
nothing.

Noor wrapped the thin foil around her against the increasing chill, and held the feeling of panic at bay. They
were lucky, she told herself firmly. Bari had been
right—they were a thousand times safer on dry land than
lost at sea on a tiny raft.

The last rays of the sun faded and darkness swept
over them, broken only by the flickering blaze of their
tiny campfire. In the darkness the silence was intense.

The rushing of the sea, the crackling of the burning wood, the cry of an unknown bird or animal in the deeper shadows of the trees, against that backdrop of silence, only told them of their aloneness.

Eight

Late in the night Bari lay awake, listening to his bride's soft breathing beside him as if it were the wind of his soul. Overhead, beyond the swathe of wedding veil that protected them, moon and stars glowed too brightly in the purple-black sky. At his feet, the sea slapped and shushed, its deep, living black painted with thick gold light. There was no horizon; he was caught in a web of spangled blackness that had neither beginning nor end.

Emotionally, too, he was caught in a web.

No, Noor, I don't love you.

That his grandfather should try to dictate Bari's choice of wife was one thing. He was an old man. Of course he expected to rule his family's fortunes in the old way, the way of generations before him. And of course nostalgia had a strong hold on his imagination.

The timing of the demand, however, was a cause almost for outrage. It was evidence of how badly Jabir al

Khalid was losing his grip that his first act, in the face of the monumental difficulties and the dedicated work that would necessarily follow the astonishing achievement of the Return, had been to track down the family of his old friend Faruq Durrani in the hopes of arranging a marriage for his grandson.

Marriage was the last thing on Bari's agenda. What time had he for the courtship and wooing that a woman had a right to expect, even in an arranged marriage? He had urgent tasks ahead of him, both as Cup Companion to a Sultan endeavouring to make an effective transition to a new order, and as the heir to the neglected family interests in Bagestan.

But his grandfather had insisted, even when Faruq Durrani's most eligible granddaughter proved to be a foreigner, born and raised in the West, into wealth and privilege without responsibility, who was very unlikely to be suited to joining Bari in his life's work.

And doubtless, Bari had pointed out to his grandfather with as much patience as he could muster, a woman who would be impatient with any attempt to arrange a marriage. As a Westerner, she would feel it her right to fall in love with a man of her own choosing, to be courted "for herself."

The old man had understood that modern concept. He had ordered that there should be no conventional overtures for an arranged marriage—no, Bari would have to woo and win the girl.

All that was bad enough, but much worse was to come. Before Bari could refuse this mad request outright, Jabir al Khalid delivered his ultimatum.

The blackmail had shocked them all. It told Bari that his grandfather was well aware that times had changed. He knew that his word was no longer law. He was not powerful in the way of his father and his father's fathers. So he was making up for the lack of moral power with threat—marry this woman or watch the family estates fall into further disrepair as cousins vie to win the prize. Never set foot on al Khalid property except as a guest of someone who cares nothing for its heritage.

The old man also knew—no one better—that his grandson had always dreamed of returning to Bagestan when it was liberated. Bari had worked with Ashraf Durrani throughout his determined, dangerous bid to restore the al Jawadis to the throne, and he intended and expected to stay and help to rebuild the country and his own family's heritage when that bid was successful.

But when the joy of the people was still ringing in their ears, when Bari might have expected congratulations from his grandfather, who had wanted nothing more than to see the al Jawadis restored to their throne, when the cup of opportunity he had worked for all his life was within his grasp…this was the agenda that his grandfather had set him: not to embark on the great task that he had spent his life preparing for, not to begin the restoration of derelict family properties, not to start on the rehabilitation of the tragically mismanaged farms and land—but to court and marry a spoiled Westerner with no sense of duty.

The first time he set eyes on Princess Noor al Jawadi Durrani, Bari had realized that fate was laughing at him. His fears of what she might be were nothing compared to the reality of the beautiful, capricious woman he saw at the coronation. A magnificently spoiled woman with a sulky, sensual mouth, who had discovered that she was a princess in Bagestan and was taking the title to heart.

Her sexual magnetism had reached him even across

the expanse of the Great Hall of the Old Palace—him and a dozen other men. It sparked out from her, wild and undisciplined, like a new star in the heavens not sure of its own brilliance.

She smiled on all, and he saw men drawn to her without volition, like moths to the brightest light. Why will ten moths all be drawn to the only lantern in a caravanserai, when each could have the exclusive light of one of numerous lesser candles?

So it was with Noor.

In spite of his furious inner rejection of all his grandfather's interference, he could not help the jealous possessiveness that had invaded his spirit at that moment.

If she was to be his, then she would be all his.

For the first time in his life, Bari understood the instinct that had driven his forefathers to cloister and veil their women. He had not wanted her, did not choose her—but she was his. Those other men's eyes, caressing her, the smiles they received, he could hardly bear. They stole what was his—he felt the instinct of his blood rise up and tell him it was so.

He had found his reaction incomprehensible—some primitive instinct in his blood he had never before encountered engulfed him, and all for a woman he didn't know and half despised!

But wanted. Her dress was designed for maximum erotic impact—with glittering jewels clinging to her neck and breasts and clouds of green tulle cloaking and revealing her soft skin in tantalizing unpredictability.

If he had been worried about his ability to woo her, however, the worry was short-lived. She might be a Westerner in her contempt for arranged marriage, but love was no more on her agenda than on his. She was flattered by his interest, she preened herself in the in-

tensity of his focus on her—but it hadn't taken him long
to discover that she *felt* nothing.

He had attractions enough to win her. He was rich,
his blood was noble, he was a Cup Companion and he
socialized with the rich and famous from her world and
his own.

Those were the traits she admired in him.

So he had showed her his family's wealth and position, instead of his hopes and dreams, as he might have
done with a different woman. He had introduced her to
celebrities and princes instead of his inner self. He had
showered her with gifts instead of the undelivered kisses
that burned him like live coals and acid.

For that was the worst torment of all—his desire for
her. There was no rhyme or reason to it, and no reasoning, either, could change it.

He kept the other men away from her. She had not
guarded her virginity all this time for him to lose the
prize at the end. One look was usually enough, from
Bari al Khalid. But if it was not—well, he knew how to
enlighten a man's wilful ignorance.

He had known that she was sexually aware of him.
Had known that she feared her own weakness, if he decided to press her. He had laid his plans as carefully as
Prince Ashraf had in his bid for the throne of Bagestan.
Noor had only one shield against him—the shield of
only-with-my-husband. Well, then, he would remove
that shield—he would build her to a pitch of desire,
then propose and make love to her at once.

She would not say no to him sexually once he had
stripped her of her shield, and equally she would not say
no to marriage once he had deflowered her.

She would be caught in a trap she had made herself.

It had never once occurred to him that, having been

so neatly caught, she would execute an eleventh-hour escape. How could he have dreamed that, having accepted and agreed, their bargain sealed with lovemaking, she would change her mind and bolt?

At first he didn't know how to credit the reason she gave him for her flight. Why would she, who had shown no sign of love for him, no interest in his feelings, run when she learned that his grandfather had ordered him to marry her? Why should she balk at the thought of an arranged marriage, who had so ruthlessly "arranged" her own?

But now he saw the truth with chilling clarity. She had fled the wedding because she wanted everything, this woman who gave nothing, and she had learned at the last moment that she was not getting quite everything. How dared she assume that, in addition to everything else, she had his love—love she hadn't tried to return, hadn't even troubled to ask for, but nevertheless expected as her due?

It was not her due. No more than wealth and an easy life was universal admiration her due. *It behooves those to whom life has been generous to cultivate humility in the face of their good fortune.* He had learned that from an early age. It was the hallmark of a Cup Companion to offer service in exchange for such good fortune as noble birth and inherited wealth.

Noor stirred and sighed beside him, and he turned to watch her again. Under the foil sheet they shared she was wrapped in the white silk that she had cut from the skirts of her wedding dress. Above her head her wedding veil protected her from insects. He shook his head. Her wedding finery had made the same journey as his own hopes. They, too, had been abased.

Her eyelashes cast long shadows on her moon-whitened cheeks, giving her the fragile delicacy of a moon creature. The old romances talked of the jinn, a race of creatures made of fire, as humans were made of earth. Just now, with the pale glow playing over her flawless skin, it seemed as if the moonlight came from within. If Allah was moved to make creatures from earth and fire, Bari found himself thinking, then surely he must also have created some from moonlight. And such a being would look like this—her skin translucent, as though her light reflected on the heavens. As if the moon were her reflection.

Did the moon have a heart? Or was its pale light symbolic of cool heartlessness?

He had to marry her. Whatever her reasons for running from the wedding, he had to find the way back. That was the price of everything he had worked towards, all that he had dreamed for his family. That was the price of fulfilling his father's deathbed request—*go home, my son, and rebuild what we lost.*

He had given his father his word, at the impressionable age of fifteen, and the promise had thereafter consumed his life.

But there was another dream, too.

He wanted a partner in life. A woman to share its joys and sorrows with him. A woman capable of the giving and the sacrifice that marriage and family demanded. Not a woman of the careless selfishness Noor exhibited.

Once he had hoped that, in spite of everything, Noor had a heart and it was not out of his reach. That she would learn to love him, and he her. That whatever its beginnings, with time they could forge the kind of marriage that would be a strength to them both.

Her flight had awakened him from a blind and brazen foolishness. What if she had no heart to reach? Or what if he was not the one to touch it? Either way, there was misery in store, not just for him, but for any children they might have. For his mother and sisters, who would suffer, too.

Unless Noor had more heart than she had shown so far, one of his dreams he must give up. Either the dream of fulfilling his promise to his father and his duty to the family, or the dream of a good marriage. He knew he could have only one. He must betray either his heritage, or his own heart. He had to choose.

Bari looked out at the jewel-spangled darkness that surrounded them. Noble birth and wealth and beauty were useless commodities here on this deserted island. Only the real inner qualities of the person mattered now…and here, too, would they not be revealed?

His eyes narrowed, staring out, as if the future might lie concealed in the blackness of the night. *The true heart is revealed in adversity.* It was a proverb in his family, which had been recited many times during the decades of suffering when Ghasib remained in power.

Noor was dreaming. He watched a frown chase across her brow, then the whisper of a smile drawing at one cheek. Unexpectedly his heart kicked, and his body leaped with hunger. If he reached for her now, if he drew her into the hungry embrace of his body and arms, if she awoke to his kiss and his desire—could she reject him?

He knew she couldn't. Even without the drug of sleep invading her mind and limbs, even without the magic of the stars overhead, the silence, the scents of nature on the breeze—she would be his. The fire in his blood would heat hers.

She was a naturally passionate woman. He had learned that during their one heady afternoon and evening of delight. Whatever lies she had held in her heart, her body had told another truth.

His flesh pulsed painfully, wanting her. Wanting that soft breathing to change, as it had before, into hungry moans of desire and delight. Wanting the taste, the smell, the touch of her, the inner flame and welcoming moistness that had almost sent him over the edge with the first thrust of possession.

The smell and the sound of the sea was a piercing reminder of that afternoon he had stolen from reality. Involuntarily he lowered his face towards the curve of her throat. The scent of her skin after their hard labour was pungent with musk and, remembering, his body tightened convulsively.

She should have been his. This was by rights his wedding night! If she had not been such a little fool, he would now have every right to awaken her with the kisses that burned his mouth, to stroke the firm, soft swell of her breasts that only the moonlight now caressed, to feed the growing hunger of her blood with his mouth, his tongue, his hands, and finally his body.

He would have the right to push his hardened flesh into the soft depths of her—his wife, his other self. To thrust and thrust in a repeat of that wild seeking—the wildest he had ever known, to feel her answer in her flesh as surely as he heard it in her throat.

Bari lifted his head with an effort and gazed out over the moon-kissed sea.

He was nearly certain that the island they were on was the most remote of the Gulf Islands, a straggler at the very tip of the chain, called Solomon's Foot. If so, it was well out of the way of any major shipping lanes. And all small-boat traffic among the islands had ended with the evacuations. The only vessels visiting the islands now were the dhows and ferries that supplied the Gulf Eden Resort. Their route would bring them nowhere near this island.

If the proverb were true—if the truth of her would be revealed in adversity—what better opportunity for it could he ask than this? To be alone with her, in a place where they would be utterly dependent on themselves and each other. For everything. Food, shelter, companionship, security…pleasure.

And if she did have a heart, what better opportunity could he hope to find for learning whether it could ever be his? There was another saying among the men in his family: *a man opens a woman's heart by repeated knocking at the door of the womb.* It was a reminder that sexual prowess is any lover's most powerful asset.

The moon climbed higher in the sky, white and pure and unshockable, as Bari made his plans.

Nine

Noor awoke as those who live in the natural world have done since humankind's beginning—with the rising of the sun. It came up out of the sea like a knot of molten gold serpents, flaming and twisting against the blushing sky.

Bari was standing looking out over the water.

"Awake?" he murmured as she stirred and lay watching the spectacular unfoldment of the first scene in the drama of the day. Birdsong rippled over them from the forest.

Noor yawned and leaned up on one elbow. "Who could sleep through this!" She dragged the makeshift mosquito net down and moved to sit up, then winced and moved more carefully. Every muscle seemed to have taken a beating.

"Oooh," she groaned weakly. "I think I need a chiropractor. Everything feels out of place."

Bari watched as she lifted one arm to admire an

angry bruise. "There will be something for that in the first aid kit."

Noor nodded and got to her feet. "At least it won't be permanently disfiguring."

She stretched gingerly. In spite of everything it was invigorating to spend a night in the open when the air was so fresh. She tried an experimental bit of jogging on the spot. Nothing hurt too, too much. She'd actually felt worse after days when her personal trainer had been in a mean mood.

"I don't know how I'm going to manage my work-out," she murmured thoughtfully. Without her gym equipment, how would she get the kinks out?

Suddenly she noticed the expression on Bari's face. "What's your problem?" she challenged him.

He shook his head, laughing. "Not a word, Princess. Would you like a drink?"

In instant answer, Noor's stomach growled, and she discovered she was ravenous.

"My God, so this is hunger!"

Bari collected the water jug from the raft and measured out a small amount for her in the plastic cup.

She swirled the rainwater around on her tongue. How weird it tasted! As if no taste at all could result in a bad taste. She looked into Bari's amused eyes and decided not to share that little experience with him.

"I'm starved. Let's eat!"

"It will be best to forage before the day gets hot," he agreed. "Afterwards we must—"

"Forage?" she repeated blankly. "What are you talking about?"

His eyes opened with a look that made her want to hit him. "About going to hunt for something to eat. Isn't that what you said?"

Noor laughed in merry disbelief. "Oh, sure! A little stroll down to Cocoa's for some skinny latte and a fat-free muffin!"

"We won't know how difficult it is until we try." He took an equal measure of water himself and tossed it off in one mouthful, then glanced up at the sun now making a fiery ascent up the cobalt-blue sky. "We should start now. It will get hot quickly."

"You have to be joking! What am I supposed to do—pick berries into a palm leaf?"

"Unless you have more aggressive survival skills."

"Is *that* what you call it!"

Bari looked at her in frowning, silent consideration for a moment. Then he half smiled.

"Noor, this is not a joke. How are you proposing to eat until rescue arrives?"

"We've got rations. I saw them." She knew he knew they were there, so what was his game?

He stood in front of her in an easy pose, his feet firmly at home in the soft grey-white sand, his arms crossed over his chest, the little plastic glass dangling from one finger. His silk jacket was creased and stained, and so were the white trousers, but he still had the proud, unmistakable bearing of a Cup Companion.

It had always thrilled her before. Now it seemed to be turned against her, and she found the condescending reproof of his nod seriously irritating.

"Yes, a very few rations were in the plane's grab bag. We must save them for emergencies, however. I am sorry, but with a little luck—"

"This feels like an emergency to me," Noor interrupted stiffly. "I'm starved!"

"Nothing like appetite for sharpening the hunter-gatherer instinct," Bari said, in the manner of a tolerant drill sergeant with a lazy new recruit. He turned and put the water back into the life raft, and closed the Velcro fastenings. Then he turned. "Come."

"I don't have any shoes, or have you forgotten? Or clothes."

He looked down at his own bare feet, and then at her, with an expression on his face that irritated her royally, and took her wrist in a strong, careless, but unmistakably autocratic hold.

"Your feet will soon toughen up."

"I don't want my feet to 'toughen up'!" She was sure that he was playing a game. She dug her heels into the sand, pulling her hand from the firm clasp of his own. "And I'm not going hunting barefoot and in my underwear!"

A sudden peal of birdsong underlined the silence.

Bari rested an assessing gaze on her. "What, then? Do you prefer to go hungry?"

"Can't you bring me back something?" she demanded. "You're the big, strong primitive male, after all! You're the one with the ceremonial sword!"

Some change in him made her shift uncomfortably. But really, it was ridiculous! What was she supposed to do half-naked, shoeless and weaponless, in a forest?

"By tradition, yes, I should be your protector," he said. "But yesterday you rejected tradition, and you rejected me. I am nothing to you now, and you—" his eyes narrowed "—you are nothing to me, Noor. You can't run from me one day and demand my protection the next. If you want breakfast, you will have to help find it."

She knew she was on dangerous ground, but unaccustomed hunger was making her mulish. "I have found it! It's in those neat little plastic packs of emergency rations over there in the raft! And that's all the hunting-gathering I'm going to do this morning, thanks!"

She stepped forward, but his hand on her shoulder, very firm now, stopped her.

"I think we have already established that in a battle between brains and brawn, brawn inevitably wins. Do you care to put it to the test one more time?"

She looked at him and saw nothing but implacable determination. His eyes were the colour of volcanic lava—the surface black, but with lines of glowing light hinting at a fierce, banked heat within. Was it her imagination, or was that red-gold line of fracture a little wider now?

She used to imagine that what she saw was a deep dynamo of passion—but he had been faking that. What was the source, then, of that half compelling, half dangerous heat?

She was convinced that the man who had yesterday been prepared to marry her would now watch her starve without a flicker of conscience. Noor could just imagine him taking pleasure from eating his bloody kill in front of her without offering her a morsel. Yet the Bari she had known until yesterday—thought she had known—would have acted very differently in these circumstances.

That curious sense of two time streams brushed her again. Suppose she had married Bari, and suppose they had taken off for their honeymoon and been brought down by the storm, ending up here, exactly where they were. How would he be treating her now?

She laughed aloud. "You know, all things considered, I'm pretty lucky! It's not very nice learning that a man's a monster, but it could be a lot worse, couldn't it? I could be discovering right now that I was *married* to a monster!"

"A man protects his wife," he contradicted her in a gravelly voice. "You are not my wife, by your own choice. Why does that make me a monster?"

Something like regret reached for her, but she shook herself out of its stealthy grip, bent to toss aside the gold foil sheet, picked up the rectangle of white silk she had slept on last night, and wrapped it around herself. It didn't offer much more actual protection than the skimpy teddy underneath, but psychologically, just here and just now, it was almost as good as putting on armour.

She pulled the knot of her makeshift sarong tight above her breast, staring at him as she did so.

With an arrogant blink that was his excuse for a nod, Bari turned and went over to the beached raft again, bending to search inside. When he straightened, he was tucking the knife into his waistband.

"Not packing the ancestral sword today?" Noor commented brightly.

"It is a battle sword," Bari told her softly. "It would be sullied by the blood of the hunt." She wasn't sure if he was joking, or speaking for effect, or telling the simple truth.

"Common sense somehow suggests," she remarked sweetly, "that a hunter has to get a lot closer to his prey with a knife than with a three-foot blade, but I'm not going to argue with the great warrior!"

"It would be a waste of time, and you are hungry," he agreed pleasantly. Noor stifled her reaction to that, except for the flashing glance that bounced right off him.

He led her along the beach towards the rocks and the higher ground at the southern tip. He wanted to measure out the island, get more of an idea of where they were, before he risked a trek in among the trees.

It was a beautiful walk along the increasingly rocky beach in the morning sunlight, with birdsong coming from a forest that was much more extensive than it had appeared—a giant oasis.

Noor resolutely refused to voice her surprise. But Bari answered the unspoken question.

"The islands, like the coastal regions of the Barakat Emirates and, to a lesser extent, Bagestan, are very fertile," he explained. "Even after thirty years of Ghasib's mismanagement. Several herbs that grow only here are known for their healing properties and used to be exported to the mainland by the islanders."

Reluctant laughter burst from her. "I thought that was just my parents' fantasy of the old country! They always said it was the Garden of Eden."

"There is good rainfall here, probably the same climate that covered a much larger area in antiquity. Some geophysical archaeologists suggest that a huge area—from the Mediterranean to the mountains of Parvan—once was as lush as this tiny area of the gulf. But catastrophic climate change affected the rainfall and, bit by bit, turned the once-fertile land into desert."

She was tacitly agreeing to a truce, perhaps because the nature of their expedition made them both feel they should be united. Exploring an unknown world, however benign it might prove, made comrades of them.

"No one knows why this tiny area escaped the march of the desert. The prolonged drought in Bagestan has raised fears that the process of desertification may even be starting again. But for the moment, we live in the last corner of the paradise that Adam and Eve knew."

Paradise. Alone in paradise with Bari al Khalid.

I don't think so! Noor told herself dryly.

The black rock, when they began to climb, wasn't as hard on her bare feet as Noor had feared. It was smoother than she had guessed from a distance, a little glassy, as if, perhaps, from a long-distant volcanic eruption. And she supposed it was exercise of a sort, if not as regimented as her workout.

"This rock is mysterious in origin," Bari continued in tour-guide mode. "It exists in the Gulf of Barakat and nowhere else on the planet. Experts argue as to its origins. There is little agreement."

They found a trail, narrow but freshly used, as they climbed higher.

"Do you think there's someone living here after all?" Noor asked, a little breathless with exertion and hope.

Bari shrugged.

"If so, they have arrived only recently. After Ghasib leased the development rights for all the islands to the Gulf Eden Resort chain a couple of years ago, the inhabitants of the islands were forcefully evacuated, and their homes and villages destroyed. The developers planned to create an isolated luxury resort for tourists."

"It was a big story at home," Noor remembered. "People were so outraged."

"Yes, an international outcry delayed the development, and now the Sultan is under pressure to turn the islands into a wildlife sanctuary. But the evacuees have to be considered. Many had lived on the islands for generations. Since the Return, some have been trying to re-establish their homes on the islands."

Noor looked hopefully around for signs of human occupation. People meant boats. Boats meant getting away from her ex-husband-to-be and his insistence on a return to stone-age living.

Bari knelt to examine some spoor. "Sorry," he told her dryly, as if her face had been too revealing. "This path has been created by animals. Goats, possibly."

"Not my lucky day, then," said Noor sharply.

They couldn't climb very high—the slope was too

steep. When they had got as high as they could, accompanied by the screech of seagulls wheeling and banking around the stony peak, they stopped to get their bearings.

The island, a small, somewhat squashed oval, was lying roughly northeast-southwest. It was generally flat, except at the southern tip, where it pushed upward into a peak of rugged black rock.

It was a breathtaking sight. At their backs the peak seemed slightly concave, a petrified wave arcing over them. They stood in the lee, just where the vegetation lost its hold. Below they could see the goat track they had been following trace the curve of the hillside and then lead down to the forested slope below.

White sand beach curved around more than half of the oval. The southern third, under the peak, was black rock. On the opposite side to the beach where they had landed was a reedy area which Bari said was a mudflat. Within the protection of the rocky peak nestled a green paradise of trees, birds and flowers. The sound of water told them there must be a stream nearby, and down below, a regular break in the rich greenery indicated its path.

A brightly coloured bird shrieked and flapped up towards the sun before tucking its wings and diving back down in among the trees.

Bari suddenly pointed to a spot at about their eye level. After a moment she saw it, a large bird, its wings outspread, riding the currents.

"A falcon," he said in satisfaction.

"Why is that good?"

"It means there are small animals."

But however they strained, in whatever direction, there was no sign of land.

After a few minutes they followed the track along the

lightly treed slope, with the sound of running water getting closer and closer.

Suddenly there it was in front of them: a small, delicate waterfall like a bridal veil tumbling down to where it was captured in a sparkling stream a few feet below them in the black rock. From there the water ran in a series of streams and tiny falls down to the forest floor below.

A small black-and-white goat stood precariously on the rocks, drinking from the water swirling in the bowl-shaped cavity of a rock.

It had not noticed their approach. Bari and Noor stood watching, silenced by the little animal's vulnerability. It was so totally trusting, eyes closed, nose deep in the life-giving stream, the perfect embodiment of that state of grace which allows the Arabic language to assign "peace" and "submission" the same word.

Noor glanced at Bari and exchanged a rueful smile. By wordless agreement, the two humans sank silently to the ground and waited for the goat to finish its drink. The animal's complete trust was somehow compelling—beautiful and deeply touching.

"How easy it is to love creatures who trust," Noor thought, and was a little surprised to find that she had whispered the words.

Bari's gaze rested on her thoughtfully, but he did not reply.

The goat lifted its head and gazed at them for a moment before turning to spring up the few feet to the path. Then, as they watched in silence, it wandered unafraid among the trees and began to forage.

Noor glanced down at the knife tucked into Bari's waistband, then up into his face. He laughed as if reading her thoughts.

"I'd have to be a lot hungrier," he agreed.

Noor laughed with him, and for a moment it was the way it used to be between them, and she remembered with sharp nostalgia how she had imagined that they were well suited. That their sense of humour matched.

But all the time they had been laughing at different things. Bari had been laughing at her.

Her gaze returned to the delicious little waterfall. After a moment's pause they simultaneously began to strip off and, leaving their clothes, clambered down the rocks to stand under the lacy tumble of water.

It was cold enough to seem icy on their exercise-heated bodies, and Noor involuntarily gasped as the fat drops pelted her.

His ears heard, and his body remembered, that it was the same gasp she had given the first time he entered her. The flesh of her breasts tightened, too, in a way he remembered in that very different moment. Bari stood under a strong, steady fall of cool water, his back to her.

"What a relief to get the salt and sand off my skin!" Noor cried.

Nervousness pitched her voice high and thin, but she hoped Bari wouldn't notice. She had to struggle not to devour him with her eyes. They had made love only on that one long, never-to-be-forgotten afternoon, and one afternoon, she discovered, wasn't long enough to create an immunity to the sight of him naked.

His body was like an aftershave ad, water droplets passionately clinging to perfect proportions. It was hard to keep her eyes from drinking him in in the same way they had everything else this incredible morning—with gratitude for the beauty.

Bari barely glanced at her. "It's good luck that we have a source of fresh water." His voice was as distant as his eyes.

After a minute Noor reached for the teddy that she had left on a rock, and began busily scrubbing it between her knuckles as she stood under the flow.

Bari put his head under, then emerged spluttering and shaking his head. Vital animal grace emanated from him so powerfully she felt it like a physical touch. Water streamed down his face and body, tracing every curvature of muscle and bone with loving attention, as though nature herself were memorizing his shape in order to produce so fine a work again elsewhere.

Noor's womb clenched with the primitive, unconscious understanding that her own body might serve as nature's workshop for such a project. What hit her then was a bolt of electricity that seemed to come not from the sky, but from the rocks under her feet, inescapably shooting up through her body to her scalp.

There was a moment of stillness all around them then, during which the lacy waterfall seemed to capture the sunlight and multiply it into a thousand diamonds tossed and tumbling over the rocks onto their heads.

In that moment, strong and strange, a man and a woman gazed at each other, and through each other into a world of possibility. The soft wind whispered to them that their two selves held the key to the great secret. The man put out his hand, and the woman's hand would have been unerringly drawn to its embrace, even had she been blind.

Their bodies sparkling with diamonds and gold, he led her to a soft sun-kissed place, and drew her down to lie with him.

Ten

A shock of heat embraced her as she lay on him, her legs entangling with his as naturally as if they had met this way over a thousand lifetimes past. Her body, resting against his aroused flesh, melted with anticipation, and in answer his hand gripped the firm mound of her behind and held her ruthlessly as his hips rose of their own accord to lift against her.

His fingers slipped around her thighs and began to tease and stroke the delicate folds of the flower, and his eyes watched her face, devouring every sign of her desire for him.

She was so moist, inviting the long, strong fingers to slip inside that almost-virgin space and warn her body of the delights to come.

Meanwhile the fingers of his other hand cupped her head, weaving through the damp tangles of her hair and drawing her face down to his waiting mouth. The hungry kisses that he had been holding back for too long burned up to scorch his lips as his mouth took possession of hers.

"Bari," she murmured, half protesting, but he smothered the sound with his kiss.

Noor felt the touch of those knowing, tender fingers ignite a hot sweetness that melted all through her, and her legs spread with pulsing hunger, falling wide to give him access to the deepest part of herself as honeyed urgency tightened her skin.

His fingers vibrated in her, his tongue following suit in the moist depths of her mouth, until she tore her lips from his with a cry, lifting away to arch her back into the pleasure building in her. His other hand moved down then, pressing her, moulding her lower body against his hardened flesh, until, with soft panting cries, she welcomed the flooding heat that coursed through her.

Her face to the smiling sky, she groaned out her gratitude, but the hypnotic motion of his hands paused only a moment, and then began anew.

"Again," he commanded.

This time the explosion came more quickly, and then leaped to another buildup, and another, while Noor writhed with increasing openness, her cries of completion and excitement grew louder, the pleasure more intense…and her desire for more grew greedier.

Her throat was wide open, her head back, her body arched, her thighs clenching, her hunger deep and animal. She was just where he wanted her—in that land where she recognized only sensation. Heat was here, and rippling pleasure, and shivering joy, and delicious moistness—but she knew no more than that.

He watched with his hunger written on his face, a hunger he could not disguise. Her head was back, her eyes squeezed shut, all her being focused on pleasure like nothing she had known existed.

Finally he could wait no longer. His control whipped from his grasp like a cable that breaks under too much weight, and his hands lifted her, opening her for him, and his body leaped in one fierce thrust. And with that sudden, hard urgency, there was what she had been seeking, what her hunger had waited for: the fierce plea-sure-pain of his body ruthless in hers, and the soaring desire that swooped and wheeled with the motion of the falcon above.

He pulled her knees down beside his hips, fixed his strong hands around her waist, and taught her the mo-tions of that primitive dance: down and up and down and up, over and over, wild and free, until the god answered, and pleasure rained down on them.

As soon as the last heaves of satisfaction had died in her, Noor started kicking herself inwardly. What kind of fool for punishment was she? Bari al Khalid had cyn-ically taken her virginity when he didn't love her, had tricked her—what kind of stupid, masochistic weak-ness was it to let him get to her all over again? She lifted his arm from her and sat up.

"I suppose you think that proved something," she said.

Only with my husband, she had always promised herself. And since she wouldn't marry Bari now to save her life, she shouldn't have made love with him again. She turned and looked down at him.

His head was turned towards her, the black eyes half-lidded. He said nothing.

What really made her bitter was the little voice that said that since she was no longer a virgin it didn't re-ally matter anymore, and the pleasure was worth it. That was exactly the attitude that she had despised in her friends. *Who do I hurt? It's not a diminishing commodity. We only get one life.*

She had thought she was safe from all that. But it seemed sex was like a drug. Once you got a taste of it—

Her anger suddenly shifted its target. How dared he make love to her, after what he had said about her? And why?

Noor got to her feet and tied the sarong over her breasts.

"Just more cynical manipulation," she accused as she picked up the wet teddy and wrung it out with an angry twist.

"Why would I want to manipulate you?" His voice was expressive of nothing so much as boredom, and her outrage flared.

"Your grandfather's estates *are* still an issue, I suppose!" Noor responded sharply.

"Oh, that."

She smiled, showing her teeth.

"My grandfather will have the good sense to realize that however good the tree, some fruit is always spoiled. When he learns of it he will not wish me to marry a woman who has acted the way you did."

Noor flinched but stood her ground. "So it was just a freebie, then?" she mocked. "Just the typical male grab-it-while-you-can?"

"And what was it from the typical female point of view? Rape, I suppose?"

She was too angry to answer.

Under the white *shalwar* he had been wearing a snug thong, and it seemed that was all he meant to put on now. He slung his wet shirt and trousers over one shoulder.

"Very Tarzan," Noor said, mock-admiringly. "I ad-vise you not to mistake me for Jane again, if you don't want a very uncomfortable surprise."

"Who the hell is Tarzan?" Bari asked, as if it was the last thing he cared to know.

They breakfasted on fresh herbs, raw dates and baked turtle's eggs eaten off palm leaves. Not exactly a meal for the gods, but she was hungry enough to swallow every morsel. She could have eaten more, but Bari had insisted on taking only a few eggs out of the nest they found.

"But there are hundreds of eggs there!" Noor had protested.

"And there is a reason for that. We are not the turtle's only predators. And they are a rare species."

She couldn't argue with that, but a couple of eggs didn't make much of a meal when there was no bread or salad or anything else to accompany them.

Licking her fingers, she looked around. "Well, what now?" she wondered aloud. "Think we'll see a boat soon?"

"The first necessity is to build a shelter."

She looked at him, suspecting a trick. "What's wrong with the raft?"

"It's too small, and it gets too hot. Over the long term, psychologically, we need—"

"But we're bound to be rescued!"

"Possibly, but what if we are not? Do you expect the world to rush to save your life when you will do nothing to save yourself?"

"You're just trying to scare me. You want to punish me for running away and you think hard work will do the trick!"

It was close enough to the truth to wring a dry smile out of him. He crossed well-muscled arms over his naked chest and eyed her levelly.

"I think it won't hurt you to put some effort into your own continued existence," he agreed.

"I've already had the hunter-gatherer lecture this morning, thanks. I think that's enough for one day. Build your own damn shelter!"

He regarded her in silence for a long uncomfortable moment. Noor put her chin up.

"This is not television, Noor. There is no camera, no crew. We don't get airlifted out if we get stomach cramp. This is real life."

She lifted her eyebrows expressively. "So?"

"Cooperation is the first rule of survival."

"Really! I'm sure there's a second rule."

He wasn't rising to the bait. He said, as if she had asked in good faith, "The second is, elect one person as leader, and then obey his commands."

"Let me guess. You've been elected."

A little voice in her suggested how unwise it was to embark on such a futile battle. *No stupider than his insistence on building a shelter,* Noor dismissed it.

Bari smiled, showing strong white teeth in the smile that she used to think was handsome. Now it just made him look like a wild animal.

"Brawn gets fifty-one percent of the vote, I think we agreed."

"Well, brawn can just go ahead and build one hundred percent of the shelter! Brains is going to do the logical thing and use the life raft when necessary."

"Wrong again. We'll take the canopy to waterproof the roof of the shelter."

"Oh, brilliant! Cut up our shelter in order to make a shelter!" she mocked admiringly. "Well, at least you're not claiming the monopoly on brains!"

"Can you possibly be imagining that your continued

mulishness is a sign of intelligence? You are acting like a fool! What do you know of conditions here? We may be completely out of the shipping lane on this island. It might be days, weeks, bef—"

"I don't believe for a minute it will be weeks, and I happen to think the raft is a good enough temporary shelter."

"No. What you think about a shelter is nothing to do with this. You are resisting what I say because you feel cheated. You blame me for not being in love with you."

"Wrong!" Noor carolled hotly. "Since we are no longer going to get married, I couldn't care less what you think of me."

"But this is not the time for such resistance," he went on, as if she hadn't spoken. "We must act to survive. You know this. Even if only psychologically, shelter is of crucial importance to us both. Now, I will give orders and I expect to be obeyed."

"You seem to think you've got me at your mercy. Suppose I disappoint your expectations?"

"Then I will leave you here and go and establish my camp elsewhere. You will not be welcome there."

She knew he wouldn't. He couldn't! But his black eyes held an expression she didn't trust. As if he *wanted* her to give him the excuse to abandon her.

"I must have been totally deluded to imagine you loved me!" she said bitterly, capitulating.

"But self-delusion is almost a way of life with you," Bari replied softly.

The next few days were sheer, unrelieved hell. Bari was a slave driver. On a diet of baked turtles' eggs, raw dates, and some berries that hardly deserved the name, he expected her to hew trees, haul branches, salvage the blackened remains of a tragic little village, and act as general dogsbody in his grandiose building scheme.

Her nails became unbelievably grimed and filthy, her legs and arms scratched and bruised and streaked with black that wouldn't wash off, the skin of her face so dry and sunburned she was sure it would never recover its tone, her nose peeling, her hair matted so she couldn't even get her fingers through it. And as for her palms and soles—how could blisters get blisters?

She looked like a total bag lady, and she knew it. The orange "moccasins" she had been forced to make for herself, cutting pieces from the leftover bits of the rubber-and-canvas canopy of the raft and painstakingly stitching them together with the fishing line, were ugly and uncomfortable. Also scant protection from snakes, the thought of which terrified her. On her head and over her fading and greying teddy, she wore a succession of soiled, stained scarves and sarongs that offered her insufficient protection from the sun, especially on a breezy day, got filthy the moment she put a fresh one on, and mostly got in her way when she was doing the menial, degrading work that Bari constantly assigned her as her share of their survival task. Her hips and abdomen and breasts were now tanned with the pattern of the lace on her teddy, which she scrubbed and put on again every day.

Bari, naturally, had a change of clothes. The emergency grab bag from the plane had contained not only a lighter, an all-purpose Leatherman tool, and a large spool of plastic tape, all of which were proving seriously useful, but also a pair of denim shorts.

That was all, just shorts. But there were days when Noor would have paid any price for the luxury of a zipper closing.

Worst was the lack of anything approaching civilized toilet facilities, even paper, and although Bari had promised to build something when the shelter was closer to complete, it seemed a long time coming.

It was the first time in her adult life that Noor had spent even twenty-four hours without liberal applications of soap, shampoo, deodorant and perfume, never mind toilet tissue.

The only relief she had from this life of horrors was a toothbrush and miniature tube of toothpaste, also from the grab bag. Since there was only one, they shared it, and the toothpaste was severely rationed, but the daily taste of civilization was all that stood between Noor and an irredeemably primitive existence. Some days she almost wept from sheer gratitude as she brushed her teeth.

They rested in the hottest part of the afternoon, because not even Bari could force anyone to work in such crippling heat. But even so, Noor didn't rest. Every day, no matter how exhausted she was, she made the trek up the mountain—and it seemed more and more like a real mountain with each trip—to take a freshwater shower in the magical little waterfall. It always soothed her to be in such a peaceful place. But it was impossible to get really clean, and by the time she had returned to the campsite she was pouring with sweat again.

In the catalogue of woes of this castaway existence, Noor found that the worst came at night. Not only was sleeping on the sand uncomfortable, not only was she often too cold to sleep, but when she did sleep she would be startled awake by the strange noises. After what had happened at the waterfall, they slept apart. Nights, she learned, were cool, and Noor had nothing to put on except the thin teddy and her homemade sarongs.

No matter how snugly she wrapped herself in a foil sheet, when a breeze blew, as happened nearly every night, it succeeded in lifting the sheet. All her built-up body heat could disappear in a second.

Chivalry dictated that Bari should offer her his jacket at night, but Bari, it seemed, wasn't going to be dictated to by any code of gentlemanly conduct. He wore the jacket on his head during the day, and as a shirt at night, and Noor was left to make do with her bits of silk. She had tried wearing the bodice of the wedding dress, but it wasn't practicable—the sleeves were awkwardly tight when she turned it back to front, and it was covered with pearls, and there were no buttons.

"I've already told you—you rejected my protection. On what grounds do you make a claim for it now?" he said when she raised the subject one evening, after a particularly gruelling day, as the sun went down and she faced another sleepless night.

"Do I have to explain ordinary civilized behaviour to you?" Noor cried.

Bari laughed with biting mockery. "Yes, let me hear Princess Noor's explanation of ordinary civilized behaviour!"

She wanted to tell him where he could put it, but the trouble was, she needed him and his masculine protection, however little she wanted it.

"You're bigger and stronger, and men have more reserves of body heat, or something," she said. "You've also got the warmest piece of clothing. Doesn't that equation suggest to you that you should share?"

When she saw the expression on his face, she knew she'd let herself in for something, but it was too late to recall the words.

"And you, Noor—you are beautiful, and graceful, and extremely charming when you want to be. And yet—how much generosity of spirit did you show to my mother and sisters? Did you share that charm with them?"

"Oh, will you leave it *alone!*" Noor exclaimed impatiently, jumping up to stride around the fire that was cooking today's fish.

"All right! I acted like a spoiled brat, I admit it, all right?" She flung out her hands. "I was wrong and selfish...and pretty damned stupid, if you want the truth. So stupid that I didn't even realize I was making them dislike me! Does my confession satisfy you? I'm *sorry,* but now I'm stuck on this island, and I can't do anything to make amends to your mother till we get back to civilization! I promise you, I'll abase myself to everyone I've insulted as soon as we get out of this hole! In the meantime, I'm freezing to death at night and not getting any sleep, and I have no stamina to get through what you'll admit is a pretty hellish existence, with you constantly badgering me and making me do the dirty work!"

"All the work is dirty work," Bari said flatly.

"All right, yes! You're working just as hard—harder! I agree. But I am not used to it, and you're not exactly making it easy for me, are you?"

"How would you like me to make it easy for you?" he asked with silky calm. "By doing everything myself?"

She could hardly keep the lid on. "No!" she shouted. "*Not* by doing it all yourself, though I know that's no more than your opinion of me! But would it hurt you to empathize a little?"

She was striding up and down, flinging her arms around for punctuation. "If it's my job to clean the fish, or gather wood, or hold a rope while you put up a wall, do you think you might say so courteously? Does it always have to come out of your mouth with contempt, as if you're utterly convinced that I resent lifting a finger to look after myself?"

"And don't you?"

For a moment the quiet question flummoxed her. She stopped and gazed at him across the fire.

"You act as if you resent lifting a finger to look after yourself, Noor. You seem to blame me for the deprivations you suffer, but who caused us to be in this situation? And as for the necessity to work, it is survival itself that makes these demands on you, not me."

Would he always succeed in putting her in the wrong? "I—I know that!" she faltered.

"If you really know it, then why do you not take on the responsibility for your existence as an adult, instead of responding to every demand like a spoiled child who prefers to play?"

"Do I do that?"

He was silent, leaving it to her own conscience to answer. Noor heaved a breath, trying to calm her jangled feelings.

"Do you think your constant bewailing of our position makes it easier for you, or for me?" he continued after a moment. "Why do you not accept the situation, Noor, instead of always regretting it? We are here together, and we need each other. You seem to want me to remember that fact, while you ignore it. But it takes two, Noor. Just like marriage."

Tears sprang to her eyes suddenly, but the sudden snapping of her overstretched emotions had nothing to do with that word *marriage*. She didn't regret not marrying Bari in the least, however much she might wish she'd found a better way to avoid it.

It was fatigue and stress and hunger that were the cause of her losing it like this. That and Bari's constant

determination to hold up a mirror to her least attractive
traits, and make sure she looked closely at them!

"I wish I could make *you* see yourself," she said, as
tears spilled down her cheeks in spite of her fierce efforts
to contain them. "You're not perfect, either, you know!"

"No," he agreed. "I'm not perfect, either. So what do
you want from me, Noor?"

She sniffed. "I can't sleep because I get chilled.
That's all."

"All right, I can warm you at night. Is that what you
want?"

His rough, dark voice sent chills of a completely different kind through her. Whatever her conscious decision, she couldn't seem to get her body to agree that
Bari's touch was poison to her.

Her eyes widened. What was he offering? "I—" She
licked her lips. "What, you mean…"

He let the half words hang painfully in the silence,
while the fire crackled merrily. His eyelids drooped,
and he reached out and used a stick to prod the fish
cooking on a palm leaf. Then he turned and gazed at her.

"Do you want sex?" he asked baldly. His voice was
heavy with reluctance, and Noor cringed inwardly. If his
tone expressed any approximation of his feelings…

"No!" she said, half-panicked at the thought that he
should imagine she was angling for his lovemaking. "I
told you!"

"So you did," he agreed in a bored voice. He nodded.
"Although we are not the best examples of the fact, the
most efficient warmth is human warmth," he said with
ironic humour. "I will give you the jacket to wear in bed,
since you ask so nicely, and I will share your bed for
warmth only. Is that what you want?"

She felt unbelievably humiliated, without knowing

why. "Yes, please," she whispered. Then she had a thought. "Bari—"

"Noor?"

"I could…if you liked, I could make you a djellaba from my—my dress. I could braid some strips into a rope, too. Wouldn't that be easier than your jacket?"

His eyes blazed with an expression she hardly dared to read as approval. "Yes, it would be much easier. Thank you, Noor," he said gravely, and her heart swelled.

"I don't know why I didn't think of it days ago!" she exclaimed.

Bari smiled. "Don't you?" he asked.

Eleven

"Please let me find some soap," Noor begged as she gingerly lifted another blackened mud brick and tossed it onto the growing pile she was collecting.

They had found the site of the destroyed village on the second afternoon, and had immediately begun the dirtiest salvage operation she ever hoped to undertake. And here she was yet again, under the watchful eye of the little black-and-white goat, who had taken to following her whenever she was in the forest, but still was nervous about visiting the campsite.

Something had shifted for Noor. Although the work was still tedious, she experienced a sense of purpose. To be working to provide for her own needs gave her an odd kind of satisfaction—what she did, every minute of every day, was useful, necessary work. Bari was right. Without cooperation they would not survive, and there was pleasure in knowing that he needed her as much as she needed him, and that her work contributed to a larger, common goal.

Even the little goat seemed to need her, and she guessed that he had been a family pet and was lonely for human company. She was slowly teaching him that she could be trusted, and that there was nothing to fear at the campsite. And every day he trusted her a little more, and that was a surprisingly powerful source of comfort.

Still, she was almost constantly hungry. And their diet was unbelievably boring.

"The food is terrible—*and* there's not enough of it!" she joked to the goat now. The little animal gazed at her, chewing contentedly on a bright green leaf—one of the special herbs that Bari had pointed out to her, she saw.

"Oh, yeah, *you're* all right, Jack!" Noor said dryly.

They had found another turtle's nest, and every day they took a few eggs from one or the other, and carefully covered up the rest. They alternated between fish, the small animals Bari sometimes also caught, and eggs, and the root vegetables they sometimes found digging in the overgrown, deserted gardens in the village. Sometimes herbs lent a welcome piquancy to the food.

Noor had been driven almost crazy by the lack of salt until Bari pointed out that the sea was full of it. After several frustrating attempts, she had at last been rewarded by the sight of a few white crystals on her palm leaf. The taste had brought tears of relief to her eyes.

Her emotions were much too volatile, of course.

The growing torment now was the lack of soap. Her hair got more matted every day. A couple of times she had tried to see herself in a section of the foil sheet, but she was almost grateful that it was too wrinkled to reflect her image. Really, she had only to look at Bari to

get a fair approximation of her own state. Bari's facial
hair had progressed from shadow to stubble to bristles,
and was now on the way to becoming a genuine beard.

He looked wild and uncivilized, his skin getting
darker every day, his face dry and cracked, as hers must
be. His strong, expressive hands were as grimed and callused as any construction worker's.

At least, thank God, however badly they needed soap,
they couldn't really smell each other. Or at least, what
she could smell of him was only pleasantly, if sharply,
masculine.

She fervently hoped she returned the favour. Right now
Noor would have traded her entire newly inherited fortune
for one day—one hour!—in her favourite health club.

"Full-body Shiatsu Massage with Cucumber and
Nine Essential Oils," she called lyrically to the little
goat, straightening for a moment to ease her aching
back. It was astonishing how little a regular workout
seemed to have prepared her body for real work.

The goat stopped chewing and gazed at her with
wide, half-fascinated eyes. "Manicure with Peach Essence Nail Rejuvenation Cream." It was a comfort just
to hear the words, to remind herself that a civilized
world existed, and she would get back to it one day.
"Pedicure with Sea Salt and Rosemary Footbath and
Aro...no, wait a minute—sea salt and rosemary—isn't
that the flavouring of those organic chips I love? You'd
probably like them," she confided to the little goat.

The little goat contentedly considered the proposition.

Noor tossed another brick into the salvage pile. Whoever had been assigned the task of destroying the few
modest little homes that had once graced this clearing
among the trees had done no more than knock them
down and put a torch to the ruins, but though Noor and

Bari had searched diligently in the wreckage, they had found almost nothing, apart from the half-burned bricks, worth salvaging.

The inhabitants must have taken everything of any use with them when they were moved out—or maybe the people sent to destroy it had scavenged the site.

A rusted axe with a partially burned handle was their biggest prize so far, but the fire-blackened material that had once formed walls was very useful in their own building projects, and Bari was happy with that.

Noor, however, still had hopes.

"Please, God, just one little sliver of real soap!" she begged, returning to her work quickly, because the sun was getting higher and soon it would be too hot. There was no point in slacking, because Bari needed this stuff for the toilet he was now building.

She was working at the outer edge of the little village, where the fire hadn't burned so fiercely and the remains of a shattered house promised good pickings. With difficulty, using the stout stick Bari had found for her, Noor heaved up a sheet of corrugated iron. That would probably be very useful, but she wouldn't get it back to the campsite on her own. Bari would have to come and help.

Underneath was a piece of wood almost untouched by fire. Noor shifted the sheet to one side and let it fall, dragging her sarong up to cover her mouth and nose from the inevitable dust and soot thus stirred up. Then she bent and looked more closely at her find. It must be the door of the little house, and hardly touched by fire!

With a cry of excitement that had once been reserved for finds in designer sales, Noor snatched up her stick again and poked it under the board, moving it back and forth to scare off any snakes that might have taken up residence there. Then she levered the board upright.

Then she stopped, breathless, staring down at the flattened earth that had once been a family's living space…to the little rag doll that lay sprawled and abandoned there.

Noor's hand was trembling as she reached down to pick it up. She let the board fall back into place as she gazed at her discovery.

People were so outraged. International outcry.

The little doll was homemade, from a long sock stuffed with wadding. So simple, she noted absently. The toe is the head, the heel is the bum, slit the fabric from the top edge of the sock to the heel and stitch into legs. Make two arms with a bit of leftover fabric and stuffing and attach to the body under the head.

And with loving care, watched by an eager child, turn this basic shape into a personality with neatly embroidered black wool eyes, a smiling red mouth. Attach wool hair and braid thickly. Tie with a scrap of gold braid. Make a little floral-pattern tunic that matches the child's own dress.

Let the child dress and undress it, feed it and put it to bed, cuddle it and love it.

…Then, one dark day, it will fall unseen from the top of a hastily packed box of your precious belongings, or from the arm of the child, screaming because she sees her parents frightened and powerless as you are dragged from your home by brutal, uncaring strangers.

Noor could see the scene, could almost hear the shouts, the terrified wailing of children, the pleading of women, as if the anguish had imprinted itself into the little doll, into the broken bits of wood and brick, on the air, into the very earth.

Humanitarian outrage. Until this moment they had

been only words to her, and she realized it with shame. Noor Ashkani had always been quite sure she had a conscience. She gave to charity as religion dictated, and even went so far as to think the division of the world's riches unfair.

But as for real understanding…

"Why can't I go?" She could hear her own sulky voice arguing with her father, and remembered with deep, pulsing shame that when the resort on the main island had opened a few years ago and several of her wealthier friends had returned with stories of a holiday in heaven—she had wanted to vacation here.

Her father had put his foot down. That had been long before the international outcry had started, but he had tried to tell her the truth. Noor had sulked for weeks.

Now the human tragedy seemed to clutch at Noor's heart, as if with the child's desperate hands. The people to whom this had happened were her own people, but they were not alone in their suffering. She wondered how many ordinary people over the course of the past hundred years had been driven out of their ancestral homelands—by one means or another—in order to create playgrounds for the wealthy. Or military bases. Or cattle pasture. Or dust bowls.

And she herself was no better than a vandal now, scrabbling through the wreck of human lives for something to make her own life more comfortable.

To hell with it. Bari could be as scathing as he liked— she wasn't doing any more scavenging today. Noor dusted off the little doll as best she could, straightened its stained, mouldy dress, picked up her stick, wiped her eyes, and ran away from the wretched sound and stench of human misery created by other humans in the name of greed.

Noor returned to the campsite laden with fresh palm leaves to line the floor of their shelter, expecting to find Bari working.

But he wasn't there. The almost completed hut at the edge of the forest was deserted. So was the toilet, further in among the trees. His tools were flung down haphazardly in the sand, and a burned board he had been attaching hung askew.

Anxiety gripped her. Bari was methodical in his building, neat and precise with his few precious tools. What could have caused him to simply toss his work aside like this? Noor dropped her load and left the protection of the trees to look down the beach.

A few yards away, tossed in a heap, lay the weather-faded white djellaba and rope she had made for him. Noor gazed along the beach, then out over the water. It was a moment before she noticed the flotsam that was spread over a broad area, being carried towards the island.

She gasped in mingled surprise, excitement, and fright. Did this represent a wrecked ship, or only a cargo lost overboard? What was in those boxes and crates?

The sea sparkled in the afternoon sunshine, lifting its tainted offering in a brilliant, tantalizing dance.

Might there be soap? Food? *Chocolate?*

From where she stood, she could see a large crate, a plastic-wrapped cardboard box, a cluster of rope, and dozens of lusciously bright, merrily bobbing oranges. It was probably only a matter of time before it all washed up on the beach, but Noor wouldn't be waiting for the tide. She untied her sarong and dropped it at her feet. The teddy was getting more frayed every day, but it served well enough for a swimsuit.

It was only as she was plunging into the water that

she saw the rest. Further along the bay, another cluster of boxes and crates was heading towards the rocks. Noor stood for a blank moment, staring. The surf was rough around the rocks. It was probably a hopeless task. And dangerous, if she got caught in an undertow.

And it might not even be worth it.

But in a choice between things that would probably come ashore on an accessible beach without her intervention, and rescuing what would otherwise be smashed against the rocks…

Where was Bari? Had he seen this? Biting her lip, her hand shading her eyes, Noor gazed up and down the beach, out over the water, hoping for some sign of him.

"Baaaari!" she called. "Baaareeee!"

No answer.

She turned and looked again at the precious cargo being driven towards the rocks. For the first time she didn't have Bari to tell her what to do. Should she go after those boxes, or was it too risky? And how? Most looked too big and cumbersome for her to simply grab hold of and then swim home.

Maybe it was a hopeless task. Maybe she should just wait and drag in the stuff that came right to this beach, make sure it landed safely.

But—

Making up her mind abruptly, Noor turned and ran to the life raft, where they kept their supplies, and snatched up a coil of nylon rope. Slinging it over her shoulder, she ran along the beach towards the rocks as far as possible, then went into the water and struck out for the nearest item.

It was a difficult and frustrating task. First she had to get the rope around the thing and tie it snugly, which was less easy than she'd have guessed. Then she had to

get back to the beach. Noor had never engaged in a real
struggle with nature, but now she became immersed in
it, fighting the capricious sea for possession of the
bounty it had brought so tantalizingly close.

She heaved a sigh of exhausted triumph as she landed
a small wooden crate safely, untied the rope and immediately went back in the water for another. It was then
that she saw Bari in the water, much further out, grap-
pling with a large crate. She had no idea how long he
had been there.

After that, there was only the burning heat, the painful glare and sparkle of sunlight on water, the wrench-
ing discomfort in her arms and back and legs as she
pulled and pushed, dancing out of the way when the surf
suddenly bounced a crate along the sand, returning to
the struggle the moment she had one safely landed.

"Noor!"

She looked up, out of a dream, unsure how much
time had passed. The beach was littered with salvage.
She had been vaguely aware of Bari dragging a chain
of smallish items ashore at least once—he tied several
pieces to the rope and then landed them all together.

She looked around. He was in the water, well out
from shore.

"Throw me your rope!"

There was something in his voice that compelled instant response. Her heart kicked as she dragged the rope
from the box she had nearly beached. She coiled the
rope as she dashed back into the water and half ran, half
swam in Bari's direction.

"Don't come any further!"

The sunlight was dancing on the ripples, painfully
bright and beautiful. Bari's arm was outstretched in the
water, his fist gripping the end of his rope. At the other

end was a cluster of three crates. The water had already dragged them to the fullest extent of the rope, and she could see that he was exhausted with the struggle to hold them.

"Stand firm, hold one end tight and throw me the other end," he ordered calmly.

Something was wrong. Noor gasped, her heart pushing into her throat. A sense of danger and threat seemed to fill the air.

"Bari!" she shrieked. "Let it go!"

"Throw it!"

She gripped her rope with shaking fingers. "Leave it, Bari—whatever it is, it's not worth it!"

If he was dragged toward the rocks, caught in the surf—

"Throw the damned rope!"

With a prayer for strength, Noor tossed the curl of rope in a backhander like her best tennis swing. It snaked out, painting a long grey line in the air before landing with a soundless splash a few yards from him.

She could see the other rope pulling him from his target.

"It's too dangerous!" she screamed. "Let it go!"

His arms stretched to their fullest extent, he at last snatched up the rope she had tossed. Then he lifted the other rope end, and against the buffeting of the waves, she saw, was struggling to drag the other rope closer in order to tie her rope to the one that held the packages. But the drag on the packages was too strong, and he was being constantly buffeted by waves.

She couldn't give him any more rope without getting drawn into the breakers. Already she was being dragged along the beach towards the rocks; she was knocked almost off her feet when a bigger wave caught Bari and he went under.

"Bari, it won't reach!" she screamed. "Let go of the crates!"

If he was dragged against the rocks, he would be so badly smashed up—why didn't he let the damned crates go?

The weight suddenly eased and Noor saw the three crates sailing away, the end of the white rope curling and swirling in a little eddy. Relief flowed through her so hot her knees almost buckled.

"Oh, thank God, thank God!"

"Can you pull me in?" Bari called.

He worked his way towards the sandy beach at an angle, not fighting the current directly. Slowly he got away from the rocks, while Noor, keeping a tight grip on the rope, dragged him in. It was a little like reeling in a wild stallion.

When he stood up out of the waves at last, staggered towards her and then fell again, she saw blood streaming from a long gash in his thigh.

Twelve

He was heavy, almost a dead weight on her, and that terrified her. Bari wasn't a man to show weakness, but he was leaning on her hard, grimacing with every step, dragging the wounded leg as if unable to put any weight on it at all. His breath rasped in her ear, sending shivers of blank terror through her. If he was seriously wounded, what would happen to them?

She helped him up the beach to the little hut, where he sank down onto the foil sheet with a stifled groan. Gripped by horror, Noor stared helplessly at the long wound running down his thigh.

"Ya Allah!" she moaned, her mother's favourite expression in the face of trouble. Thoughts of infection, gangrene and amputation danced grotesquely across her imagination. How dreadful to think of him losing a leg, and all because she—

"First aid kit."

His voice was a whisper; he was clearly in pain. Noor came abruptly to her senses. He was the wounded one— he shouldn't have to do the organizing! But she was the only other person available.

She had to concentrate.

First aid kit. Noor ran to the overturned life raft, under which they stowed their equipment, scrabbled wildly for the first aid kit, then, from the diminishing pile of white silk she had salvaged from her carefully demolished wedding dress, grabbed a medium-sized square.

Back at the shelter, she knelt beside him. The bleeding was already slowing. At least he wasn't going to bleed to death! Her panic subsiding somewhat, she began to tear the silk into strips. Such basic action made her feel more competent and confident.

"I'm sure it needs stitches," she told Bari, though she had nothing more than television hospital dramas to go on.

"Never mind. The important thing is to get antiseptic onto it."

She was sure she should use boiled water to wash the wound first, but there was no possibility of that. Even if she had a pot to boil it in, she had already proved hopeless at lighting the fire.

The fire! They had lighted it every night for a signal, as well as the psychological and physical comfort it offered. But who would light it tonight?

"The drinking water in the emergency kit will be sterile," Bari said, sending her dashing back to the raft to search for some of the tiny little plastic packs of water which they hadn't had to touch yet.

What followed was the most nerve-racking half hour of her life. Under the patient's quiet but clear instructions she washed the ugly wound, made sure it was clean, bathed it with antiseptic, then drew the edges of the gash together, applied sterile pads, and taped them as neatly as she could. Then she bound his thigh with a clean bandage and, afterwards, strips of silk. Finally, to protect the bandages, she wrapped and taped a plastic bag around the whole.

"Does it feel all right?" she asked at last.

"It feels fine. Thank you," Bari said, still breathing in a way that frightened her. "You made a very work-manlike job of it."

Even though she knew it wasn't true—some of her taping looked like a five-year-old's craft project—Noor was swept with an unfamiliar sense of accomplishment. She'd done it! She'd actually managed it! Something had desperately needed to be done, and, however inex-pertly, she had done it!

"Thank you," she said, with real humility. She smiled down at Bari, feeling a strangely touching connection with him because she had been able to help. "I'm really glad I could do it."

"So am I."

After all the cynical looks in the past, his approving smile now was like rain on new roots. They gazed into each other's eyes for a moment of silence. In the forest the birds began to sing the sun down.

"Do you want a painkiller?"

"No," said Bari. His mouth contorted. "Yes."

She pressed a tablet out of the bubble pack and gave it to him with a little water. He drank it and lay back with a little grunt of pain.

"How did it happen?"

"I didn't see whatever it was. I was kicking hard against the current and it was in my way. A jutting rock, maybe."

Her breath hissed in sympathy. "Do you—" She blew her breath up over her forehead, sending a tendril of hair dancing. "Is it broken?"

He was silent for a moment. "No. The bone may be bruised. It'll be a day or two at most before I can put weight on it."

She wasn't sure she believed that. Might he be lying to keep her calm, or was he maybe in a state of denial?

"Ya Allah," Noor whispered again, her eyes wide, as the full extent of what his injury would mean began to unfold in her mind.

"Tomorrow you'll collect some herbs for me. Good thing the shelter is nearly done," he muttered drowsily. Reaction was setting in. "You'll be able to manage."

Manage! She stared at him in mute protest. Bari's eyelids fluttered, and Noor's heart fluttered in response. If he lost consciousness—! The weight of the world seemed to be on her shoulders all at once.

"Bari! Do you want anything?" she cried, just to see him open his eyes again. To know that he could.

He took a long time to collect his thoughts, gazing at her with a frown. Then he shook his head.

"Do we have any food?"

At the mention of the word her stomach growled. Because of the salvage operation Bari hadn't gone fishing today. They hadn't foraged for eggs. The sun was very low now. Behind her, the birdsong was at its evening peak. She would have little chance of finding anything in the dark.

"There are dates," she remembered, getting to her feet. She had laid some dates out in the sun in the hopes of drying them.

But as she stepped out of the shelter, she stopped short.

"The salvage! I forgot all about it!" she cried jubilantly.

She dashed back inside the shelter and snatched up the little knife.

"Take it easy with that thing," Bari protested.

But Noor barely heard. A moment later she was half-way along the beach, bending over one of the biggest boxes. The slanting sun picked out the delicate Arabic letters she had not had time to examine before.

"'Al Bostan luxury food importers!'" she translated with a happy shout. "Food! I knew it!" With hands made clumsy by excitement, hunger, and fatigue, she finally managed to slit the plastic packaging, and then the packing tape. Eagerly she pulled up the cardboard flaps.

In the sunshine the cellophane-wrapped packages were unmistakable. Her heart lifted with crazy joy.

"Lettuce!" she shrieked, as excited as, in a former life, she might have cried *Moët et Chandon!*

She reached in and drew one head of lettuce out of the neatly packed box. Then she glanced back towards the shelter and frowned a little. Wilted lettuce. Not exactly the meal of choice for an invalid.

"I suppose the tinned soup went straight to the bottom," she muttered darkly, as if the soup would regret that choice one day.

She chose a smaller box and renewed her attack, much more proficient with the knife than she would have been even a few days ago, if she had been in a state of mind to notice….

It was like a joke, but somehow Noor couldn't laugh. She had half killed herself, and Bari had ripped up and maybe broken his leg, and all they had to show for it was…

"What's that howling?" she heard from the shelter. She got up and walked over to where he lay.

"Two boxes opened so far," she reported in a flat voice. "And the score—we are now in proud possession of two dozen severely wilted heads of romaine lettuce and a few thousand plastic swizzle sticks."

A shout of laughter met her ears as she dropped one of each on the ground beside him.

She laughed with him. It was that or cry.

Bari picked up the swizzle stick and frowned at it in the fading light. "I thought so," he said after a moment, and held it up. "See the logo? The shipment was destined for the Gulf Eden Resort. They bring fresh food and supplies over from the mainland on a daily basis. One of the dhows either sank or had to cut loose the cargo during the storm."

"It's taken a long time to beach, hasn't it?" Noor asked.

Bari shrugged. "The currents among the islands can be very difficult, particularly after a storm. Every sailor learns that quickly. And that blow we had last night might have had something to do with it." Last night there had been a horrible wind and high rough seas smashing up the beach. "The wooden crates may contain less perishable food," he suggested.

"From your lips to God's ears!" Noor said, reaching for the axe and hefting it like a pro. She scarcely noticed how the burned handle blackened her callused hands.

A little later Noor stumbled up the beach into the hut with her arms full. She dropped to her knees beside Bari and spilled the riches on the sand.

"It's really hard to prise open those crates!" she cried. Her hands were bruised, bleeding and filthy, but she was exultant.

"But you managed?" Bari asked.

"Two of them, plus a couple of the boxes, and I've got the knack now— I can do the others tomorrow!" Noor said jubilantly. "And look what I found!"

"What?" He smiled at her, and Noor blinked on an in-drawn breath. She had never seen quite that expression in his eyes before, and somehow it made her heart skip.

"*Ta da!* Smoked salmon!" she cried, holding it up, too excited to save the best till last.

"What a relief to know the civilized world still exists."

"It's food, isn't it?" Noor said defensively, reacting to the irony. "I love smoked salmon, and we've got *pounds* of it, in packs that are good for *years!*"

Bari laughed, his eyes alight with that strange warmth. "I did say we might be stranded for a while, but I hope…"

She was too focused to appreciate his irony. "I know, Bari, but the point is, it's good for as long as we need it. It's good now. Not like the lettuce."

"*Alhamdolillah,*" he said.

"And rice! Bags of it. Who'd have thought that would float? And water biscuits, and a huge carton of potato chips, look, and—" she scrabbled happily among her treasures "—oh, and *coffee!* Isn't that just *so* fantastic? I'm almost crazy for a cup of coffee!"

"All we need now is the cup," he teased.

"And a pot for boiling the water! I haven't found anything useful like that yet, but there must be some way to make something that'll work."

She didn't see the expression that crossed his face. "You think so?"

"Not everything was for the hotel kitchens. There's some stock for different boutiques. Haven't you noticed?" She lifted a hand and struck a pose.

"You have a new forage cap," he said admiringly.

"Not just any forage cap, either! This is the last word in desert chic." Noor turned her head to display the canvas flap that protected her neck, as if she were a member of the French Foreign Legion. "Notice the discreet Gulf Eden Resort logo! Only the truly discerning— well, the obscenely rich—will recognize that, of course."

"Of course," Bari agreed gravely.

"I'll bet the shop sells bikinis to match, too! I'd love it if I found one. This thing I'm wearing is just about at the end of its very short but traumatic life span. But it'll be dark soon—I had to stop. How hungry are you for dinner?"

"Homicidal," Bari allowed with a grin.

"Smoked salmon and crackers?"

Noor had cut little squares from the plastic that sealed the boxes, which now she laid over pieces of board chopped from a crate, to serve as plates.

She peeled open a pack of smoked salmon and a box of water biscuits, poured water into their one plastic cup and set it carefully in the sand, then sat back, as proud and satisfied as if she had produced a five-course meal.

"Doesn't that look delicious?" she cried, her stomach growling in anticipation.

"Best offer I've had all day," Bari agreed.

They fell on the food as if it were a feast. "Oh, the taste of *salt!* And who'd have believed a simple cracker could be so satisfying?" Noor demanded, munching, when they had demolished most of the meal in silence.

Bari nodded, picked up the cup of water, and offered it to her.

As she reached to take it, Noor suddenly noticed her hands. She always scrubbed her hands with sand and seawater at the end of every day, not with much success. But tonight she had been too busy. Dirt was packed around the ragged nails, the callused palms were black with soot from the axe handle, the skin of her fingers raw and scraped with the effort of opening the crates.

She shrugged. Well, she had worked hard, and it was no surprise if her hands showed it. As her fingers closed around the little cup, she felt a curious pride, as though the dirt of hard work were a badge that marked her kinship with women all over the globe, the women who wrest a living from the earth.

Suddenly she felt how much she deserved the drink. For the first time in her life, Noor unconsciously made the connection between work and self-worth. Always before, she had been given whatever she needed by right. Because her father was rich, because she was who she was.

Today she had earned the food she had eaten, and this drink of water, and she felt the difference.

They were lying together in the shelter, with a foil sheet over them. Noor was restless and couldn't sleep, but there was absolutely nothing she could do to amuse herself. The darkness was intense, she had discovered, when there was no city glow to lighten it.

She sighed unhappily. For the past three days, everything had fallen on her. Bari said his leg was improving daily, but he still couldn't stand on it for longer than a few minutes at a time, so he wasn't doing much in the way of work.

He could give her instruction and advice, though, and Noor was learning fast. She had learned to light a fire, though not without first wasting too much of the fuel in the little cigarette lighter. She had even caught a fish in the net Bari had made from her wedding veil and a pliant branch. With nothing but his verbal description to go by, she had found the right healing herb in the forest, and made a paste to put on his wounds.

Nearly every day new packets from the lost cargo

washed up on the beach, and every day she invented
new uses for frustratingly useless artefacts from a way
of life which seemed increasingly distant and
incomprehensible.

She had constructed a backgammon game for them.
For counters, from the dozens of tiny fridge magnets she
found in one package, she had chosen fifteen bearing a
miniature Old Palace, and another fifteen of the Great
Mosque. The board she created out of the cardboard box
itself, outlined the points with Bari's knife, and then
stained alternate points with crushed berries.

She had brought Bari small bits of dried wood and
instructed him to carve them into dice. In the evenings,
when darkness descended, they lay by the fire, playing
while the flame faded to glowing ash.

On an impulse she couldn't resist, Noor had threaded
the pearls from her wedding dress onto a piece of fishing line, and made a necklace, first for herself, and then
for the little rag doll she had found, whom she had
named Laqiya. Bari had admired them both with apparently equal approval.

This morning she had opened a huge box addressed
to a boutique in the resort called MemorArabia to find
a half dozen replica beaten brass bowls and a couple of
large replica hookahs, all wrapped in enough plastic
bubble wrap to build a tent. The hookahs she had set
aside with a snort of contempt. "What would anybody
want with them?" she demanded indignantly. "What
use would they be?"

Bari laughed. "It's a good thing you don't work in
the tourism industry."

"But what a *waste!* I mean, someone will take that
home and put it on their mantelpiece and it'll collect
dust for three months and then be given to charity, and

someone else will take it home and put it on their coffee table, and that's its story. It's excellent quality—I bet
it's a functioning hookah—but who's ever going to
smoke it? And look at all the materials that have gone
into it! This is real brass tubing. It could have been…"

With a little indrawn breath, Noor fell silent. And a
couple of hours later, she had extracted the tubing from
several hookahs and mounted it over the fire, supported
by stones at each end. On the little platform thus created she put a replica beaten brass bowl from the same
shop, and so boiled water for the first time.

"Coffee!" she sang as she stirred the powder into the
steaming water. Her ladle was the plastic cup from the
emergency kit, and she carefully decanted several measures of the hot coffee into another brass bowl and offered it to Bari, before doing the same for herself.

"Isn't that heaven?" she demanded as the scent teased
her nostrils and she waited for the liquid to cool. "I feel
as though I grew the stuff and ground it myself!"

Maybe it was the coffee that stopped her sleeping
now, she reflected. After so long with no caffeine, it
might have had an effect on her that it didn't use to have.
She was utterly exhausted by the day's work, so what
other explanation could there be?

She wished she could snuggle up against Bari, but although they slept close under the same foil sheet, he
never offered to actually hold her. Sometimes when she
awoke, it was to discover that she had wormed her way
into his embrace in her sleep, but she had never done it
in cold blood.

His breathing told her he was awake, too. Her pride
had taken a bad beating when she'd discovered his true
opinion of her, and although their relationship had now
improved out of all recognition, she was still nervous

of what his reaction would be if she asked him to hold her. She had asked him once before and been harshly repulsed, and the humiliation was ever fresh.

In the darkness she felt him fold his arms under his head. "Can't sleep?" he murmured softly.

"No. Isn't it ridiculous? Every muscle is screaming for a rest, too." Belatedly she remembered that he had even more reason to complain. "What about you? Is it pain that's keeping you awake?"

He grunted without answering, and she supposed he felt it was unmanly to admit to suffering.

"Do you think your leg is healing properly?"

He didn't answer, and Noor felt a shiver of dread. What would she do if he suffered complications? What if the wound became infected? The mess of herbs he had asked her to apply to the wound had looked positively toxic, and she didn't have even first aid training, let alone any medical qualifications.

"If we ever get out of this, I'm going to take a first aid course," she vowed fervently. "And I'm going to get some kind of practical training in something, too."

Bari was silent for so long she wondered if he'd fallen asleep. But then, in an odd voice, he asked, "What sort of practical training?"

"I don't know yet. I'll have to look around. Plumbing, maybe!" She laughed a little. "Something useful. You know, Bari, it's like—here we are on a desert island, and only certain skills count. And only certain things are useful, and the useless things are just so much garbage clogging up our campsite—and the island. And it's what you said—there's no room for anyone who doesn't pull their weight, and if we don't cooperate, we die. But you know what I've just realized?"

"What?"

"The whole world is a desert island. It's no different than what we've got right here. It's just—easier to overlook the truth out there."

There was another long pause, but this time she knew he had heard.

"I see," he said softly.

"So when we get back—*will* we ever get back?—I want to start doing something useful. Something like engineering, or medicine, or…I wonder if it's too late to start. Do you think I'm being silly?"

"No," he said softly. "Why would I think it silly to want to make a contribution to the world?"

Noor laughed in sudden recognition. "That's what it is, isn't it? I hadn't thought of it just like that!" She laughed again. "*Ya Allah,* I've become a do-gooder! Do you think I'll turn into a poor-little-rich-girl who runs around orphanages wringing her hands?"

Bari laughed, too. "Not unless you want to."

"Well, I don't. I want to do something *practical.*"

"From the evidence of the past few days, you might consider becoming an inventor," he offered, only half joking.

Noor was silent, absorbing that. "I think that's the biggest compliment I've ever had," she said softly.

And it was in that strangely sweet moment that she realized she did love him, after all. Had she loved him from that first moment? Had her own self-absorption simply hidden the truth from her? Or was it only since she had come to the island that her heart had opened enough to let love in? She couldn't say when the seed had been planted, but the full-blown plant was unmistakable.

She had a terrible, powerful urge to tell him so, but fear stopped her. He had pretended to love her when in his heart he felt contempt. And his reasons for marrying her hadn't changed: he still wanted to please his grandfather. He wanted to inherit the family estates.

If she told him of her love, would he pretend to love her again? She was almost certain that he liked her better now, but what if he didn't?

Noor was feeling desperately confused all at once, and she shifted restlessly. "Oh, what I'd give for a portable DVD player and a good movie!" She cried out her frustration in the darkness.

"Is that what you normally do when you can't sleep?"

"I don't have much trouble sleeping usually, but when I do, yes, I get up and watch a movie. Or read. Or write e-mails to my friends. That's the problem with technology—where is it when you really need it?" She laughed, her heart stretched with pain and confusion, when she wanted to weep. "I wonder what primitive cultures do for insomnia?"

"The same, only without the technology," he suggested. "Would you like me to tell you a story?"

Noor gave a little grunt of surprise. "My father always used to tell me stories! I'd almost forgotten. Does your story have jinns and fairies and giant rocs?"

"Of course." Her heart beat with sudden urgency as she felt him lift an arm and offer to slide it under her head. Wordlessly Noor slipped up to rest on his bare shoulder as his arm drew her in against him.

"Is your leg comfortable?"

"It's fine," Bari said mildly. "Now be quiet and listen."

Thirteen

"**O**nce upon a time, there was a king who had an exceedingly beautiful daughter, named Zarsana. The girl was so beautiful, and so sweet natured, that everyone said she could hardly be human. Among themselves the servants called her the Fairy Princess. She was the joy of both her father and her mother.

"One day, the King said to the Queen, 'Although it will pain us to lose her, it is time that our daughter was married. We must find her a suitable husband. In our pleasure in her company we have already delayed too long.'

"The next day, the King visited his daughter in her rooms in the palace, and told her his thoughts. But Princess Zarsana smiled at her father and said, 'Why should I leave you and my mother when we are so happy as we are? Do not seek to change things, but let us remain together.'

"Her father insisted that it was the fate of every young

woman to marry, and at last the Princess said, 'I will marry only a man who has visited the City of Gold.'

"Her father was astonished, for he had never heard of the City of Gold. He tried to dissuade his daughter, but the Princess was adamant. At last the King went away and consulted with his viziers.

"None of the viziers, not even the Grand Vizier, had ever heard of the Golden City. But as ignorance never holds back an expert, they consulted together and advised the King.

"'You must invite all the eligible princes of the world to visit, and ask which of them has seen the City of Gold,' they advised. 'Whoever says he has made such a trip shall marry the Princess.'

"But when the King invited all the princes of the world and asked each of them in turn if he had visited the City of Gold, none had even heard of the place. And they all returned to their homes none the wiser regarding the reason of the visit.

"Then the viziers said, 'Your Cup Companions are all men of the highest nobility. Ask them whether any has succeeded in visiting the Golden City, and whoever says he has shall marry your daughter.'

"So the King ordered a feast, to which he summoned his Cup Companions. When they had eaten and drunk, recited poetry and discussed philosophy and love in the usual way, the King spoke.

"'Which of you has visited the City of Gold? For whoever has done so shall marry my daughter, Zarsana, and I will make him Crown Prince.'

"Of course all the Cup Companions wished very much for such a fate, for Zarsana's beauty and good nature were well-known, and whoever was Crown Prince would inherit the kingdom in the course of time. But each had to confess that he had never even heard of such a place as the Golden City.

"When the King summoned his viziers again, they scratched their heads. 'No other man can be sufficiently noble to marry the Princess, even if he has seen the Golden City,' they agreed. 'The Princess must give up her determination to marry such a man.' And they had no more advice to offer.

"So the King paid a visit to the Princess again, and explained the difficulty. 'No one has even heard of the City of Gold. How is such a man to be found? You must give up your determination and let me choose a husband for you.'

"But the girl refused.

"'Let a proclamation be made in the streets,' advised Princess Zarsana. 'Say that I will marry that man, whatever his birth or rank, who has visited the Golden City.'

"The worried King did as his daughter had instructed, and messengers were sent out into the city to announce that whoever had seen the City of Gold should travel to the palace, where he would marry the Princess Zarsana and be made Crown Prince.

"The announcement caused great excitement in the kingdom, and the news was passed from lip to lip, but not even the oldest of the King's subjects had ever heard of such a place as the Golden City.

"At last the news came to the ears of a handsome young man named Salik, the son of a silk merchant who had died leaving his son enormously rich. Salik had squandered all his father's wealth on gambling and vice, and now he was very miserable. His false friends had abandoned him when they saw that all his money was gone, and he was too ashamed to approach any of his father's old friends in his present state.

"When he heard the proclamation, Salik said to himself, 'Since no one knows of this city, who will be able to challenge me if I say I have seen it? This is the way to mend my fortunes, for I can sink no lower than I already am.' So he went to the palace and said to the guards, 'I am the man the King seeks. I have visited the City of Gold and seen it with my own eyes.'

"Salik was taken before the King, to whom he repeated the false claim. The King in turn sent him to the Princess. Princess Zarsana said to Salik, 'Have you seen the Golden City?' 'Yes,' replied Salik. 'While I was on my travels in search of knowledge, I reached the City of Gold.' 'And by what route did you travel there?' she asked.

"Salik was undaunted. 'From my home in this city I travelled for many days, till I came to the great city of Isfahan. From there I made my way through the Dasht-i Kavir, and after great struggles found my way to Zanzibar. From there I went to Bokhara, and thence to Samarkand. From Samarkand through the mountains, I made my way to the shores of the sea. I entered the City of Gold, which is as beautiful as paradise. There I studied for many months, and at last made my way home.'

"The Princess smiled. 'What you tell me is wonderful, and it is clear that you have indeed seen the Golden City. Tell me again how you travelled there.'

"Feeling pleased with his success, Salik began to embroider.

"'From here I journeyed with great difficulties to Isfahan, and from there I joined a caravan through the Dasht-i Kavir. In Zanzibar I left the caravan and travelled with a friend to Samarkand, and what adventures we met with along the way I shall entertain you with at a later date. In Bokhara I met a wise man, who gave me advice and directed my footsteps through the mountains to the Golden City.'

"The Princess ordered her servants to throw Salik out into the street, and when her father came to ask after him, she chided him for not realizing that the young man was a rogue. 'Do not be impatient, Father,' she advised. 'For this may take time.' So the King ordered that the crier should walk the streets of the city every day, making the announcement that any man who had visited the City of Gold would marry the Princess.

"But as for Salik, he was in very low spirits. He was now in a much worse case than before, for not only had he lied and been found out, earning everyone's contempt, but at his first sight of her he had fallen deeply in love with the Princess. And he had failed to win her.

"The young man wandered for some time, bewailing his fate and regretting the Princess. At last he decided that, as he could not live without her as his wife, he must do what was necessary to win her. He made up his mind to go through the world, searching for the City of Gold until he found it, or died in the attempt.

"So Salik set out on his journey, and travelled until he reached the forest of Aghaz, which was home to wild animals and robbers, and which seemed to extend before the traveller, however fast he moved. Salik journeyed through the forest, and at length came to a tree under which a very ancient dervish was living. The hermit welcomed him and served him with food and drink, and asked where he was going. Salik told the dervish of his quest, but the dervish could not tell him anything of the City of Gold. He sent Salik to his older brother, who was also a hermit, in far distant mountains.

"But the sage of the mountain also had not heard of

the Golden City. He in his turn advised Salik to travel to the seashore, and thence to a far distant island in the ocean, named Jariza. Jariza was ruled by a rich foreign king, Ashabi, who was known for his foreign travels, and who might know of the City of Gold.

"So Salik proceeded to the seashore, where he obtained passage to Jariza with a merchant ship. But when the ship had almost reached its destination, a black storm blew up, and the ship, lashed by winds and waves as high as mountains, broke up. Salik and the merchant were tossed into the sea, and Salik was immediately swallowed whole by a giant fish.

"Soon after, the fish was captured by fishermen, and because it was so big, they took it as a wonder to the King of their country. In the King's presence the giant fish was cut open, and to everyone's amazement, a handsome young man emerged.

"At the King's enquiry, Salik introduced himself and explained his mission. 'And now,' he finished, 'I am on my way to the court of King Ashabi of the island kingdom of Jariza, for he is a great traveller and seafarer, and he may know of the City of Gold.'

"The King laughed in amazement and said, 'I am Ashabi, and this island is Jariza,' and everyone was astonished at this outcome of the fishermen's gift.

"The King had heard of the City of Gold as being situated on a far distant island, but he did not know where. But on an island not far away there was a shrine, and to that shrine, in a week's time, would come pilgrims from all over the islands. The King offered to take Salik to the pilgrimage, in order that he might question the pilgrims about the City of Gold.

"So Salik remained with the King until the time came, and then they set sail for the shrine. But as they

voyaged, they passed an island on which stood a giant
tree with a thick trunk and broad, low-hanging branches.
Salik asked King Ashabi about the tree, but the King
said, 'We dare not approach closer, for there is a great
whirlpool which lets go of no boat once it has been
trapped.' And just at that moment they felt the boat
tremble beneath them; the whirlpool had captured the
boat. As the boat was drawn into the vortex, it came
closer and closer to the island and the giant tree. Salik
was able to leap up and pull himself up into the branches
of the tree. There he hid himself, watching the boat disappear into the whirlpool, and wondering what to do.

"When night fell, a flock of giant rocs came to roost
in the tree, and Salik discovered he could understand
their speech. The rocs were discussing their activities
of the day and their plans for the morrow. After some
time, one of them said to the others, 'Today I have
feasted in the Golden City, and tomorrow I will do the
same, for the gardens are so lush there I see no reason
to travel further.'

"Salik was elated to hear this, and when the rocs
were fast asleep, he climbed up onto the back of the one
who had spoken of the City of Gold, and hid himself in
his feathers. In the morning the roc flew to the Golden
City and alighted in a beautiful garden.

"Salik slipped from his back undetected and wandered about the garden until he met two women. He
asked them what the place was, and the women told him
that it was the City of Gold, ruled by a fairy princess
named Perizan for her sister, Queen Marifa, who was
absent, and that they were the Queen's gardeners.

"They conducted the traveller to the palace and into
the presence of the Princess, who asked him for his
story. When he had told her everything, Princess Peri-

zan said, 'Your story interests me very much and I
would like to know more. However, I must go with my
women on a visit that cannot be delayed. I shall be away
two days. You will be comfortable here in the palace—
order whatever you wish. But on no account go into the
Inner Pavilion.'

"With that, Perizan and her women departed, leaving Salik to wander through the beautiful palace and its
magnificent gardens. He was delighted, for the palace
was the most wonderful thing he had ever seen, with pil-
lars glittering with precious stones, and walls of beaten
gold. In the gardens grew plants the like of which he had
never seen, of enchanting beauty, visited by birds of
brilliant hue and thrilling song. Whatever he asked for
was brought to him instantly, and the food was
flavoured with spices so delicious every meal was an
enchantment.

"But on the afternoon of the second day, as is the way
of mortals, he began to wonder why the Princess had
forbidden him the Inner Pavilion. And at length the
young man's curiosity overwhelmed him, and he made
his way to the central courtyard of the palace, where the
Inner Pavilion stood in its own lush garden, its golden
dome glowing like a sun. Salik climbed the staircase and
found himself on a broad terrace encircling a glittering
pagoda that was composed of sweeping arches and the
domed roof, all studded with mirrors and laced with
gold. In the centre of the pagoda was an eight-sided
chamber. And in one of the sides, Salik saw a door.

"When he opened the door he found himself in a
chamber even more beautifully and richly decorated
than all that had preceded it. The walls glowed from the
sparkle of a million diamonds, and were hung with pictures painted with rubies, emeralds, sapphires, tur-

quoises, amethysts, and a strange jewel, black as ebony, that glittered like a serpent's eye.

"Eight arched windows carved into the domed roof let in a mysterious light that fell upon a divan resting upon a raised dais in the centre of the chamber. The divan was covered with magnificent cloth of gold embroidered all over with diamonds and pearls.

"It covered the form of a beautiful woman, who lay absolutely still. Her black hair cascaded down behind her to the floor like a curtain, threaded with gold, in each curl a perfect pearl. In the centre of her forehead a large diamond on a band of woven gold seemed to capture all the mysterious light from the windows and send it flashing out to every corner of the chamber.

"Salik shielded his eyes from the bright rays and, as if hypnotized, approached the sleeping woman to look down at her face. With amazed bewilderment, he beheld the form of his beloved, the Princess Zarsana, whom he had seen in the palace so many months before.

"He called to her, but could not rouse her. Not knowing whether she was sleeping, dead, or merely an image, Salik wandered disconsolately out of the chamber to sit on the terrace overlooking the garden and consider, trying to make sense of what he had seen.

"He looked down into the garden and discovered a lake he had not noticed before. Beside the lake was a magnificently caparisoned horse, whose coat was black as the night sky, bearing a richly jewelled saddle of red gold, but without a bridle. Blinking in wonderment, Salik descended into the garden and approached the horse. But when he tried to mount it, the horse kicked him, so hard that he was sent into the centre of the lake. Salik sank under the surface, and when he rose again, he discovered that he was in the lake of a garden in his own city.

"Troubled and astonished, Salik emerged from the lake and left the garden. And as he walked the familiar streets, wondering what had happened to him and whether it had all been a dream, he heard the town crier beating the drum and announcing, 'Whoever has seen the City of Gold will marry the Princess and become the Crown Prince.'

"Immediately he went to the palace and said to the guards, 'I have seen the Golden City. Take me to the King.'

"The guards led Salik to the throne room, but when he was admitted to the King's presence, the Cup Companions and courtiers and viziers at once began to cry, 'This is the very villain who came before, and whom the Princess had thrown into the streets for his insolent lies!' And the King, too, remembered him, and threatened him with severe punishment if Salik persisted in his falseness.

"But, though frightened, Salik stood firm. 'Take me to the Princess,' he insisted, 'and if she rejects me again, I accept death as my fit punishment.'

"The King consulted with his viziers, but their advice was confused and contradictory, and for every one who advised one thing, another advised the opposite. And at last the King sent a message to the Princess Zarsana, who came to the throne room accompanied by her women.

"'Father, do you listen to more lies from such a rogue?' she asked the King.

"But Salik stepped forward and cried, 'Tell me how it is that I saw your lifeless form in the Inner Pavilion of the palace of the Golden City, and yet see you here alive!'

"Then the Princess smiled and, turning to the King again, said, 'He speaks the truth, and he will be my husband. But he will not become Crown Prince here in your kingdom, for he must return with me and live forever in the City of Gold.

"'Know that my true name is Marifa. I am Queen in my own land, and in my absence my sister rules in my stead. I was cursed to be born among mortals and live as one of you until a mortal man should, for love of me, visit the Golden City and see my true form there. Now he will become one of us and rule my kingdom with me. And he will henceforth be called Asheq, for his love is true.'

"And hard upon her words, the wonderful black horse flew in through one of the tall windows of the palace and came to rest in front of the Princess. Salik mounted the horse, with the Princess in front of him. And to the wonderment of all in the throne room, the horse mounted into the air and flew out of the window, all the way to the City of Gold.

"Queen Marifa and King Asheq arrived in the City of Gold amid great rejoicing, and they ruled there for many years, and Allah sent them peace and happiness."

Fourteen

His voice faded into silence, and they lay without speaking for a long moment. Then Noor said, "Thank you, that was lovely," in a drowsy, sensually charged voice, and it seemed the most natural thing in the world that Bari should lift his head and bend over her.

Her hand was pressed against his naked chest, half in fear, as deep, urgent need flowed through her. She licked her lips and her eyes tried to pierce the darkness to see his expression. But the last glow of the fire was almost gone, and the first light of the moon had yet to make its appearance.

"Noor," he murmured, in a voice that melted her, and when he felt the long, responsive sigh, his mouth came down and brushed her eyelid and her cheek in a tender quest for her mouth. Noor sighed as his lips teased and nibbled and at last took possession of hers, and of their own accord her arms slipped up to encircle his neck.

His hand pressed hard along the length of her back, and then he moved his fingers to the neckline of the jacket she wore, and slowly, expertly, began to unbutton it.

It was dark, they were guided by touch and scent alone, but still she saw a golden glow as his hand found her breast, and then his mouth lifted and laid a tracery of kisses down her throat, and she responded with hot melting as his tongue tasted her skin.

She kissed his neck, stroked his firmly muscled chest, cupped his head, feeling the silken curls cling around her fingers. Then her hand clenched as his touch shivered along her stomach and abdomen and he found his way unerringly to the nest of clustered nerves at her centre.

Pleasure poured through her, as if liquid gold shot from his fingers, and Noor told him her delight with low, panting cries of gratitude and release. She reached for him then, her hand enclosing his aroused flesh, and gasped a little breath of hungry recognition.

His skin was silken marble, warm and pulsing, and the cry that came from his throat was the sign of her female power, and melted her into fainting pleasure again. They stroked and pressed and kissed until the pleasure was like a madness. And then at last, with a rough groan, his hips slipped between her hungrily welcoming thighs, and his flesh into that place that had already become home to him.

He rose up above her, and behind his head the moon also climbed, gilding their lair with white-gold fingers, brushing his velvet curls, her forehead, her ear, as he moved in her. And for both of them the light seemed to enter their bodies, liquid pleasure that built with each stroke of him inside her, till they were blinded by the brightness, burned by its heat.

Then unbelievable pleasure forced its way through every vein, into every cell, and fountained up in her throat in a wild cry as free as the wildest animal's call. Over and over, down and down and down, pounding, grinding, the mortar and pestle of their bodies breaking the fresh herb of passion to produce the pure essence, the pungent rich oil of deep, immeasurable ecstasy.

The perfume of it burst through their being then, for they were in the world of separation no longer. "I love you," they heard on the air, half fainting, not knowing whether it was her throat or his, or Love itself, that formed the words. And there was no duality, no past and future, no I and Thou; there was only the One.

Bari stood at the water's edge, watching the first rays of the sun divide the black of the sea from the black of the heavens.

He was caught in his own trap. He had wanted to make her love him, and instead… He laughed in soundless mockery at his blind hubris. A woman like her, vital, beautiful, with a quick intelligence and a heart now revealed as good and true—how had he left his own heart out of his calculations? What arrogance had blinded him to his vulnerability?

He loved her. Fire seemed to burn where his heart had once been, a fierce black fire that consumed him. What other woman would have responded to the test in such a way? She had been reluctant at first, but in the end her true worth had shone forth. Underneath that self-absorbed exterior that he had so arrogantly despised was a woman of enormous heart, of powerful courage, with wit and humour in the teeth of adversity…and with all that, she had imagination, vision, ingenuity.

Now he had seen her true self, the human soul that

had been disguised by the trappings of a too-easy life, by the tarnish of self-absorption. The circumstance he had helped to create had rubbed the tarnish away, and the precious metal glowed with its true colour.

She was pure gold, and he felt now that the touch-stone of his heart had always unconsciously known it. Like Salik in the story he had told her, he had seen the image, and had determined to find his true beloved and make her his own.

How could he have imagined himself immune to her?

He shook his head. He had told himself that Noor needed to have the veneer stripped away, but had ignored the fact of his own blindness. He too had needed a stripping away—he had needed to remove the cold reason by which he had judged her, and see her as his heart saw her. He had had to learn that he, too, had a heart. And that his heart was a better judge of truth than his intellect.

She belonged to him. That was a central truth, flowing like golden lava from an eruption in his heart. He looked back on his grandfather's command now as an impertinence. How had the old man dared to order Bari to love his own heart's breath, his own life, his eyes? He felt now that even his grandfather's wanting him to marry her was theft.

What a fool he had been, risking everything in the madness of this enterprise! Could she love him now, when he had imposed such unnecessary suffering on her? When he had ranted at her, blamed her, and told her the great lie—that he did not love her? Would she ever understand that he had not known his own heart till now, but still had been driven by its dictates?

Had she whispered her love last night, or had he dreamed it? He had cried his heart's truth, and heard her cry in the same moment, and joy had flooded him till he nearly wept.

But now he doubted. Had he only heard what he wished to hear, that simultaneous echo of his feelings?

He had to get them off the island. He had delayed too long already. He had proved her over and over again, her strength, her soul, her courage—but had he made her love him, or hate him?

He shook his head in weary resignation at his own stupidity. What woman would love a man who had reduced her to such circumstances? How had he imagined the great magic would occur here, where he offered her nothing but hunger and uncertainty and backbreaking work?

Perhaps it had been his heart ruling him, even then. Faced with her determination not to marry him, offered the chance to keep her to himself, away from the world—had it been that?

Such blind foolishness was over now. If only it were not too late.

He lifted the object in his hand and turned a switch to test the function. A soft red glow told him that the machine was alive. He paused there for a moment, trying to foresee the consequences of this tiny movement of his thumb, but the future was blank. He could not see it.

Still, it had to be done. Bari broke the wire and pressed the switch. There was no going back now. A helicopter would be scrambled within the hour. Depending on their position, rescue would probably arrive by midday.

That would give him time, he hoped. Time to state his case, to learn if what he had heard in the night had been her own voice.

"Wow, you're really walking!"

The sleepy voice came from behind him. He restrained the impulse to hide what he held, his heart sinking. "Walking?"

"You've come a long way down the beach, you know. How does your leg feel?"

"Oh—fine. Much better. Noor…"

Sleepy, sensually drugged, Noor stood blinking in the glow of sunrise, trying to wake up. Bari had something bright yellow in his hand. It had an aerial and its red eye was flashing with life. Weird. Could a working mobile phone have washed in on the tide?

"What's that?"

"Ah—"

"Let me see?"

She reached for the object, and with a kind of helpless resignation he let her take it from his hand.

She read the letters stamped in the yellow plastic without comprehending for a moment, and then gasped. At once she was wide awake, adrenaline rushing through her.

"My God, it's an EPIRB! Where did it come from?"

The jolt of excitement made her heart thump. Bari was still silent, and she looked up at him with a broad smile. "Is it transmitting? Do you think it came from the same ship that lost all that cargo? My God, what *luck!*"

EPIRB meant Emergency Position Indicating Radio Beacon, she knew. Wherever it had come from, if it was indeed working, rescue wasn't far off!

Noor whooped with excitement, relief and sheer happiness. "They'll track it! They'll come, won't they? How soon, do you think? I wonder what ship it's from! Isn't this amazing? Did it just arrive on the tide?"

Her relief was tinged with just the lightest brush of disappointment. She had been happy here in a way she had never experienced in the outside world—the happiness of self-sufficiency and self-worth. And she had a sudden premonition that such happiness might not survive a return to the world. That what she had learned and decided here might not be sustainable in the whirl and pressure of that other life.

Bari was gazing out over the water, curiously still.

"Noor," he said softly. "Noor, I—"

"That's funny," she noticed absently. "The tide's only just starting to come in. When did this thing land?"

She peered at the yellow case in the early light. There was quite often an identifying label on an EPIRB, she knew from her yachting friends.

Al Khalid. Aircraft call sign ISQ26. Aircraft registration...

"What on earth—!"

Noor's eyes widened, narrowed, and then squeezed tightly shut, her face twisting into denial as she understood.

"Is this—*yours?*" She opened her eyes again and gazed at him in disbelief.

"Yes," he said, and in one bright flash she saw it all. The whole picture.

"You *can't* have!" she breathed. "You *didn't!*" Her voice broke on anguish. "Oh, God!"

"Noor, I love you," he said, too late.

He tried to draw her into his arms, but like a wild animal she wrenched herself free of his hold and stepped back, staring at him, her face white.

"You had an EPIRB the whole time?" she whispered. "Right from the beginning, when we were in the raft? *Tell me!*" she shouted when he made no answer.

"You know it," Bari replied, taking it from her trembling palm and setting it on the sand to beam its message to the stars.

"We could have been rescued as soon as the storm was over. Before we even got to the island!"

She stared at him, her mind spinning with confusion and misery.

"What was it—an experiment? You were trying to see if you could break me? You wanted to—to... And now, for some reason—" she gestured to the EPIRB "—now the game's over and you're letting me go home! I wonder why?"

"I love you," Bari said urgently, for how could he believe that his love, which had changed everything for him, would have no power over her?

"No, that's not it!" she said in dismissive contempt. "That's not why you're calling a halt." She frowned, her mind whirling, trying to see her way through the jumble of impressions. "No, what changed between last night and this morning? Just one thing—I told you I loved you."

Noor closed her eyes, the ice-water truth of it coursing through her blood. "That's what you were waiting for, isn't it? That's what you planned here—a little *Taming of the Shrew*. Brainwash her, break her down, and *hey presto!* She'll think she loves you!"

"No!" he protested, but it sounded like a lie.

"Rescue was going to arrive by chance, wasn't it? You'd have found some explanation, and I'd never have known! Only, I woke up early."

"I hadn't even considered what to tell you," he said levelly. "Please lis—"

"*Bullshit* you hadn't! You'd considered the whole damned thing from beginning to end! You started plotting this—when? When we were still in the plane? Boy, nobody crosses you and gets away with it, do they? What was it—the breaking of Noor Ashkani's spirit as prelude to a loveless marriage?"

"You are not broken," he said, emphasizing each

word. "And I planned nothing. I took advantage of the situation. I admit it. But—"

"I suppose you even faked the wounded leg!" she accused.

He suddenly lost his grip on himself. "Try to keep your accusations within limits!" he advised angrily.

"You're walking now and you look pretty comfortable!"

"I've been able to walk for the past—"

"And I notice, belatedly I admit, that last night it didn't give you many problems!"

Last night. Her breath hissed in through her teeth. "You really wanted to make me your slave in every way, didn't you?" she whispered. "Did you enjoy having me fetch and carry for you? Are you happy? Was revenge tasty? And now we'll go back to civilization—though nowhere can be called civilization, exactly, if you're there—and then what?"

He abandoned his anger and said urgently, "Noor, don't take it like this. Think of what you learned during this time. Think of what you know!"

"Learned? I learned what kind of...of self-satisfied, arrogant *bastard* you are!"

His jaw clenched. "That is not all you learned."

"Screw you."

She turned away, taking in the sight of their campsite, the little shelter, the fireplace, the stacks of salvage...the place that, she realized suddenly, had come to mean home to her, because Bari was there. The place where she had learned to rise to the challenge, where she had responded to necessity with invention, where she had learned what she could do, where she had discovered...

Now she suddenly saw it as an outsider would see it: a primitive place—a filthy, half-blackened, jerry-built shack, a stack of ragged boxes, an overturned half-de-flated life raft, the detritus of the fire, the bubble wrap that served as their mattress…. And most primitive of all—herself, a half-naked savage with ratty hair, peeling face, scratched, scabbed arms and legs, sunburned skin, wearing a dirty scrap of once-white silk…

And a pathetic, handmade string of pearls around her neck.

That, suddenly, was the worst humiliation of all.

Noor's stomach heaved. She had been so pleased with it, with herself for making it, had modelled it for Bari with such pride!

With choking revulsion, she lifted her hands and tore at the necklace. The fishing line was too strong to break, but at her ferocious jerking the knot slipped and gave at last. The pearls spilled into the sand at his feet, one by one.

Noor turned on her heel and headed toward the hut.

"Listen to me!" His hand caught her wrist, and he forced her to face him again.

Her jaw was clamped tight against tears, but her eyes were shuttered, showing no way in.

He had to try. "Did I have no excuse for what I have done, Noor? I don't say I was right. It was an insane thing—but remember what had happened. Remember your own actions when you remember mine. I offered you marriage in good faith, believing that, if we didn't love each other, still we could make a strong partnership. I had made up my mind that you were my life's partner, the mother of my children. The whole of my world was there to witness that. And then the guard came to tell me you had been seen driving away in the limousine…. Did I have no excuse for anger? For madness, even?"

It made no impact, he could see that. Noor stood

straight and cold. "You've had plenty of time to get over it, too. Are you trying to tell me you only now came to your senses?"

"Perhaps. They call love a madness—they say a lover is a madman. But for me perhaps it is the other way. Maybe learning that I love you brought me to my senses at last. Because I have learned it."

She snorted. "Oh, do me a favour!"

"Noor, let us stop this before it leads to a path that neither of us can turn back from! We have each done terrible things to the other. Let us forget those hurts, in the name of love. I love you. You are my woman, my wife."

"Oh, this from the guy who wouldn't even lend me his jacket till I got on my knees and begged!" she recalled with renewed bitterness. "What it means to be the woman of Bari al Khalid, eh?"

"You love me," he said. "You said it, last night."

She laughed mirthlessly. "Don't you believe it! Aren't you the man who said women always talk like that during sex?"

"Not you, however."

"Ah, but I've been trained by a master! And I'm a quick study, as you've noticed yourself. But don't forget you also once called me heartless. If you brought me here in the hopes of breaking me down to the point of being willing to marry you," Noor said, opening her eyes at him, "sorry, but you were a little premature with the EPIRB. Maybe you shou—"

She broke off when he wrapped his arms around her and dragged her tight against his body. Fierce black eyes burned her for a moment, and then his mouth smothered hers.

Her blood went up like gunpowder, but before the heat could reach her brain, Noor tore her mouth away.

"Don't touch me!"

"Show me how you have been hurt by what I did, and I will let you go!" he declared fiercely, delivering kisses behind her ear, on her throat, in her hair as she twisted her face away. "Noor, I love you!"

Even in the heat of her anguish, his mouth could ignite her blood. Her heart beat in a wild, thrilling tattoo, as if it believed his love. Her body felt the strength of his hold, the hunger of his hands, read the passion in his eyes, and leaped from desire to hunger to drowning passion in a moment. She was melting for him as if she had made no terrible discovery between last night's lovemaking and this moment.

"Marry me, Noor!" he begged, his voice growling in his throat. "I love you, I want you. You are mine!"

From some distant coldness in her, she found the strength to thrust him from her. "Don't touch me again," she ordered coldly. "Don't even speak to me."

Fifteen

"**O**w! Ah, ooh! Oh, don't stop, Rudayba, it's wonderful! *Yow,* that hurt! Oh, did I ever—*aaah!*—miss this!"

The full-body Shiatsu Massage with Cucumber and Nine Essential Oils was just what Noor needed, and if it brought tears to her eyes, who would look further for the cause?

Her cousin Jalia, that was who.

"So what now—you're not speaking to him?" Jalia was sitting on the sofa by Noor's head, lazily flicking through a pile of newspapers and magazines. The two cousins were in her suite in the palace, hiding out from Bari and, incidentally, from the media. Noor's adventure was the kind of fodder the tabloids and celebrity magazines fed on, and they had smelled blood.

"Do you *expect* me to speak to him?"

Jalia shrugged. "I don't get you. You were willing to marry him when you didn't love him and he'd never said

he loved you. Now he insists he's crazy about you, and
you're breaking your heart for love of him—"

"I am not!"

"—but now you won't hear of marriage. There's a
certain lack of fundamental logic, isn't there?"

"I told you, Jalia," Noor repeated doggedly. "When
I said I'd marry him, I was so hypnotized I didn't even
realize that what I felt wasn't love. On the island I
thought I'd learned to love him, but that was just brain-
washing, wasn't it? It's not real love."

"Keep saying that, and you might even come to believe it. There's more than one way to get indoctrinated.
You can even do it to yourself."

"That is just so ridiculous!"

"You're a very different person from the Noor I used
to know. I told you before. Your eyes smile. You're…con-
siderate. Is that why you're so mad at Bari?"

Noor took a deep breath against the pain Rudayba
was inflicting. "No," she said softly. "No, I'm…I'm
aware of that, and I'm grateful for it. But that doesn't
mean—" She blew out a hopeless breath.

Jalia shrugged and lifted up the magazine she was
flicking through to show Noor the double-page spread.
RETURN OF THE CASTAWAY PRINCESS!

There were several photos of Noor and Bari climbing out of the rescue helicopter, their faces strained and
worn, enveloped in the robes their rescuers had given
them. In one of them the little rag doll was visible on
Noor's arm—the only thing Noor had carried with her
from the island.

A few library photos filled up the rest of the space,
the magazine's attempt to disguise the fact that there
was nothing apart from the fact of the rescue to write
about. Neither Noor nor Bari had given any interviews

yet, in spite of pestering that amounted to persecution. And considering her own family's response to her story, Noor wasn't at all eager to make explanations to the broader public. Her mother hadn't spoken to her for an entire day.

"They want the next instalment, and they won't wait forever. What are you going to tell everybody? The truth?"

"Ow! Ow! Rudayba, that one's really—*Ya Allah!* Ooh, that's good! No, are you kidding?" Noor continued to Jalia in English without a break. "The truth? *He Never Loved Me, Sobs Broken-Hearted Princess?* I *don't* think!"

"Of course, you could always sue him." Jalia tossed the magazine aside and picked up a newspaper. WEDDING FLIGHT MYSTERY STILL UNEXPLAINED, Noor read. "They'd love you if you did."

"Sue him for what?" Noor demanded irritably.

"Involuntary forced confinement, of course. The media would gorge on that. You could give them all the details of the hardship your villainous, mercenary fiancé put you through, trying to break your indomitable spirit."

"Rudayba, that's enough digging for one day, thanks," Noor said suddenly. The masseuse stopped, wiped her hands and discreetly left. Noor clambered off the table, wrapping the gigantic white towel around her. Cleanliness still seemed an unparalleled luxury.

"I'm going to take a shower."

Jalia obediently followed her into the bathroom, where Noor examined herself in the mirror. After several days of serious facial and skin rejuvenation work, she was looking human again. Her hair squeaked, her hands had been soaked and scrubbed till her fingertips were nearly raw, the nails were neatly rounded and glossily polished. Her feet were similarly restored.

Various bruises and scratches were fading along with the aches and pains. In fact, it was back to her old life again.

The only things that didn't fade were the memories. When she closed her eyes she still saw Bari's face, felt his hands, his mouth...when she breathed her heart still ached.

"So, you want to call a lawyer?" Jalia flung herself into a plush chair as Noor started the shower.

"Don't be ridiculous. I'm not going to sue Bari!"

"Why not?"

Noor smiled sweetly. "Because that would require seeing him in court."

"That bad, huh?"

Noor stepped under the water and picked up the plastic bottle of perfumed shower scrub. She stood looking at it for a moment before shooting the soft green liquid into her palm. How she had yearned to be here then, but somehow now...she would give anything to be back on the island, falling in love with Bari and believing that he was falling in love with her.

She felt tears burn her eyes and quickly pushed her face under the stream, rubbing the lather into her breasts, her neck, her arms, her stomach, fiercely trying to blank out the memory of that day by the falls.

But a brand isn't got rid of so easily.

"If you don't agree to see me, I'll give an interview to the media," Bari's voice threatened. Noor tried to pretend to herself that she could listen to his voice without melting.

"And why should I care?"

"You might not like what I'm going to tell them. I plan to say you ran away because you were only mar-

rying me for my money, and at the last minute you
learned the family property was less than you
thought."

"What? Who'd believe that?"

"The media don't care about the truth, they care
about a story. I can make the story look good. On the
other hand, if we were to talk, we might come up with
an even better story to give them."

"Are you threatening me? Is this blackmail?"

"You aren't surprised, are you? You already know I'll
stop at nothing."

"Why are you doing this?" Noor shouted. "What do
you *want?*"

"That's easy. I thought you knew. I want you. Now,
and forever."

Her heart thundered. "Well, you can't have me,"
Noor said doggedly. Then, because she couldn't resist,
"And anyway, how would telling a bunch of media types
that I was marrying you for your money help you?"

"Isn't it obvious? The only way you'll be able to re-
deem yourself in the world's eyes after a statement like
that is by marrying me."

She slammed the phone down.

"Princess, how do you feel about Jabir al Khalid's
ultimatum?"

The journalist had cracked her cell phone code and
Noor had been fooled into answering. Now she was
trapped.

She hesitated, wondering how to get the maximum
information from the journalist while giving the minimum away. She was not experienced in dealing with the
media, and she knew she should get off the phone as
quickly as possible without offending the woman.

But she was wild to know what Bari's opening salvo was.

So she laughed lightly. "I don't really know what you're referring to. Ultimatum?" Had Bari told the media about his grandfather?

"I'm talking about his discovery that you aren't, after all, the granddaughter of his old friend."

Noor's jaw fell open. "That I'm…what?"

"Didn't you know, Princess? It seems the old man thought you were the descendant of his best friend, and that's why he approved of the marriage between you and Bari. But now he's discovered that he had confused the names. Not so surprising at his age, I imagine. It turns out your grandfather, Faruq Durrani, was the Sheikh's fellow Cup Companion, all right, but not his special friend."

"Really?" Noor prompted, curious to know where this was leading.

"In fact, as I understand it, your grandfather was actually Jabir al Khalid's rival in love. And Faruq Durrani won. Somehow Jabir al Khalid got the name of his enemy confused with the name of his friend."

She paused compellingly.

"I guess memory can do funny things." Noor knew enough to fill the gap with a platitude. She was unsure whether to believe this, but what was the point?

"Now that he's remembered, apparently, he doesn't want his grandson to marry you?" the reporter said, on a rising note.

"What?"

"Jabir al Khalid has changed his mind about wanting Bari to marry you, apparently."

Noor sat stunned, the phone pressed to her ear. Was it true? Bari forbidden to marry her? Her heart nearly stopped at the thought. She lifted her mouth away from the receiver and tried to breathe quietly, sucking in gulps of air, fighting for calm.

"Uh, it's a surprise to me," she said when she could.

"It's not true? Are you and Bari still engaged?"

"I think that's for Bari and me to decide."

"Because I hear the man who really was Bari's grandfather's friend has five granddaughters, and Bari is supposed to choose from them."

"No comment," Noor whispered.

"Why didn't you and Bari get married, Princess?"

Noor put the phone down.

She paced the suite, racked with indecision and torment.

Could it be true? Had the old man made such a discovery? Or was this just the first salvo in the war Bari had promised her?

But when her mother called to tell her the same story, she had to believe it: Bari's grandfather had made a mistake. He now saw the halting of the wedding—whatever had caused it—as a gift from God. And he intended to accept the gift. Bari was forbidden to marry Noor, who was the granddaughter of a villain.

Noor's mother had been furious enough before. Now her air of reproach was almost more than Noor could stand.

"Do you think—will he do it?" Noor asked, trying for calm.

"Of course he will obey his grandfather, as is fitting. He did so before—why should he resist now? If he wants the property, he must!" her mother said bitterly. "You have thrown away such a man, Noor, and your choice is sadly very final. If the marriage had been completed, the old man would probably never have remembered his error, or if he did, it would have been when he had a great-grandchild on his knee, and too much happiness to regret it. Now—"

It was the first time her mother had ever spoken to her in such a tone. The first time, she supposed, that she had ever seriously disappointed her mother's very low expectations of her. What had been asked of Noor? That she enjoy herself and marry well. And she had screwed up.

What a fool she was. She understood herself now, when it might be too late. Because the thought that Bari might marry *her* simply in order to inherit the family estates was nothing compared to the horror of thinking he might marry some other woman for the same reason.

Sixteen

Noor dressed carefully for his visit, in a neat navy linen suit with a pencil skirt that emphasized her slimmed-down figure, a white tank top under the smart jacket, bare legs and sling-back stilettos.

She was sitting at a table by the window, examining an engineering college course catalogue, when Bari was admitted by her maid. She pretended not to notice his entrance, turning a page noisily.

A dark hand entered her field of vision and closed on the page. A second later the book was ripped from her slackened grasp and sent flying across the room.

Noor's eyes swept up and hungrily took in the sight of him for the first time since they had left the island. The beard was gone, the dark hair neatly cut and curling. He was wearing casual Western dress—tan jeans, loafers and a black polo shirt that revealed his dark, muscled arms, his smooth throat.

She opened her mouth to complain, but Bari beat her to it.

"I don't have time for your games," he warned. "You called me here. What do you want?"

He gripped her arms and drew her to her feet. In her high heels, her eyes on a level with his, she gazed into the black depths with expectant alarm.

Muttering an oath, he swept her into his embrace, and his mouth clamped itself to hers, firm and silky, hungry and hot. His arms imprisoned her, velvet-covered steel: at the same time hard, so that she couldn't escape, and soft, so that she didn't want to.

Her blood boiled up under his touch; her mouth felt swollen with pleasure and yearning. His tongue teased its way past her tingling lips with tender electricity that ran everywhere through her body. His arm clamped her waist, his other hand cupped her head, the fingers threading through her hair.

It wasn't, it just wasn't possible to resist him, Noor admitted helplessly. This might be their last kiss. Was it their last kiss? Was he going to marry someone else?

His kiss grew fiercer, more possessive, his arm sliding behind her head and locking her in the curve of his elbow, the other hand gripping her waist, then her hip, then wrapping right around her back under the jacket to clasp her tightly against him. Noor found herself tilted crazily backwards over his arm as he kissed her ruthlessly. She was half fainting from pleasure and the fact that the world was upside down.

Her arms encircled his neck in luxurious hunger, her breasts pressed against him. She moaned as his mouth left hers and trailed down her neck to the perfumed pulse in the base of her throat.

"At least I smell better than the last time you kissed me," she said stupidly.

"Do you think I like perfume better than the scent of your body?" he growled, and his mouth moved up to smother hers again.

It was some time before she could ask him the questions she had summoned him to ask, and when she got around to it, she was on his lap, while he sat on the sofa. Her shoes were off, her skirt hiked up, his hand caressing her inner thigh, just above the knee, with a touch that melted her.

"It's no setup," Bari said, shaking his head at her accusation. "Grandfather made a mistake. It was while the media were asking questions about us when we were missing, and he began to talk about his old friend, that he suddenly got the names straight in his mind. And he remembered that your grandfather wasn't his dear friend after all, but the one who had stolen his lady love, one of the al Jawadi princesses, and married her."

"How could he make such a mistake? Didn't he have the details checked out?" Noor protested.

"He got the two names confused in his memory, that's all. It was a long time ago, and he's an old man. I have an idea that subconsciously he wanted me to marry the granddaughter of the woman he once loved. But now that he's realized the truth, he won't be acting on an unconscious motive any longer. And he's as determined as ever to run my life."

She held her breath.

Bari drew her hand to his lips and kissed the knuckles, then the palm. "He forbids our marriage, Noor. In marrying you, I'll lose my birthright. I'll have little to offer you materially. What my father left me doesn't compare with what is in my grandfather's control. But the task is still the same—to rebuild the country, with the tools that come to our hands." He looked up into her face, his love written in his eyes. "Will you do that with me? Will you marry me?"

Noor bit her lip. "Why don't you just—marry that other man's granddaughter, the way your grandfather wants?"

"Because I love you," he told her, giving her a little shake. "Because you are a woman without equal, and I want to be the father of your children. Because life is empty without you, Noor, and the palaces and lands and wealth I would inherit if I obeyed my grandfather could not fill the emptiness."

Her heart kicked so hard her breast ached. How she wanted to believe him. But…

"Oh, Bari!" she whispered, her eyes troubled.

He breathed deep, as if she had struck him a blow over the heart. "I understand," he said. "Will you listen while I try to explain, Noor? It isn't much of an explanation, but…I'm asking for your understanding—and forgiveness."

She gazed at him wordlessly. His hand gently stroked her hip.

"I was very angry with you, Noor. It's no good trying to gloss it over. So angry that even when I was hiding at the back of the plane, and heard that the airport was socked in, a part of me was hoping the shock would teach you a lesson. Even at that point I was tempted to leave you in the dilemma for a while. So you see the idea was already in the back of my mind, that you should be allowed to lie in the bed you had made."

He paused, gathering his thoughts. "I had forgotten that there was an EPIRB in the plane's grab bag. I suppose I didn't think of it because there wasn't much urgency about it. No one could have scrambled a helicopter during the storm even if we had been transmitting. Whereas what we were doing was immediately essential to our survival."

"But when the storm was over, I asked you about an EPIRB. I remember."

"And I remembered then, and lied about it. Almost instinctively. I thought—this situation is a learning opportunity, but the lesson hasn't hit home with her at all."

She nodded ruefully. "I was just expecting that life would get right back to normal and I wouldn't have to adjust, so what was the point?"

He drew her hand to his mouth and kissed it thoughtfully. "I didn't get the whole picture at once. I just decided to see how you would react to a little more hardship. It wasn't until that night that..."

He paused.

"That night?"

"I want to tell you a part of my life that I haven't told you before," Bari offered softly, and when she nodded intently, he began.

"My father died when I was fifteen. It had been the dream of his life to return to live in Bagestan one day. When he was dying, he asked me to promise that I would help to further the royal family's attempts to regain their throne, and one day, when it became possible, return and restore the family property and make my home here. He knew his father would leave me what would have been his own inheritance. I swore to him that I would do as he wished. I meant it. I became committed in that moment."

Noor thought of her own parents' passion for their troubled country, a passion that had survived time and distance, and that, without her consciously realizing it, they had passed on to her.

"I know," she said softly.

"It was always understood between my grandfather and me that, while I would certainly not inherit all the family property, I would undertake to reclaim and restore it on behalf of us all. And I would have the money to do it.

"After the Return, my grandfather suddenly made conditions. I proposed to you, Noor, believing that I had no choice. I owed it to my own hopes, to my father and the promise I had made him.

"But that night on the island, I began to consider whether I was prepared to sacrifice my hope of a happy marriage for the sake of that promise. Whether my father would have wanted me to make such a sacrifice. If I was going to make you change your mind again—"

"Oh, just like that?" Noor said dangerously.

He smiled unrepentantly and touched her cheek. "You'd changed it once already, remember. It was at least possible. But—should I make the attempt? That was the question. When I proposed to you, I had believed that in spite of everything you were someone with whom I could make a good marriage. When you ran from the wedding…"

Noor bit her lip. "You should hear my mother on the subject!"

"…I asked myself if that judgement had been mistaken, if we were too different in outlook to make the kind of partnership I envisaged happen. And it was while I was turning that over in my mind that I realized that—" he paused "—that I had been given an opportunity to find out who you truly were."

"Not to make me love you?"

"That, too, if I could." He stretched up and kissed her. "What I didn't realize was how much of an opportunity it would be for me to learn about myself. And my own heart."

They were quiet for a moment. "And so you...you just decided to keep me there till...what?"

"I didn't think that far ahead. I just went from day to day, and after a while I almost forgot about the EPIRB. It didn't seem relevant. Until the day we got the flotsam. I was out there in the water with my leg cut open, fighting to hold that rope, determined to get those crates, and I suddenly thought—what the hell am I doing? There could be sharks out here, and I'm risking that for a few crates of food when we can call for rescue any time?"

A laugh escaped her. "Why didn't you get the EPIRB then? You were badly hurt. Weren't you scared?"

He kissed her again. "Can't you guess? Because I couldn't walk to the hiding place! I'd have had to tell you about it, and I knew how you would react. How hurt you would be. I thought—I can never explain it. But even then I didn't understand that I couldn't hurt you because I loved you."

His hands tightened on her, but Noor resisted. "But later, when you were walking again? It must have been uncomfortable. Why not then? Where was it hidden?"

"It wasn't far. But by then, Noor, you were in the middle of a metamorphosis. You were suddenly finding what you could really do. And I couldn't interrupt your journey.

"Now tell me your side of it," he said.

Noor heaved a sigh. "I learned so much, Bari. You're right, it was a kind of metamorphosis. I hated a lot of it, but—I guess that was the price of change. And I can't be sorry it happened."

"Do you forgive me, Noor?"

She smiled into his eyes. "How can I be grateful for

what happened and still blame the person who caused it? Yes, I forgive you. Can you forgive me?"

For answer, he wrapped her head with strong, possessive hands and lay back, drawing her down to his hungry kiss. When she lifted herself away from him again, he held her face and whispered, looking into her eyes, "And...do you love me? Will you marry me, Beloved?"

She closed her eyes against the thundering of her own heart, then opened them again.

"No answer?" he begged hoarsely.

"I love you, Bari." The words seemed torn from her throat. "Yes, yes, how could I say no?"

The strength roared into him, and he kissed her with a rough and hungry passion that ignited her blood, burned her, melted her. They slipped down into the soft sofa, arms and legs entwining, wild hunger in their hearts and mouths.

After a moment, he drew his head away. "First things first," he whispered, reaching into his pocket. When he lifted his hand, he was holding the beautiful diamond solitaire that had been her engagement ring.

Noor suddenly remembered the piercing, painful moment on her wedding day when she had torn it off her finger—a different woman, in another lifetime.

"Give me your hand," Bari commanded in a gravel voice. Noor breathed deep, lifted her left hand and put it in his.

With a look of passionate possessiveness, the Sheikh slipped his ring back where it belonged.

A long time later, he murmured, "Do you remember the day I took you sailing down the coast?"

She was on the bed in the curve of Bari's arm, leaning over him on one elbow as he lay back against the pillows, sweat-damp curls falling on his forehead, his eyes lazy with love.

She gave him a look. Remember?

"The house up above—do you remember it? It is a beautiful place, or it was once."

"Oh!" Noor whispered. "And it's—your family's?"

"That particular property was left to me by my father. I meant to show it to you that day. But—we did other things."

"Did we? I've forgotten," Noor teased, and then fell down onto his warm chest and was thoroughly kissed for her pains.

"It will fall into the sea if repairs are not undertaken soon," he said then. "Although of course we must have somewhere in the city, I would like to restore that as our home. Will you come with me now and look at it, and see if you would like to live there?"

"Yes, but what are we going to tell the media? They're all out there, and when they see us together…" Noor gabbled anxiously.

"We can't let them publish the truth," he said.

She nodded in vigorous relief. "It would make me look like such an idiot. I mean, I *was* a fool, but do I have to be exposed as one in front of the world?"

Bari leaned up and kissed her. "Don't call my beloved names."

"Not in public, anyway," Noor agreed with a grin. "Is there some explanation we could make that would satisfy the media and put them off the scent?"

Bari's eyes glinted thoughtfully. "My grandfather's foolishness has had many uses," he mused. "With his first decree, he found you for me, and with his second, he brought you back to me. And I really don't think he will have the right to complain if we make use of him again!"

Epilogue

"THE PRINCESS I LOVE!"
Forbidden Wedding Will Go Ahead!

The marriage of Cup Companion Sheikh Bari
al Khalid and Princess Noor Yasmin al Jawadi
Durrani, which was dramatically halted in
Bagestan last month when the bride and groom
mysteriously disappeared, is on again, accord-
ing to sources.

The truth behind the mystery of the wedding couple's disappearance, only minutes before the ceremony was due to begin, has at last
come out. Sources close to the couple have revealed that the Princess and her fiancé fled because Sheikh Jabir al Khalid, the groom's
grandfather, dramatically withdrew his per-

mission and barred the union at the eleventh hour. The couple fled, intending to undertake the ceremony elsewhere. But their plane was forced down in a storm, and the rest is history. The couple spent what would have been their honeymoon on an uninhabited island, surviving on turtle eggs.

Their disappearance, the search, the dramatic rescue, and the couple's continuing devotion have had no influence on the old Sheikh's decision, however.

Bari al Khalid will be forced to sacrifice his expected inheritance, consisting of vast property in Bagestan, in order to marry the woman he loves. The legacy will now probably go to a cousin.

"My wife and I will build a new legacy together," the handsome Cup Companion has been quoted as saying. The wedding is expected to take place next month.

* * * * *

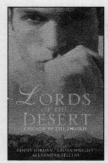 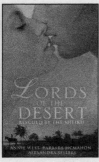 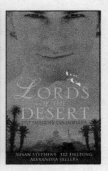

millsandboon.co.uk Community

Join Us!

The Community is the perfect place to meet and chat to kindred spirits who love books and reading as much as you do, but it's also the place to:

- **Get the inside scoop from authors about their latest books**
- **Learn how to write a romance book with advice from our editors**
- **Help us to continue publishing the best in women's fiction**
- **Share your thoughts on the books we publish**
- **Befriend other users**

Forums: Interact with each other as well as authors, editors and a whole host of other users worldwide.

Blogs: Every registered community member has their own blog to tell the world what they're up to and what's on their mind.

Book Challenge: We're aiming to read 5,000 books and have joined forces with The Reading Agency in our inaugural Book Challenge.

Profile Page: Showcase yourself and keep a record of your recent community activity.

Social Networking: We've added buttons at the end of every post to share via digg, Facebook, Google, Yahoo, technorati and de.licio.us.

www.millsandboon.co.uk

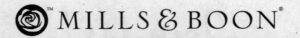